Where I Found You

"What a delightful read. I devoured this novel. I couldn't put it down because the storyline drew me straight in. Where I Found You has it all: a family feud, enemies to more, relatable characters, a treasure hunt, a second chance, and forced proximity."
—ALLYSON, GOODREADS

"This is a very well-rounded book that has all the things I like in a good read: wonderful characters, enjoyable setting, great humor, swoony kisses (and then there's all the almost kisses...), realistic personal growth and development... not to mention the feud between their families, a treasure hunt with difficult clues, and past hurts that need healing. I thoroughly enjoyed reading it and can't wait for the next book!"
—MARGARET, GOODREADS

"The world needs more of these books that emphasize redemption and the value of looking beyond first impressions and living authentically. Prepare for a binge-read and for goodness sake, don't start this one on an empty stomach!"
—THE LITERATE LEPRECHAUN

"This was an entertaining read. There is a strong, reassuring message woven in of how God's love lifts us out of sin and repairs broken relationships."

—DEB, GOODREADS

Where I Found You

· MAGNOLIA BAY ·

BOOK 1

Where I Found You

BETSY ST. AMANT

sunrise

PUBLISHING

Where I Found You
Magnolia Bay, Book 1

Published by Sunrise Media Group LLC
Copyright © 2025 Betsy St. Amant Haddox

PRINT ISBN: 978-1-963372-48-9

For more information about Betsy St. Amant please access the author's website at the following address: www.betsystamant.com.

Published in the United States of America.
Cover Illustration and Design: Raya Decker

· MAGNOLIA BAY ·

Where I Found You
No Place Like Home
Meant for Me

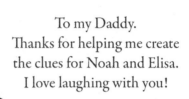

To my Daddy.
Thanks for helping me create
the clues for Noah and Elisa.
I love laughing with you!

Love lifted me! Love lifted me!
When nothing else could help
Love lifted me.

One

NOAH HEBERT NEEDED TO GET BACK home—he didn't have time to watch paint dry.

"You got the wrong blue." Peter, Noah's apprentice at the Blue Pirogue Inn, clearly felt confident enough to point out the obvious as he stood beside Noah, his scrawny arms crossed.

"I can see that." Noah pushed one hand through his hair as he stared at his mistake—one of many over the past several months he'd been fixing up the inn since his grandfather's funeral—and sent a scattering of sawdust onto the taped off floor. The humidity of his coastal Louisiana hometown wet Noah's flannel shirt and stuck it to his back, despite the spring breeze rustling through the pine trees outside. Not that the humidity was much better in north Louisiana.

Figured. They were finally at the finish line of these endless renovations, meaning his return to Shreveport and his real job as a land man in the oil and gas industry was in sight . . . but now he was being mocked by slate blue and—

"Sky blue. How did you even do that?" Peter squinted up at him beneath his side-swept dark hair. The kid had chosen to work a trade instead of going to college, and had proven to be a hard worker and fast learner. Noah could trust him to notice details.

Especially this one glaring at them in matte finish.

"Lot on my plate, kid." Noah checked his watch with a grimace. "And now I'm late for an appointment with the one man in Magnolia Bay who probably hates me the most."

Peter's eyes widened. "Must be a Bergeron."

"Isaac Bergeron, and if you're a praying kind of person, you might start working on that now."

"That bad, huh?" Peter made a *tsk* with his tongue.

Worse than the kid knew. But some parts were public. "As county inspector, Isaac's the one holding the keys to this kingdom." Noah gestured around them, at the multitude of mostly-finished projects, at abandoned tools lying on heaps of folded tarp that hadn't been put away yet. And now even more projects would be delayed, all because of the stupid paint. "I'm hoping I get the inspection certificate from this meeting so we can reopen and call this a wrap." And never have to see the wretched man—or his daughter—again.

Not that Elisa Bergeron would be at the Magnolia Blossom Café today. Just the ghost of her memory.

Peter clasped his hands in front of him in a posture of prayer. "On it."

Noah headed for the front door, stepping over a discarded roll of painter's tape. "I'll grab the right blue on my way home."

"Slate blue!" Peter called after him.

Noah shot him a thumbs-up over his shoulder as he hurried outside. He steered around a crew member perched halfway up a ladder on the porch, measuring for the decorative trim left to hang. Better him than Noah—he'd never been a fan of heights.

He breathed a gulp of air not thick with sawdust as he hurried down the porch stairs, careful to avoid the rotten spot on the second step. No, wait. That had been fixed, along with the shingles that begged for attention the past year. Everything was finally coming together, just in time for tourist season.

Assuming Isaac Bergeron didn't hold a grudge and did his job fairly.

There's more where this one came from. Noah might not ever get Isaac's last words to him—or the sight of the bitter man cleaning a shotgun on his porch, out of his mind. And now he had to sit down with him for coffee.

He started toward his grandfather's Chevy truck that had become his along with the inn during the reading of his will. For the first time in a long time, Noah's chest didn't tighten at the sight of the tired but sturdy three-story structure he'd inherited—the lingering symbol of a family feud multi-generations thick. That'd be one way to market for the upcoming tourist season. *Come see where the infamous Bergeron/Hebert battle first began . . .*

His cell vibrated in his pocket, and he pulled it free before hauling himself into the truck cab. Hopefully his backorder of tile hadn't been delayed again. He snorted at the display indicating a string of missed messages. Thankfully, none from the tile guy.

Noah opened the group text labeled "GONE FISHING."

CADE
Fishing tonight at 7, right? 🐟

Linc
Aye. I'll bring the cold ones.

Owen
You always bring the beer, Linc. 🍺

Linc
Only because we never know if Noah is gonna bother to show.

Noah winced. Yet lately, the accusation wasn't inaccurate. He typed back.

<u>Noah</u>
I'll be there this time, I promise.

<u>Owen</u>
Hey guys, I might need to borrow some bait again.

Noah dropped his phone into the console cup holder. The familiar scent of Armor All mixed with the evergreen air fresheners he kept dangling from the rearview mirror wafted over him. Partly his scent now, partly his grandfather's. Grandpa Gilbert used to keep candy orange slices in the glove box. There were probably still melted traces of them clinging to the interior.

Noah gripped the steering wheel and took a breath. Time to get this over with. He started the engine just as his phone rang.

Noah grunted as he reluctantly hit the speaker feature. "Yeah?"

Cade's voice filled the cab. "Just making sure you're really coming tonight and not blowing smoke."

"I'll be there. I could use the break . . . after I get this certificate and slate blue paint, anyway."

"Sure you don't want to stick around Magnolia Bay a little longer? Enjoy the hard-earned fruits of your labor at the inn?" Cade's grin was evident in his voice.

Noah looked both ways at the end of the drive. "I'm sure. This town is too small for Bergerons and Heberts to coexist again."

"Especially with a certain blond one?"

"I didn't say that."

"Didn't have to." Noah turned off the private road, the bay in his rearview. "Three months of working on the inn has been plenty. I need to get back to Shreveport ASAP."

For several reasons, and fine, maybe one of those reasons was blond. Not that Elisa Bergeron lived in the Bay anymore—she was probably a famous chef somewhere on the mainland by now.

But he'd seen her memory more around town in the time he'd been back than he had in the twelve years prior combined.

Cade sighed. "That's too bad, man."

Noah cleared his throat. "You know I was just here long enough to get the Blue Pirogue fixed up for tourist season." He ignored the pinch of guilt that always followed that fact. He *should* keep the inn—it was his favorite childhood landmark, his safe space growing up during his parents' tumultuous marriage. It was his grandfather's legacy.

But he couldn't live in a town that judged him. Judged his family.

He pressed the gas. "I have a real job in Shreveport." One he'd been on hiatus from. He didn't have a boss to go back to, since technically, he was self-employed as a landman, but the project manager might not trust him with future projects if he stayed gone too long.

"Running an inn is a real job. Regardless, you're good at construction—I've seen what you've been doing at the inn."

The compliment might have sunk in if there hadn't been so many mistakes made the past few weeks. "Don't worry. I'll hire someone to keep the Blue Pirogue running for me. I definitely don't want to sell."

Cade's voice dropped in understanding. "To Isaac?"

"To any Bergeron, but definitely not to him." The thought of Noah's beloved childhood inn going to that man was inconceivable. Grandpa Gilbert would flip over in the grave.

"Don't worry about meeting Isaac today, by the way. I think he's mellowed a little over the years."

"Maybe to you. You're not a Bergeron . . . and you didn't break his daughter's heart."

Cade snorted. "I think that breaking part was a bit mutual, if I recall."

Noah's grip tightened on the wheel. "Water under the bridge."

WHERE I FOUND YOU

And if that statement didn't remind him of the time he and Elisa would walk the beach to the coastal bridge onto the island, picking up seashells, throwing back the broken ones and collecting Elisa's favorite in a little mesh pouch he'd bought her just for that purpose . . .

"I guess you'll see." Cade chuckled. "She might be there, you know."

"What?" Noah hit the brake harder than he meant to at the stop sign. "She's back?"

"Been back, bro. She manages the café."

Impossible. "I thought she went off to culinary school." Not that he kept up. But small towns talked, and some gossip threads strung all the way up the state to North Louisiana.

"She came back."

Noah's foot slipped off the brake pedal and he quickly stomped it again. "You could have warned me."

Cade laughed. "What do you think this is?"

"I meant sooner."

"If it's water under the bridge, what's it matter?"

If Noah could reach through the phone and wipe the smirk off his friend's face, he would. With his fist. "Thanks a lot." He eased off the brake and turned onto Village Lane, Magnolia Bay's main drag, flipping his visor down against the mid-morning sun.

"You haven't seen her around town at all the past few months?"

"Been keeping to the inn and the hardware store." And eating enough Chinese take-out to merit his jeans fitting tighter, all to avoid public restaurants and the chance of running into . . . well, anyone.

"She didn't come to the funeral, did she?" Cade asked.

"No. But I wouldn't have expected her to. She owes me nothing." And he probably owed her even less.

He coasted into a parking spot in front of the Magnolia Blossom

Café, then killed the engine. The truck idled into silence. "I'm here, man. I'll see you on the pier."

"You got this," Cade coached. "Get in, get the certificate, and get out."

"From your lips to God's ears." Maybe the Lord would hear one of them.

Noah sat for a moment, slowly withdrawing the keys from the old ignition and stalling as he took in the café's front. Not much had changed in the past decade plus. The turquoise curtains tied back in the front windows had faded and the welcome sign on the porch now hung slightly crooked. The potted flowers celebrating spring were new, though, as was the cheery yellow paint on the door.

His erratic heartbeat was also new. How many times that fateful summer had he coasted up to this very parking lot, waiting for Elisa to get off work so she could hop in his truck? Hit up the drive-in movie the park hosted every June, toss popcorn in each other's mouth and miss. Share a large soda and fight over the last of the Milk Duds.

Noah reluctantly released his seat belt. Of course Isaac would choose this spot to meet—probably got free coffee from his daughter, if she ran things now—and Noah wasn't in a position to argue the specifics.

He pushed through the front doors, the turquoise walls immediately closing in on him in a rush of memory. He avoided looking at the patrons seated at the spinning barstools at the serving counter—more so, at anyone potentially *behind* said counter—and scanned the crowded room for Isaac. The unmistakable aroma of waffles and syrup wafted over him like an air freshener someone needed to invent. He inhaled deeply, then moved through the maze of various-sized yellow tables toward the back, where Isaac was most likely to be seated. He definitely didn't want to draw attention to himself lingering in the doorway.

The breakfast crowd was in full swing. Forks clanked against dishes, the abrupt holler of "order up" sounded through the swinging doors behind the bar, and the chatter from townsfolk eager to start their day filled the diner with a low hum.

Despite Noah's determined attempt to keep his gaze away from the counter, it traitorously darted there anyway, ping-ponging back and forth until he was certain Elisa wasn't one of the two aproned people pouring coffee.

Relaxing, he walked past Sadie Whitlock, owner of the local used book shop, who sat at a table reading a hardback and nursing a glass of chocolate milk. She'd always been kind, a little older than him, and usually had her face in a novel. "Hey, Sadie."

"Noah! Good to see you out and about." She looked up from her book with a smile, her green eyes bright. "How's progress on the inn?"

"It's getting there. You'll be seeing less of me around here soon." Noah's grandfather had been a regular at *Second Story*, devouring American history texts as far back as Noah could remember. He'd accompanied Grandpa Gilbert into that used bookstore more times than he wanted to that last summer spent on the island when he was eighteen.

"That's too bad, but I understand. Not everyone can take over a business suddenly, like I did from my great-aunt." Sadie gestured with her book—what looked to be a romance novel, judging by the cover. "Surely I'll see you before you leave."

Old Farmer Branson—who looked exactly the same as he had a decade ago—raised his head from a plate of bacon as Noah passed, but didn't nod. The grizzled man had always been close with the Bergerons, taking their side in the ongoing feud over who rightfully owned the inn's grounds. Most people in Noah's generation seemed mature enough to realize the majority of that beef had occurred in the past, but some old-timers still liked to play favorites.

Especially if they'd only ever been told one side of the story.

"Noah! Fancy meeting you here." August Bowman, his grandfather's probate attorney, stepped in front of Noah and held out his hand. "Come for the pancakes?"

So much for avoiding conversation. He liked August, though, as far as lawyers went. "No, sir." He returned the handshake, noting the older man's signature tweed blazer. The man had been born in the wrong century. "I have an appointment—Blue Pirogue business."

"Speaking of the inn, I was going to call you later this morning, so this is rather fortuitous." August set his briefcase on the empty table beside them, then pushed his glasses up his nose. The man's untamed salt-and-pepper hair was the only thing about him that wasn't always perfectly in order. "Could you come by my office this afternoon?"

Noah hesitated as the dozens of unfinished tasks on his calendar filled his mind, including finding slate blue paint. "I'm afraid I've got a full—"

"Here, take my card, in case you need a refresher of the address." August handed over the rectangular business card. "It won't take long, but it's important."

"I'll try, but—"

"Great! Two o'clock?" August clapped Noah on the shoulder before he could protest. "See you then, son."

Noah was more likely to be August's grandson than son, but he didn't get to protest that or the fact he couldn't come by before the older man scooted toward the exit.

Great. Noah needed to find Isaac, before he got swept into any more obligations.

He scanned the café a final time, his gaze bouncing off the various magnolia blossom centerpieces, the kitschy teal and yellow wall art, and the hardened stare of Sheriff Rubart—another Bergeron fan—until . . . *there.*

Isaac Bergeron sat with his back to the restroom wall, his iPad on the table before him next to a mug. The Magnolia Blossom Café had never used a designated set of coffee cups. Delia Boudreaux, the long-time owner and town "mama," had told Noah when he was a kid that she was clumsy and would end up breaking them, so if they never matched, no one would know.

The thought brought a smile. Maybe he'd missed this quirky town just a little.

Isaac looked up from his iPad, squaring his shoulders under his dark polo shirt. His face was clean shaven save for a tidy goatee peppered with gray. "Noah. Glad you could make it."

Noah's burst of generosity dissipated. He dipped his chin as he slid onto the bench seat across from Mr. Bergeron, then remembered a childhood's worth of Delia's reminders to take off his hat during greetings. He tugged his favorite ball cap free from his head and nodded again. "Sir."

Isaac wasn't a gambling man, but his poker face could have won him a bundle. He revealed zero hint of how sharing a table with a Hebert affected him, if it did at all. Especially this particular Hebert.

Noah, however, worked hard to keep his thoughts off his expression. He replaced his hat and searched for polite conversation. "Have you ordered?"

"I had a bagel. Would you like some coffee?" Isaac cocked one brow, the intentional movement creating the exact intimidation factor Noah was sure he intended.

"I think I'm set, thanks." He wanted a stack of pancakes, but not at the expense of making this meeting longer than necessary.

Under the table, Noah flexed his hands against the worn denim of his jeans. During the inspection last week, they'd kept their distance. Isaac had done his official thing, while Noah hovered just close enough to be reached if the inspector had any questions. Thankfully—for both of them—there had been few, and their forced interaction hadn't taken long.

Isaac took a leisurely sip from his mug, and Noah dug his fingers harder into his knees. Surely Isaac wanted to get this over with as much as Noah did. But the older man didn't seem in a hurry to hand over the coveted contents of the closed manila folder sitting on the table.

"As you might expect, I have some news for you." Isaac set down his mug, then draped one arm across the length of the booth seat.

There was the poker face again. He braced himself for a request to tweak a few things. But Noah knew the inn, knew the work that had been done with his own sweat and blood, not to mention the crew he'd hand-picked that had come highly recommended. He'd had a tight budget to work with from his construction loan, but he'd gotten the best and even bartered a handful of favors when finances got tight.

That reminded him—he owed Peter a few bass.

Noah cleared his throat. "I'm ready."

"I have to warn you, it might not be good news." Isaac drummed his fingers on the bench as if it were a regular day, not as if he was holding Noah's golden ticket just out of reach. "But it's how these things go sometimes."

So it was as he'd feared. Noah gritted his teeth, keeping his gaze on the syrup-sticky menu between them rather than on Isaac's smug expression. "I assume there are some changes you'd like to see?"

"Only one big one." Isaac finally reached for the folder and slid it across the table to Noah, then flipped open the cover. The bold stamp boasting the words FAILED INSPECTION met him like a red-inked slap in the face.

Noah's mouth went dry. He stared at the unexpected words until they swirled against the other type. "I don't understand. How?" His renovations couldn't have failed. Noah had personally attested that everything had been done up to code.

But he did understand, didn't he? He should have known a Bergeron wouldn't play fair.

Noah wished he could rip the paper into tiny shreds and throw it in Isaac's face. Wasn't that what his grandfather had preached all those years of Noah's childhood, as he grew up in the inn? That the land under the Blue Pirogue was rightfully Hebert property, despite their petulant claims otherwise, and that the Bergerons were simply "too lazy to make their own good business deals"?

Isaac's face was less than sympathetic—in fact, that appeared to be a smirk hovering around the corners of his mouth. Then the man schooled his features and picked up the condemning paper before Noah could give into temptation. "I'm sorry it wasn't what you hoped."

"I bet." The words slipped out before Noah could censor, but as a flush of heat crawled up his chest, he realized he didn't want to. This was injustice. "There is nothing wrong with those renovations, and we both know it. I followed all the rules."

"What are you implying?" Isaac tilted his chin a degree, his gray eyes narrowing.

"More like assuming. I'm assuming the fact the Blue Pirogue happens to be on the exact acreage our families have been feuding over for generations has nothing to do with this." Noah jabbed his finger at the folder.

"Of course it doesn't," Isaac snapped. "Are you questioning my professionalism?"

"Yes, along with about a dozen other things right now." Namely, what in the world had he taken on with this inheritance? Hadn't his dad, who'd been successfully managing a luxury hotel chain in California for the past fifteen years, warned Noah when Grandpa got sick the first time? *He's going to pawn that old dump off on you in his will, you know. It'll be a money pit. You don't have to accept it.*

But Noah had. And until this moment, he hadn't regretted it.

Isaac's eyes flashed.

Noah took a deep breath, trying to regain control. He laid both palms flat on the table, releasing his breath. "Let's just say I'm questioning the timing. You've had your eye on that inn since before Grandpa started chemo."

"That has nothing to do with this and you know it." Isaac's voice turned to steel. "In fact, if you'd bothered to read the report before making accusations, you'd see there's a good reason the inspection failed." He nudged the paper closer to Noah. "Black mold."

Noah's fire tempered a bit. "That's impossible." He'd have seen it.

"Afraid not." Isaac pulled a few photos free from the folder pocket and turned them around for Noah.

His heart dipped in his chest as he stared at the evidence in the walls. Not so impossible after all. He picked up another glossy image. "How did I miss this?"

"It probably happened after the storm. You know Hurricane Anastasia didn't play favorites last summer." Isaac's haughty expression sobered. "Left more damage in its wake than a Kardashian."

"I know. It even hit us in Shreveport. Mom and I have lived there for fifteen years, and we'd never seen anything like that reach so far up north."

Was it his imagination, or did Isaac's eyes narrow at the mention of his mother?

"Regardless of where it came from . . ." Isaac began stacking the photos. "The mold exists. It'd be *unprofessional* to approve this inspection before the problem is fixed."

Noah stared at the way Isaac calmly slid the photos that were ruining Noah's life back into the folder pocket. He'd thought the Blue Pirogue hadn't taken much damage during the storm, and what little there had been had easily been swept into the round of renovations.

He'd thought wrong.

"Black mold is a massive liability." Isaac leaned back in the

WHERE I FOUND YOU

booth, his expression tight. "You clearly can't operate with guests until the mold is taken care of."

"But I can't afford this." He'd barely made budget on the renovations needed to get the inn up to date—and up to code—for the pending tourist season. The inn's books had been in the black—barely—when Noah took over, but having to close temporarily for the repairs had given the dwindling business account a hit. So far, he'd managed to keep his own meager savings out of it, hoping to get the inn back up running before he decided whether or not to keep it.

Isaac shrugged a little, downing the last of his coffee. "Maybe if you hadn't expanded the third-story suite, you'd have some money left over for emergencies."

Noah stiffened. The last thing he needed was yet another person telling him how to manage and market the Blue Pirogue. "Not that it's your business, but that expansion was necessary to draw honeymooners and guests who want more space." He folded his arms over his hammering heart. "Statistics prove it'll pay for itself in a few years."

"That's great—except you can't start the clock until this is handled." Isaac tapped the folder.

He was aware. Noah cleared his throat. These next words were going to taste like sawdust. "Then what do you suggest I do? I don't have that kind of money left." Or energy. Or time. The inn was supposed to be finished in the next few weeks so he could figure out his next steps in life.

Not take several backward.

"Do like everyone else does—get a loan." Isaac raised his eyebrows in challenge as a slow grin curved the corners of his mouth. "Or you could always sell."

Noah's gut tightened. "Nice try."

Isaac leaned forward and lowered his voice, all pretenses gone as he braced both hands on the table. "If you don't handle this one way or another, I'll call Judge Morrow. You'll have a cease and desist slapped on you faster than you can say—"

"Afternoon, gentlemen." A slender, tan arm stretched past Noah and started pouring coffee from a carafe into Isaac's mug. The familiar scent of vanilla and honey hit Noah like a two-by-four from the past and he didn't need to look up to know.

Elisa Bergeron.

But he did look up, because there wasn't a man on the planet who was unable to spare Elisa a second glance. He swallowed hard, watching her pour her father's coffee, his gaze skimming over her high cheekbones and pink lips. Her blond hair, shorter than he'd ever seen it, was tucked back into a tiny ponytail, revealing her slender neck.

"And can I get you anything, hon?" Elisa's voice, twangy with a southern drawl just as he remembered, trailed off as her eyes met his. Just as blue as he remembered, too, though they darkened as recognition paled her cheeks. She jerked the carafe upright. "Noah Hebert."

He spread his arms in a slightly exaggerated, resigned gesture. "That's me." And that had always been the problem between them, hadn't it? His name. What he represented.

She lifted her chin, her smile wobbly around the edges. "Well, I'll be. It only took you four months of being back in town to stop in here, didn't it?"

"I've been pretty busy with the inn." He waited. Elisa had always been a master at keeping her emotions in check. Hard to tell if her words carried a genuinely pleasant undertone . . . or if she was contemplating stabbing him with the fork resting near Isaac's mug.

She resumed pouring, her back rigid but her tone fluid as if he hadn't spoken at all. "I didn't think men who wore flannel every day were afraid of anything."

He scooted the fork out of reach. "Never said I was."

"You're right. You didn't say much of nothing, did you? Some things never change, I suppose." Her voice flowed like molasses, but the look in her eyes as she met his gaze full on packed a punch he hadn't expected.

And just like that, he was eighteen again, sitting on the pier out by the bay and memorizing the curve of her sun-kissed shoulder beneath his arm. The smell of sunscreen and vanilla wafting off her hair, lapping over him like the waves beneath their feet.

Naively believing that summer would last forever.

He held her challenging stare. "And some things do." Unfortunately, and fortunately, all at once. He watched a hurricane of emotions flicker through her eyes, but he couldn't have named a single one.

And he refused to look away first.

"Elisa!" Isaac yelped.

She finally broke eye contact, looking down with a gasp. Coffee spilled over the brim of Isaac's mug and formed a river on the table, cascading toward Noah. He jerked back, but not before a stream of scalding brown liquid struck the leg of his jeans.

Forget Hurricane Anastasia—Elisa would always be the biggest storm he'd ever encountered.

And it looked like his brief respite from the rain was over.

Two

ELISA BERGERON HAD ALWAYS HATED surprises—because they were usually bad. And if Noah Hebert sitting in a coffee-soaked booth wasn't further proof of that, she had no idea what was.

"I'm so sorry." She jerked the carafe away, but the damage had been done. And maybe she didn't feel entirely all that bad about it, save for the accident gave away the fact that Noah Hebert still affected her. After all this time.

Bless it.

She fisted a handful of napkins from her apron pocket and tossed them on the coffee, but it felt a little like tossing a sponge into Magnolia Bay. Embarrassment heated her throat. "Here." She handed a few more to Noah, but he was already sliding across the booth, wincing. Okay, so maybe she did feel bad. That coffee was *hot*.

He moved to the end of the seat. "I think this requires a trip to the men's room."

"Of course." She stepped back to give him space, but not before he crowded her at the edge of the table, smelling like a mixture of spicy soap and a forest after a hard rain. Good gravy, but she hadn't smelled that particular mix in over a decade. Not since the last time she'd snuggled in close to his neck on a beach blanket, stretched across the bay's sand.

Then he stood, taller and more imposing than she'd remembered, and her mouth dried at his flannel-coated proximity. "It's that way." She pointed to the restroom.

"I've not been gone *that* long." He raised a dark brow at her.

And now she was back to no longer feeling bad. "Well you know what the Good Book says about a day being like a thousand years—"

"Elisa, why don't you get us a towel?" Dad's expression revealed nothing—how did he always do that?—as he calmly moved his work folders out of the way of the spreading puddle.

"Right." Guilt from reacting poorly in front of her father washed over her like—well, like a massive coffee spill. She avoided Noah's eyes as he stepped past her to the restroom hallway. "Be right back."

Once he'd cleared the wall full of various inspirational sayings Delia had framed over the years, she dashed for the kitchen, attempting to look more like she was on a mission for a towel than a personal quest to hide her burning cheeks. Her pulse accelerated, and she shoved through the swinging doors, nearly slamming into her co-worker, Trish Gamble.

"Whoa!" Trish pulled back a round tray of water glasses just in time. "I'd ask where the fire is, but it seems to be burning your face. You okay?"

Elisa fanned her flushed cheeks with her free hand as she set the carafe on the stainless-steel island. "I dumped coffee on table fifteen."

"See? This is why they shouldn't let managers do a waitress's job." Trish set her tray down with a grin, looking more like a college student than someone in her late-twenties. "Isn't that right, Mama Delia?"

Delia Boudreaux cocked one rounded hip and laughed as she

stirred the black beans simmering on the industrial stovetop. "I plead the fifth." Tendrils of graying hair had freed themselves from Delia's trademark blue handkerchief, and her furrowed brows did nothing to hide the amusement dancing in her wise eyes.

"Cheater," Trish teased. She cast Elisa a sympathetic look. "Want me to go clean it up so you can save face?"

"You'd be a daisy if you did." Elisa braced her elbows on the island and buried her face in her hands as Trish grabbed a rag and bustled out of the kitchen. But her shut eyes only provided a backdrop for the last few agonizing minutes to replay in slow motion. Along with a few replays from one particular summer—a movie she hadn't indulged in for quite some time.

Several minutes ticked by and she realized she was afraid to move.

"You okay over there?" Delia's familiar voice held a smile, though Elisa couldn't be certain with her closed eyes.

She slowly raised her head, straightening to a half-draped position over the island. "That man could intimidate the petals right off a tulip."

"Oh, what man?" Trish was back, tossing the coffee-soaked towel into the giant hamper under the back row of counters. Her red ponytail skimmed her back as she checked over one shoulder, as if said man might be in the kitchen with them.

Delia pointed the long-handled spoon at Elisa. "Your father?"

Elisa snorted. "That depends on who you ask."

"Now I'm pleading the fifth." Trish raised both hands. "Not that I know him well. But he can be scary."

"Dad used to be a lot gentler before . . . well. Before Mom died." He used to be a lot more of a lot of things before her mother passed. "But no, I wasn't talking about Dad. Even though he's out there right now . . . with Noah Hebert."

Blood roared in her ears at his name, and she tried to temper her visceral reactions. *Be a good girl and calm down.*

"Noah's out there?" Delia perked up at the stove, even as she reached around and massaged her lower back. Though forever young in spirit, Delia's age seemed to be creeping up on her, but she remained determined to keep cooking for the café. No one else would remember to put love in her recipes, as she put it. "What did he say?"

"Nothing. I was pouring Dad coffee, then I spilled it. Not a lot of opportunity for chit-chat." Not that she'd wanted to give Noah any. This diner was her safe spot—and he was an intruder.

"Who's Noah?" Trish crossed her arms over her apron-clad waist. "You know, this is one of the downsides to being new in a small town. I get zero tea."

"There's sweet tea in the fridge, hon." Delia gestured toward the double fridge across from the industrial sink.

"Not that kind of tea. Gossip. You know . . . like, spill the tea?" Trish gestured with her hands, as if pouring from a teapot.

"All that slang. Your generation makes communicating so much harder than it needs to be." Delia waved one hand in the air and resumed stirring with the other. "Noah moved away when he was a teenager but spent every summer here with his grandfather at the Blue Pirogue Inn. Noah and Elisa were . . . well. They were—"

"We just *were*. Once upon a time. Past tense." Elisa hated labels. Especially ones that were impossible to define.

Trish wiggled her eyebrows as she headed for the kitchen door. "I've gotta check him out."

"Trish!" Her protest was in vain. Her redheaded coworker was already peering through the rounded window in the dou-ble-hinged kitchen door. "Didn't you see him when you cleaned the table?"

"No one was there except your dad." Trish tilted her neck as she squinted to see. "Noah must have been drying off. That was a lot of coffee, Elisa. What'd you do? Trip and throw the entire pot?"

Elisa joined her at the second of the two doors and peeked

through the circular glass pane. Noah wasn't back yet. "I was startled."

Mostly by the force of his direct eye contact, but Trish didn't need those details. Hopefully Elisa had managed to save face. She didn't have much left by way of Noah Hebert, but she had her pride. Didn't she?

"Speaking of coffee spills, I appreciate your extra help today, even if you did try to drown my customers," Delia called from behind them.

"Anytime, Mama Delia." As manager these last three years, Elisa didn't often wait tables, but they were short-handed when she'd arrived that morning and it was packed as usual for the morning rush. Her father could have warned her that rush was going to include meeting up with Noah Hebert.

She turned back to the window. "Why didn't Dad warn me he was meeting him here?"

And why had no one warned her Noah's hair had gotten deliciously longer?

Trish sucked in her breath as Noah approached the table once more. "That's got to be him. Dark hair?"

"And flannel shirt." As always. Funny how it never used to annoy her so badly.

"Mmm, like the guy in those paper towel commercials." Trish made a *tsking* sound. "I'd have been flustered too, sister."

Elisa frowned, pulling back from the window to glare at her friend. "Not like that."

Delia coughed, and Elisa shot a warning look over her shoulder. "Mama Delia, you got something in your throat over there?"

She hummed. "Don't mind me. Just wondering how long your nose is going to grow."

Trish let out a burst of laughter. Elisa turned back as Noah looked up—straight at them. "Duck!" She grabbed Trish's wrist and yanked her down.

Delia kept talking, as if her two best employees weren't currently performing deep squats in front of the kitchen doors. "When did you see Noah last, honey?"

"Twelve years ago?" Elisa shifted her weight, waddling like a crab away from the window before she resumed standing. "He came to town for his grandfather's funeral six months ago, but we didn't attend." Bergerons and Heberts never expected that of each other.

So yeah, she hadn't been privy to Noah up close and personal in about twelve years now, Yet today, she'd been close enough to count the hairs forming his not-even-close-to-five-o'clock-yet shadow to notice the few that were already turning gray in a sophisticated lumberjack-type way . . .

Bless it, he *was* like that paper towel guy.

"So what did Noah do when you flirted with him?" Trish performed the same side-step crab walk away from the door, amusement lighting her freckled face as she awaited Elisa's answer.

"I didn't flirt."

Confusion etched between Trish's brows. "But you flirt with everyone."

Elisa bristled. "That's different."

"Why don't you take Noah a plate of pancakes? To apologize for the spill." Delia plated a short stack from the oversized griddle next to the stove. "I've got a few ready right over here."

"Me or her?" Elisa and Trish pointed at each other as they spoke simultaneously.

"I've been called many things in my years, but never a busy-body." Delia lifted her chin as she returned to her beans—a special recipe that was the perfect side for the café's famous Cajun breakfast tacos. "I'll let you two decide."

"I like paper towels." Trish grinned.

"Be my guest." Elisa gestured toward the diner, ignoring the completely misplaced twinge of jealousy sparking through her veins.

Delia waited until Trish had backed out the swinging door, plate in hand, before catching Elisa's eye. "Seems to me those proverbial tulips you mentioned earlier aren't the only things affected by Noah's presence today."

"*Delia.*" Elisa tossed her apron on the counter and crossed her arms. "He's a Hebert. Not to mention the last person I'd ever trust again."

"Hebert, hmm? Sounds a little like '*Montague*' if you ask me." Delia pointed at her with the spoon again, thick sauce dripping back into the stock pot. "Ms. *Capulet*."

"You know how it is with our families. Most kids got bedtime stories growing up." Elisa yanked open the dishwasher door, desperate to do something productive. "I got stories about the feud between the Bergerons and Heberts."

"You're doing that thing where you angry clean." Delia cranked off the burner and turned to face Elisa. "Which means—you *are* still hung up on this man."

Elisa grabbed a plate from the stainless steel sink opposite the stove, providing the perfect opportunity to turn away from Delia's all-knowing assessment. "Don't be ridiculous."

"I'm an old woman. I can be anything I want."

"What's that?" She hastily loaded two more plates, the dishes clinking together. "I'm sorry, I can't hear you, Delia."

Not deterred, Delia simply raised her voice. "I pay someone else to do that."

"As the manager. I oversee all operations—including labor." Elisa jammed another coffee mug onto the top rack. Delia had given her a job as a waitress in her late teens, cheered for her when she went off to culinary school with the dream of one day starting her own restaurant, and welcomed her back with open arms into a management role when all those dreams—and her heart—had

WHERE I FOUND YOU

dissolved. She owed Delia a lot. The Magnolia Blossom Café felt like home because of the woman's generosity and kindness.

"Tell me. What is it about Noah?" Delia abandoned the stockpot and headed to her favorite cutting board on the island.

Elisa shut the dishwasher door, then glanced around the clean kitchen. She was officially out of distractions. "What do you mean?"

Delia lined up a carrot on the wooden board. "You two got along quite well for a time if I remember correctly. Feud or no feud."

"That was a lifetime ago." Elisa rarely allowed herself the luxury of remembering that summer. When sunsets stretched long and lazy, when fireflies filled the humid evening air like fairy dust and late-night bonfires on the beach transitioned into early morning kisses . . .

"Well, you know what the Lord says about time—a thousand years is like a day, and all that." Delia began chopping.

Elisa zipped the charm on her favorite necklace along its dainty gold chain, ignoring the words she'd just used on Noah. "That feud runs deep in these parts, and you know it. Sometimes I wonder if Sheriff Rubart isn't even more upset about everything than Dad."

"I think Noah's adolescent escapades might have contributed to that." Delia smirked. "When Sheriff was a deputy, he had to clean up quite a few messes after Noah and Gilbert. He's a good boy, though."

Elisa tilted her head. "You never took sides, did you?"

"It's just land, darling." Delia shrugged as she worked the knife against a celery stick. "Plus, I wasn't around when the whole thing started before my time. I surely don't see any point in punishing anyone for their last name."

If only the rest of the town shared her sentiment.

Delia examined the knife in her hand, then dug a sharpening

tool from the drawer under the island. "Trish was right, by the way."

"About Noah looking like a paper towel ad?"

"About you flirting with everyone." Delia glanced up from the knife.

Elisa crossed her arms and stared at the chipped tile near the sink. "It's harmless. And serves a purpose."

She'd learned right quick after a decade of waitressing, culinary school, and restaurant management that being the one to flirt first created an ideal barrier—one *she* could control. Leave 'em guessing, treat 'em all the same. She kept her male customers at arm's length, and they kept the tip jar full . . . and her heart safe. Win-win.

Except she'd never attempted that formula on someone she'd truly liked.

"Maybe it has a purpose." Delia tested the knife's sharpness on the carrot, then began chopping. "But Noah's different, isn't he?"

He was, but not in the positive way Delia kept implying. Maybe that was Elisa's way out—maybe she needed to reverse tactics and flirt a little bit. Put Noah in a category she could handle. He'd flustered her, but if she treated him like everyone else, maybe she could hide the truth.

She leaned one hip against the countertop, fiddling with a floral-print oven mitt. "Noah is a puzzle."

"Good thing you like puzzles, then, Ms. Treasurer of the Puzzlers Club." Delia's smile turned into a wince as she rubbed her lower back. "Crank that thermostat down a few notches, will you, honey? It's warm in here."

It wasn't any hotter than usual in the kitchen, but Elisa obeyed anyway, moving to the unit on the far wall. "For the record, Noah is the kind of puzzle you buy only to discover all the pieces aren't in the box." Detrimental to one's plans and sanity, at worst. An aggravation, at the least.

"I bet." Delia shot her a knowing glance, then her face contorted in pain.

"Are you okay?" Elisa tossed the oven mitt on the counter and started toward her boss.

"Of course. Just the old hip acting up—" Delia's leg suddenly gave out and she grabbed for the counter, but missed, slapping the long handle of the butcher knife instead. It flipped into the air as Delia grasped for a hold on the cutting board, the island, anything—yet only found air.

"Delia!" Elisa lunged, but couldn't reach her before the older woman disappeared behind the island. The knife clattered to the ground, along with the cutting board full of vegetables.

Then everything went deathly silent.

Three

E HATED THE WAY THIS DAY WAS
going. And he especially hated that it was hard to feel confident and capable with a giant wet spot on his jeans from
his clean-up attempt in the men's room.

Noah had finally gotten his coveted short stack, but despite
sitting there staring at the rivulets of syrup, all he could think about
was how Elisa had cut her hair. The last time he'd seen her, that
blond mane had been long and flowing halfway down her back,
skimming the tie on her swimsuit top as she'd jumped off the dock.
Today, that short little ponytail only served to draw attention to
her eyes, wide and blue like the bay first thing in the morning.

Stop. The last thing he needed right now was distraction—
especially the distraction of Elisa. He stabbed his fork into his
pancakes.

"So, where were we?" Isaac moved a discarded, coffee-soaked
napkin farther away from his iPad with a grimace.

Noah set down his fork. "You were threatening me with the
local judge." Too bad the coffee spill hadn't taken out that blasted
inspection report. Just for the poetic justice of it all.

Isaac released a sigh that would have sent two of the three little pigs scurrying. "That wasn't a threat."

"I know what you're doing here."

"You gentlemen need anything else?" The red-haired waitress—Tammy? No, Trish—paused at their table once again, carrying a jug of water. She'd already brought a towel, pancakes he hadn't ordered, extra pats of butter, and a miniature pitcher of syrup. If he didn't know better, he'd think she was hitting on—

He looked up at her fluttering eyelashes and stifled a sigh. "I think we're all set here." He kept his tone polite, but firm. She was friendly and attractive, but he wasn't interested—after all, he would be leaving town once he got the mold situation under control.

"Let me know if you change your mind..." The young waitress trailed one hand along the edge of the table.

Noah blinked, and the redhead's image was replaced with Elisa's that one summer, bringing him a milkshake and jokingly sliding two straws across the table before shooting him a wink. How different might things be if he'd resisted her then, too?

He attempted to drown the memory with more syrup. Noah had a lot of practice getting Elisa Bergeron out of his thoughts—though some efforts worked better than others. He poured faster, avoiding Trish's eyes.

She finally gave up and took the water pitcher to another customer.

"I must say, that was nicely done—extricating yourself from that one." Isaac shook his head. "At least you seem to be an apple that rolled a bit farther from the tree."

"What did you say?" Noah's fork clattered to his plate. Sadie looked up from her book, and a middle-aged couple Noah didn't know cast them curious glances.

"Calm down." Isaac lowered his voice, holding up both hands as his gaze darted around the room. "That was a compliment."

Sure it was. "If you're aiming for a compliment, then tell me I'm pretty." Noah tossed a napkin on his uneaten pancakes, which were soggy with excessive syrup. He'd had enough. Isaac Bergeron was never going to help him—he was wasting his time. Maybe Isaac held all the power in this situation with the mold, but he wasn't going to sit there and let him talk about his family like that.

However much his old man might deserve it.

Noah abruptly stood—wet spot and all—and reached for his wallet. "Thanks for the inspection. I'll be in touch."

"Oh, come on. Sit—"

A sudden clatter rang from the kitchen. Noah, along with most of the patrons, looked up, forks paused en route to their mouths.

Isaac, however, appeared unfazed. He took a slow sip from his full mug. "Good ol' Delia. Clumsy as always."

That might be true, but Isaac said it more like a slam than a loving endearment. Noah liked Delia. She'd never played favorites in the feud between the families, taking a rare Switzerland position in Magnolia Bay. And yes, she always joked about breaking mugs.

Still, Noah's gut twisted as he stared toward the swinging doors. Something didn't feel right—that didn't sound as simple as a dropped glass. He hesitated, waiting for a confirmation laugh or "it's okay" to sound from the kitchen like he'd often heard in restaurants after a dish broke.

It didn't come.

He strode toward the kitchen, ignoring Isaac's protest. Sadie and several other customers shot each other concerned looks as Noah pushed behind the counter. Everything was probably fine. Delia would lovingly fuss at him for invading her space, then wrap him in a big hug and chastise him for not stopping by sooner.

But just in case.

He wasn't certain what he expected to see when he walked through the double doors into the kitchen, but it certainly wasn't Elisa bent over Delia, who lay unmoving on the floor by the island, her eyes shut tight as blood trickled down one arm. A smattering of vegetables covered the floor around her.

Noah's heart ricocheted against his throat. He dropped to the hard floor beside Elisa. "What happened?" He gently touched Delia's neck, searching for a pulse. *There.* His shoulders sagged with his exhale.

Tears tracked Elisa's cheeks. "I don't know. She was talking to me, and then suddenly, she was . . . she—" She shook her head, cutting off her explanation as she gestured toward Delia's still figure, wringing her hands.

He released a slow breath. "We need to find a clean towel, see how bad this wound is on her arm." He sat back on his heels, looking around for anything they could use. "And we should support her head."

"Right. We need a pillow." Elisa drew a shaky breath as she stood, and for a wild, unexpected moment, he wanted to comfort her. To offer assurances he didn't have, to pull her into a hug for old times' sake, to smooth that furrowed line between her brows.

And to explain that the kitchen probably wasn't going to have fresh bedding at her disposal.

He looked up, following her movement toward the counter, and noticed for the first time a busboy and a blond waitress hovering helplessly near the stove. He redirected his towel statement to the busboy as Elisa hurried across the kitchen on her misguided search for a pillow.

"Has anyone called for help?" Noah's question was only met with wide, blank stares.

He addressed the shaken waitress. "Call 911. And see if there's a nurse anywhere in the café."

She quickly obliged, pulling a phone from her apron pocket and rushing out the kitchen doors.

Then Elisa was back, crouching beside him and holding out an apron. "Will this work?"

BETSY ST. AMANT

"I think so." Noah folded the thin fabric several times to provide a cushion and gently slid it under Delia's head, careful not to move her neck more than necessary. He knew that much from television shows, at least.

"I can't believe I didn't immediately call 911." Elisa sat on the floor next to him, crisscrossing her legs. Guilt troubled her eyes and her chin, streaked with dark makeup trails, trembled. "Wake up, Delia." Her voice crested with panic as she gently tapped Delia's shoulder.

The same shoulder that Noah had cried on when he was a young teen, the day his dad had taken that age-old family feud and doused it with gasoline. Yet Noah had been so selfish since he'd been back in town, consumed with the inn and forgetting those who had helped him when no one else would.

"I should have visited the café sooner." His whisper slipped free—half to himself, half to Delia. Could she even hear him?

Then the busboy handed him a towel and Noah pressed it against Delia's arm wound. "See? It's not as bad as it looks." He didn't know that, but hope was a good thing to cling to until the professionals arrived.

"Why is she unconscious?" Elisa gingerly took Delia's hand in her own and rubbed the woman's wrinkled knuckles.

"She must have knocked herself out when she landed." Noah removed the towel long enough to see the bleeding had thankfully stopped. He nodded toward the butcher knife laying a few feet away on the tiled floor. "And that must have fallen with her. Looks like only a nick. Hit on a bad place, is all."

"She'd been chopping vegetables when it happened." She frowned. "Whatever 'it' was." New tears filled her eyes and her voice broke. "What *do* you think happened?"

A throat cleared from across the room. The young busboy looked about as uncomfortable as Noah felt—he needed an escape.

Noah shot the guy a sympathetic look. "Why don't you stand

43

guard and make sure no one else comes in the kitchen except the paramedics. Or a nurse, if your co-worker was able to find one." The last thing they needed was anyone crowding Delia.

The busboy eagerly took his post, what looked like relief crowding his expression as he hurried through the swinging doors. Then they immediately swung back open as Trish rushed inside, her eyes wide and her face pale. "What happened?" She covered her mouth with her hands when she saw the blood-stained towel.

Elisa shrugged helplessly. "We don't know. She just went down."

"What can I do?" Trish's voice shook as she squatted beside them.

"The first responders will need her insurance card." Noah studied Trish, who seemed up for the task. "Why don't you go find her wallet?"

Trish stood slowly, her gaze darting between Elisa and Noah. Then she nodded stiffly. "Of course. She usually keeps it in the storage room."

Noah turned back to Delia, who hadn't moved.

"Is she stirring?" The hope in Elisa's voice nearly undid him. Then her countenance crashed as she answered her own question. "I don't think so. Never mind."

He briefly touched her hand. "Don't worry."

"I hate blood." She squeezed her eyes closed, her breathing shaky.

Oh, how he knew. "Hang on." Noah took the opportunity to toss the stained towel off to the side, around the corner of the island. "Okay. You can open your eyes now."

She did, focusing right on him, and Noah realized his mistake in the suggestion. Her baby blues, now red-rimmed, met his gaze with more vulnerability than he'd ever seen. It nearly knocked him backward.

"I need her." Her tone pleaded, as if he had the power to give her what she wanted. And for a half-cocked minute, he wished he did.

"I know. Come on, Mama D. Wake up for us." He shifted into a more comfortable position on the floor, avoiding Elisa's eyes. Vulnerable or not, she was not his ally.

"The paramedics should be here any time now." The seconds felt like minutes, the minutes that had already passed, like days. His mind raced with what to do next. Right—the medics would want details on Delia. He shifted positions, trying to get the tingles out of his right foot. "Do you remember if she was slurring before she fell? Could it have been a stroke?"

Elisa adjusted her hold on Delia's limp hand. "I don't think so. We were talking about—" Then she abruptly rolled her lips together.

He followed the movement by habit before wrenching his gaze away from her mouth. "Talking about what?"

She lifted her chin a notch, eyes focused on Delia. "Puzzles. And the local Puzzlers Club."

That obviously wasn't the full story. Had they been back here discussing *him*? Delia had a way about her—mothering everyone in her path. Offering jobs, wisdom, hugs . . . whatever was needed, especially to the youth in the area. But you never outgrew Delia. She was one of the most respected women in Magnolia Bay, and the thought of Elisa spewing unfair details about him all these years he'd been gone lit a match in his chest.

Noah fought back his temper. He didn't want to fight with Elisa, but he also couldn't sit there pretending like they were polite strangers anymore. If they were going to be running into each other around town at all after this, they needed to set some ground rules. "Elisa, listen, we need to—"

"Look!"

Delia's eyes fluttered open and locked on Noah. "It's about time you showed up, boy."

Elisa didn't need Noah Hebert. Fool me once and all that, and she'd been fooled twice already.

But bless it, the man was hard to resist.

Elisa shoved her hair back from her damp forehead as she hovered, wanting to help the uniformed firemen but knowing she was completely in the way. Noah had tugged on her arm a moment ago, trying to edge her away from the bustling crew taking Delia's blood pressure, examining the lump on the back of her head, and bandaging her arm. But she'd shrugged him off, partly out of desire to stay right where she was ... and mostly because the touch of his fingers had her lighting up like a firefly.

Now Noah waited near the door, arms crossed as he kept an eagle-eye on Delia as the men finished their efficient routine. Noah, protective? He'd bailed on everyone years ago and hadn't looked back. He was a little late.

Even if he had been quite the hero for Delia today. The way he'd taken charge of the scene, helped Elisa breathe again, and acted cordially—as if their family's joint history wasn't more tattered than her great-grandma's quilt currently draped over the foot of her bed. As if the older firemen hadn't cast curious looks between her and Noah standing in the kitchen. Together. Montagues and Capulets.

Elisa tugged her phone free of her pocket, straining to hear the low voices of the men moving Delia onto a stretcher. She should text Mr. Bowman. The kind lawyer who always ordered bear claws had asked her to stop by his law office that afternoon, but she might need to stay at the café now. Everything that was so sure a half an hour ago felt so up in the air.

Then a muffled female voice joined the din. "Elisa?"

Oh thank heavens. Delia was awake again. After she'd looked

up at Noah and spoken those few cryptic words, she'd drifted right back out.

"I'm here!" Elisa shoved her phone back in her pocket and shot forward as the firemen secured the older woman onto the gurney. "She's talking. That's good, right?"

They ignored her question, but as she met Noah's gaze across the room, she watched a wave of what seemed to be relief wash over his face. So it *was* a good sign, even if the paramedics couldn't admit it. For the first time in what felt like an hour, Elisa took a full breath.

"Elisa? Is that you?" Delia's head was secured into a position where she could only look at the ceiling.

"It's me!" She knelt next to the lowered gurney and took Delia's clammy hand, trying to lean into the older woman's limited view while staying out of the way of the fireman working the straps. Then she looked up. "Wait. Where is she going?"

"Magnolia Memorial." Captain Sanders impatiently adjusted the brim of his cap and then gestured for two of the men to hoist the stretcher. "Come on. Let's get her loaded."

The hospital. Elisa's throat tightened. "Why?"

"You know I can't tell you that, Ms. Bergeron. Protocol." Captain shrugged. "You're not next of kin."

Elisa reluctantly stood and moved away from the stretcher as Noah cleared his throat. "Elisa is close enough to family, and everyone in the room knows it."

Elisa stilled. Noah Hebert, defending her? Somewhere really far south had just frozen over. She wasn't sure how she felt about that—and on second thought, it was probably best she *didn't* feel a single thing about it.

And she sure didn't need him coming to her rescue twice in one day.

Ignoring Noah, she rested her free hand on the captain's arm, working up a soft smile. "Darlin', Ms. Bergeron was my mama. You call me Elisa."

"Of course. Elisa." Captain dipped his head, shifting his weight beside the now raised stretcher. His arm warmed beneath her hand.

She looked at him from beneath her lashes. "Now, Evan . . . of course I respect you as captain and all . . . but you know you used to pull my hair in fourth grade. I think we're beyond *protocol*, don't you?" She cocked an eyebrow and widened her smile.

Heat flushed the man's tanned cheeks, and he coughed. But the sudden banging of the kitchen doors sounded before he could answer. Elisa whipped her head to see who had left.

Noah.

She shook her head, returning her gaze to Evan. "Her arm is bandaged and that nice gentleman there"—she pointed to one of the firemen with a Scripture reference tattooed on his forearm—"said there weren't immediate signs of a concussion. So why the need for the hospital?"

Captain shuffled his feet. "Elisa, I can't—"

"Good heavens, I'm right here. I can tell her myself." Delia waved her hand between them. "Elisa, who needs a watchdog when I have you?"

Captain smirked, then looked chagrined as he ducked out of Elisa's sharp gaze. "We'll, uh, we'll give you a minute."

"You'll give us two minutes," Delia said, clearly coming back to herself.

The other firemen stepped back, whispering with their captain, who was still flushed.

"Delia, what's going on?" She should be relieved Delia was her normal fiery self, but something still wasn't right. Normally, Delia would be shrugging off the fuss and returning to her black beans.

"Honey, all this stuff they fixed was a side effect of my fall." Delia pointed to her bandage and then gestured toward her head. "There was a reason I fell."

"So they're going to run some tests? Rule a few things out?" Elisa gripped her hand. "I can tag along, if you need me to."

Delia gave her a knowing look. "Now you don't really want to go to the hospital. I know it reminds you of your sweet mama."

"Oh, I'll be fine." Elisa shook back her hair. "I became a fan of those M&Ms in the vending machine on the chemo floor—finally figured out how to get D4 to work." She smiled, even as tears filled her eyes. Of course Delia would be more concerned about Elisa's memories than her own current health crisis.

Delia squeezed her hand. "Maybe so, but I want you to stay right here and close up the café. Make sure everyone gets their ticket and maybe give out the rest of the donuts as apology for shutting down early." Then she closed her eyes, as if faced with a sudden wave of pain.

Elisa sucked in her breath. "What aren't you telling me? Why did you fall?"

Delia opened her eyes, with what looked like a mixture of embarrassment and pain shining with the lingering tears. "My leg went out on me."

"That happens sometimes, though, right?" She hadn't wanted to point out how often, but if she knew, then Delia must.

"I think this was the last time they're going to let it." Delia licked her dry lips and focused on Elisa. "I can't keep putting off my surgery, hon."

"Hip replacement?" Elisa swallowed hard. That would be a massive undergoing, on top of the extended recovery afterward. How would the café survive without its chef that long? But Delia's health had to come first. "I'll help any way I can. Just tell me what to do."

"That part I don't know yet. Financially, this isn't something I can take on right now and you know how my insurance is."

"Yes, and I also know your aversion to doctor's offices." This

WHERE I FOUND YOU

911 expense would be a big enough headache—but hip surgery? It would be completely out of reach.

"The Lord will provide." Delia's voice deepened as it often did when she spoke about her relationship with God—one Elisa never could quite relate to her despite years of trying. "But do you understand what I'm telling you, honey?"

Elisa frowned.

"Ma'am, we need to go." Evan's firm captain voice didn't leave room for argument this time, not even from Delia Boudreaux. He gestured to the crew to take the stretcher again and they quickly obliged.

She grasped for Delia one more time. "I don't—what are you talking about?"

"I don't want you to panic, and I know how much this place means to you, but Elisa . . ." Delia's gaze locked with Elisa's as they began to steer her out of the room. "I might have to sell the café."

Four

I F THE STRESS OF THE DAY WASN'T GOING to do him in, the lyric-less soft rock playing over the law office speakers was sure to take him out.

Noah leaned forward in the faux leather waiting room chair, resisting the urge to glance at his watch a third time as a lazy ballad blared overhead and August Bowman's paralegal, Peggy, prattled on the phone across the lobby. Instead, he raked his fingers through his hair and stared at the worn area rug beneath his shoes.

August had asked him to be there at two o'clock, and it was already ten after. He'd give the man about five more minutes, then Noah had to get on with his day. Namely, finding the right color paint for Peter, and getting his insurance agency on the phone about the mold issue. The claims department had yet to call him back despite his repeated messages. The incident with Delia had temporarily distracted him from the bad news he'd received from Isaac, but now that he knew she was conscious and being taken care of, the weight settled back on his shoulders and made itself comfortable.

He released a tight breath. Maybe his first instincts were off, and his policy covered a surprise like this. The inn had hurricane coverage, which he'd already tapped into for the damage that occurred last summer. The problem might be in proving the mold came from that named storm. But maybe they'd have an additional stipend he didn't know about. Maybe it wouldn't be as detrimental as he feared.

Sure. And if wishes were crawfish, he'd have a nice bowl of gumbo about now.

Noah grabbed a nearby fishing magazine from the end table and flipped through the glossy pages as Peggy babbled about a recent nail salon experience. But all he could see were the events of the day in place of each article. That dreaded FAILED stamp. Elisa's startling blue eyes. The half-chopped carrot lying next to Delia's still form.

Elisa flirting with that fireman.

He shifted in the chair. Not that it had *bothered* him—he just didn't want a front row seat to this game she seemed to be playing. Since when did she get her way by flirting? It wasn't Elisa.

Though to be fair, how was he to know who she was anymore?

Noah tossed the unread magazine back on the table. He had bigger catfish to fry without getting all affected by Elisa—like his grandfather's legacy and his own inheritance hanging in the balance. Maybe if insurance wasn't going to help with the mold, he could extend his existing loan. But his buddy Owen, who was a loan officer at Magnolia Bank & Trust, had warned him four months ago when he took out the construction loan that Noah was near his approved lending cap.

One way or another, he'd figure it out. He wouldn't quit until he did.

He wasn't Russell Hebert.

"August shouldn't be much longer." Peggy finally hung up the phone from behind the counter and took a loud slurp of a nearly-empty drink. The middle-aged woman had a penchant for her new granddaughter and Schnauzers, if the collage of photos covering her workspace was any indication. "He's usually very punctual."

Noah responded with a brisk nod, but that apparently didn't curb her need for small talk.

"It's good to see you again." She pointed a blue pen at him, despite the one already tucked behind her ear. "I guess you haven't been back in this office since the estate settlement, have you?"

"No, ma'am." He hadn't had a reason to. And he didn't want to think about what the reason could be now. Whatever August needed, he would have to say no. Noah's plate was already overflowing with tasks, and his chest hurt thinking about his to-do list, which now included the insurance hassle.

And if this song didn't stop in the next five seconds he might—

The lobby door swung open and a woman rushed inside. "Sorry I'm late. There was an emergency."

The woman's gaze landed on Noah the exact moment her identity registered. Blood roared in his ears. He started to stand, then sank back into his seat. Twice in one day. Magnolia Bay was shrinking. "Elisa."

"Noah." They stared at each other.

"*And Peggy.*" The receptionist finished off the name declarations in a sing-song voice before cracking up. She wiped at her eyes, still laughing. "Sorry, I watched that Hamilton musical for the first time last week. I couldn't resist."

Noah watched the same rod that felt suddenly attached to his spine stiffen Elisa's posture as she hovered in the doorway. They should have cleared the air between them back in the diner while they had the privacy, but he hadn't wanted to stay and watch her show with the captain.

So now what? A dozen options flashed through Noah's head. Offer Elisa a chair? Pretend their reluctant bonding in the kitchen over Delia had never happened? Be friendly?

Peggy's gaze darted between them. "Well, look at you two! Back together again."

Elisa sank onto the chair farthest from Noah. "Coincidence, I'm sure." She crossed one jean-clad leg over the other, a gold sandal dangling half off her foot. "But you never know, do you?" She winked at him.

Noah narrowed his eyes. He wasn't Captain What's-His-Name, and he wasn't interested in joining Elisa's list of admirers. Especially not when she'd shot down his effort to help her earlier and resorted to flirting instead.

Peggy laughed again, the overeager sound of a woman who hadn't had quite enough conversation for the day. "Those were the good ol' days, huh? You two, shoving that family feud where the sun don't shine." She tilted her head and squinted. "I was only in my, what, mid-thirties back then? But I remember that star-crossed season like it was yesterday. Y'all were a real-life Romeo and Juliet—with a less tragic ending, of course."

That point might be debatable.

Elisa kept a steady smile trained Peggy's way, but Noah caught the flash of emotion skittering through her eyes before she tempered it. "All good things must come to an end."

Noah raised an eyebrow. "Good?" Not the word he would have chosen to describe that summer. Heated. Reckless, maybe. Foolish, for sure.

"And look at you now." Oblivious to the tension, Peggy tucked her hands under her chin. "All grown up. I mean, I see Elisa around town now and then—you know I can't stay away from the café's bread pudding. Obviously." She patted her hips. "But Noah, you've been a stranger around these parts for years! And apparently even since you've been back."

"Been busy with the inn." His throat felt as dry as his rote answer. *Where* was August?

"I can't wait to see what you've done with that old place. Everyone loved Gilbert, you know. Was such a shame what happened to him but I'm glad you're taking up the helm." Peggy pointed with the pen again. "Now, inquiring minds will want to know—including my niece. Are you single?"

His dry throat suddenly felt clamped in a vise. Was it his imagination, or had Elisa leaned forward a little in her chair?

The phone rang, the shrill alarm a blessed rescue. He exhaled enough to create a draft.

"Oops." Peggy uncapped her pen as she reached for the phone. "Hold that thought, now."

Definitely would not.

Elisa released a low whistle. "Saved by the bell, huh?"

He didn't smile back. The last thing he wanted to discuss with Elisa—or anyone, for that matter—was his relationship status. Which, for the record, hadn't changed since he'd been back in Magnolia Bay or even for the past two years before that.

But Elisa was watching him, as if waiting for a response. Fine. He'd give her one. "What are you doing here?"

Her hesitant grin faded. "Not following you, if that's what you're implying."

"I wasn't." He was, but he refused to feel guilty for the white lie. This Elisa he didn't know, and despite their earlier shared crisis, he wasn't about to start trusting her now. Not after her father's tricks—and definitely not with Peggy casually bringing up their past like it was a local trivia game.

Elisa tilted her head, studying him warily. "If you must know, I have an appointment with Mr. Bowman. Sort of." She glanced at her phone display. "Everything got all turned around on me after Delia's collapse, though. I might not have gotten the time right."

Okay, now he felt a little guilty. "How is Delia?"

Elisa tucked her phone back inside her purse. "She's at Magnolia Memorial."

He nodded stiffly. "They running tests?"

She hesitated. "It's not my place to say."

He snorted. He saw what she was doing now. The fire captain could be a pawn on Elisa's chess board, but Noah refused to pick up a game piece. Not again. "Let me guess. *Protocol*, right?"

Elisa blinked twice at him with blue eyes that would stop any other man in his tracks, her long dark lashes fluttering against high cheekbones. He steeled himself. Noah wasn't any other man. He was a Hebert. Maybe he'd forgotten for a moment earlier in the day, but he wouldn't again.

"Protocol?" She leaned one finger into her cheek, drawing his eyes to the dimple adorning her jaw. "What are you talking about?"

He shouldn't finish his thought. There was no reason on this entire storm-affected bay to finish his thought. And yet . . . he'd never been great at saying no when it came to Elisa. "That if you're expecting me to try to woo information out of you next, don't hold your breath."

"Excuse me?" Her eyes flashed as her hands dropped to her lap.

He was too far in to back out now. "Like you did earlier today with What's-His-Face. I'm not playing your games." He leaned back and crossed his arms over his chest.

"What *games*?" The words exploded from her lips, then suddenly, that same shell he'd seen at the diner slipped into place. She tossed back her hair, her expression now soft and controlled. She opened her mouth, but the sudden clatter of the phone hitting its base stopped her short.

"Oh, you two," Peggy giggled as she gestured with her drink. "It's not even Fourth of July and just look at all these fireworks!"

"I'd say more explosion than sparks." He cut his eyes toward Elisa.

"You must have me confused with someone else, sugar." Unfazed, she leaned toward Noah, holding his stare as her accent deepened. And like a sailor with a siren, he couldn't look away. Her pink lips parted, and a thousand traffic lights couldn't have stopped his gaze from following the movement. He felt her pause and short intake of breath in his own chest.

She didn't break eye contact. "I never once asked you to woo me."

The double meaning slammed his gut.

"You know, for a minute, back in the diner . . ." Elisa's voice trailed off. She shook her head. "I thought maybe we could get along—for Delia's sake, at least. But apparently not."

Then the interior door to the lobby opened and August appeared in the frame. "So sorry to keep you waiting. Come on back." He held the door ajar.

Gladly. Noah stood, his throat heated. Whatever August had to tell him would be better than this stroll down memory lane at gunpoint. He took a step forward, then hesitated. "Me? Or her?"

The same question was written across Elisa's stoic face as she perched on the edge of her chair, tucking her purse strap up on her shoulder.

"Both of you, of course." August hurried them along with a wave of his hand. "This way."

Elisa settled onto one of the hard wooden chairs across from Mr. Bowman's desk. She'd never encountered a grizzly bear, but she imagined they'd be a lot like Noah Hebert—temperamental, unpredictable, and overly scruffy. The man needed a haircut as much as he needed an attitude adjustment, and she had little hope of him receiving either.

She avoided looking at the man-bear taking the seat to her left and tried to focus on the grandfather clock tucked in the corner of Mr. Bowman's office instead. The air conditioner kicked on overhead, sending a welcome draft across her flushed cheeks.

What in the world had happened to the kinder version of Noah that comforted her in the kitchen after Delia's collapse? The man who distracted her from the sight of blood and took charge when she couldn't?

Some burr had nestled up in his saddle blanket, that's what. Well—maybe bears didn't wear saddles. She was mixing metaphors, but that's what trying to communicate with a man like Noah did—confused someone senseless.

Once upon a time, he'd kissed her senseless, but that was a memory she hadn't entertained in a decade and certainly wasn't going to start again now. She lifted her chin.

"I'm sure you're both wondering why you're here." Mr. Bowman folded his hands atop a thick file resting at the center of his tidy desk.

"More curious as to why she is," Noah muttered. "Is this about my grandfather?"

"Indeed." Mr. Bowman pushed his glasses up on his nose. "There's been a rather peculiar turn of events, but Gilbert was always a little peculiar himself, wasn't he?" He smiled fondly.

"I actually didn't know Gil—Mr. Hebert very well." Elisa frowned. "He came to the local puzzlers club meetings, but we rarely talked."

She was the only Bergeron in the club, and he had been the only Hebert, so by default they gravitated to opposite sides of the room. Sort of like all of her and Noah's extended family members did at church. Every Sunday was like a wedding, split with a groom's side and a bride's side. Maybe Delia was right, and no one cared that much anymore. But habits ran deep in Magnolia Bay, and those church pews might as well be branded with family crests.

"Well, Gilbert seemed to know *you* better than you might realize." Mr. Bowman leaned back in his chair, the worn leather creaking.

"What's this all about?" Noah's impatience shone through his clipped tone.

She'd wanted to ask the same thing, but leave it to Noah to pave the way with rudeness. "I'm sure he's getting to that, sugar."

Noah's eyes cut hard to her profile, but somehow she resisted the urge to look back. She kept her gaze trained on the lawyer.

Mr. Bowman tugged at his shirt collar with one finger. "I know this is unconventional. But Noah, I do have good news."

Noah leaned forward in his chair, his elbows resting on his knees. His jeans were dusty, and blue paint flecks she hadn't noticed earlier dotted his right forearm. "I could use some good news today."

She could too. Did he really think he'd had a harder day than her? He hadn't watched Delia hit the floor, hadn't had to process the fact that his entire life might be about to change with the potential sale of the diner. But Elisa wasn't about to make this a competition—or a scene. She sat quietly, tucking back her instincts to protest his claim.

Her father would be proud.

"There's a stipulation to your grandfather's will. Now that six months have passed since his death, I'm free to disclose it." Mr. Bowman picked up the file lying on the desk but didn't make a move to open it. "There's more inheritance to be had."

"What?" Noah sat up straight. "How?"

"Like I said, it's unconventional."

Elisa frowned. More money given on the anniversary of a death? That was more than a little unconventional. But she wasn't there to judge. To that point, she still had no idea why she was there at all. Other than she was clearly making Noah uncomfortable, and that was a bit of a win. She allowed a small smile.

"This is great timing." Noah rocked back on two chair legs, his eyes wide as the announcement visibly sank in. His face practically shone with relief. "You have no idea how great."

WHERE I FOUND YOU

"Hang on there, son." Mr. Bowman's tone grew cautious. "There's a condition." He swung his gaze toward Elisa. "This is where you come in."

She froze.

Noah's chair legs landed with a thud. "I'm sorry?"

"Me?" Her voice squeaked and she cleared her throat. "I don't understand, Mr. Bowman." She felt as confused as Noah looked.

He offered a patient smile. "Call me August."

"August," she obediently parroted, still perplexed.

The tension radiating off Noah, however, was clear as the bay on a summer morning. "How in the world does my grandfather's will have anything to do with Elisa?"

"Good question." August pulled a sealed envelope from the file and handed it across the desk to Noah. "The remainder of the inheritance is hidden away. Inside that envelope are clues to its location."

"Clues?" Noah sputtered. "Like a treasure hunt?"

"I'm afraid so."

Noah pulled a single card from the envelope, his brow furrowed. "This says Clue #1, Part 1." He squinted into the envelope's depths. "Where's the rest?"

August hesitated, then rolled his shoulders back as if bracing for a blow. "Well . . ." He reached over and handed Elisa a second envelope.

Even before she opened the flap, she knew. So did Noah, judging by his horrified stare.

Sure enough, she reached inside and pulled out a card. Clue #1, Part 2.

"You've got to be kidding me."

She didn't speak the words out loud, but she matched Noah tone for tone in her head. None of this made sense. Everyone knew Elisa liked puzzles. She enjoyed her monthly meetings with the Puzzlers Club and heading up the annual Magnolia Bay Scavenger

Hunt every year. This treasure hunt could be fun to solve, but not like this. This felt more like the type of puzzle where all the pieces *seemed* to fit at first, but the picture didn't line up on the seams and you realized it was all wrong.

This was all wrong.

"This has to be a joke, right?" she pleaded with August.

"No joke." The older man shook his head and busied himself straightening the fake succulent on his desk, taking care to line it up with his beige pencil holder—and avoid their eyes. "You're supposed to work together to solve the clues."

Together.

Elisa's eyes locked with Noah's. Her heart stuttered, panic swelling her pulse into her ears. No way. Today only proved they had zero business doing anything together, ever again. "Here." She thrust her envelope toward Noah. "I can just give you mine."

"I'm afraid that's very generous but prohibited." August gently *tsk'd* a finger at them. "It will forfeit you both from the inheritance if you cheat." He peered at them over the rim of his glasses. "And I will be watching, as I was instructed."

Good gravy.

Her thoughts bounced like a ping pong ball inside her tired brain. Gilbert Hebert had left inheritance for *her*? She wanted to ask how much money, but that seemed irrelevant. Right now, any amount could help Delia . . . could possibly save the Magnolia Blossom Café.

But like this? She didn't even know Mr. Hebert. It felt wrong.

Helping Delia felt right, though.

Elisa stared at her envelope, unsure what to do next. And judging by the seconds ticking loudly off the grandfather clock behind August, everyone else in the room felt the same.

Finally, Noah exhaled and broke the silence. "Listen. My grandfather could be eccentric, but he was never without purpose." He tapped his envelope against his knee as he squinted at August. "What else do you know?"

"Nothing I'm at liberty to discuss, I'm afraid." August spread his hands wide in a helpless shrug.

The envelope tapped a faster rhythm. "So you're saying we don't have a choice?"

"Not if you want the remaining inheritance."

Noah's Adam's apple bobbed. "And she gets part of the treasure?"

Elisa frowned at the offended tone of that "she." Like she was gum on the bottom of his boot. Though honestly, she couldn't fully blame him right now. She had no idea how she'd feel if her family member had suddenly passed and included Noah in their inheritance.

August nodded. "That's what's listed in the will. As executor of his estate and as his lifelong legal counsel, it's my job to see the will is upheld according to the specifics of what my client"—he paused, softening his rapid legal verbiage, and met Noah's gaze—"what your *grandfather* wanted."

Elisa shot Noah a look, feeling strangely affected by the way he seemed so unaffected. His back, ramrod straight, didn't even move with his breath. He kept his eyes trained on August, profile still, eyes slightly narrowed as if he were absorbing a beating. Like he'd win a prize if he showed as little emotion as possible.

She knew what that was like.

"Listen." August crinkled his nose at them both. "I know this is not typical. But that was Gilbert. And that's part of his charm and why we all loved him so dearly. Right?"

Noah's voice stayed tight but controlled. "Right. Sure."

Elisa risked a second look at the man-bear, and that's when she saw the truth. She recognized that mask he wore—she'd put it on herself almost every day for a decade.

Noah had never grieved his grandfather.

A surge of unexpected empathy welled in her chest. And suddenly Noah wasn't her mortal enemy, he was that awkward kid in middle school who turned bright red when the teacher called on him. The quiet teen who moved away in the midst of scandal and then reappeared as a man some four years later and swept her off her flip-flops.

"We can make this work." She shifted to face Noah, noting from her peripheral August's surprised straightening in his chair. But Noah continued staring at the succulent on August's desk. She ducked her head, trying to make eye contact with him. "I'm good at solving puzzles. Together, I'm sure we can—"

"Absolutely not." Noah suddenly stood, his chair shoving back a few inches. "Thanks for your time, Mr. Bowman." Then his eyes finally met Elisa's. "But I'm afraid it was all for nothing."

Then he simply walked out of the room.

Five

H E'D FORGOTTEN THE PAINT.

Noah opened the bait and threw his line into the sunset-sparkling waters of Magnolia Bay with a little more force than necessary. After the whopper of a Wednesday he'd had, was it any wonder he'd forgotten to go to the hardware store? No matter how fast he worked or how many notes he made in his phone app, he couldn't get ahead.

"Resorting to scaring the fish out of the water?" Cade Landry joined him at the far end of the west pier, the one only a half mile from the Blue Pirogue and the one they'd all unofficially claimed for their fishing nights. Cade's title of City Development Director—not to mention his status as the mayor's son—casually protected their holy grail of fishing spots.

"Might work better than the bait I used last time." Noah adjusted his hold on his rod, his jaw tight. His mind raced with all the things he still needed to accomplish, but if he had stood the guys up tonight, they'd never let him live it down.

He didn't need the list of people he was disappointing to get any longer.

Owen Dubois and Linc Fontenot strolled up the dock toward

them, Linc toting an ice chest in one burly hand while Owen walked faster to keep up, clutching his favorite ball cap against a gust of wind. The tired but sturdy wooden planks creaked under their combined weight.

Linc set the ice chest down on the pier with a thump, his man-bun shifting with the abrupt movement. "Drinks are here."

"Look who actually showed up." Owen grinned at Noah and then held out his hand, palm up, toward Linc. "Told you he'd come. Where's that fiver?"

Linc stared briefly at Owen's outstretched hand before making an about-face and picking up his rod.

"You can pay me later." Owen shrugged good-naturedly, pushing up the sleeves of his discount red hoodie. "Did anyone bring any extra bait?"

Cade toed his army-green tackle box toward Owen. "Help yourself."

Owen began digging through the colorful lures while Cade and Linc set up their rods—Cade's being a brand new designer pole he'd mentioned in the group text last week.

Noah took a deep breath, rolling his shoulders down and back as he stared toward the glittering blue depths. Maybe the guys wouldn't pester him and he could fish in silence, clear his mind of stress. Maybe he could watch the gold-tinted waves lapping against the thick beams of the pier. Admire the seagulls swooping down to try to find the fish before they did. Appreciate the spring wind blowing off the bay—

The crack of a can opening echoed across the open water. "How'd it go with Isaac?" Cade took a drag from his soda.

So much for that. Noah drew in his line to recast. "It went, that's for sure."

"Not good?" Cade swiped the back of his mouth with his hand. The sun glinted off his dark blond hair, the wind threatening to muss the perfect gel job he always prided himself on. "What happened?"

"Wait—Sadie came to the bank today and mentioned something went down with Mama D." Owen's brow furrowed as he stood, fumbling with his bobber. "Is she okay?"

"Of course she is. That woman is indestructible." Linc's deep voice refused any room for arguing. If he decided it was true, it must be—and usually was.

As Linc took Owen's lure and showed him how to set it properly, Noah shrugged. Last I heard, she was at Magnolia Memorial and doing all right. I don't have any details."

"So did you get your government invasion report, or what?" Linc shot him a side-glance.

"His what?" Owen laughed.

"His piece of paper proving something he already knows about his own property." Linc gestured with the lure in his hand. "A man should be able to run his own business without interference from the government."

Cade nearly spewed his drink as he laughed. "You do remember my dad is the mayor?"

"Aye." Linc glowered. "I said what I said."

"So did you get it?" Owen took his pole to the edge of the pier.

"I got it all right." Noah balanced his rod between his legs and pushed up the sleeves of his flannel shirt. Despite the wind, it was getting warmer. Or maybe having to admit failure flushed him even more than seeing Elisa had. Hopefully they wouldn't connect *those* dots—

"I heard Elisa Bergeron spilled coffee all over you, too." To his credit, Owen tried to hide his smile but failed.

Noah clenched his jaw as he reclaimed his fishing rod. "Sadie sure was chatty today."

"What can I say? Business accounts take a while to open." Owen cast his line into the water, making Linc duck and glare. "But back to the inspection—what happened? You're not as chipper as I'd imagined."

"Maybe because you just used the word *chipper*." Linc stepped back to give Owen room as he yanked on his line.

"I got something!" Whatever it was sure didn't want Owen to reel him in.

Linc went to help him while Cade sidled closer to Noah. "You good, man?"

"About the meeting with Isaac?"

"You know what I mean." Cade turned up his soda can for another swig. "You haven't seen Elisa in . . ."

Noah kept his focus on Owen's struggle with the fishing pole and Linc's futile efforts to take it from him. "Twelve years."

"That had to have been a shock."

"The hot coffee pouring into my lap sure was."

"What are y'all whispering about?" Linc asked, stepping back toward the cooler.

Cade fished around in his tackle box. "Elisa Bergeron."

"Dude." Noah shot Cade a look. "Come on."

"Y'all's past isn't really a secret anymore." Cade gestured to the town behind them.

Linc pulled free a drink. "What happened between you two?"

"You actually care?" Surprise lit Owen's sunburned cheeks.

Linc shrugged one massive shoulder as he popped the top. "If we're going to be out here gossiping, I'd like to be in the know. I was off at college when this drama went down, apparently."

"Noah saw Elisa for the first time in forever today," Cade explained.

Owen nodded eagerly. "And she was so upset she dumped coffee on him."

"That is *not* what happened." Noah groaned. "How did this fishing trip turn into narrating my life like a bad audiobook?"

"Hang on. Here are the facts—Noah and Elisa had this whole

Romeo and Juliet thing going on the summer we were all eighteen." Cade nodded his head toward Linc. "Not you, obviously. Old man."

"I'm two years older. Shove it."

"Just let us know what the view looks like when you hit forty first."

Linc flexed, his bicep nearly bursting through his shirt sleeve. "Oh, it'll look fine."

Cade ignored him. "Anyway, it ended really bad. The whole family feud thing . . . her dad obviously didn't approve of them sneaking around together, and it all blew up one night while he was cleaning his shotgun."

Owen's eyes grew wide as he tossed his line into the water. "He shot you?"

"*No.*" Noah sighed. "We just didn't get a lot of closure after that, and I went back to Shreveport. See? This is why I never talk about it." Not to mention it wasn't a pleasant topic to revisit. Then fragments of memory, coated with Elisa's vanilla perfume and sunkissed hair, skittered across his mind.

Okay maybe the memories weren't *all* bad. Just what they turned into.

"We were kids. We should have known better—maybe we did. Maybe the forbidden element is what made it what it was." Noah shrugged. "Regardless, it's over, and Elisa didn't pour coffee on me on purpose. Let's set that rumor straight."

"What is this whole feud about, anyway?" Linc asked. "I guess I've missed that too. Just know your families hate each other."

"Elisa's ancestors accused mine of stealing land from them, all the way back to patent in the 1800s. It's been a bone of contention ever since."

"That's dumb," Linc declared.

"I agree. But it's the land the Blue Pirogue is on, so it affects me. Especially now."

Cade leaned against the pier railing. "I've always leaned your way on that whole thing—namely, because I know how Isaac can be—but I can't hate on Elisa. We go all the way back to our elementary school days."

"Yeah, I know. We all hung out together in middle school. Braces, acne, Cade's endless pranks, and all." A grin worked its way up to the surface. "Those yearbook photos would make for excellent blackmail."

"And then you moved." Cade rolled his eyes. "Just *had* to break up the party."

"Obviously that wasn't my choice." Noah shook his head. "Definitely my father's."

Owen frowned. "I thought your parents divorced?"

"They did. After my dad's infidelity, my mom pulled me out of ninth grade early on and moved us to Shreveport." Noah scoffed. "Nothing like starting a new high school in a new city."

"Yikes." Owen scrunched his face in sympathy as he adjusted his line.

"Well, personally, I'm glad you're in town again, even if it is temporary." Cade clapped Noah on the shoulder. "And even though you stubbornly refuse to stay."

"I know, man." The encouragement took a bit of the edge off Noah's day. "Thanks."

"If you two are done being mushy, there's more fishing to do." Linc glared as Owen turned and held up the tiny snapper he'd snagged.

He handed Owen a different lure from Cade's tackle box. "You're baiting the next one yourself, show-off."

"Now that you have the inspection report clear, what's your plan? How long until you abandon us again?" Cade asked.

Owen went to work with a metal jig while Noah reeled his own line back in. He let out a slow breath. "I *don't* have a clear inspection report. Isaac failed it." Noah set his rod down. Time for a cold one.

As if reading his mind, Linc handed him a drink from the cooler. "That's low, man. He should be more professional."

"The worst part is . . . I think he was." Noah shut the cooler lid and sat on top of it. It'd be easier to blame the rejection on Isaac's longstanding beef with his family or even on those threatening letters the man sent to the inn that summer when Noah was with Elisa. But the proof was in the photos. "The Blue Pirogue has black mold."

"From Hurricane Anastasia?" Cade picked up his rod from the pier, casting a questioning look over his shoulder at Noah.

Noah nodded. "Most likely. Going to be hard to prove that was the cause, though."

"Insurance company won't like that." Linc crossed his arms over his dark red shirt. "Might not cover it without evidence."

"Way to help, Pollyanna." Cade snorted as he cast his line. It zipped cleanly through the air and landed in a patch of water highlighted with the sun's reflection. "Pretty sure he's aware of that."

Linc shrugged a beefy shoulder. "The truth is the truth."

"And the truth will set you free." Owen, still attempting to bait his line, glanced up at them.

"Is that in the Bible?" Linc squinted down at him, arms still crossed. "Or is that another one of those 'God helps those who help themselves' assumptions of Scripture?"

Owen shifted his kneeling position on the dock. "It's in there. Out of context for this conversation, maybe, but check John 8 next time you crack open the Word."

"Leave it to the PK to know for sure." Cade tugged at his line.

Owen grinned good-naturedly, though the pastor's kid references had to get old after a while. "You guys could know as much, too, if you read a little more."

"I know Scripture, but I'm bad at the references." Cade shrugged.

That was more than Noah could say. He was bad at all of it. In fact, his grandfather's funeral had been the first time his rear had landed in a pew in nearly a decade.

After all, if he couldn't fully trust God, it was probably better to stay off his radar.

"So what are you going to do?" Linc brought the conversation back around to its unfortunate origin. "Is Bergeron shutting you down?"

Noah shook his head. "Isaac technically can't, but he did point out I can't operate until it's handled. Threatened to go to Judge Morrow to make that official if I don't take this seriously. And right now, the inn *seriously* can't afford any more loans."

Cade sighed. "I'm afraid Bergeron's right on that one. And my father is big on safety, especially post-hurricane. So I couldn't get him to sweet talk Morrow for you if that happened."

"At this point, I'm hoping insurance will kick in." Noah drummed a nervous rhythm on the cooler. "They covered some of the earlier repairs right after the storm, but I'm not sure if this is going to qualify."

"What about your dad?" Cade asked.

Noah cut his eyes hard to his friend. "What *about* him?" He heard the poison dripping from his own voice, so it was no surprise Cade immediately shot him a "never mind" look.

Russell Hebert might be making a name for himself on the west coast with his hotel chain, but he wasn't an option for borrowing money—and not only because he would probably say no.

"Sorry." Noah took a deep breath. "I decided years ago I didn't need him, and I'm not going to start now." Their semi-annual phone conversations were plenty. Even then, it was hard to shut out Noah's teenaged urge to earn his dad's attention.

But his father had made his choices years ago—ones that didn't include Noah.

"It's all good, man." Cade adjusted his line. "Just making sure it wasn't an option."

"You never know about insurance coming through." Owen sprang to his feet, holding his successfully baited line like a prize. "Life can surprise you sometimes."

"That's for sure." Noah hesitated. Did he really want to reveal the next surprise of the day? Might as well get it over with—they'd hear eventually. He stood and ambled to the edge of the pier with his rod, bracing one hip against the low wooden railing. "I got another one of those life surprises at August Bowman's office today. Turns out my grandfather left more inheritance for me."

"Dude!" Cade slapped him on the back, jostling his fishing pole. "That's huge! Why didn't you lead with that? Won't that solve your money problem?"

Noah winced. "It's a bit of a game to get it. Literally." He took a deep breath, flinging his line into the waters as he rattled off the next words. "I have to solve clues to find it. Like a treasure hunt."

"That's not so bad. Kind of fun, huh?" Owen squeezed past Linc to the ice chest.

Linc scoffed. "Aye, your grandfather was a character. I'm not surprised at all."

"It'd be almost *more* surprising if he didn't have some kind of last laugh from the grave." Cade chuckled.

That was true—frustrating, but true. Noah watched as his red and white bobber danced on the waves. Grandpa had always been eccentric—the kind of man equally as likely to scold Noah for lying as he was to invite him onto the roof of the inn with a paper towel roll to watch for pirates. Or spend an afternoon out on the boat, rowing and offering brain teasers for Noah to dissect, like his favorite quote from *The Count of Monte Cristo—To learn is not to know; there are the learners and the learned. Memory makes the one, philosophy the other.*

He missed him.

"That's not all." Noah cleared his throat and tightened his grip. "I have to do the hunt with Elisa Bergeron."

Silence filled the space between the men. Only the cry of a seagull interrupted the sudden stillness.

"Okay, so maybe you can appeal the will." Cade raised an eyebrow at Noah. "That's a thing."

"I'd have to ask August."

"Seems to me if that was an option, he'd have presented that in the moment." Linc shrugged in that annoying, no-nonsense way he did when he was right.

"I agree. Just play it out." Owen rummaged around in the cooler and retrieved a can of sparkling water.

"Aye." Linc cast and stared stoically out into the water. "Besides, what kind of grandson would you be if you tried to blatantly override your grandfather's wishes?"

Owen dropped his water can and gaped.

"Linc!" Cade exclaimed. "Come on, man."

Noah scrubbed his hand over his chin. "He's right." Brash, but right. "I'm stuck, and Grandpa knew it."

"*Knows* it, maybe." Owen chased the can as it rolled a few feet down the pier. "He could be watching all this, too."

Cade pulled an errant weed off his line before recasting. "Does Pastor Dubois agree with your theology on that one?"

Owen cleaned the top of the can with his shirt hem. "There's actually a lot of theologians who believe our loved ones can see—" Sparkling water spewed in his face as he opened it.

"Before we start arguing religion or politics, can we get back to my problem?" Noah set his rod on the pier as Owen swiped his face with his sleeve. Enough fishing for one day. He turned to Linc. "So you think I should do this?"

Linc met his gaze and held it. "I think your grandfather had a plan and it's worth respecting."

Noah flinched, his fists clenching at his sides as if on autopilot.

"There wasn't a lot of respect when he refused to tell me his cancer had come back until the last minute."

Linc, for once, stayed silent.

Noah bit his bottom lip until he tasted blood. Why had he said that? He hadn't admitted that to more than the mirror in months. But if he'd only known the remission was over, he could have—

Cade set his pole down with a clatter and came to Noah's side. "Look, I know it's been a rough year."

"I've had worse." Like the year he was fourteen, for example, and learned how bad his dad sucked at being a family man. But this year had also been up there—and it kept escalating. "I'm just overloaded with renovations for the inn."

"Before tourist season starts." Owen nodded in understanding, taking a careful sip from his dented can.

Noah waved a hand at Cade. "You should understand that. You've been working with your father the past six months on fundraisers for all these rebuilding efforts."

"Well, sure. I think we all understand busy." Cade gestured toward Owen. "On this pier alone, we've got a loan officer in the middle of a city financial crisis, and a fisherman—"

"Aye." Linc rolled his eyes. "For the hundredth time, crawfishing is not the same as fishing."

"—*crawfisherman* trying to maintain a living in an economic dip," Cade continued.

"Exactly." Noah exhaled. "So you guys can see how I don't have time to work in a wild goose chase . . . which I'm horrible at, by the way. I might have inherited the inn, but not Grandpa's puzzle-solving skills."

Owen furrowed his brow. "Maybe that's why he wanted Elisa to help. Isn't she in the Puzzlers Club?"

Cade nodded. "She heads up the annual town scavenger hunt, too. She's great at that stuff."

Noah shot a look at Cade, who lifted both hands and shrugged. "Just stating facts, man."

It didn't matter. "I don't want her help. We *can't* work together." They couldn't even have a conversation together, if the run-in at August's office had been any indication. "Besides, if he knew I couldn't do it, then why even start this in the first place? He could have willed whatever he wanted from the beginning."

"I don't know. It sounds to me like this might be God solving your money problem with the Blue Pirogue." Owen's eager smile did not match Noah's opinion of the idea.

"Whether the Lord is involved or not—it doesn't sound like you have a choice if you want the money." Linc, the only one still fishing, kept his eyes on the water. "So it comes down to what's the inn worth to you?"

That wasn't fair. The inn had been the one constant in Noah's childhood—the one thing he could count on in his troubled teen years when he couldn't depend on anything else. No matter how unstable things were between his parents as a kid, or how hard it'd been finishing high school in north Louisiana with a bitter single mom, he could always come back to the Blue Pirogue for the summer.

He couldn't fail it now. Was he being prideful in resisting the help? Grandpa had arranged it like this for a reason.

He just couldn't for the life of him figure out why.

"That man-bun gives you much wisdom." Owen teasingly swiped at Linc's hair but could barely reach the balanced knot at the top of the guy's six-four frame.

"It's *not* a man-bun," Linc growled, jerking out of range. "It's just my hair."

"I agree with Owen. I think this might be the Lord working. But maybe the insurance will come through, and it won't be such a pressing decision for right now." Cade opened his tackle box and rifled through the colorful assortment. "We can always hope, right?"

He'd been a little short on hope lately. But Cade was right. There wasn't necessarily a decision to make today. Besides, Elisa might not even want to work with him after he'd charged out of Mr. Bowman's office like a bat out of an exceptionally hot place.

"I'll see what my insurance company says and go from there." There. Decision *not* made. And somehow that felt like enough for now. Noah took a deep breath of salt-laced air.

But blast if he didn't still smell traces of vanilla and honey.

Elisa's best friend and roommate, Zoey Lakewood, set a white bakery box of beignets on the vintage trunk-turned-coffee table between them before plopping onto the dark gray sofa. "I brought leftovers. You know what I always say—can't dish without a dish." She tossed back her long black hair and grinned.

Elisa leaned forward in the floral armchair she'd had since college—the one Zoey had kept for her while she was away at culinary school—and plucked a powdery treat from the pile. Zoey opened Bayou Beignets a little over a year ago and had already won local awards for best dessert on the island. "Thoughtful as always."

She started to take a bite, but Zoey lunged forward, arms extended, nearly knocking over their water bottles. "Wait!"

Elisa froze, beignet halfway to her mouth.

Zoe's bright blue eyes widened. "Remember the cardinal rule of beignets."

Right. Don't inhale or exhale. Elisa held her breath and shoved half the beignet into her mouth. Powdered sugar melted on her tongue and provided a delicious reprieve from her thoughts. Her mind kept churning up worry like the silt at the bottom of the bay.

"I've successfully sugared you up. Ready to talk now?" Zoey tugged a navy polka-dotted throw pillow into her lap and settled in.

They'd shared many a chat in this living room over their past two years of rooming together—an extra blessing for Elisa, since having a roommate meant she'd only had to stay with her dad for a brief time after leaving culinary school. If these walls—which were mostly covered in framed canvases of Zoey's black and white photography prints—could talk, they'd have more than a few secrets to share.

Elisa finished chewing before speaking. "I know you heard about Delia falling at the diner."

Zoey waved a dismissive hand. "The whole town heard." She leaned in. "Did you really hit on Captain Sanders?"

"*No.*" Elisa reached for a second beignet, then thought better of it and sat back against the chair. "I . . . convinced him to give me information."

"I bet." Zoey plucked a pastry from the box and chomped into it, powdered sugar providing her with a temporary mustache. "So how is Delia? That I haven't heard."

"Physically, she's going to be fine. Eventually." Elisa had left Mr. Bowman's office and gone straight to the hospital to check on Delia before visiting hours ended. The sweet woman had been a little groggy from pain meds but coherent enough to confirm Elisa's worst fear.

"Great!" Zoey clapped her hands, sending another puff of sugar into the air. "Praise the Lord."

"Amen." Elisa licked leftover sugar from her finger, then hesitated. She wished the story ended with the praise. *Because I am grateful, Lord.* The silent prayer lingered in her heart.

But there was more to the story.

She inhaled a tight breath. "The surgery will be what Delia

needs, but she's going to have to sell the café to afford the operation."

"What?" Zoey's hands fell to her lap. "She can't sell the Blossom. That place has your blood, sweat, and tears seeped into every surface." She wrinkled her nose. "Maybe scratch that specific description, but you know what I mean."

"My reaction was the same, trust me." Elisa swallowed hard, dusting her hands on the plaid pajama pants she'd changed into upon arriving home. She needed all the comfort she could get tonight—especially considering the other blow Delia had delivered.

The one she hadn't even had time to process for herself yet.

"Is there no other option?" Zoey clutched the pillow to her chest.

"She offered to sell it to me." Elisa's stomach twisted. "That's the worst part. I can't begin to afford it."

Nor could her father, even if she found the courage to ask. He made a decent living now, but they'd never had extra growing up. The medical bills had piled up for her mother, along with the unexpected funeral costs. Elisa had worked her behind off to send herself to culinary school . . . just to throw it all away.

Not that Trey had given her a choice.

"Ugh. I hate that." Zoey frowned, her dark bangs nearly obscuring her sympathetic gaze. "Buying the Blossom would be so perfect for you."

In theory, yes. In reality . . . "Even if I could, it wouldn't be the same without Delia. She's the talent."

Zoey pursed her lips. "You went to culinary school. She's not the only one with skills in the kitchen."

Elisa rolled her eyes. "I haven't cooked in years. I'm a manager now for good reason." Reasons she wasn't about to discuss tonight. The day had been emotional enough without fixating on her memories with her mom.

"I heard a few other interesting things today." Zoey quirked an eyebrow. "Word got around that the Bergerons and the Heberts were mixing."

Elisa tugged at the suddenly confining neck of her zip-up sweatshirt. "That's the last thing I need right now."

"You know small-town gossip chains—and you guys are two popular links right now." Zoey smirked. "So what happened?"

Elisa filled her friend in on the moments after Delia's collapse, where Noah had rushed to her aid like—well, like a friend.

"That's good, right?" Zoey frowned. "Why are you telling me this like I should be upset?"

"Because I *hate* that I opened up to Noah." Elisa pulled the hood of her sweatshirt over her head and sank into it. "I thought maybe something had shifted a little between us, into, I don't know— mutual acceptance?" Heat flushed her throat. "But he was right back to being awful afterward. I'm a fool."

"You're hardly a fool." Zoey shifted positions on the couch. "You were in a state of crisis."

That was one way to put it. Fear struck hard when Delia hit the floor. "I froze. Watching the firemen, with their stabilizers and blood pressure cuffs and bandages . . . it all looked so official. So necessary."

Zoey tilted her head. "It *was* necessary. That's their job."

"I know. I meant . . ." Elisa fiddled with her hood string. Her throat tightened and she squeezed back the unwelcome emotions. She couldn't—wouldn't—break down. She'd stayed strong for Delia—once she was awake, at least, since she hadn't managed to do so while she was unconscious—and hadn't reacted poorly at the hospital. She'd even kept her cool with Noah, hadn't let him see how much he fazed her.

She couldn't fall apart now.

Despite Elisa's silence, recognition lit Zoey's eyes. "The incident today reminded you of your mom." Her voice dipped in compassion.

Elisa burrowed further into her sweatshirt until the knot in her throat loosened. "I don't know why."

"It's understandable."

She squinted at her friend. "Fainting and hip pain aren't the same as cancer."

"Trauma is weird." Zoey shrugged. "No one can hold you responsible for what you said in the middle of a trigger. Not even Noah Hebert."

"I was so afraid I was going to lose Delia too." Elisa edged the hood away from her face. "She's going to be okay. But the café..."

"So you're still potentially losing something you love." Zoey sighed.

"My mom worked at that diner. How can I let it go without a fight?"

Zoey twisted her lips to the side. "There's got to be something you can do."

The rest of the afternoon blipped back on Elisa's radar, shooting off welcome sparks of indignation. "Well, it wouldn't have to be like that, if Noah would get his head out of his stubborn—"

"Not feeling so vulnerable and crisis-y anymore, are we?" Zoey snorted.

"Noah has a way of making all good feelings vanish." She updated Zoey on Gilbert including Elisa in his will and the treasure hunt stipulation. "In a way, I don't blame Noah for being upset. I *am* a Bergeron."

"Yeah—and Gilbert was a grown man who could do what he wanted." Fire lit Zoey's blue eyes. "I'd be happy to point that out to Noah. I can't believe he's refusing to do this hunt when you need the money for such a good cause."

"To be fair, he doesn't know I need the money to pay for Delia's surgery. And it's his grandfather. His decision to make." Elisa bit down on her lower lip. "Unfortunately."

"Do you know how much you stand to inherit?"

Elisa shook her head. "I didn't want to ask. I figured if we were supposed to know, Mr. Bowman would have told us in the meeting."

"An unknown inheritance. Could be anything." Zoey's eyes sparkled with curiosity. "What if you did the hunt and only got fifty bucks?"

Elisa grinned. "Then I'd get to watch Noah grow a second head."

"He deserves to be pranked from the grave, honestly."

Zoey's loyalty radar had always flared high—it was one of her best qualities as a friend. "I appreciate that. And these." Elisa finally gave in and snagged another beignet. "It's frustrating to have a solution so close, yet out of reach. But like you said, we don't even know if my share would help make a dent in Delia's hospital bills."

"You could do the hunt and find out."

"Not solo. It was clear we work together or not at all." She bit into her dessert, staring aimlessly at her favorite canvas of Zoey's—a close-up of Delia behind the counter at the Magnolia Blossom, head tilted back in wild laughter—as she let herself imagine what the hunt would entail. Following clues, solving riddles . . . It would be fun, if it wasn't with someone who hated her guts.

"Convince Noah, then. Turn on that charm of yours." Zoey deepened her voice and upped her southern twang. "*Sugar.*"

"Oh, stop it." Elisa tossed the chair pillow at her roommate, who batted it onto the navy pinstripe rug. "I think Noah's immune to me."

"He wasn't that one summer." Zoey caught the pillow and wiggled her eyebrows.

"No fair." Elisa gestured with her beignet. "That summer is off limits. And so is he."

"It's too bad, really. You guys made a great couple while it lasted."

"Try telling that to my dad." Elisa rolled her eyes. "Not that Noah would be interested anymore anyway after getting run off my porch with a shotgun." Not that that was the whole story.

Zoey scrunched the pillow into her chest. "It probably wasn't as dramatic as you remember."

"Dramatic or not, the end result was the same—Noah walking away, and never coming back." She could still see the stretch of his T-shirt across his back even now, if she closed her eyes long enough. Funny how a short relationship so long ago could linger like yesterday.

"Regardless of shotguns and past summers . . . you know what you need to do." Zoey eyed the beignet box, as if debating going for another pastry. Then she met Elisa's gaze. "For Delia."

"I know." Elisa pulled the hood up over her head again. Maybe she could burrow into this jacket a little farther and find a back door into Narnia . . .

"So go do it. Swallow your pride."

Elisa grimaced. "I don't think I have any left when it comes to Noah Hebert."

"Here." Zoey tossed a water bottle at Elisa. "This will help wash it down."

Elisa caught the bottle and stuck out her tongue. "Cute."

"Noah sure is."

"That has zero bearing on anything!"

"Except making the scenery better when you beg him to do the treasure hunt."

Elisa frowned. "Who said anything about begging?"

"I misspoke." Zoey uncapped her bottle and paused. "When you *charm* him into doing the treasure hunt."

Elisa laughed, but her hands shook as she twisted the lid on the bottle of water. She clearly no longer had any effect on Noah Hebert.

But for Delia's sake, she had to try.

Six

HE WAS SEEING THINGS.

Noah set his tackle box on the shelf of the inn's garage and scrubbed his eyes with his palm. He blinked twice, but the image of Elisa Bergeron rushing through the twilight across the front lawn of the Blue Pirogue, wearing an oversized sweatshirt and red plaid pajama pants, didn't diminish.

He turned to fully face her—or perhaps her apparition—but she didn't seem to notice him as she pushed up the sleeves of that giant hoodie. She angled away from the garage, dodging a paint can Peter left out in the grass, and hopped over a discarded stepladder.

In the distance, headlights flashed then vanished as the slow rumble of an engine faded.

What in the world?

This day couldn't get much weirder. He'd thought the call from the claims adjustor he'd just received dropping the bomb that his insurance payout for hurricane-related claims was maxed had been the final nail—but he might have assumed too quickly.

He edged out of the garage, keeping to the shadows as Elisa continued her dogged mission down the walkway bordered by overgrown bushes—he kept meaning to trim them back—to the front door of the inn. There she squared her shoulders, lifted her chin, raised her hand to knock . . . and froze. Fist lifted, back straight, unmoving.

She'd chickened out.

He smirked and leaned one hip against the corner of the inn, crossing his arms over his flannel shirt as he waited.

Her arm lowered to her side, and she shook back her hair, the blond bright against the deepening dusk. She raised her fist again, inches from the door, then exhaled loud enough to disturb all the fish they hadn't caught in the bay.

Oh for crying out loud.

He straightened. "Christmas called. It wants its pants back."

Elisa shrieked, jumping backward like a cat and stumbling over the concrete step. She planted one hand against her heart and bent over, chest heaving as she glared. "Bless it, you scared me."

"You're the one creeping around in the dark." Noah stopped a few feet away on the walk. "In your pajamas." He gestured toward her buffalo plaid sweatpants.

She closed some of the distance between them. Crickets protested the interruption from the unattended flowerbeds alongside the porch, and the evening wind that rustled her hair sent a welcome rush over his slightly sunburned neck.

Elisa's cheeks were pink, but he'd bet money it wasn't from a sunburn.

"Sweatpants aren't seasonal." She peered up at him, her crossed arms making her look tiny beneath the sweatshirt's bulk. "I have a pair with ice cream cones that I wear in the winter."

"Noted. Was there anything else you came here to say?" He glanced at the driveway, which was empty save for his own vehicle and one of the work trucks the crew left behind. "Walked here, apparently, to say?"

"I didn't walk." She stabbed her hands through her hair, pulling it away from her cheekbones as she released her breath. "And yes, I'll say it as soon as my heart rate returns to normal."

Elisa standing a few feet away from him in her pajamas was causing his own arrhythmia. Good grief, did the woman sweat vanilla? How did she always smell that good?

He focused on the small patch of pale skin between her eyes, refusing to let his gaze drift the length of her. It wasn't fair how time had only added to Elisa's charm. Nope, he'd memorize every dip of that little furrow in her brow before he allowed himself to remember what it felt like to press his hand against her lower back and tug her close—

"We have to do the treasure hunt."

He blinked. "I'm sorry?"

She lifted her chin, squaring off with him as if her next suggestion might be a duel. "We don't have a choice."

After getting the bad news from the adjustor, he agreed—but he couldn't give in that easily, not after his dramatic exit from August's office earlier that day. "Why's that?"

"Because I need the money. And after talking with my dad this evening, it sounds like you need it, too." She jerked her head toward the inn.

Great. A flare of bitterness sparked in his gut. "Isaac told you about the failed inspection?"

"I asked him why you two were meeting at the diner." She shrugged. "It's not a secret."

"Not for the inspector's daughter, I guess." He slapped an errant mosquito on his arm.

"Sugar, I couldn't care less about black mold. It's not shameful."

He clenched his jaw. "I'm not your *sugar*." Hadn't been for a long time, and he sure wasn't interested in re-upping for the role.

"Well you could stand some sweetenin'." She quirked an eyebrow at him.

He took a deep breath. Neither he—nor the inn—could afford

for his pride to stand in the way. He'd booked two reservations for the summer just that afternoon, unwilling to tell the potential customers there might not be an inn to stay at come June. If insurance wasn't going to help, and he couldn't open for tourist season before fixing the mold issue, the remaining inheritance was his only option to fund the mitigation.

But still. "What do you need money for?"

"I don't see how that's your business." Her tone, while matter-of-fact, somehow wasn't rude, which only aggravated him more.

Did she ever get mad?

"Well, you know why I need the money. If we're going to be partners, then it's only fair I know where you're coming from." He didn't know why he cared what she did with it, except for the fact that Elisa even having a stake in this game still irked him.

"Wait. You said partners." Her blue eyes lit with hope. "Does that mean you'll do it?"

His resolve flickered. "Like you said—I think we have to." He studied her delicate features, and considered the red flags going off in his brain. This was such a bad idea. Why had his grandfather thought it a good one? "But if we do, I think we should keep this on the down low."

"*Down low*?" Her lips curved up. "Apparently the 1990s called, too. Want their slang back."

"You know what I mean. If anyone realizes we're working together, it'll raise eyebrows. I'm not up for the drama." Or a write-up in the Magnolia Chronicle.

"Me neither." Her expression sobered. "Especially from my dad."

One thing they could agree on. Was she, too, remembering a particular night twelve years ago, much like this one? When the moon was full above their heads, and the cicadas sang in the treetops and the grass folded cool under bare feet?

When black tears tracked Elisa's cheeks and her father made it incredibly clear to Noah how many shotguns he owned?

He cleared his throat, pushing back a summer best forgotten. "So . . ." The past was the past, despite its sudden attempt to convince him otherwise. It needed to stay solidified in history, where it belonged. Tonight, the hunt was all that mattered. Saving the inn. Proving he wasn't a failure. Red flags aside, they had to go for it.

He held out one hand to shake. "Temporary truce?"

Elisa rolled in her lower lip, peering up at him with cornflower blue eyes as if gauging his sincerity. Then she shook his hand. "Temporary truce." Her palm was small and warm in his, and his brain had to tell his hand to let go twice before his fingers complied.

He hooked his thumbs in the back pockets of his jeans. "And only people who *need* to know will know."

She nodded, her hair swinging in her face. She brushed it back. "Right."

The word had barely left her lips before an engine puttered. Noah squinted at the road. A dark car inched by, headlights off. A familiar silhouette sat in the driver's seat, her pale face illuminated by the full moon. He sighed as he angled back to Elisa. "I'm guessing Zoey Lakewood is on that need-to-know list."

"Told you I didn't walk." Elisa grinned sheepishly. She waved, and Zoey guided the car up the driveway.

Noah watched as Zoey rolled down the driver's side window. He didn't know the woman well—she'd been a grade younger than him in school—but he'd bought some pastries from Bayou Beignets for his crew a few weeks ago, and they'd been a big hit. "If she was your ride, why did she leave?"

"Because I told her to. I didn't want to chicken out and lose."

Lose?

Gravel crunched as Zoey shifted the car into park. "Hey, Noah." She leaned out the open window and wiggled her fingers.

"Zoey." He tipped his head at her and frowned. "Your headlights are off."

"I know." Zoey clicked them back on. "So, did you do it?" Her dark brows disappeared into her thick bangs as she looked eagerly at Elisa.

Elisa headed for the other side of the car. "Yep. You owe me ten bucks."

"Did you do *what*?" Were the shadows playing tricks, or had Elisa's smile turned downright sassy?

She opened the passenger door and paused, one arm braced on the frame as her gaze mingled with his. "Why, convince you to do the treasure hunt, *sugar*."

He narrowed his eyes.

She slid inside, shut the door, and leaned over to talk to him through Zoey's window. "Zoey bet I couldn't, so now, I can treat both of us to Burger Barn fries on the way home."

"Slay." Zoey slapped her a high-five. "Cash is in my coin purse on the console, there."

Noah clenched his fists. He'd made a mistake. Less than an hour ago he'd been on the pier with the guys, most of whom had completely understood his need to *not* get involved in this hunt with Elisa. Now, after ten minutes in her presence, he'd shaken hands on the opposite—*and* become the subject of a bet at the same time.

He stifled a growl.

Zoey waved as she yanked the gearshift into reverse. "Thanks, Noah!" Clouds shifted overhead, revealing more of the moon. The glow illuminated the front yard, pushing back the shadows as she backed up and cut the wheel, gravel skittering.

"Meet me at August's office tomorrow morning!" Elisa hollered out her open window before they gunned it out of the drive.

Noah crossed his arms and stared after them as the vehicle zipped away, Elisa's arm weaving a pattern in the wind as they sped off. Yep. That smile had definitely been sassier. She'd gotten the best of him, and she knew it.

And he'd just agreed to work with her.

"I have to admit, seeing you two here is a surprise." August Bowman handed Elisa a ballpoint pen and pointed to the legal documents spread across his desk. "Considering the way we left things yesterday."

Elisa leaned over the desk and signed her name in her best cursive, intentionally ignoring Noah's tense posture next to her. "He had a change of heart." She hadn't expected said change to come that easily. She'd barely even flirted. Was Noah warming up to her?

"More like I had a heavy dose of reality." Noah plucked the pen August offered and scrawled his own name in a barely legible chicken scratch under Elisa's. "Is that it?"

"Initial page three." August accepted the pen Elisa handed him. "And that should do it! You're officially on the hunt and in agreement with the terms." He stacked the papers carefully before sliding them into a file. "I'll get Peggy to scan and upload these, but I'm old-school—I like having paper copies too."

"Seems reasonable." Elisa hoped her manners would make up for Noah's lack of.

As if reading her mind—bless it, wasn't that a scary concept—Noah cleared his throat as he stuffed the pen back in the desktop holder. "I apologize for my grumpiness. I didn't get a lot of sleep last night." A muscle twitched in his jaw. "Had an unwelcome guest late into the evening."

Elisa's eyes widened. So much for warming—his tone could freeze water.

August frowned as he tugged his ever-present tweed jacket down over his slacks. "I hope they didn't vandalize anything. You have enough going on over at that inn of yours."

"I thought people would realize that, but alas." Noah cast Elisa a sidelong glance. "So far, no permanent damage done."

She opened her mouth to tell him exactly what she thought of his innuendo, then clamped her lips shut. *Be a good girl and calm down.* She lifted her chin and flashed her best smile at August. "Thanks for all your help. I'm sure we'll be updating you with our progress."

"Right." August snapped his fingers, looking down so fast his glasses slid across his nose. "Speaking of progress, you need your first clues." He shuffled through the folder and pulled out the envelopes he'd shown them yesterday. "Here you are. There will be four clues to follow. Five locations."

"Great." Elisa eagerly accepted hers. This was going to be fun— she hadn't had a good puzzle to solve in ages. Or rather, it *would* be fun, if Noah wasn't being a living, breathing Eeyore about it all.

Noah was slower to take his packet from August. "Thank you." At least he was polite this time.

"We'll be in touch." Elisa hoisted her purse on her shoulder and clutched her packet to her chest. Best to get Noah out of there before he dove for that file folder of paperwork, wielding liquid Wite-Out. Neither of them could afford to back out now.

"Best of luck to you." August began ushering them toward his office door. "Remember the rules, and call if you have any questions. But I'm sure you'll do fine."

Elisa felt confident as well, but Noah's drawn expression indicated otherwise. "Absolutely." She tugged at Noah's sleeve—flannel again?—and beamed for August's sake. "In fact, we'll go get started right now." Maybe if she stayed upbeat, Noah would eventually follow suit.

Noah allowed the contact on his sleeve until they were out of the office, then pulled his arm free. He held open the exterior door to the law firm. "Don't you have to go to the café?"

They stepped out into the morning sunlight. Elisa smirked. "Trying to get rid of me already?"

Noah squinted as he looked left and right before crossing Magnolia Bay's main drag. "Don't tell me Delia is already back at work today."

Elisa fell in step beside him on Village Lane, pulling sunglasses from her purse. "No, she's still at the hospital for monitoring since her blood pressure was having trouble regulating. But we got the morning shift at the Blossom covered, and I arranged for a limited menu with a temp chef Delia recommended. I just need to go help him during the lunch rush."

Noah grunted his acknowledgment of her update as they strolled the landscaped sidewalks in silence, bees buzzing in the bordering flowerbeds filled with tulips. The hanging *Second Story* sign creaked on its rusty hinges as it swung from the porch ceiling of the used bookstore, freshly painted eggshell blue. Next door, Sawyer Dubois was heading inside the coral-colored Spin Shop, where he worked part time selling vinyls in exchange for discounted gear.

Despite the recent rebuilding efforts, effects of Hurricane Anastasia still lingered. For every storefront or stretch of street that seemed back to normal, there was a broken tree or patched siding. A few neighboring fences boasted new planks of wood, mismatched from their weathered counterparts. Some of the more unfortunate businesses still had tarps on their roofs.

As they walked, Noah shrugged out of his flannel, revealing a fitted tee beneath. Elisa slid on her sunglasses, grateful they hid the way her eyes kept finding the curve of Noah's biceps. "So, where to?"

Noah glanced at her, a strand of dark hair flopping over his forehead. Why she wanted to move it out of his eyes was beyond her. "Don't tell me you're actually looking forward to this."

"Why, Noah Hebert, are you still mad at little ol' me? It was just a bet." She thickened her accent, partly out of habit and partly because she knew it would irk him.

She wasn't disappointed.

He stopped, crossing his arms. "Define mad."

She tapped her chin. "Pretty sure Webster calls it 'very angry.'"

"Then no. I'm not very angry." He picked up the pace again, dodging a woman in workout clothes walking a corgi, and didn't wait as Elisa quick-stepped to keep up.

"Irate?"

"No."

"Infuriated, then." Man, he walked fast. She was out of breath, despite her somewhat frequent gym visits.

"Aren't those both worse than very angry?"

Goading him was fun—it gave her the upper hand. She needed to find her flirting pattern with him. Maybe it was sarcastic banter. "Depends on who you ask." She nearly ran into his back as Noah stopped and spun around.

"Listen." His gaze seared right through her sunglasses and his tense posture radiated enough heat to rival the sun. "We have a job to do. And the sooner we do it, the better."

She was losing that upper hand. Elisa found her best smile despite the sting of his words. "Did you know that when you're mad, you get all stiff and straight like a cypress tree growing right out of the bayou?"

"I'm not mad, though, remember?" He didn't move, didn't even seem to breathe as he studied her, seemingly completely unfazed.

Bless it, this wouldn't do at all. Elisa blinked behind her sunglasses, praying he couldn't read her eyes through the darkened lenses and interpret the sudden cacophony blaring inside her head. She wasn't entirely sure she wanted to interpret it, herself. "Then what are you?"

He didn't answer, just kept watching her, reminding her of the time that summer they'd had a staring contest on his grandfather's old boat. The winner was awarded a kiss, and Elisa had never been so happy to lose a contest in her life.

She licked her suddenly dry lips. The spring sun overhead continued to warm her bare arms, but she'd heated up way before that. Ridiculous, but true. Maybe she could stay in denial with others, but it was much harder to pretend with herself.

She returned Noah's stoic gaze, unable to move away from it and not even sure how willing she was.

Noah's lips parted, and his gaze softened. Then a shadow flicked across his expression, removing all traces of compassion, and he clamped his mouth shut. "What am I? In a hurry, is what I am. And you should be, too." He turned again, abruptly. "Chug a Mug is right up here. Good a place as any to get started." Then he walked away.

Elisa pulled off her sunglasses and hesitated on the sidewalk, watching as the distance between them increased. She could call after him and remind him this was *her* town, that she knew good and well where the best coffee shop was. That she hadn't been the one to leave and never look back, like he was doing right now. Or she could go after him, grab his arm, and demand to know what that look had meant, the one she'd felt clear down to her freshly painted toes peeking out of her gold sandals.

But she wouldn't do any of those things. Elisa slowly slid her sunglasses back into place.

She was a good girl, and she'd stay calm.

Even if Noah had the potential to churn deep waters faster than any hurricane.

Seven

THE HEADY AROMA OF ROASTED BEANS and some kind of hot pastry wafted from the Chug a Mug. The coffee shop was situated across the street and two doors down from the Magnolia Blossom, which Noah figured Elisa would appreciate. As soon as they wrapped up this first clue, she could head to work.

And he could get back to the inn and finish planning his way through this mold fiasco.

He started to open the coffee shop door.

"Hold on." Elisa's hand snaked around Noah's bicep and tugged him back a few steps.

He tensed, an electric current pulsing from his upper arm down into his fingers. That was the second time she'd touched him today, and the second time he'd felt the contact straight through his sleeve and into his soul.

"What?" Hadn't he said they were in a hurry? He'd also said they needed to lay low, and her holding onto him like this was definitely not keeping a subtle profile.

Yet none of those facts made him shrug out of her grip.

She leaned in, her voice a tense whisper as her gaze raked the tinted windows. "We don't know the weather report."

"Warm. Partially cloudy." He gestured with his free arm to the sky, where the evidence shined above them.

"That's not what I meant." She released him and shoved her sunglasses up into her hair. The abrupt motion only highlighted the dimple in her cheek, which once upon a time he'd used as target practice for his lips.

He stepped aside as a handful of teenagers, obviously *not* concerned about the weather, hurried inside the coffee shop. "Then what are you talking about? I've been here before." Once. The brew hadn't been great, but then again, he had been too busy with his to-do list to care.

She gestured over her shoulder toward the building they were still not entering, and he still didn't know why. "You've got to know the weather report before you order."

He pointedly looked up at the clouds drifting in front of the sun.

"It's code." She waved one hand, directing her gaze back to him. "The barista, Miley Mitchell, is the owner's daughter. But Mr. Mitchell is always traveling. He owns a bunch of other businesses . . . anyway, she's in charge, and her moods affect the coffee."

He scoffed. "That's crazy."

"That's Magnolia Bay." Elisa lifted one slim shoulder in a shrug.

"No, I mean, that's scientifically impossible. One wouldn't affect the other."

She squinted at him. "You've never heard of cookin' with love?"

"Of course. But that doesn't mean it's true."

"Well, in Miley's case, it's the opposite."

Noah sighed. "We're wasting time."

"Suit yourself." Elisa tossed her hair back and reached for the door, catching it as Sadie Whitlock exited.

"Hey." Sadie's gaze darted curiously between the two of them before she smiled at Noah, tucking a thick book under her arm. "How is that old inn shaping up?"

He dipped his head. "It's getting there." Sadie had been in her late teens when he'd first accompanied Grandpa to *Second Story* in his youth, and was often there, helping her aunt with the store. Seeing her now up close, it was impossible to disconnect her from the memories of his grandfather.

From the doorway behind Sadie, Elisa quirked one eyebrow at him, her expression clearly reading *I thought you were in a hurry.*

He was. But Sadie was still talking. "I know I saw you at the memorial service, and we didn't get a chance to speak yesterday at the diner, but I wanted to express my condolences again for your loss." She tilted her head, her curly brown hair brushing across the knotted straps of her brightly patterned sundress. "Your grandfather is very missed."

An unexpected ball of emotion rose in his throat. Noah swallowed. "I appreciate it. I know he enjoyed your family's store."

Sadie's friendly gaze softened as she adjusted the hold on her novel. "You should stop by—for old times' sake."

"I don't have a lot of spare time for reading right now, with the renovation." Noah reached to take the weight of the door Elisa still held open. "But I'll try."

"Of course. See you around." Sadie dipped her head in acknowledgment of Elisa as she turned to leave, polite but distant. If Sadie's family had been friendly to Grandpa all those years, it only made sense they'd be cooler to the Heberts. It was the Magnolia way.

Noah gestured for Elisa to go inside. *Now* they could get started.

But Elisa stepped back out of the shop, raising one arm after Sadie, who had already moved several paces down the sidewalk. "Wait!"

Sadie turned at her call, her brows arched.

Elisa darted a glance at the tinted window of the coffee shop. "Weather report?"

Noah suppressed a sigh.

But Sadie smiled, her green eyes softening as she leaned in and whispered, "*Very* cloudy."

"Perfect." Elisa gave her a little wave. "Thanks."

He gave up trying to figure it out and joined Elisa in the short line extending from the cash register. The whir of an espresso machine and the aroma of freshly ground beans filled Noah's senses, mingling with the low hum of chatter from the patrons scattered around the cozy space. Everything was black, silver, or brass—the high serving counter, the coffee tables situated around oversized chairs, the light fixtures. The far wall appeared to be a giant chalkboard, filled with various scribbles and quotes from patrons. Something else he hadn't noticed in his quick run-in the other week.

Elisa followed his gaze. "They erase that wall every month and start over. Everyone is free to write what they want until then." She grinned. "More than one teen relationship has ended by someone seeing someone else's initials in hearts."

Noah snorted. He could think of much more traumatic ways to breakup as a teen—

"Next!" The barista with short dark hair and giant hoop earrings, wearing a black apron and a striped shirt with rolled-up sleeves, gestured impatiently for them to move up in line.

Noah approached the counter. That must be Miley. A pencil was tucked behind one ear, and a dainty tattooed vine of flowers peeked out of her sleeve and wrapped around her forearm and wrist.

She turned bored eyes on Noah, attitude seeping from every piercing. "Well?"

Suddenly, he wished he'd taken the weather report a little more seriously. "Um." He cleared his throat, casting a glance at Elisa. "I'll take a small—"

Elisa shook her head, but it was too late.

"We don't have *small*," the young woman barked. She seemed more suited to a studded dog collar than the thin gold chain adorning her neck. A tiny music note dangled off the end. She jerked one finger toward the cup sizes lining the counter. "We have the mini mug, the mug, and the chug a mug. Or you can bring your own mug for the Mug Me discount."

Noah had never been much of a tea drinker, but the idea was growing on him.

Miley narrowed her eyes. "And no, none of that was my idea. My dad is unapologetically corny."

"Right." Noah shifted his weight, noting her stud nose ring. "I'll take a small—I mean, a *mini* mug of coffee."

"Black or blond?" Her dark eyes bored into his.

Noah blinked.

Elisa hissed at his elbow. "Black."

He repeated the command as if Miley hadn't already heard her. "Black."

"Cream?"

He glanced at Elisa, who shook her head, eyes wide. He cleared his throat. "No."

"Foam?" Miley punched buttons on the iPad register.

Elisa barely grazed his arm with hers.

"Yep."

Miley hovered one finger over the keypad. "Flavored syrup?"

Elisa sucked in her breath.

He was on his own for this one. He took a shot in the dark. "Nope."

Miley's face relaxed a smidge, and she punched one final key on the register. "Four twenty-seven."

Noah released his sigh as he relinquished his debit card. He wasn't entirely sure what he'd just avoided, but he'd clearly avoided something.

Elisa gave her order next, then Miley curtly addressed them both before turning to the shiny coffee maker to her left. "I'll call your number when it's ready."

Noah frowned. "But you didn't give me a num—"

"Just go." Elisa half-pushed him toward an empty group of

chairs in the back corner by the chalkboard wall. Once they were out of earshot, she smiled. "Get ready for the best cup of coffee you've ever had."

Noah slid his card back inside his wallet. "But she seems like she's in a bad mood."

"Exactly. The forecast was cloudy, remember?" Elisa plopped down on one of the black slip-covered chairs and pulled her legs up under her.

He sat stiffly on the wide seat next to Elisa, a low table angled between them. "So the coffee is better when Miley is upset?"

"Every time."

Was this still Magnolia Bay, or had he stumbled after a rabbit with a stopwatch? "In Shreveport, you just order coffee and it's the same every time."

"What can I say? Magnolia Bay has character." Elisa shrugged.

That was one word for it. Regardless, he could use that coffee. Noah rubbed his hand down his face. "Where's the first clue?"

Elisa raised her eyebrows. "You have it."

Oh, yeah. He pulled his envelope from his back pocket and wrestled the thin paper free.

Elisa craned her head sideways to read the card alongside him.

One, if by land, and two, if by sea;
And I on the opposite shore will be . . .

He leaned back in his chair. "That's helpful."

"Is that your grandfather's handwriting?" Elisa's tone gentled as she ran one finger lightly over the ink.

There went that knot again. "It is." He closed his eyes as images of that exact writing filled his memories. Scribbles in the margins of books. Notes posted on the fridge and stuck on the bathroom mirror. Tags on Christmas gifts. Even when Grandpa had written *Santa*, Noah knew. Yet he'd always played along.

He abruptly opened his eyes. "What does yours say?"

Elisa opened her envelope.

Hang a lantern aloft in the belfry arch
Of the North Church tower as a signal light . . .

Noah groaned. "They're both pieces from a poem."

"Paul Revere's Ride." Elisa's eyes lit with excitement even as Noah felt his own energy seeping away. This was already impossible. What was Grandpa thinking?

"The lines are out of order. I wonder if that's significant." Elisa tapped her chin with her finger, the whirring of the espresso machine competing with her words.

Noah leaned forward, bracing his elbows on his knees. "What do you mean?" He had so much to do at the inn, and here he sat, waiting on coffee from a moody college kid and contributing nothing to the challenge at hand.

He didn't need more opportunities to be set up for failure.

"You have the first part of Clue #1. But in the poem, the lines from my clue—Clue #1, Part Two—come first." Elisa tucked a chunk of hair behind her ear. "Might be nothing."

"It's got to be a church, right?" Noah pointed to the wording on Elisa's paper. "North Church tower . . ."

"But none of the churches around here have bell towers." Elisa tilted her head. "Maybe it's symbolic?"

Noah pinched the bridge of his nose. "You'd think the first clue would be easier."

"Don't give up. We have to let it percolate a bit." She gestured around the shop. "Like a strong coffee."

It was a nice thought, but the truth remained. "We don't have a lot of time."

"Let it steep."

"So first it's coffee, now it's tea?" He shot a look at Elisa. "Why are you *not* frustrated?"

She rolled her eyes. "I don't know. Maybe the same reason you're frustrated *all* the time?"

Easy for her to say. Elisa didn't have the fate of an entire family legacy hanging over her. If they couldn't figure this out, the money would remain where it was—locked away, and doing no one any good. Time wasn't something they had a lot of.

This partnership didn't need to last any longer than it had to.

He cast a look toward the counter, hoping their order was almost ready, and caught Miley pointing right at them as she spoke with a female customer. He groaned. So much for keeping a low profile.

"Let me think." Oblivious to the gossip chain starting at the counter, Elisa held up one hand. "Your grandfather liked history, right?"

Noah nodded. "He collected early American memorabilia and thrift books. And the man memorized the lyrics to the Hamilton musical before it was cool." He snorted at the mental image of Grandpa rapping the lyrics to "My Shot" while vacuuming the foyer of the Blue Pirogue.

That gave him an idea. He shifted in his seat as a mom and two toddlers scooted past their table. "I think he's got a collectible Paul Revere spoon somewhere in the library at the inn. Maybe that's a lead?"

"Maybe." Elisa scrunched her nose. "Though that seems too easy."

Easy? He was surprised he'd even thought of it in the first place. He cleared his throat, trying not to be offended. "Got a better idea?"

She took the clue from his hand and held the papers side by side, squinting. "I'm working on it."

They needed progress, not perfection. Noah scrubbed his palms down his jeans. "I can check the inn when I get home tonight, see if there's anything in the collector's case."

"It wouldn't hurt to rule it out." Elisa was still squinting, almost like she was patronizing him.

"Number twenty-seven," Miley bellowed from the front.

"That's probably us." Elisa started to stand, but Noah beat her to it.

"I'll get it." He turned to head for the counter, when something dark caught his eye outside the window.

Smoke.

Billowing out the front door of the Magnolia Blossom Café.

Elisa stood unmoving in the middle of the diner, surveying the damage with her hands shoved into her hair. Water dripped from its tangled ends, much like it dripped off everything else. The chairs had toppled over in everyone's rush to get outside once the overhead sprinklers turned on. The magnolia flower centerpieces she'd so carefully crafted were wilted, their drowned petals sagging onto the tabletops.

"Man." Noah's deep timbre sounded beside her. He'd been the first one to sprint across the street and race inside, as well as the one to ensure the fire department had been called as her staff stumbled out, coughing. Now they were being corralled across the street until the fire department determined the scene clear. "What a mess."

"That's sort of like saying the bay is wet." Water seeped into Elisa's sandaled feet as the acrid scent of smoke lingered in the air. A piece of soggy hamburger bun floated past her.

"You were lucky." Captain Sanders shrugged out of his bulky fire retardant jacket as he approached. "It's only water damage. The sprinklers did their job." He looked around the saturated café. "I know it seems like a lot right now, but it'll clean up."

Elisa fought back a smirk. Clean up. Right. With her and what army? She forced a smile, wrapping her arms around her middle as a sudden chill racked her body. "Does Delia know?"

Captain Sanders shrugged, holding up one finger as his walkie talkie squawked. "We haven't told her." Then he walked a few steps away, speaking into the device in low tones.

Delia couldn't know about this yet—she had enough to worry about with her health. Though keeping it a secret from her wouldn't be possible either. Maybe Elisa could put off the inevitable until she had time to get the bulk of the water out.

She thought about the singular mop in the storage closet near the bathrooms and a strangled half laugh, half sob emerged from her throat. Talk about understatements.

"Ms. Bergeron, I'm so sorry." The diner's temporary chef, Lucius Sanchez, pushed through the open café doors, a protesting fireman at his heels. Lucius still wore the white chef's coat he'd insisted on wearing for his shift.

"Sir, I've got to insist you leave the premises." The young fireman clamped a firm hand on the chef's arm.

Lucius shook off the uniformed man's grip as his thick dark brow furrowed with regret. "The fried pickles got away from me. I've done them a hundred times, but the oil . . ." He flapped his hands helplessly at his sides. "Then when I was dealing with that, there was a grease fire that grabbed the towel. From there— *whoosh*." He demonstrated with both hands.

Elisa's shoulders shook as the sudden, uncanny urge to laugh gripped her. What in the world—was this grief? She snorted, then sputtered. Then the laughter burst free. Oh bless it, she couldn't stop. Her upper body trembled under her wet shirt.

"Um, Chef . . . why don't you go on home?" Noah looped an arm around Lucius's shoulders and steered him toward the exit. Water slurped under their shoes, which only made Elisa laugh harder. Noah angled Lucius through the door. "You can dismiss the waitstaff, tell them to not come back until they hear from Elisa. It'll probably be a day or two."

"Or a hundred." Elisa guffawed, bending over at the waist as her body convulsed with laughter. This was worse than that time Zoey had made her laugh in church, and she shook the entire pew with her attempts to control herself. She tried pinching her own arm, but it didn't help. And she was cold. So cold.

"Elisa . . . you okay?" Captain Sanders slid his walkie talkie on his hip holster, concern sketched across his expression.

"Just peachy, Captain." Elisa pressed her lips together as tears burned her eyes. The giggles wouldn't stop.

"I think she's in shock, sir." The young fireman next to her gently touched her arm. "Why don't we do a vitals check?"

"I'm fine." She snorted again, and pressed her fingers to her mouth to catch the next one as she shivered. "It's been a stressful few days, is all." The last thing she needed was people fawning over her. She had work to do—starting with that mop.

The snort burst free.

The fireman frowned. "I think we should—"

"She said she's fine." Noah turned to the captain, his commanding tone dismissing any further discussion. "I assume you turned the electricity off? What can we expect over the next few days while we clean up?"

Noah, once again taking charge on her behalf. She hated that and appreciated it, all at once. It was confusing. Sort of like how confusing it was to be this cold when she'd been practically sweating outside a few hours ago.

Elisa didn't catch all of Captain Sanders's instructions, something about breaker boxes and getting the water removed. All she could think about was how appealing Noah looked with his hair dripping down his forehead, his soaking wet T-shirt clinging to his muscled torso.

And then suddenly there was light, and shadow, blurring. Her vision, narrowing. She took a deep breath. Shivered. What were those swirls? She reached out to touch one . . .

And fell into sudden darkness.

Eight

"LET ME GET THIS STRAIGHT." ZOEY shoved a plate with a strawberry-lemon beignet across the black iron table to Elisa before taking the other chair for herself. "Noah Hebert ran into a burning building for you?"

The fairy lights clustered in fleurs-de-lis shaped wall vases across the sage-colored walls blurred in Elisa's tired eyes as she skimmed her thumb over the dish's stamped Bayou Beignets logo. After her morning, she didn't have much appetite for the fuchsia and yellow street staring up at her. Her head hurt, and her arms ached from cleaning. "Well, a smoking building, technically."

"Hey, where there's smoke, there's fire. And in this instance, I mean literally *and* figuratively." Zoey folded her arms over the table and leaned forward. "I heard you swooned in his arms?"

Good gravy, Magnolia Bay's gossip mill churned faster than the Pioneer Woman made butter. "Don't even go there. Captain Sanders said it was a mix of shock, low blood pressure, and skipping breakfast that rendered me unconscious."

Of course, Noah *had* brought over a sump pump he'd had in storage at the inn, which was sort of hero-like and made the cleaning that morning go much faster. But telling Zoey would only feed her friend's delusion.

Zoey wiggled her eyebrows as she bit into her cookie-topped beignet, the bangles on her wrist jangling. "Sure. Low blood pressure . . . and chemistry."

Elisa pinched off a piece of her dessert. "I *fainted*. I didn't get hit in the head." Which is what it would take to fall for Noah Hebert again—sump pump or not.

Zoey tilted her head. "Or maybe Noah isn't as bad as you've been told your whole life."

"I'm starting to regret agreeing to Trish's suggestion that I take a break before we get back to cleaning." Elisa popped a bite into her mouth. "Besides, you were the one threatening to remind Noah about what a jerk he's been. Let's go back to that."

Zoey lifted both hands. "Look, you know I'm on your side. But Noah seems to be helping you a lot suddenly." She grinned. "Can't we all just get along?"

Elisa snorted. "Try telling that to the multiple generations of two families who both think the other stole their land."

"Did they?"

"Someone's in the wrong. I've been told it's the Heberts, of course."

"I don't get it. It was such a long time ago." Zoey shrugged. "Why not just accept the fact that whoever holds the current title is the legal owner, and move on with your lives?"

"I'm not hung up on it, personally. I couldn't care less about the land around the Blue Pirogue." Elisa pressed her thumb against a rogue piece of fuchsia icing. "But it became about more than the land. You know it got personal for a lot of people—especially Noah's generation. After his dad, well, you know."

Zoey nodded. "Oh yeah. Scandal of the decade, apparently."

"You'd think it'd been the scandal of a century. Besides, it's not just the feud or the stories I've been told that have given me my opinion about Noah." Elisa jerked her gaze to meet her friend's. "I also have personal experience, remember?" The lending of one sump pump didn't negate a decade of history.

"Maybe." Zoey pointed at her with a ring-adorned finger. "But I also know what I saw when I pulled up at the inn the other night—and it wasn't two people looking at each other like they were locked in an eternal battle."

"Then you need glasses." Elisa leaned back in her chair and crossed her arms. "You'd be cute in them, actually."

"Don't change the subject. Though you're right." Zoey ate a piece of cookie off the top of her pastry. "I've known you long enough that I've earned the right to point out the obvious now and then."

Elisa pinned her friend with a stare. "And what's so obvious that I'm missing?"

"Easy." Zoey swiped crumbs off the table onto the floor. "Feud or not, history or not—you're looking forward to this collaboration with Noah."

Elisa sat straight, her chair squeaking on the tile floor. "I am not—"

"You're trying to convince me—and yourself—that you're not, but you are." Her friend nodded. "You're into this, aren't you? Tell the truth . . . and don't make me pull the scout's honor card."

Elisa frowned. "We were never scouts."

"Well, I was, for a day back in sixth grade. Then I realized I hate camping and brown isn't my color." Zoey grinned.

Elisa's head pounded too hard to argue. "Maybe I *was* looking forward to the hunt. But only because it had the potential to be fun. Following clues, solving a mystery, finding treasure . . . it's a puzzler's dream." Her eagerness to get back to the clues surged just from speaking about it.

Then reality diffused the spark. "But I'm not sure how much

it's going to matter. We're stuck on the first clue." And now she had the soggy diner to deal with.

"Stuck already? That doesn't sound like you." Zoey furrowed her brow. "Though to be fair, it doesn't sound like you had much time to solve it before the café caught fire, either."

"True." She could still remember the stricken look on Noah's face as he grabbed her hand and hauled her off the Chug a Mug sofa, the way he'd blocked the café's door with his arm to keep her from going in first . . .

So maybe it was more than the sump pump.

"The annual Scavenger Hunt is coming up this summer, right? That's not scratching your puzzler's itch?" Zoey stood from the table as a middle-aged couple strolled inside the shop, the chimes on the door jingling in their wake. She called to them, "Be right with you!"

"The Scavenger Hunt is a good time, but it's a lot of work. And it's a puzzle I have to plan for everyone else." Elisa hesitated as the truth of her next words hit hard. "This one was planned for me." Which didn't make sense considering her lack of relationship with Gilbert Hebert. Still, she couldn't deny that it made her feel special.

"Planned for you . . . and for Noah." Zoey arched an eyebrow at Elisa. "*Together*." Then without waiting for a response, she headed for the couple perusing the display case in their matching Magnolia Bay tourist T-shirts. "See anything you like?"

Before the couple could answer, the chimes sounded again, and Linc Fontenot barreled inside, a scowl sketched across his face. "Zoey Claire!"

Zoey jerked at his bellow. "Jumpin' June bugs, Linc! What's your problem?"

Elisa smirked. She might technically be Zoey's best friend, but Linc had always been a close second. And Zoey might be the only person on the bay who could get away with talking to Linc like that.

He came to stand directly in front of Zoey, his eyes narrowed. "You told me the beignets were almond-free."

"The ones you got were." She crossed her arms, clearly not intimidated by his towering frame.

"Aye. Does this look almond-free?" He raised the hem of his long-sleeved T-shirt, revealing a six pack of abs covered in pink hives.

The middle-aged woman standing at the counter gawked until her husband nudged her. Elisa covered her mouth to hide her grin.

Zoey tugged his shirt down, then grabbed Linc's arm and steered him a few feet away from the counter. "I'm with customers."

"I'm a customer. A loyal one, at that." He scowled again. "Who you tried to kill."

"You are not *deathly* allergic to almonds. I told you there was the possibility of cross contamination—along with that sign in bright red letters." Zoey pointed to the counter by the cash register.

Linc lifted his chin. "You never warned me."

"Maybe if you hadn't been complaining about my prices, you could have heard me. Besides, this could be from anything—like laundry detergent or soap." She planted her hands on her hips. "Do you have any Benadryl?"

He growled. "I don't take medicine."

"Then be itchy. Preferably somewhere other than my store." She attempted to turn his broad shoulders toward the exit.

Linc, unfazed, didn't budge. He lowered his voice, ducking his head. "What kind of medicine did you say it was, again?"

"*Benadryl.* Oh my word, Linc. Look, I'll swing by Magnolia Grocery and bring it to you as soon as the part-timer gets here to relieve me."

"Okay." Linc, still scowling, reluctantly moved toward the door. Then he called over his shoulder to the couple still standing wide-eyed by the display case, "Don't get the lemon tarts." He lifted his shirt again in warning.

"Out!" Zoey shoved him through the door, shutting it behind her with a clang of the chime.

Elisa caught Zoey's eye and raised one brow, her spirits suddenly lifted. "Speaking of *together*..."

"Speaking of *don't even go there* . . ." Zoey pointed in warning, then adjusted her logo T-shirt and smiled at the stricken couple. "Now, where were we?"

"Harold likes strawberry." The woman, who sported a fanny pack, gestured to the display. "I wanted to try a chocolate, but I was afraid it might melt in the car."

"Too messy on the seats." Harold nodded, his straw hat askew. "We're not used to hot spring temps like this up in Michigan."

"Our traditional beignets probably handle the heat best." Zoey moved behind the counter and grabbed a pair of tongs. "Or maybe you'd prefer caramel?"

As their conversation droned on, Elisa pulled out her phone and sent Trish a text letting her know she'd be back soon. She still needed to figure out the best way to break the news to Delia, if someone hadn't beaten her to it.

The chit-chat continued from the serving counter.

"Where are you two headed next?" Zoey tucked the cardboard flaps inside the bakery box.

Harold pulled his wallet from his shorts. "We have a tradition—every new town we visit, we see a lighthouse if we can."

"It's silly. But it's our thing. Isn't that right, dear?" The woman hooked her arm through Harold's. "Every year for thirty years."

Harold handed over his payment. "She likes the lights in those big ol' structures. Finds it romantic, somehow."

"How can you not?" The lady sighed. "Lighthouses are pure poetry."

Elisa frowned. The word *poetry* niggled her brain, sparking an idea just out of reach. Paul Revere. The poem. Clue #1.

And I on the opposite shore will be . . .

Her eyes widened.

Hang a lantern aloft . . . as a signal light . . .

"That's it!" She shoved her chair backward. Her heart thudded a frenetic rhythm in her chest as she grabbed her purse. "Zoey, I'll call you later."

She'd solved the first clue.

His grandfather's personal library was the only space in the Blue Pirogue that Noah couldn't bear to update.

He strolled the perimeter of the room, his gaze roaming from title to title on the cherrywood shelves. Afternoon sunlight poured through the narrow windows lining the west wall, sending dust particles dancing across the beams. He'd come to test his theory on the spoon collection, but stepping foot in the room for the first time in weeks and looking—really *looking*—slowed down time. Like maybe Grandpa wasn't gone. He was just at a Puzzler's Club meeting or picking up those orange hard candies he liked from Magnolia Grocery, and would be back any minute. He'd laugh and his bushy eyebrows would creep up his head as he regaled Noah with some exaggerated tale.

But there were no footsteps heading into the library. The spoon collection sat in a display case near the window, but lethargy and nostalgia held Noah back from checking. Not yet.

Running one finger down the spine of a hardback copy of *Johnny Tremain*, Noah took a deep breath, imagining he could still smell peppermint and cigars. Most likely, though, he smelled the smoke from the diner clinging to his own hair.

What a day. He'd put in several hours at the café with Elisa, setting the diner back to rights in hopes of giving Delia the smallest shock possible when she came home from the hospital.

He'd also spent a portion of that clean-up time trying not to notice how adorable Elisa looked sopping wet. Trying not to remember the time they'd overturned his boat, and she'd popped out of the waves, sputtering for breath with her hair plastered over her face like it'd been while standing under those fire sprinklers. He'd peppered her nose with relentless kisses that afternoon in the bay until she'd laughed and forgiven him.

Not that he'd wanted to attempt the same today. It was a memory—one out of a million from that summer.

His hand skimmed over several American history texts, then stopped at the empty spot on the shelf. Odd—Grandpa's collector's edition of *The Count of Monte Cristo* wasn't in its usual place. Maybe he'd read it more recently and left it elsewhere in the inn.

His fingers then landed on a dusty frame of Grandpa and Noah standing on the dock, taken when Noah was eleven. In typical preteen fashion, he'd refused to smile for the camera, but even now, he could see the joy he'd felt that day fishing—and it'd had nothing to do with the impressive bass dangling from the end of his line.

"I wish you were here." The whispered words seemed to ricochet off the matching cherry desk with the antique lamp and the old-fashioned letter inbox. Grandpa never had adjusted to the concept of email, preferring to do things "as our capable forefathers did" when it came to communication. Of course, he did eventually learn to play Solitaire on the boxy desktop computer he'd finally been persuaded to buy.

If he could ask his grandfather for advice now, he would. He'd already spoken with two mold mitigation people, and one wanted a large deposit up front—a payment that would take the remaining money in the inn's account plus a chunk of Noah's personal savings, which he was currently living off while on hiatus from his landman work running title. He could ask his project manager for a new project and start working half-days from his laptop, but that would delay progress on the final restoration, which would then delay his return to Shreveport.

And he needed to get back to Shreveport.

"I guess if you were here, I wouldn't have to figure all this out, would I?" Noah released a humorless laugh. The second mitigation company was booked up for months—not surprising in the wake of Hurricane Anastasia. But they didn't require nearly as high of a deposit, having adjusted their fee schedule out of sympathy for their sudden influx of customers.

So Noah could pay more and get it done sooner, or save money and be forced to stay in Magnolia Bay longer—assuming the treasure hunt would deliver funds that would cover the remaining balance on either option.

"Everything feels like a catch twenty-two lately." Noah set the framed photo on the shelf. Grandpa couldn't hear him, but it still felt freeing to release the concern into the air. Maybe God would hear instead and send some sort of inspiration or solution.

Not that Noah deserved it.

He ambled to the desk, pulled the miniature key to the collector's case from the drawer where Grandpa always kept it, and slid it into his pocket. There was another key next to it, bigger and half-buried under a pile of envelopes. What in the world did that go to?

Then his gaze caught Grandpa's ancient letter opener, the one with the carved pelican—the Louisiana state bird—on the end, and Noah smirked. When he was a kid, he liked to play with the items on Grandpa's desk, so Grandpa told him a spooky story about a cursed ghost pelican living in the bay so he'd be too scared to pick it up and risk cutting himself.

He'd believed that story until he was nearly thirteen.

Noah chuckled under his breath, picking up the time-dulled

blade. "I think I believed almost everything you told me." The stillness of the library absorbed his declaration, the statement disappearing into the numerous volumes of words surrounding him. "There are several stories now I sure wish I could hear again."

Such as the time Grandpa pranked everyone in his first puzzler's club meeting by pretending not to speak English. And when he took a cross-country road trip in his twenties with his brother—Noah's Great Uncle William, now deceased—and ended up having dinner with two well-known celebrities but didn't realize it until halfway through the meal.

Or why he divorced Grandma Edith when Noah was seven.

He drew a tight breath and set the letter opener back in its case. Hebert men were known to be quitters in all the ways that mattered, and Noah refused to let history repeat itself.

The story about the cursed ghost pelican might not be real, but that generational curse sure was.

Noah's cell buzzed in his pocket, providing a welcome relief from his thoughts. He checked the display—unknown number. He silenced it and slid his phone back into his pocket, then crossed the floor toward the spoon case. Might as well get to work.

He unlatched the glass door and searched the rows of antique silver until he found the collectible Paul Revere spoon. Nothing seemed out of the ordinary, and the dust patterns in the case didn't appear disturbed. Still, to be sure, he carefully lifted the velvet display tray and peered under it.

Nothing. He'd been wrong.

Which meant Elisa had been right.

His cell buzzed again, same number as before. He sighed and answered as he put the tray back into place. "Hello?" Probably a spam call.

"Noah, finally."

Elisa? His gaze darted back to the spoons. Had his being wrong

114

somehow sent an invisible radar pulse to alert her? "How did you get this number?"

"That's not important." Her breathy tone indicated excitement—unless she was jogging. "Are you ready to go?"

"Go where?" He peered cautiously out the front window to make sure she wasn't running across his yard again.

"To get clue number two." Victory crackled through her tone. "I figured it out."

Of course she had. "Where are we going?"

"You'll see. Be ready in ten." Her voice pitched higher. "No, five."

He headed for the library door, flipping the light switch, and pulled the door shut behind him. "I'm ready now."

"Good, because I'm here." He could hear tires crunching the Blue Pirogue's gravel drive. "Bring some cash."

What was she up to now? He patted his pocket for his wallet. "Got it."

Her voice wavered. "And maybe some lavender oil."

He tensed. "That's oddly specific."

"You'll see when we get there."

Oh, brother.

Nine

THE LIGHTHOUSE ON THE SOUTHERN END of Magnolia Bay had been a staple in Elisa's life as far back as she could remember. And yet, she did *not* remember the drive there taking this long.

She gripped the steering wheel with both hands, having long abandoned her nervous run of chit-chat and settled for awkward silence instead. The extended proximity with Noah made her hyper aware of his masculine scent, the warmth of his presence, the way he tapped a steady rhythm on the passenger door handle—like maybe he was nervous, too.

"I think we're at an impasse." The words blurted free before her lips could catch them.

Noah shot her a sidelong glance, his dark hair falling across his forehead. "The turnoff to the lighthouse should be another few miles up the way."

"I didn't mean geographically." She waved one hand in the air before returning her death grip to the wheel. The road carved a gray path toward the horizon, the lighthouse still much too small in the distance for her liking. The late afternoon sun teased the clouds, casting long shadows across the water lapping on either side of the concrete bridge. "I meant . . . us."

"What *us*?"

That honest question shouldn't sting, but a prickle ripped down her spine anyway. Elisa shifted in the driver's seat as she checked her side mirror. There was hardly any traffic, but it gave her something to do with her gaze while she felt Noah's fixed on her. "It's weird, you know? We're not friends. But we're not really enemies, either, now that we've called a truce." She shrugged as she needlessly glanced into her rearview at the dotted white lines blurring behind them. "It's like we're in the void."

He laughed, a small sound in the back of his throat that reminded her of slow dancing on the beach, with fireflies and the moon as their only light. "That's one way to put it."

"And how would you put it?" She braved up enough to meet his eyes, briefly, since she was driving. And also briefly because she sure didn't want to be responsible for steering her car straight into the bay if he happened to be looking at her like he had during those summer nights.

He wasn't.

They were safe.

He stretched his long, jean-clad legs against the floorboard as she slowed down to make the turn to the lighthouse. "I'd say it's complicated."

She pressed her lips together as she clicked on her blinker. "Like a social media status."

"Hopefully less drama than that."

She cut him a look as she turned right. "We have a personal history and an entire family feud, sugar. I think we're *more* drama than that."

"Why do you do that?" He pulled at his seatbelt, turning slightly to face her. "The whole sugar thing."

"To bug you." She shot him a smile, one that hopefully masked the telltale thumping of her heartbeat under her floral tank. "Is it working?"

"It is now."

Good. Nice and safe. "Don't you think we should get along, though?"

"We do get along."

She stopped at a four-way and tilted her head. "No we don't. We're always arguing."

Noah sighed. "You do realize we're only arguing right now because I disagreed with you that we don't get along?"

Point taken. She tapped the steering wheel with one finger. "Maybe the truce should be a little more defined."

"Sure. Name your terms." He leveled his gaze at her, shadows playing hide and seek across his face, and for the life of her, she couldn't remember which pedal would get the car moving again. "What do you want?"

She swallowed, avoiding his eyes. Such a loaded question. In all honesty, she wanted her life back before he popped up in the diner with her father, before he swept in to help her with Delia... before he discombobulated what had taken her years to regulate after that summer.

But she couldn't say that. Luckily, she'd had years of practice toning down her real emotions. "I think we should work as a true team. With good communication." The pedal on the right, that was it. She glanced both ways and eased down onto the gas. "And leave the past where it is."

Hopefully he wouldn't ask her to clarify whether she meant their past or their families' past. The answer was both, but it seemed rude to specify.

"Works for me." Noah stared straight ahead, his gaze fixed on the lighthouse drawing ever closer. "So how'd you figure this clue out?"

"I don't know if I'm right." She pulled up to the looming white tower, weatherworn despite a fresh paint job a few years ago. The hurricane hadn't done any true damage to the time-honored structure, but it sure had tried. "A couple of tourists in Bayou Beignets were talking about the lighthouse, and the woman mentioned how poetic they were. It got me thinking about the poem, and the lines about light and shore . . ." She shrugged.

"My mind would have never connected those dots." Noah shook his head. His hand rested on the door handle, but he made no move to get out as he studied her. "That's impressive."

Warmth flushed her neck. It was much too dangerous to let his compliment seep in—especially when he was just trying to be civil, maintain their truce. She cleared her throat. "I could be wrong. But it seemed worth investigating."

"I think you're right." A muscle twitched in his jaw, and for a moment, Elisa wondered if he was referring to more than the lighthouse lead. Did he really want to work with her, for real and not only for survival? Maybe work toward a semblance of friendship again?

She weighed the pros and cons of such a move as he maintained eye contact, his brewed-coffee gaze slowly deepening to espresso. He opened his mouth, then shut it and offered a tight smile. "Shall we?

He popped open his door, and she quickly followed suit, shutting her side with one hip and meeting him in front of the vehicle. The lighthouse stretched above them, tall and proud, as waves lapped against the nearby shore. A plaque on a stand boasted the lighthouse operated for over a hundred years in official capacity before retiring and settling into the status of tourist favorite. Even now, a couple stood down the sandy beach by the water as a photographer knelt in front of them, capturing the lighthouse in the background.

"So, teammate." Noah's hands rested on his hips. "If you were a clue, where would you be?"

"That's easy." She gestured to the guard shack near the base of the tower. "Did you bring that cash?"

Noah frowned, then he scanned the lighthouse from bottom to top. Understanding etched across his features. "I don't like heights." He pressed his lips together as he stared upwards, his gaze shuttering.

"I know." She tugged his sleeve, urging him toward the ticket stand. "That's why I mentioned the lavender oil."

"Do I look like the kind of guy who carries essential oils in his pocket?" Noah's worry turned into a scowl that proved he must have been spending time with Linc lately.

"I don't know." Elisa gave him a reassuring pat on the shoulder, trying not to notice the way his muscles, coiled with anxiety, clenched tight beneath her hand. "But lucky for you, I *am* that kind of girl." She produced a vial from her jeans pocket and uncapped it. "Smell this, sugar. You'll be fine."

He stared at her, just long enough to make her wonder if he was going to get right back in the car and lock the door. Then he reached out for the oil, like maybe he did trust her, like they were friends again. Or at least heading in that direction?

Their fingers grazed as he took the vial from her hand. She cleared her throat as he held the tiny bottle under his nose and breathed deep.

Because wasn't friendship what got them in trouble the last time?

After he inhaled several breaths, she took the vial from him and recapped it, hoping he didn't notice how her fingers trembled.

Maybe *neither* of them would be fine by the time this wretched hunt was over.

He'd paid twenty dollars for this. Handed over two tens to the bored-looking guard sitting in the ticket stand, then followed like a sheep as the man lumbered over to the access door at the base of the tower with a key ring that looked as ancient as the lighthouse itself.

Noah steadied himself on the rickety spiral staircase stretching up . . . up . . . up, and tried to control his breathing. Elisa, on the other hand, scampered up the stairs several paces ahead of him, reminding him of the Bible verses he'd seen crocheted on a pillow in Magnolia Grocery—something about hinds' feet and high places.

"You coming?" Her voice echoed in the round structure, only serving to remind him how narrow and confining the winding staircase was. The steps weren't wide enough for two people, and if anything was going to make him start praying again regularly, it would be the thought of what would happen if someone attempted to climb down while he was going up.

He gritted his teeth, biting hard on the stick of gum he'd popped in hopes he could release his adrenaline. "Right behind you."

One look down on her part through the open slated stairs would prove that wasn't true, but it gave him something to strive for. Sweat pooled on his lower back as he forced his legs to move onto the next stair. Done.

One more. Done.

Elisa's blond head poked over the railing, two levels up. "Do you need more oil?"

He needed to get out of this suffocating hot box, is what he needed. Needed the ground. "I think you slicked me up plenty good enough in the parking lot."

While he'd been trading cash and his sanity for two tickets, she'd swiped oil down both sides of Noah's neck. Elisa swore it had calming effects, but all he'd noticed was that his nervous sweating smelled better than it probably would have otherwise.

One more step. Done.

At this rate, they'd find the next clue by Christmas. How many stairs had the guard told them—177? He'd zoned out after that. Was the inside of this tower shrinking, or was that his vision tunneling? He squinted.

"Hey, Noah?"

He grunted, still unable to see Elisa as he gripped the railing in his damp palm. One more step. Done. Six million left to go. He tried to widen his eyes, but it didn't help the shadows crowding his vision. His heart raced. "What?"

"Did I ever tell you I went to culinary school?"

He blinked, attempting to focus on the next step beneath his feet as it swam. "I heard."

"Ah, that figures." Her voice lilted from above, giving him something to climb toward. "Well, anyway, I obviously didn't stay."

He wondered how she'd ended up back at the same diner she was waitressing at before she left, but why was she telling him this now? He climbed a little faster as his vision cleared. Two more steps. Done. He sucked in a long breath. "What happened?"

"A lot, actually. I sort of got screwed over by a boy—by a co-worker who took my graduation job lead out from under me."

Noah released his breath. "Boyfriend?"

There was only silence above, and the sound of his own breathing. Then . . ."I didn't mean to say that."

He took another step toward her. "But you did." So she had a boyfriend betray her.

The thought stung a little—did she count Noah on that same list of betrayals?

"Well, doesn't matter anyway, because I realized I wasn't as into cooking as I thought I was." Her voice softened, though the echo still carried in the tight space. "Just because my mom cooked didn't mean I had to, you know?"

Three steps. Done. "That's baloney."

Elisa had always loved cooking. Even when they were eighteen, she'd fixed a picnic for them to take to the beach. He'd expected

PB&J, maybe a few bags of chips. But she'd made three-cheese grilled flatbread sandwiches with her own secret Creole sauce, homemade garlic and pesto chips, and fruit salad with marshmallow cream. And those southern teacake cookies she'd claimed were her mother's recipes.

A decade later, he could taste the maraschino cherries, picture the hunk of bread that got caught in her hair during an impromptu food fight with the leftovers.

Another four steps. Done. "No, really. I like being manager." Her easy tone filled the space again, urging his feet forward. Another four steps. Done.

And now he was really trying not to imagine Elisa cooking for the jerk who double-crossed her.

"Being manager is the best of both worlds. I can be around the food but not have to make it."

But her accompanying laugh didn't sound genuine, and suddenly, Noah wanted to see her face. Wanted to see if her expression matched her voice.

Wanted to see if she meant it.

He rounded the final curve at a near jog. Elisa waited for him at the top level leading to the observation deck, the sunlight through the wall-to-wall windows catching her blond hair and making it gleam. The lighthouse's original Fresnel lens the guard had yammered about earlier filled the center of the space behind her.

Elisa smiled, and he felt silly for needing to check on her. She was fine.

"Odd time for story hour." He braced his hands on his thighs as he caught his breath.

"Was it?" She raised an eyebrow before leaning down to unlatch a low window marked EXIT. "Seems like it was the perfect time to me." Then she shimmied out the opening before he could reply.

She'd done it on purpose. He bit down on his lower lip as he cautiously hunched under the low frame of the window and moved into the sunshine. That made twice in two days that Elisa Bergeron had tricked him. Except this time, he hadn't minded the trick nearly as much.

A fact which disturbed him far more than the nerve-wracking view from the top.

Noah risked a step toward the security railing to see the ocean, and his stomach pitched. Nope. He plastered his back against the lighthouse wall. A bird swooped past the curved deck, doing little to settle Noah's rush of adrenaline. He closed his eyes.

A warm, steadying hand rested on his arm. "You good?"

He opened his eyes. He couldn't quite feel his legs, but he wasn't about to let Elisa know that. He sniffed, squaring his shoulders as he avoided her gaze. "I'll be fine."

She grinned. "I won't let you fall."

The wind lifted a strand of her hair and sent it fluttering away from her cheeks. Something stirred within him, something terrifyingly like old feelings. Noah clenched his hands into fists to prevent his fingers from tucking that rogue lock behind her ear, from cupping her cheek in his hand and reminding her how pretty she was.

Silly impulse. He blamed the lavender oil.

Then their eyes met, hers with a teasing, compassionate spark, and his stomach flipped.

It was no longer the lighthouse that had him concerned about falling.

Ten

NOAH DIDN'T LOOK SO GOOD.

In fact, under his pale expression, he looked almost . . . well, *friendly*. And if that wasn't a red flag for his mental state while standing at the top of the tower, Elisa didn't know what was.

She removed her hand from his arm and turned to evaluate their surroundings. She needed to find this clue, and fast. For Noah's sake, of course. Not because touching his arm and standing this close, where she could fully appreciate the depths of his scruffy jaw was messing with her own head. "Do you see anything on the window ledge?"

Noah shifted, slowly, toward the frame they'd crawled from and ran his fingers around the edges. "No."

She'd have to check it better to know for sure, but at the moment, she didn't want to risk crowding him. "I'll walk around the perimeter. Do you want to come—"

His wide-eyed stare answered her unfinished question.

"Right. Be right back." She maneuvered the outside of the observation deck, trailing one hand over the tower wall and one over the outside railing as she walked. Nothing felt out of place, loose, or otherwise messed with beneath her fingers. Where would Gilbert have put their clue? Were they looking for a note card like the first clues had been written on?

She was flying blind—and with a lame duck waiting for her, to boot.

Lord, I could use some help here. And if you could keep Noah from having a panic attack, that'd be extra helpful.

"Noah?" She lifted her voice above the wind as she made her way around the circle toward him. The sun inched its way toward the water, sending beams of light dancing across the top of the waves. Thank the Lord no other tourists had bothered to come to the lighthouse this close to closing time. "You good?"

He called something from around the curved platform, but the wind snatched his words. At least he was still on the deck and hadn't crawled back inside. Progress.

"Remember that time I tried to get you up here?" Seemed a bit dangerous to reference their summer together outright with him, but keeping Noah calm took first priority until they found the clue. "You refused. Claimed it was a tourist trap and not worth the money."

"Oh, I remember." His voice was faint, but she thought she heard a hint of humor in it.

"You probably thought you were so slick, hiding your fear of heights." She continued her search, winding her way around the platform toward where she'd left him. "But I figured it out after that impulsive trip we took to the Ferris wheel on the boardwalk."

She completed her search and stood planted in front of him.

He met her eyes, shook his head. "Lot harder to find excuses not to go on a free carnival ride."

"I'm just glad you made it out of the cable car before you threw up." They shared a grin.

Then Noah's face clouded, and he looked down, then away from her. "Any luck?"

Right. Enough reminiscing. She straightened her shoulders. "Nothing obvious. But, then again, I didn't expect obvious."

"There aren't a lot of places to put anything." Noah was clearly avoiding looking at the railing—or at her—but he did at least reexamine the window frame a little more thoroughly. "Do you think the lighthouse isn't the right site?"

She appreciated how he phrased that so vaguely, rather than simply stating she could have been wrong. Though the nicety could be proof of his waning emotional state being up this high.

"I'll go back in and look around the top floor. Maybe the clue is inside, out of the elements."

Noah shrugged, one hand digging into the wall, the other attempting a casual pose on his hip. "I had my eyes on the ground the whole time coming up here, and I didn't see a thing."

"I'm sure it's hidden pretty well. If it's here, it's obviously been up here for a while. Gilbert would have had to stash it while he was still healthy enough to come do it, but recently enough that he knew about his—" Oh, good gravy. She'd put her sandal in her mouth again.

A muscle in Noah's jaw flexed and she wished with everything in her she could retract the careless statement. "I'm sorry." She touched his arm. "Did you . . . know the cancer had come back?"

One quick jerk of his head confirmed her suspicion. *Oh, Noah.* She swallowed and squeezed his arm. "Don't worry. We're going to find it."

He nodded, a bit of color coming back into his cheeks. He drew a ragged breath, and before she could assure him it wasn't necessary, he swung back through the opening into the top floor. She quickly followed suit.

But he seemed better now, stronger. More focused. "Could he have left it with the guards at the ticket stand?"

"Maybe. We can ask when we go back down." Elisa rolled in

her bottom lip. "You know your grandfather best. If he was here, what would he be drawn to?"

Noah surveyed the small space. "He was quirky, but he had purpose. And he wouldn't have made it impossible—that defeats the point. He wants us to find these clues." He sighed. "We just have to think like him."

Elisa had a sudden idea. "How tall was he?"

Noah shrugged. "Five-ten, maybe? Under six feet, for sure. I passed him up in high school."

"Well, that doesn't help me. How tall are you now?" She gestured for him to come closer. "I'm about five-six."

He moved to stand in front of her, near enough she felt his warmth and nervous energy. "Six-one."

His voice dipped deeper, but that was probably his phobia talking. She, on the other hand, had no excuse for the rapid increase in heart rate or the sweat dotting her palms.

"So, about . . . here." She forced herself to focus on Noah's forehead as she held one hand flat, indicating where Gilbert would stand between their two heights.

"Yeah." His breath, warm and minty, fanned her face. "Close enough."

Too close. She took a step back. "What could he reach easily? He would have hidden it quickly, so no one would walk up on him."

"Yeah, and it's not like he dragged a ladder up here." Noah turned slowly, his eyes scanning the space. His back was rigid but his shoulders weren't as tense as they'd been on the way up the stairs. "Maybe we should re-read the clue."

Elisa recited the first one from memory. "One, if by land, and two, if by sea; And I on the opposite shore will be."

Footsteps sounded below, faint but distinct. She met Noah's stricken look, certain her own face reflected the same panic. She recited faster. "Hang a lantern aloft in the belfry arch of the North

Church tower as a signal light . . ." The footsteps grew louder. "What words jump out at you?"

Noah ran a hand through his hair as he paced. "Opposite?"

"Me too." Elisa nodded. "And lantern."

"Hang a lantern . . ." Noah muttered.

On cue, their gazes drifted over to the Fresnel lens.

Noah quirked one eyebrow. Elisa shook her head as she considered. "It's all beveled glass—nowhere to hide anything. So what would be opposite the lens, or the light?"

"Typically a lantern hangs from up high, right? So, maybe the floor?"

They looked down. No evidence of a trap door, secret compartment, nothing. Just smooth concrete beneath their feet.

The footsteps came closer, along with voices. They were running out of time—and privacy. "I just thought of something." Elisa gripped Noah's arm. "Would your grandfather have even been able to climb all the way up here? In his . . . condition."

"I didn't think of that, either." Noah's face paled. "I don't know. Maybe not."

She sighed. "So it could be downstairs."

"There wasn't anything downstairs, remember? Only the staircase."

Then their gazes locked as the approaching footsteps grew louder. "The stairs."

"He could have taped the clue under one of them, and no one would ever think to look." Noah's brow furrowed. "But which one?"

Bless it. There were only 177. But wait. "The clues contained numbers. *One* if by land, *two* if by sea . . ."

Hope lit Noah's eyes. "So the first step? Or the second?"

Adrenaline tingled through Elisa's fingers. She loved this—the thrill of solving clues, figuring out secrets. Maybe Noah would come to appreciate it once they had a taste of victory. "Let's try both."

Two college-aged guys popped in the doorway, out of breath and joking with each other. They nodded at Elisa and Noah as they maneuvered around the lens to the observation deck.

Elisa jerked her head toward the door. "Let's go." They should have enough time to get back to the bottom and check under the steps before the men attempted to come back through.

Noah gestured for her to descend the narrow stairwell first. "I'm just glad we didn't pass them on the way down."

"Do I need to tell you more of my life journey stories?" she half-joked over her shoulder. But his steps were keeping up with hers this time. He must be motivated to get to the first floor—not that she could blame him.

"Thanks for that, by the way." His voice was so low she almost missed it over their rhythmic footfalls.

Her heart stammered again, and it wasn't from the exertion or the thrill of the hunt. She carefully schooled her words. "You'd have done the same for me."

His silence made her wonder, but she refused to turn around to check. Probably best she didn't see his face—or let him see hers.

They made it to the bottom of the lighthouse in half the time it'd taken to reach the top, and Elisa eagerly turned to face the first step. She knelt on the hard floor, running her hands under the rough bottom of the stair. "Nope."

Noah squatted and searched under the second step, a hint of anticipation in his eyes. Then his face fell. "Nothing here either."

Elisa sat back on her heels, out of breath. Dust motes floated upward in the sunbeams scattered across the circular tower. She followed their journey, thinking. "Your grandfather was always so patient at the puzzlers club meetings."

"I didn't inherit that trait, if you hadn't noticed." Noah joined her, sitting on the concrete floor by the start of the winding staircase. "Maybe your hunch was wrong."

Maybe. She closed her eyes, running back through the clues, the conversation she heard at Bayou Beignets, what she knew about Gilbert. "He often said in meetings, when newcomers would get frustrated, that the answer was usually right there in front of them. They just had to wait until they saw it."

"So we're waiting on something—we don't know what—to reveal itself." Noah scrubbed his chin with his palm. "Seems like a solid plan."

She shot him a look. "Do you have a better one?"

"Sure." He scoffed. "Maybe we could count to three, say *abracadabra*, and—"

Elisa grabbed his arm and sucked in a tight breath. "That's it."

"The heat must be getting to you." He pressed the back of his hand against her forehead. "Grandpa wasn't a magician, *sugar*."

"Not that." She crawled forward on her hands and knees, ignoring the intentional bait of his word choice. "Count to three. One if by land, two if by sea . . . Three is the next step. Literally." She reached under the third stair, feeling the rough plank from one end to the other, hope soaring in her chest until—

There. She ripped the envelope free and held it up with a grin.

Eleven

IT'D ONLY BEEN TWO DAYS, BUT IT FELT like two months since they'd signed papers in August's office and started the hunt. And Noah wasn't entirely sure he wanted it to end this quickly.

He picked up the clue card from its spot on the coffee table next to a half-empty box of pizza, and spun it between his fingers. "No more stalling." His fingers itched to rip open the envelope, even as he wished time would slow down. Just a bit.

"I'm not stalling, I just want to revel in the win a little longer." Elisa pushed her hair out of her face, leaving a streak of tomato sauce across her jaw. They'd come back to the Blue Pirogue to eat dinner and review the next clue together, riding the high of their victory. Elisa had insisted they not open the next clue until they'd properly celebrated finding it. A large pepperoni and two-liter of soda later, here they were.

Sitting next to her on the floor, eating a late dinner, brought back a wave of nostalgia. How many times had they done that together over the summer? Like the time when she'd doctored up the cartons of Chinese take-out he'd bought with several spices, claiming they weren't Cajun enough. And the time she'd presented him with hand-torched marshmallows, toasted to the perfect degree of crispness for s'mores skewers.

"Does reveling involve finger painting with pizza?" He leaned toward Elisa from their shared spot in front of the coffee table, then thought better of it and handed her a napkin. A truce—or even a fledgling friendship—didn't require that level of intimacy. And being alone here in the inn, with his crew gone for the evening and the haphazard mix of construction dust, scattered tools, and lingering paint fumes, somehow felt exactly that—intimate. "Your face."

She scrubbed north of the sauce, then arched her delicate jaw toward him. "Did I get it?"

Freckles dotted her high cheekbones, and her blond hair waved perfectly away from her ear, despite the heat of their earlier climb. And yep, she still smelled like vanilla and honey, even with cheesy bread sitting two feet away from him.

Noah cleared his throat, hoping she hadn't noticed him staring. "So you can find a clue hidden in a hundred-year-old lighthouse, but you can't find food on your own face?" He took the napkin from her. "Some puzzle master you are."

"You're just jealous I found the clue first." She lifted her chin in mock arrogance.

"Only because of something I said. And you better be nice, or I'll let you walk around town like this." He gestured to the sauce still dotting her jaw.

"You did help back at the lighthouse, I suppose." She raised one eyebrow at him. "With all the not-fainting you pulled off."

"Okay, have it your way, pizza-face." He started to stand up, and she burst into laughter. The sound washed over him like waves against his favorite fishing dock, twice as comforting.

"I'm kidding!" She grabbed his arm, and he fell back the few inches he'd risen onto the rug. He landed closer than before, and the warmth of her arm heated his side.

"I surrender. Fix me." She arched toward him again, waiting, chin extended.

He slowly brought the napkin to her face. This was new. The bantering, the jesting—all in good fun, rather than exchanging actual digs. He kind of liked it.

Which was a huge problem.

Their former dynamic was frustrating in its own sense, but this one . . . this one felt dangerous. Heady.

Sort of like he was standing on the lighthouse deck all over again, staring out at his future, once upon a time.

He wiped her face and crumpled the napkin into a ball. "Truth or dare?"

Surprise lit Elisa's eyes, a spark he felt in the depths of his stomach. She squinted at him. "If I say dare, are you going to make me cartwheel down that hallway?"

"I guess we'll find out." What was he *doing*? This wasn't like him—or rather, not the Noah of late. That Noah was always stressed and overwhelmed, forever behind on his endless list. But today, Elisa made him want to slow down and smell the roses—or rather, smell the vanilla.

And he desperately needed a change of pace.

"No, we won't find out." She grinned as she reached for another breadstick. "Because I choose truth."

"Chicken." He couldn't help but tease her, even though he had no idea what he would have requested if she'd chosen the dare. "Okay . . . ready?"

"I was born ready, sugar." She fluttered her lashes at him and her southern twang, while exaggerated, coated him like the molasses on Grandmother's homemade cookies.

"Why don't you cook anymore?"

She blinked. "You go right for the gut, don't you? I told you, culinary school fell through and my ex—"

"No, I get all that. But culinary school and cooking aren't inexplicably twined."

Her gaze dropped.

He wasn't trying to upset her. But she had been too good to quit so easily. It didn't make sense. "I guess I'm saying I want to hear the rest of your story. After our climb today, I've got blood, sweat, and tears invested in it, remember?" His sweat, at least, was most certainly back on those lighthouse stairs.

"I should have known my good deed of helping you would reach around and nip me in the behind." Elisa released a short laugh. "Fine. But I get to ask you truth or dare next."

"Fair." He'd cross that bridge when it came.

She drew a breath, leaning her head against the couch as if settling in for story hour. "I don't cook anymore because it felt like a lot of it was tied up with the school, and all my failure there." Her voice hitched as if she'd struck a nerve in her own memory. "I guess I could have gone somewhere else, searched for a job on my own. But I wanted to come back home."

Noah nodded. "To your dad?"

"And Delia." She was quick—maybe too quick—to clarify as she stared up at the ceiling.

Vague answers. And they still left an obvious question. "So why don't you cook for the Magnolia Blossom? You have all that education and time put in."

"Delia's not interested in branching out—she's been making the same southern favorites for years and her customers love it." Elisa shrugged, head still against the couch. "It's not my place. Besides, I like managing."

Like she kept stating . . . or rather, overstating. But it didn't feel right to pry further—she didn't owe him any answers. He went for lightening the mood instead. "I suppose you were always good at telling people what to do."

She elbowed him in the ribs, and he folded into his side, laughing. "I'd say I'm kidding, but . . ." He caught another elbow to the ribcage. "Ow. Okay, truce."

"Another one? I'm going to need to start a list." She met his gaze in challenge. "My turn." She rose to her knees and faced him, anticipation lighting her gaze. "Truth or dare?"

"Dare." Whatever she came up with had to be far safer than admitting to anything she might ask. He'd rather streak Bayou Boulevard than admit he'd missed her even a little the entire past decade. That he'd compared every woman he'd dated ever since to her, and they all came up lacking.

Elisa's eyebrows lifted, but she quickly recovered from the surprise. "I *dare* you to answer my question."

He sucked in a tight breath. Clever. "Let's have it."

A somber expression slid over her face as she sat back on her heels, giving him her full attention. "Why is the Blue Pirogue so important to you?"

Speaking of going for the gut. But at least she hadn't asked about their former relationship. He cleared his throat. "It's my heritage."

"There's more to it than that." She tilted her head, studying him as if she'd never fully seen him before. "It's not only a building to you."

"Of course it's not." Which was something Elisa's father and grandfather, the men who'd been actively attempting to take it away from Noah's family for decades, would never understand. It wasn't about an age-old feud or who owned what property rights the inn rested on. It would always be more than that.

He had to give her something, though. She'd never give up as easily as he did. All part of that good ol' Hebert curse.

Quick to quit.

Elisa waited, watching him closely, and he hoped she couldn't read the myriad thoughts scattering around his brain.

Noah sighed. "The Blue Pirogue is my childhood. It's a testimony to my family through the ages . . . all my favorite memories are here. Grandpa would make up silly adventures for me when I was a kid. He always had some kind of puzzle going in his study—usually a 3D one, or a two-thousand-piece puzzle." He smirked. "None of that easy five-hundred-piece junk, as he'd say."

Elisa smiled softly. "That sounds like him."

Her encouragement—and the safety of the inn around him—loosened his tongue. "He was there, you know? I could always count on Grandpa to show up when my dad—" He cleared his throat. "When no one else could. Like for Little League games. JV ball tryouts. Whatever I was doing." Noah swallowed. "The inn represents that, somehow."

Elisa nodded. "Consistency." The word, heavy with southern accent, stretched between them. "That makes sense."

"Grandpa never quit on me." Noah looked down, wishing he could reel the words back in like Cade with his high-end fishing rod.

"You two always seemed close."

"Very." He stared at his hands in his lap. "That's part of why it was so hard when he and Grandma Edith divorced."

Elisa's voice dipped with compassion. "What happened between them?"

"Honestly, I'm not sure." Noah shifted into a more comfortable position on the floor. "Grandma was there for the early years of my life, with her molasses cookies and patterned aprons. Always smelling like cinnamon and offering warm hugs. Then she was gone, and all the adults were hush-hush about it." He shrugged. "I just put two and two together when I got older, figured out he left her." He shot her a look. "This might shock you, but Hebert men aren't particularly skilled in the relationship department." He only had to look at his own dad to see that. "Grandpa was a terrific grandfather—but apparently not such a great husband."

Elisa nodded. "I guess we all have our hang-ups."

Some more than others. Noah swallowed.

WHERE I FOUND YOU

"So if the inn is so important to you, why aren't you staying?"

"I need to get back to Shreveport." The words flew off his tongue as if they were rehearsed. Yet the meaning behind them didn't feel nearly as strong as it had even earlier that morning.

The inn was already working him over. Or was that Elisa? He needed to tread carefully. He cleared his throat. "Ready for the next clue?"

She picked up the envelope—the one he'd been so eager to open moments ago, yet nearly forgot about during their impromptu game. "Do you want to do the honors?" She extended the card.

"Sure." He took it from her, scooting a few inches away from his spot on the floor, resting one shoulder against the couch and facing Elisa so he could keep his distance as he read. Thankfully this time he knew to brace himself against his grandfather's handwriting.

The origin of that fateful command
Lives among us even today
Search the books if you want to find
The truth to end a fray. (UJC)

Elisa pulled a little black band from her wrist and began wrapping her hair into a short ponytail. "Read it out loud."

That wasn't going to help. *Oh, Grandpa.* He muffled another sigh as he repeated the confusing words for Elisa.

"Huh?" She frowned, her hands slowly falling from her hair.

"Yeah, exactly."

She snatched the card from his grip, re-read it, then looked up. "This isn't a poem."

"It's a bad one, if it is." They were back to square one all over again. Make that square two, technically. Now what?

"Maybe it's about the poem from the first clue." She licked her lower lip, her gaze running back over the handwritten words. "That fateful command . . . what command? What books?"

"Grandpa has a library." Noah pointed behind them down the long hallway. "Maybe he means one of his history books?"

"Maybe. And this UJC." Elisa shook her head. "It's in parentheses. Would he mean that as an afterthought? Like a sub-clue?"

"Or that part isn't even important." Noah shrugged. "Maybe it's optional."

"Or it's further explaining the last line somehow." Elisa sighed. "This one will be a doozy."

He snorted. "I thought that was my line."

"Maybe being an Eeyore is contagious." She handed him the card, then stood.

Noah did so as well, his left foot tingling from sitting on the floor so long. "Wait a second. You think I'm Eeyore?"

"Well, you're sure not Tigger."

"I guess that makes you Piglet, then." He was starting to see why teasing was so much fun. In fact, if he was in fourth grade, he might just reach out and tug her ponytail. Instead, he caught her wrist as she started past him.

She turned, glancing down at his grip, and her soft hand warmed.

He opened his mouth to tease her further, but couldn't remember what in the world he was going to say. Her smile waned as awareness hit her eyes.

His breathing shifted, subtly, until their rhythms matched. She inched closer, or maybe he drew her in—didn't matter. Only inches separated them, giving him a close-up view of her freckles and those cheekbones that itched to be traced.

He obliged, dragging one knuckle gently across their length. Her breath hitched off rhythm, and she licked her lower lip.

So much for treading carefully.

Red flags waved across the back of his mind, but he didn't want to think about them. Or about impossible clues, or about losing the inn because of stupid mold.

He just wanted to feel eighteen again.

Good gravy—Noah Hebert was going to kiss her.

A dozen voices stammered at Elisa to run. But she ignored them, drawn toward Noah like a moth to an open candle. A masculine candle that smelled like the sun on the bay and the forest after a heavy rain and all her favorite things about the island.

The back of his hand grazed her cheek, and she turned her face into his touch, breathing in his warmth and the caress of his knuckles. He held her eyes with his deep brown gaze, drawing her chin up and providing her a better view of his whiskered cheeks. She wondered if they felt as rough as they looked, and her hand longed to find out.

Before she could, his fingers continued an exploration along her jaw, then trailed quickly down the side of her throat until his hand cupped the back of her neck. She remembered that move. The first time he'd kissed her that summer, it'd been the exact same progression. A less secure woman would wonder if he'd pulled such a thing on every woman he'd dated since, but the smolder in his eyes assured Elisa it was reserved for her.

The warmth of his hand sent contrasting shivers down her spine, and she stepped closer toward the fire—toward being burned. Her finger buried into his shirt, knotting the material with both hands. One palm came up to graze his cheek. Just as prickly as she imagined . . . as prickly as she *remembered* . . . yet she wouldn't change a thing.

He ducked his head and she arched toward him on her toes, her body operating completely on autopilot as if the past twelve years had been an unfortunate blip on the radar. This was bad.

But so, so good.

Her breath hitched. She should move. Abort.

But she might as well have been chained to him, chained to the past. Her eyes fluttered closed.

"Elisa Bergeron!"

Her eyes flew back open at the slamming of a door. That wasn't the sweet mutterings of the man about to kiss her—it was the voice of her father.

"Dad?" Elisa's bewildered, high-pitched tone hurt her own ears as he strode across the floor. She wasn't sure if she had stepped away first or if Noah did, but sudden distance spread between them. Had her dad seen what had almost happened?

What *had* almost happened?

She stared at her father, whose red face testified he'd seen plenty. "What are you doing here?"

"I could ask you the same." Dad crossed his arms over his polo shirt. "I left several messages."

She automatically patted her jeans pocket for her cell, but it was back on the coffee table, near the abandoned pizza boxes.

"Not you. Him." Isaac's gaze swung sideways to include Noah.

Noah repeated a similar pat down, to no avail, looking as flustered as she felt.

"But I can see you were otherwise engaged." Isaac frowned.

Oh, boy. "Dad. What are you doing here?" Elisa kept her voice calm. *Be a good girl . . .*

"I wanted to check on the proceedings for the mold mitigation. When no one answered, I thought I'd swing by." He nodded toward Noah, his lips pressing into a hard line. "I can see I came just in time."

Noah cleared his throat, shifting his weight from foot to foot. "Proceedings are under way."

"Proceedings to fix the Blue Pirogue, or to weasel back into my daughter's life?"

"*Dad.*" Elisa moved to stand between them, even though they

WHERE I FOUND YOU

remained on opposite sides of the room. She stretched a hand toward both men. "Noah and I are working on a project. That's all."

Noah's gaze cut hard to her, and she averted her eyes.

Isaac lifted his chin. "I know what I saw."

Embarrassment crept over her shoulders. "You got your answer about the mold. Was that all?"

Isaac nodded stiffly at Noah. "Hope your *proceedings* are well-planned. You're going to need all the help you can get."

She quickly tugged at her dad's arm, willing him to move toward the door before he could humiliate any of them further. "I'll go with you. Come on."

She fought to hide her sigh of relief as her father turned and stalked for the front door. She cast an apologetic glance over her shoulder at Noah, who stood with feet braced apart in the middle of the lobby, his expression unreadable.

Boy, nothing like feeling eighteen all over again.

Twelve

HE CLEARLY NEEDED TO DO THIS BY himself.

Cell phone glued to one ear, Noah paced the sidewalk in front of Magnolia Bank & Trust, aware that he probably resembled a caged tiger—sans cage. The morning sun played peek-a-boo with the clouds overhead, far too cheerful for his mood. A mother walking with her toddler gave him one glance and changed their route to the opposite side of the street. Great, now he was scaring children.

Noah stabbed his hand through his hair as he verbally approved the mold mitigation company's quote.

The high one.

"Next week? Sure. As soon as possible." He turned to pace again, narrowly dodging a light post adorned with a wreath of white magnolia blossoms. If last night's meeting with Elisa had accomplished anything, it proved this treasure hunt was out of his league. Sure, they'd finally solved the first clue, but they had zero leads on the next.

More importantly, last night proved the sooner he left Magnolia Bay, the better.

After spending hours tossing in his bed, reliving the almost kiss and debating whether he'd been upset or relieved at Isaac's interruption of it, he'd formed a middle-of-the-night backup plan. He cast a wary gaze up at the Magnolia Bank & Trust sign.

Hopefully Owen remembered they were friends.

Noah thanked the agent on the other end of the line—as genuinely as one could thank someone for highway robbery—and pocketed his cell before pulling open the front door of the bank.

A rush of air conditioning wafted over his flushed skin. He straightened his shoulders as he entered the fake fern-filled lobby, hoping the sweat he felt on his back wasn't showing through his blue button-up shirt. He'd refused to wear a tie to this drop-in meeting, but figured adding a collar wouldn't hurt his chances at a loan.

A low whistle greeted him as he headed toward the roped-off line in front of the teller counter. He turned in time to see Cade strolling toward him from the row of offices on the far wall.

"My man! Looking sharp."

Noah shook his head as he returned his buddy's handshake. "Just trying to keep up with you."

"Good luck." Cade straightened the lapels of his tailored jacket and posed with a toothy grin—the one that had earned him a spot as an extra when a movie crew came through the bay a few years back.

Noah smirked. "You're fancy, even for you."

"I had a meeting with the branch manager—still working on getting some post-hurricane fundraising sponsors for a big event this summer. Got a community softball game in the works, too, among other things." Cade checked the Rolex on his wrist. "What are you doing here so early? The bank just opened."

"Need to talk to Owen."

"The hunt not going well?"

"Dude. I almost kissed her." The admission blurted free before

Noah could remember two important facts—he hadn't planned on telling anyone, and they were in a public place.

Cade's eyebrows shot toward his gelled hairline. "I'd say step into my office, but I don't have one. So we're stepping into Owen's." He tugged Noah around the corner into a glassed-off cubicle. "He's not in yet."

Noah glanced at the lobby they'd vacated. "We're probably not supposed to be here."

"You keep forgetting my dad's the mayor." Cade pointed to one of the two armchairs opposite Owen's desk. "Sit."

Noah sat, bracing his arms on the legs of his jeans. He couldn't bring himself to wear the khaki pants, but at least these were the Levi's without stains. Not that Owen needed impressing.

His gaze drifted to the framed family photo on his friend's desk, taken with Owen's pastor-father, Sunday-school-teaching mother, and his two fellow PK siblings, Sawyer and Adeline. They all smiled big for the camera, a happy blend of autumn leaves and denim shirts.

Noah's throat knotted. What would it have been like growing up with two parents who loved each other? What would have happened if he hadn't left town as a young teen, after his dad cheated and left him and his mom to face the gossip alone?

Would he and Elisa still have had that one summer together, several years later?

"So." Cade mirrored Noah's posture from the other chair. "Back to this kiss."

"Almost kiss," Noah corrected.

"Potato . . ." His friend's voice held warning.

Noah sighed. "We started the hunt. Finally figured out the first clue—well, Elisa did, anyway."

Cade squinted, but didn't interrupt.

"It was at the lighthouse."

He flinched. "You hate heights."

"I remember." Noah snorted. "So did Elisa. She helped me focus on finding the clue and not the fact I was one hundred and seventy-seven steps above the earth."

"So you kissed at the lighthouse?"

"*Almost* kissed."

"You almost kissed at the lighthouse?"

"At the inn. We grabbed a pizza and were celebrating our victory. Started talking. Laughing."

"And one thing led to another." Cade nodded. "I get it. You don't have to kiss and tell, don't worry."

"There's not a kiss to tell about." Close, though. Noah snagged a business card from the holder on Owen's desk and spun it between his fingers. So close he could still smell her, could still feel the lines of her face under his fingertips.

"You're sure worked up over an almost kiss." Cade leaned back, hooking one expensive loafer over his knee. "Did she reject you?"

Hardly. She'd been leaning toward him like the tower of Pisa. "Her dad walked in." *Then* the rejection started.

Cade's foot slipped off his knee and hit the ground with a thump. He leaned forward, chin braced in his hands. "Isaac caught you with his daughter?"

Noah spun the card faster. "Remember, we hadn't actually kissed."

"What happened?"

This was the part he hated most. Noah spread his hands. "Isaac told me off and they left."

"And Elisa?"

He swallowed. "Didn't say a word." History repeating itself.

"Man." Cade shook his head. "So you're here to get a second loan because you're giving up on the hunt."

"Maybe. Isaac resorted to drastic measures that one summer. Not sure if his ire would have calmed by now or grown hotter."

Noah bounced one leg. "I can't risk him sabotaging this inspection."

He'd never told anyone about the letters Elisa's dad had started sending to the inn that year—and there was no reason to now. The people who needed to believe him wouldn't, and the others wouldn't care.

Cade nodded. "So basically, you need to make sure Isaac doesn't stay ticked at you until the inspection passes. Which will be hard with you and Elisa working together."

"Right. So it seemed wise to come here, evaluate my options."

"You might not have many of those if it's money you're after." Owen strode inside his cubicle, his striped tie hanging crooked as he maneuvered between them to his chair. He grinned as he plunked his lunchbox on his desk. "Good to see you boys. To what do I owe the pleasure?"

"We needed a quiet place to wait." Cade shot Noah a look—one Noah returned with a solid *don't say a word* expression.

"Happy to help." Owen wiggled the mouse to wake up his computer. "Let's see what we can do. Cade, do you need money, too?"

Cade snorted, then shot Noah an apologetic glance. "I mean, no. I'm good." He stood and clapped Noah on the shoulder. "I'll let you two talk shop. Keep me posted."

Owen waved as Cade cat-walk strolled out of the cubicle. Then he typed in his computer password. "So what are we looking at?" He leaned back and pulled an old-fashioned calculator from his center drawer. "I'm assuming this is about the inn and the mold."

Noah named the total figure the mitigation company had given him. "I don't know if this inheritance is going to pay out that much—if we can finish the treasure hunt and get it in the first place." No sense in reviewing the extra complication he and Elisa had thrown into the mix last night.

Or the fact that they had yet to speak since then.

Not that it bothered him. They were adults now, not hormonal teenagers. They'd simply gotten caught up in the moment and post-victory endorphins. It was better for Noah to back out now, get some distance back between them, and forget this silly hunt.

He'd handle his finances in the more traditional fashion—by going into crazy amounts of debt.

Owen made a humming sound in the back of his throat as he clicked through records on his screen. "I've got your current construction loan pulled up, the one you took out through the business to make the renovations. The payment history is solid, which the powers-that-be will like. But you're talking about needing a bridge loan, and unfortunately that cap is hit. I'd ask for a favor except there's also the existing mortgage you're still making payments on . . ." He offered a sympathetic wince. "They'd laugh at me, honestly."

So it was worse than he'd imagined. Noah sighed. Gilbert had enough tucked back in the business account to pay the mortgage through the next several months, but without the coming tourist season, they'd be bankrupt in no time. Everything depended on the inn opening again, ASAP.

Which meant the mold had to be dealt with one way or another.

Owen pushed his glasses up on his nose. "I could run numbers on you personally, but you realize that changes the obligation on your part. You'll be blurring the lines between your business and your own finances."

Noah had feared it might come to that. But what choice did he have? He couldn't quit on the inn. Or on his grandfather. He could take the loan out himself, and pay himself back through the summer profits. Of course the treasure hunt could solve all of this, but was the cost of working with Elisa worth the risks? Worth aggravating Isaac into more revenge?

Worth stirring up things best left unstirred?

"Go ahead and see." Noah shifted in his chair. "My credit is good."

"Which will help. But remember, everyone is stretched thin right now with the hurricane." Owen frowned as he began furiously putting in numbers. "If you had a co-signer, like your grandfather did for that second mortgage years ago, it'd be no problem. Do you have co-signing options that you know of?"

"No. It's just me," Noah answered quickly—probably too quickly, but Owen didn't seem to notice as he punched a few more keys.

"Your current income-to-debt ratio isn't bad. That's good." He kept typing, then switched back to his calculator.

"Are we a go, then?" Noah returned the business card to Owen's desk, trying not to panic over the deposit due next week when the mitigation crew showed up.

"Not yet." Owen offered a tentative smile. "Luckily, you have an in with one of the top producing officers this year." He squared his shoulders.

"Congrats." Noah's phone buzzed in his pocket, reminding him his workday wasn't going to wait around forever. He stood. "I'd sure appreciate any leverage you could pull for me."

He tried to hide his smile as Owen scrambled to stand too, his rolling chair knocking into his knees and nearly sending him back down. "Of course." Owen smoothed his tie as he regained his balance. "Let me see what I can do. I should have an answer for you in a few days."

"Thanks, man." Noah said goodbye, then made his way back through the lobby, his phone buzzing with another incoming text. His heart shouted a hope his mind chastised. He had no business wanting Elisa to text him. No business hoping she'd clarify why she hadn't stood up for him last night.

It shouldn't matter. He just needed to get back to the inn and change out of this stiff shirt, make a dent on his list, prepare for the mitigation crew next week . . . anything to distract him from this page in history attempting to repeat itself in real time.

But to make sure it wasn't her . . .

He pulled his phone from his pocket and checked the display. Then he stopped short in the middle of the bank.

Delia had texted him.

Delia
_____

Trouble at the coffee shop.

COME QUICK.

"I made a big mistake." Elisa set Delia's wheelchair brake at the corner table by the window at Chug a Mug and hurried to move the extra seat out of the way. The espresso machine whirred from the front counter, and several patrons turned and offered sympathetic smiles to Delia in her chair.

"What mistake? Did you forget to order me decaf?" The older woman's brows rose as she looked up at Elisa. "Because I sure wouldn't complain." She covered an exaggerated yawn with her hand.

Elisa took the remaining seat opposite Delia. "You know what the doctor said—no caffeine. Your blood pressure has been high."

"Wouldn't yours be if you'd been stuck at the hospital the last few days while your café burst into flame?" Delia tugged a napkin free from the dispenser and wiped the table in front of her.

"You heard, huh?" Elisa winced.

"Of course I heard. It was on the news last night. That hospital TV was tiny, but not mute."

"I'm so sorry. I meant to tell you, but things have been a little hectic." To put it mildly. There'd been the hours spent cleaning up, going with Noah to the lighthouse, her father running into the inn unannounced...

Her stomach flipped. She was being such a coward, not texting

Noah after her abandonment of their victory party last night. But seeing the anger in her dad's eyes had sent her straight into survival mode—stay calm. Defuse the tension. Hide her emotions.

"I'm teasing you." Delia patted her hand. "Actually, Lucius came to me yesterday evening, owning everything. He felt horrible."

"He was a big help cleaning the diner." Elisa nodded. "He's over there again with Trish now, finishing up. We should be able to re-open for breakfast tomorrow after the health and code inspections this afternoon." She checked her watch. Hopefully they could get back to business for their faithful Saturday crowd.

She really needed some normal.

"That's what I heard." Delia wadded the napkin into a ball. "I will say it's a little odd getting secondhand information on my own diner." She glanced out the window at the café across the street. "In some ways it's like I've already sold it."

"Don't say that." Elisa touched her arm. "Everyone has been trying to let you rest."

Delia waved one hand in the air. "I fell, that's all. I'm not completely fragile."

Elisa frowned. More like fell, cut her arm, obtained a mild concussion, needed surgery, *and* was rolling around in a wheelchair with high blood pressure. "At least they discharged you this morning."

"On a handful of ridiculous conditions." Delia pursed her lips. "Speaking of my accident—have you seen Noah since?"

Elisa licked her suddenly dry lips. Time to confess. "About that . . ."

Miley appeared at their table, two coffees in hand. "Here you go!" Her smile was wide as she deposited the drinks in front of them with a flourish. "One mini mug decaf latte, and one chug a mug white chocolate mocha with almond milk."

Oh, no. Elisa offered a weak smile. "Thanks, Miley."

"Of course!" The girl tugged her tank top down over her low-rise jeans. "Enjoy!"

Elisa met Delia's gaze as the young barista practically skipped away. "The weather is apparently quite sunny."

"Well, I wasn't all that excited about decaf, anyway." Delia nudged her cup away without trying it.

Elisa risked a sip, then fought the urge to spit it back into the cup. "We better warn the others. You know Sadie comes in here every day like clockwork."

"I'll send a few texts, spread the word." Delia pulled her phone from her pants pocket. "I've learned how to use this smartphone pretty well since I've had nothing else to do—though it sure makes this old lady feel dumb."

"You're a whiz in the kitchen, Mama D. You don't need to be up-to-date with technology, too." Elisa gestured to the wheelchair. "How long are they making you use that?"

"Until after my surgery. They don't want to risk another fall." Delia wrinkled her nose as she typed out a text, like the very idea of it happening again was simply preposterous.

"Do you have the surgery scheduled yet?"

"They advised as soon as possible. But I'd like to have my ducks in a row first."

Ducks . . . meaning a buyer for the café? Elisa traced the lid of her cup with one finger, fighting to keep her tone casual. "So you're still planning to sell."

"I don't see a lot of options from where I'm sitting." She pointedly tapped the armrest of her wheelchair. "Insurance will make a dent, but the rest will be billed to me after the surgery." She sighed. "I sure hate debt. And not being able to work after the surgery . . . it makes sense to hand the Blossom over to someone else."

A confession bubbled in Elisa's throat. She wanted so badly to tell Delia about her hope to use the inheritance to cover her surgery but Delia would refuse to let her. She'd have to do it anonymously—assuming she and Noah could figure out the rest of the clues.

Maybe the second clue would make more sense when they weren't inches away from each other, fighting whatever chemistry had risen from the grave.

"Well, I know the surgery will be a hassle, but I'm glad you'll be back in shape after that. We all need you." She glanced through the window at the Magnolia Blossom. Delia came first and was way more important than the café. It held fond memories, but many of those were wrapped up in Delia herself.

"Don't you worry your sweet little blond head. You can't get rid of me that easily, now." Delia's fingers kept flying over her phone keyboard. "There. Warnings sent."

Good. Hopefully tomorrow Miley would be in a worse mood. This sure wasn't the week for Elisa to be cutting back on her own caffeine intake.

"Now, what's this you were saying about making a mistake?" Delia set her phone down and looked directly at Elisa.

She hesitated, wrapping a paper straw wrapper around her finger. She'd planned to blurt out what happened with Noah last night, but now that Delia had already asked about him, the words felt stuck in her throat like last summer's strawberry taffy.

"Out with it. I've been in the hospital for two days—I deserve a good story." Delia wiggled her eyebrows.

She drew a fortifying breath. "A lot has happened since your accident."

"Tell me, tell me. I'll just be looking out the window while you do, to make sure my café doesn't suddenly disappear into a sinkhole or some other tragedy."

"I've been named in Gilbert Hebert's will."

Delia jerked her attention away from the window to Elisa. "Say what?"

She explained the events of the past few days, ending with the near-kiss from Noah last night and her father's interruption. "So now we have no idea what to do with the next clue, haven't spoken since, and I imagine time is ticking for Noah." She wouldn't mention her own secret clock counting down to Delia's surgery.

"Good heavens." Delia eyed her full coffee cup. "I might need that after all. That's quite a load, honey."

"You're telling me." Elisa lifted one hand in a wave to Cade, who was approaching the front counter. He waved back, and she quickly sliced one hand through the air in front of her throat.

He tilted his head, frowning.

She mimicked drawing a rainbow in the air, then formed birds with her hands and fluttered them through the air.

His eyes widened in comprehension, and he slowly backed away from the counter, mouthing *thank you* before he darted out the door.

"Sweet boy, there." Delia nodded toward where Cade had disappeared. "Now. About your father." She narrowed her eyes. "How did *that* conversation go after you left the inn?"

"We haven't talked, either."

"But you left with him?"

"I made sure he left, listened to him rant a little, then went home."

"Without speaking your piece."

Busted. Elisa shifted positions in her chair, bouncing one foot under the table. "You know I can't do that."

"I know you *won't*." Delia shook her head. "Honey, you've got to speak up for yourself."

"That's never gone well. Not with Dad."

"You're an adult now. Things can be different." She reached across the table and squeezed Elisa's hand. "It's not like it was when your sweet mama passed when you were a teenager. I know how you felt like you had to hold your daddy together."

Emotion burned the back of Elisa's throat. "He didn't like outbursts. Or any strong emotion. I think when Mama died, he'd had enough of all that for a lifetime. He needed calm."

Cooking for Dad, serving him coffee, bringing him his favorite book when he got home from work . . . those were the times he responded to Elisa with positivity. When she held it together, kept calm, she earned his approval.

The rest of the time, he either stared into space or fussed at her for being emotional.

"Answer this." Delia let go of her hand. "Do you feel like you did anything wrong by spending time with Noah yesterday?"

Not this time around. Elisa swallowed. "No. We were just having a good time celebrating the first clue. It had been tough—much tougher than we expected. We were caught up in the moment." She shrugged. "But now we're stuck again, so I don't know if any of it matters."

"You're not going to get anywhere if you don't talk." Delia tapped the table with one finger. "And that applies to both of these men in your life."

"Noah isn't *in my life*." Elisa began twisting the straw wrapper into another knot. "We're in a truce. Temporarily working together."

"Mm-hmm."

"I mean, for a minute, sure, I wondered if we could be friends again."

Delia's brow arched. "Friends?"

Heat crawled up Elisa's throat. "Friends that kiss."

Delia pursed her lips but, to her credit, stayed silent.

"I should have known better than to get close. Chemistry dies hard, apparently."

"Sometimes it doesn't die at all." Delia nodded. "But why do you even need to kill it? Noah's a nice guy."

He had some redeeming qualities, but not enough to erase time. "Because our families hate each other." Elisa unknotted the paper wrapper. "Not to mention our personal history outside the feud. We've got more baggage than an airport. Maybe my dad did me a favor by showing up like that."

Delia let out a noncommittal grunt.

"If we had kissed, it'd be like opening Pandora's box. No way to stuff everything back inside once it got loose."

Delia leveled her with a look. "You already stuff more than you should." She paused. "You know the right man will love you for who you are . . . not the image you present."

The words touched a deep ache, one she'd locked up for a long time. A knot formed in Elisa's throat and she swallowed against it. "Who said anything about love?"

"That's what you want, isn't it? From your dad. And from the right man, one day."

She snorted. "Let me guess. You think Noah is that man for me?"

"I know it wasn't that snake of a man you dated in culinary school." She scrunched her nose. "What was his name? Taylor? Trevor?"

"Trey."

"Tell me, hon. Were you ever up front about what you felt when you were with Trey?"

"Probably not like you're meaning. But I made my feelings pretty clear when I stopped by his apartment to surprise him with a baked apple loaf and caught him with one of our classmates." Even now, the memory chafed like a pair of denim shorts after the log ride at the boardwalk. She'd always had a feeling about him and Sarah, but had denied the obvious far too long.

Delia narrowed her eyes. "If that apple loaf ended up anywhere other than smashed over his head, you weren't up front."

"I wish I had smashed it. Instead, I calmly placed it, and the bracelet he'd given me on our three-month anniversary, on the table and let myself out."

Delia muttered a *humph*. "See? Even in that situation you didn't think you could be yourself. Show your real feelings."

"I was trying to take the high road. Then to add insult to injury, Trey bad-mouthed me to the head teacher and took my job recommendation." Elisa swallowed. "Man, I know how to pick 'em."

"You picked a bad apple, hon. That's all."

"That apple cost me a post-graduation job." Elisa nibbled on her lip, tempted to go back to the memory and wallow a moment. "But you know all that. And I'm happy how things worked out, getting to come back to the Blossom."

"Getting back to Noah . . ." Delia waved one hand in the air, as if they'd given Trey all the air he deserved. "I think Noah is a possibility—at least one not to be cast out like yesterday's waffles."

"I'm more of a pancake girl." But Elisa's smile fell flat. "Besides, I don't even know how much longer he's going to stay in Magnolia Bay. Word is he's just here to get the inn ready and then will be moving on."

"Never know for sure until you *ask*." Delia gave her a pointed glance. "And talk about how you *feel*."

Elisa worked the straw wrapper faster, heart pounding. No way could she address the kiss with Noah. Despite what Delia was saying about being real, it was better to pretend like it hadn't affected her, to keep her emotions in check.

Being real was too dangerous.

"I hear you, Mama D. But talking to Noah or my dad seems like it'll just cause more issues."

"It's always worth having a conversation." Delia straightened in her chair. "Trust me, dear."

"Fine." Elisa dropped the wrapper and let out a defeated sigh. "Which *man in my life* do you recommend I talk to first?"

"That's easy." Delia leaned back, folding her hands across her stomach as she grinned. "The one approaching our table, of course."

Thirteen

NOAH WRENCHED OPEN THE DOOR OF the Chug a Mug and charged inside, chest tight. His adrenaline flowed, and he flexed his fingers as he gave the room a quick, frantic scan. A woman with two young kids sat near the chalkboard wall, typing on her phone as her children wrote with little white sticks. Two businessmen in suits sat on the couches with laptops, a newspaper spread across the table between them. The latest pop hit played via the speakers overhead, a tune that had Miley nodding her head to the beat as she snapped a lid on a to-go cup of coffee.

All was well.

No fire.

No masked robbers.

No armed criminals.

Delia sat at a window table with Elisa, a calm smile on her face, her arms folded across her middle. He rushed toward them, ignoring the cheerful chatter aimed his way from Miley, and towered over their table.

"What's wrong?" He scanned Delia, who seemed completely fine minus the fact she was in a wheelchair. Elisa was next—who also seemed fine as she blinked up at him . . . minus the fact his heartbeat was sliding into a completely different kind of acceleration. "What's going on?"

"Good to see you, Noah." Delia gestured toward an empty chair at a nearby table. "Why don't you join us?"

"I don't get it." He grabbed the chair and straddled it backwards, resting his wrists on the top of the curved back. "You said there was trouble."

"I did?" Delia tilted her head. "I don't recall."

Elisa's eyes widened. "Delia, what did you say in your texts about the coffee?"

"Coffee?" Noah frowned. He pulled out his phone and pulled up the message. His hand still shook from the dozen what-if scenarios that had raced through his mind. "This isn't about coffee."

Elisa craned her neck to read over his shoulder. "Trouble at the coffee shop. Come quick." And then the next text: "BTW this is Delia." She shot the older woman a look.

"What?" The woman spread her hands wide. "You said to warn everyone."

"About the coffee!" Elisa waved a hand toward the front counter and leaned in to whisper. "About Miley's mood."

"Wait. This is about the barista?" Noah pointed to his phone, his heart rate still several notches from calm. He narrowed his eyes. "I thought there was another fire—or worse."

Delia hunched her shoulders up by her neck, her smile turning only slightly sheepish. "I guess I'm still learning proper text etiquette."

"I guess so." Noah briefly closed his eyes, then looked back at Delia. Her grin was much more cat-ate-the-canary now than regretful. "How'd you even get my number?"

"You doubt my powers?" She side-eyed him.

Delia wasn't wearing a cape, but the woman had always possessed a superhero-type ability with people. His fight deflated, sagging his shoulders. "Mama D, I don't think Wonder Woman would doubt your powers."

"Good boy." She patted his arm. "I'd offer to buy you a coffee for your trouble, but I think that defeats the whole point."

Elisa offered him a sympathetic half smile. Now that his vision was clearing and his mind settling down from the adrenaline, Elisa's proximity registered quick and hot on his bare arms. Like maybe there was a fire after all.

Noah cleared his throat, drawing his arms closer to his torso as he angled away from Elisa. If he couldn't see her, he could pretend like last night didn't happen. Pretend like he wasn't still embarrassed about her rejection and desperate to finish what they'd almost started, all at the same time. He focused on Delia. "Are you going back to work today?"

"Waiting on the inspection to clear, then we'll get all that sorted out." She studied him, and her eyes narrowed. "Someone sure is looking fancy for a Friday. What have you been up to?"

Uh-oh. He shifted his stare slightly over her shoulder, out the window. From Delia's position, she could easily see down the street to the bank . . . which he'd left roughly ten minutes ago.

There was no way she could know about his request for a loan, even if she saw him leaving the building. Still, his stomach knotted. "Just errands. Then rushed here to save the day."

"You did that earlier in the week." She dipped her head toward Elisa. "*Both* of you took great care of me before they carted me off to the hospital and force-fed me cherry gelatin."

Elisa ducked her chin and averted her eyes.

Yeah, Delia was up to something. They'd definitely been talking before he showed up.

Noah drummed his fingers on the table. "Mama D, is there a reason no one else is rushing into the Chug a Mug worried about an emergency?"

"You know what?" Delia snapped her fingers. "I just remembered I'm late to meet Sadie at Second Story. She's been holding a few books for me to read while I'm under doctor's orders to rest more."

Elisa's eyes widened. "You're leaving?"

"It's down the street, dear. I'll manage." She wheeled herself back from the table.

Elisa's arm shot helplessly toward Delia. "But—"

"After all, I'm sure you two have plenty to talk about." Delia neatly dodged her grasp.

Noah nearly choked. Had Elisa told her about last night?

Delia kept rolling steadily around their table, twisting to speak over her shoulder. "You know, with trying to find the next clue and all."

The clues. Not the kiss. Noah relaxed slightly. Elisa must have told Delia about the treasure hunt, which was fine. Delia made pretty much every "need-to-know" list in the south.

But what neither of them knew was that if Owen got him this loan, he didn't plan to finish the hunt.

"Be careful!" Elisa called after Delia, who was already rapidly progressing toward the front door. A college-aged student with headphones draped around his neck stopped to hold it open for her, then lingered in the doorway as he stared toward the counter.

Noah twisted in his seat to follow the young man's gaze right to Miley, who was unabashedly dancing to the song playing overhead while singing into a bottle of creamer. The guy quickly replaced his headphones and made an about-face, the door drifting shut behind him.

He sighed as he turned back to face Elisa. "I guess word spreads quickly."

"I'm telling you—the weather report matters." Elisa nudged her cup toward him. "Try it if you don't believe us."

"Weather report is a much better phrase than 'danger.'" Noah shook his head. "Only Delia. What do you bet I'm the only text she even sent?"

Elisa smirked a little. "Last time I made a bet you got mad."

"Not mad, remember?" Oh no, they were headed back into flirty waters already. He cleared his throat, stifling the urge to pick up where they'd left off last night. "Well, I'm glad Mama D is feeling good enough to stir up trouble."

"Speaking of trouble." Elisa tugged the latest clue card from her purse. "We never got to brainstorm last night."

"Right. We were . . . interrupted."

"Right."

They stared at each other, Elisa nibbling on her lower lip while Noah battled every instinct in his body. They'd almost let history repeat itself. But then Elisa *did* let history repeat itself, by not standing up for him with her dad. It shouldn't matter as much as it had a decade plus ago. He was an adult now, not a college kid with an unstable childhood looking for security. He'd grown up, and so had she.

So why did he care?

Noah drew a deep breath, breaking eye contact. If he told her about the possibility of his quitting the hunt now, and the loan didn't come through, he'd be in a bind. Working together would be even more awkward at that point. He needed to fake it until he heard back from Owen.

But sitting here, pretending to care about this clue while fighting a dozen conflicting feelings roiling through his stomach, sounded about as pleasant as a big gulp of whatever was in Elisa's cup.

He abruptly stood. "I can't look at this right now. I need to get back to the inn." He felt like a heel but what else was new? He was a Hebert, and she was a Bergeron. The expectation was low.

Besides, she'd made her position clear last night.

Elisa's gaze flickered with hurt before she slowly stood too, pausing to loop her purse over her shoulder. "Okay. I should go meet Lucius at the Magnolia Blossom, anyway. The inspection is this afternoon."

They turned simultaneously toward the exit, crossing the coffee-scented room in silence as Miley continued her one-woman concert from behind the counter. Noah pushed open the door and let Elisa walk through first, trying not to inhale her vanilla and honey scent as she slipped past him.

He was almost clear to go back to the inn, finish his list, and focus on this mold problem. Surely Owen would come through, and then Noah could get back on his feet and pay off the debt after a promising tourist season. Easy. Drama-free.

But to do so, he'd be quitting the hunt.

His stomach clenched. Wasn't the whole purpose of restoring the inn to prove he *wasn't* a quitter? To break the generational curse? If he quit on Elisa now, he was no better than Russell Hebert. And no closer to proving Elisa's father wrong.

"Wait." Noah shot his hand out before he could change his mind, grazing Elisa's shoulder with his fingers.

She twisted to face him in surprise, the morning sun staining her hair with streaks of light. "What?"

"Let's meet up later and go over the clue. When we can both get free."

She raised her eyebrows. "You sure?"

He hated the wariness in her eyes, hated that he'd put it there, and hated that no, he wasn't sure at all. But he couldn't quit. "Yeah." He forced a smile. "I mean, the last time we researched a clue here, the café caught on fire. Better not risk it."

Her genuine grin made his own start to feel a little more authentic. "Seems wise. So . . . you'll text me?"

"I'll text you." He lifted one hand in a wave, watching as she sauntered across the street to the Blossom while willing his gaze to go in any other direction.

Definitely nothing wise about it.

She'd knocked out one convo Delia had suggested—might as well get the other one over with.

A soft ding announced Elisa's arrival to the second floor, and she took a deep breath as she exited the elevators and strode down the beige-carpeted hallway. Bergeron Inspections filled the plaque holder on the third door to the left. She pushed through it before she could lose her nerve.

Her father had only ever kept part-time employees, and sure enough, Melissa's desk sat empty in the front of the office, across from two fraying upholstered chairs. She probably took Fridays off.

"Dad?" Elisa wandered past the coffee station that boasted a sink, overflowing trash can, and a stale-smelling Keurig, and wrinkled her nose before turning toward her father's office. "It's me."

"Come on in." His door was open and he sat at his desk, furiously typing on a laptop while a golf game played silently from a TV mounted on the wall.

Elisa perched on the edge of the single chair across from him, her back stiff as she waited to be acknowledged. The single framed photo on the bookshelf behind him was her senior portrait, taken many moons ago, nestled next to a row of dusty books and a crispy brown plant. Melissa had tried, at least.

There weren't photos of Mom anymore.

Elisa looked away, folding her hands in her lap. "Bad time?"

"Nope." Dad finished typing, hit the enter key with a flourish, and leaned back in his office chair, spinning to face her, his expression unreadable. "What's up?"

And this was why these conversations were impossible. Delia didn't seem to understand that Elisa wasn't the only one wanting to avoid them. "Things got pretty tense last night." She looked away, then forced herself to hold his gaze. "We never talked about it."

Her father sat upright. "What's there to talk about? Other than your entertaining that Hebert kid again." His expression was no longer unreadable, except now Elisa very much didn't like the message it conveyed.

"He's not a kid, Dad." She swallowed back her next words, which were to point out that neither was she. That point shouldn't have to be made, though.

Even if she still felt like one.

Dad leaned forward, bracing his arms on the wooden table. The large desktop calendar page crinkled under his arms. "You know what I mean. I thought that stage in your life was over."

So did she. And judging by how strange Noah acted today, maybe it was.

"We're not starting anything back up. Like I said, we're working on a project and were grabbing a pizza after." The words felt sticky in her throat, and her father's stare boring into her—clearly searching for any half-truths—made them even harder to release.

"You know how we feel about the Heberts. They're thieves."

She let out a huff. "I know, trust me."

"Are you getting smart?" Her dad quirked a brow. "Maybe you're an adult, but you're not speaking like one."

"Sorry." Ugh, she was already caving. She straightened her shoulders. She could do this. For Delia, for herself. Maybe even for Noah. "With all respect, Noah isn't a villain. This feud had merit back in the day, but it feels pointless now. Things are the way they are."

"So we should stop fighting for justice?" Dad reared his head back to stare down his angular nose. "Just let things be, however unfair and illegal?"

She scratched her leg. "Well, no. But the inn is built. Whatever feud was going on over the rights to that property doesn't matter now."

"We could fix it if we buy it. Get the land back in the Bergeron name as it should have been from the beginning of this town—and reap those benefits." He waved his hand around his office, with its worn carpet and tired furniture. "You think this is fair? You think it was fair for you to grow up the way you did?"

Elisa frowned. "Dad, we were hardly poor."

"Well, we sure weren't rich." He shook his head. "Not like them."

Who cared? None of that was the point. "We got by fine. I never wanted for anything."

"Your mother sure did."

"What?" Elisa's gaze snapped to meet his. "What do you mean?"

"I know you two had all these expensive plans together—cooking abroad, culinary school, opening a restaurant." His lips pressed into a thin line. "She clearly wanted more."

"Dad, that's crazy. Mom was *happy* with our life." Sudden tears pressed the back of her eyelids. "We were having fun together. Making her southern teacakes and dreaming of serving them in our own restaurant one day. But she didn't care about not ever having those things."

"Well, maybe I wanted to give them to her." Dad's eyes filled with uncharacteristic emotion, and he turned back to his laptop. "I don't have anything else to say about Noah or any other Hebert."

Not fair. If he got to talk about Mom, she could talk about what she wanted to. *Just stay calm.* She clenched her hands into fists to control her surging emotions, digging her nails into her palms until the burn of tears vanished from her throat.

Now or never.

She slowly relaxed her fingers. "I'm going to be working with Noah until we finish this project, and I'm letting you know that as a courtesy."

There. That wasn't so bad.

Except her father wasn't responding, only staring.

She shifted in her seat.

He continued to stare.

But she couldn't be the one to break the stony silence first. Couldn't show a drop of emotion, or he'd call her out. So she looked past him, counting the books on the shelf as she waited. Four. Five. Six.

The silence stretched.

She dropped her gaze to the shelf below and counted dried stalks on the fern. Five. Six. Seven—

"So this is your position?"

She nodded soundlessly.

He tapped a pencil against his calendar. "Even though his family did what they did?"

"Dad, with all due respect, I'm not concerned about land rights from a hundred years ago."

His eyes morphed to steel as he tossed the pencil into its holder. "What about Aunt Rhonda, huh? You concerned about her?"

Elisa clamped her mouth shut. She hadn't prepared for him to play that card, which was foolish, because her dad always kept it tucked under his sleeve. She braced for the inevitable. Nothing short of another hurricane blowing through the bay was going to stop her father from saying his next sentence.

His words turned to ice. "You're not concerned with the fact that the Heberts killed your aunt?"

Fourteen

IS GRANDFATHER WOULD ROLL IN HIS grave if he knew how many times Noah had attempted to fix his hair before meeting Elisa that afternoon.

He scowled at the bathroom mirror as he ran damp fingers through the dark strands, attempting to make that one stubborn patch lay flat. Then again, Grandpa was the one who had thrown him and Elisa into the whole treasure hunt in the first place. The hunt Noah didn't want to finish. He was going through the motions out of some deranged sense of moral obligation that made zero sense except . . . He sighed. Except he didn't want to be a quitter.

That fact unfortunately made plenty of sense.

Noah stepped back from the newly installed vanity. Forget it. That cowlick wasn't going anywhere, and he wasn't about to gel up like Cade. He headed to his closet and grabbed his favorite navy ball cap instead—the one he'd gotten from a Louisiana landman convention last year—and tugged it on his head. There. Problem solved.

Now to see which to-do list item he could check off before meeting Elisa. Owen hadn't called with any update from the bank yet—not that he expected same-day approval, but a man could hope—and the mold repair would start next week. Until the mitigation crew determined what all needed to be done, it was pointless to work on any of the finishing touches inside the inn.

Of course, he could finish cleaning out that walk-in closet in Grandpa's old room—which he'd intentionally put on the back-burner for months because the other chores around the inn seemed more urgent.

And because, though the closet was small, the task felt enormous.

Before he could change his mind, Noah headed down the stairs to the original master bedroom on the bottom floor that his crew had turned into a luxury suite. He'd be fast about it. Sort through Grandpa's things, put aside anything worth keeping, and toss the rest. No reason to get emotional about it.

A text chimed on his phone, and Noah paused on the staircase as he glanced down. It was his project manager from work.

Chad

Hey Man, did you fall in a swamp?

He shook his head and texted back.

Noah

The alligators are all in Nola, Don't Worry.

Chad

When you coming back? I got a new project I'm parsing out. You want in?

Noah hesitated. His bank account balance wanted in, but he didn't have the time to work on anything outside the inn and this treasure hunt. He typed back.

Noah

Not yet. I need a few more weeks. I'll be in touch.

Chad
_____
Roger that. And watch out for those swamp pup-
pies.

Noah pocketed his phone as he passed by the lobby desk. Hope-fully there would be a project to join when he was ready. In the oil and gas industry, one never really knew.

But one problem at a time.

"Hey, boss." Peter met him at the front door, clutching a travel mug of coffee and wearing a nervous expression. "Whatcha got for me today?"

Oh, no. Speaking of work. Noah stopped short. "Hey. Um . . ." He looked around, started to rake his fingers through his hair and then remembered his cap. His hand fell to his side. "I thought I texted the crew to hold off until after the mitigation team comes?"

"You did." Peter nodded eagerly, shifting his weight in his worn sneakers. "I thought I'd show some initiative." He toasted him with his travel mug and let out an anxious laugh. "Impress the boss."

Noah sighed as the truth registered. Peter was in college. Which meant Peter was broke. He couldn't send the young guy away, not when Noah's motley crew had already missed so much work they'd been counting on having these last weeks. He thought fast. "How do you feel about cleaning out gutters?"

"On it." Peter offered a quick salute. "Ladder out front?"

At least that would be one thing off his list, though it could have easily waited until summer. At least Noah wouldn't have to get on the ladder himself. "Should be. Check the garage if not."

"Aye, aye." Peter shook back his unruly hair and hesitated. "And thanks."

Noah offered him a wave. "No problem." Peter was his cheapest labor, but the kid worked hard. Noah would try to find a way to help him out, even if he had to supplement the guy's paycheck with ramen noodle packages. "I'll be in the downstairs master if you need anything."

The college student hurried outside. In the new suite, Noah pulled open the door to the master closet, the one Grandpa had used for personal storage through all those years of operating the Blue Pirogue, and let the aroma of the past wash over him. Peppermint and cigar smoke.

No turning back now. He grabbed the first box he could see before he could chicken out. "It's only stuff." Talking to himself kept the nostalgia at bay. "One pile to keep, and one pile to donate." Maybe a third pile to throw away. Hopefully the "keep" pile would be small. The sooner the Blue Pirogue—and Noah—had a fresh start, the better.

Assuming Isaac Bergeron and this mold would ever give him one.

The box was heavier than Noah anticipated. He set it on the ground and pulled another one free from the top shelf, full of various paperback puzzle books. Sudoku, crossword, word search. Noah tugged one of the volumes free and flipped through the completed pages. Every single square was filled in—using ink. He shook his head with a smirk. Of course. He set the single volume aside as a keepsake and moved the rest of the box to start a trash pile.

Noah worked for several minutes, finding a stack of old college yearbooks, a collection of pocketknives he'd never seen, an entire box of mismatched socks, a clay crawfish ornament Noah had given his grandfather for Christmas in third grade, and an antique American straight razor kit.

After making a dent in the closet's contents, he returned to the first heavy box, squatting in front of it as he wiped a bead of sweat from his face. The box was sealed up tight with duct tape—a little surprising, since the others only had their flaps tucked. He grabbed one of the collectible pocketknives and sliced through the box seam, then lifted the flaps. Books—not as surprising.

But why store them here and not the library? He frowned

and removed the top layer of dusty hardbacks. Some of the titles seemed to be duplicate copies of books he'd seen on the library shelves during his perusal the other day. He didn't think Grandpa had ever gotten rid of a book, even when Sadie started offering him trade deals.

A worn black cover caught his attention—a thick leather Bible. Definitely one of a kind. He lifted the heavy tome and the faint scent of peppermint drifted up to greet him. A memory flashed, one of sitting in church next to Grandpa, tugging at the collar of his shirt and fidgeting on the pew in his uncomfortable shoes. Grandpa had pulled an orange hard candy from his suit pocket and offered it to Noah with a wink.

He swallowed hard, tempted to close the flaps and move on. But the book drew him, beckoning him to crack the spine and touch the same pages his grandfather had read once upon a time. Grandpa didn't go to church with Noah as much after he and Grandma Edith divorced, which didn't make sense at the time but did once Noah became an adult. Churches had rules, and men who left their wives weren't welcome.

He fanned through the thin pages, noting a few handwritten notes and starred verses. A scribbled comment in the margin beside Psalm 39:1 gave him pause. *I said, "I will guard my ways, that I may not sin with my tongue; I will guard my mouth with a muzzle, so long as the wicked are in my presence."*

The comment next to it read, <<H vs. B>>

Hebert vs. Bergeron.

Noah raised his eyebrows. Grandpa sure hadn't filtered his words about the Bergeron family over Noah's growing-up years. Had that begun to shift at some point in his life? Was that why he'd wanted Noah and Elisa to work together now? In that case, the Bible would be newer—one Grandpa owned more recently before his death.

Noah thumbed more pages, his gaze landing on more thin black cursive next to 1 Corinthians 13. *Love is patient, love is kind.* The handwritten text read, <<I love Edith. I wish I was enough.>>

Man. He could relate to that feeling. Maybe there was more to the Hebert curse than he'd thought.

Noah scanned a few more pages as he thought. The Bible had to be old, if Grandma was referenced. That declaration of love would have obviously been written sometime before they'd divorced, when Noah was a child. He flipped back to the title page, where Grandpa's hand-written name rested on the line under *This Bible belongs to.* Then he squinted, his heart racing as he read the next line. But no matter how long he stared, the numbers didn't change.

The year printed in the "purchased on" field was within the past decade.

"So what do you think the next clue is talking about? 'The origin of that fateful command'?" Elisa tried to steady her voice as she tucked one knee up under her on the wooden park bench. The last thing she needed was for Noah to realize she wasn't doing great. It wasn't like she could talk about her dad with him. In fact, she'd talk to the mailman before discussing her family's dirty laundry with Noah.

So why the burning need to unload her thoughts?

"I'm not sure." Noah stared toward the playground, where two young redheaded boys tripped over each other trying to climb up the slide. A mother on a nearby bench gently pushed a stroller back and forth with her foot as she talked on her phone, while Pastor Dubois and a small group in matching shirts passed out bottles of water and church invitations over by the partially repaired gazebo. A handful of spotted clouds dotted the otherwise clear sky, allowing for plenty of heat.

Noah had suggested the park as their meeting place this afternoon, away from the distraction—and the prying eyes—at Chug a Mug. Which was fine with Elisa. She could use the Vitamin D streaming onto her arms. They'd settled onto the bench in Lagniappe Park a half hour ago, but so far they'd made little progress on figuring out the next clue.

Of course, that might be because pulling words out of Noah today felt a little like trying to pull a rain boot from the muddy bottom of Pelican Bayou.

"I'm guessing the command has something to do with the Paul Revere poem, but I don't see the link yet." Elisa rubbed her finger over the dirty water stain she'd acquired on her thigh at the Blossom.

Though to be fair, she wasn't talking as much as usual, either. She hated that even after cleaning up at the Blossom for several hours after she left her dad's office, his words still lingered in her head. She'd been looking forward to moving along with the next clue, but that slap-in-the-face mention of Aunt Rhonda . . .

She pulled her other leg up to her chest and hugged her knees, surveying the copse of pines across the park. Most were intact, but several stumps remained in the ground from trees that hadn't survived the hurricane. Blemishes in an otherwise pristine setting.

She felt like one of those stumps right about now. Faking it while trying to blend in, to pretend everything was fine and she didn't feel cut off in the middle.

"What's wrong?" Noah twisted on the bench to face her, draping one arm along the back. He'd changed out of his dress shirt since that morning when he'd charged into the coffee house, looking casual now in jeans, an athletic tee, and a ball cap. Hard to determine which look suited him best.

"What do you mean?" Elisa blinked up at him, but it was evident in the thin set of his lips he wasn't falling for it.

"Usually when we discuss the treasure hunt, you light up like a Christmas tree on Village Lane."

She bristled a little under his sudden evaluation. "I could ask you the same question, sugar. Not that you're normally chipper."

He seemed to ignore that logic, dipping his chin to meet her gaze. "You've made eye contact with me twice since we've been sitting here."

"Oh yeah? Well you barely even noticed when that giant Golden Doodle chased a ball right up to our bench. Got drool all over your shoe."

Noah held her gaze in challenge, and she refused to look away. Then he broke contact to check his watch. "Is it the inspection? Are you worried about the results?"

That sure would be an easy out, but it'd also be a lie. Elisa let out a slow sigh and shook her head. "No, they came by before I met you here. We're clear to reopen tomorrow—thanks to Lucius. He's been relentless in his efforts."

"Guilt can be a strong motivator." Noah's voice deepened an octave before he cleared his throat. "Truth or dare?"

Her stomach fluttered. Noah being vulnerable again made her simultaneously want to stand on the bench and break into song . . . and sprint hard after the Golden Doodle's ball rolling into the woods. She controlled her features to remain passive. "Truth."

"Okay . . . what are you upset about?"

"Cheater." She elbowed him, his side rock-hard under her nudge. She attempted to ignore the electric current pulsing up her arm. "If you must know—I had a fight with my dad this morning. He said some pretty rough things."

Noah's expression softened. "I'm sorry." He hesitated. "Was it about this?" He waved the clue card between them. "I know the hunt is getting complicated."

That was one way to put it. "He definitely doesn't like us working together, let's put it that way."

Noah snorted. "Yeah, that impression was clear."

"He's a man of many strong opinions." Many of which were wrong, if you asked Elisa. But no one ever did. She lifted her chin. "But I told him we were working on a project together, and he was going to have to get over it."

"You told your dad to get over it?" Noah's brows shot into his hat.

She paused. "Not in those exact words." To that point, she wasn't sure if leaving the office in a sudden flood of tears counted as words at all. But she'd had plenty of them in her head.

Elisa waved one hand toward Noah before he could ask any further questions. "Your turn to play. And don't choose dare, or I'll just dare you to tell me the truth again."

"Why do you care?"

This time, her rapid blinking stemmed from real surprise.

"I'm sorry, that came out a little harsh." Noah released a hesitant chuckle, reaching up to adjust the brim of his hat. "I meant . . . why are you worried about me?"

"I think that question goes both ways, too." Still facing outward on the bench, she turned her head to meet his eyes, their faces closer than they were before. She didn't move away, and neither did he. Bless it, she was being bold—especially in light of his attitude that morning in the Chug a Mug. She could lean in a little if she had the nerve, try to re-create the moment that was interrupted at the inn. It wouldn't take much effort at all.

But it wasn't worth the risk to her heart. Noah had left before, and he was leaving again. Besides, they were only on clue two. If something shifted between them before they finished the hunt, they would lose it all.

She couldn't let Delia down.

"You want to know why I'm worried about you?" Noah's voice, still an octave deeper, shook her insides. "Are you sure about that?"

This wouldn't do at all. Elisa broke eye contact and rubbed her palms down her jeans. "Maybe that's a truth or dare for another day."

Noah let out a quick sigh—one born of disappointment or relief, she wasn't sure which—and nodded. "Agreed."

She reached for the card he held, desperate to switch gears. Solving this clue would be much easier than trying to solve the riddle that was Noah Hebert. The man ran as hot and cold as that rusty apartment sink she'd had to sweet-talk her and Zoey's building manager into replacing. "So, maybe this first line means—"

But he didn't let it go. "Have you ever believed something to have happened a certain way, and then find something later that suggests maybe it wasn't what you thought at all?"

Talk about riddles. Noah himself was starting to fit into that category, but she couldn't go there. Elisa's hand fell back to her lap. "Do you mean in general, or a specific event in history?"

"A specific event."

"Something like you thought it happened on a particular day but then it turned out it was earlier or later?"

"Not exactly." Noah leaned forward, resting his elbows on his knees. "My grandfather divorced my grandmother when I was seven. No one talked about it much, but Grandpa stopped going to church regularly after that. I remember hearing rumors when I was a kid, about yet another Hebert man quitting. This time on his marriage, apparently."

Wow. She leaned toward him, then thought better of it. "That's horrible for a kid to have to process."

"I agree." Noah shrugged. "My dad even made similar jokes about the Hebert men."

Elisa stiffened. "Your dad?"

"Yeah, and then after my parents divorced too, my mom said it even more often. I guess she forgot she was griping about Hebert men *to* a Hebert man." His lips twisted to one side. "But she saw me as her little boy, not a namesake. I'm sure it was harmless."

"Maybe not intentional, but clearly not harmless." She couldn't take it anymore. She rested her hand on Noah's arm, his skin warm under her touch. "I'm sorry."

He looked down and she followed his gaze to her fingers, pale against his tanned forearm. "I'm only telling you this because I found something in Grandpa's closet today that makes me wonder if he didn't leave my grandmother, after all."

"That's big, isn't it?"

"I think so. But I don't know how to find out for sure."

No wonder he'd been so quiet. He was trying to solve his own puzzle today.

"Maybe you'll find something else stored away that can confirm." The moment that merited a comforting touch had passed. She pulled her hand back, missing the warmth of his arm under her palm, and tucked her fingers under her legs on the bench. Just in case.

"I hope so. He'd written in the margins of his Bible that he loved her." Noah shifted positions on the bench. "He even wrote that he wished he was enough. Which I can relate to. I always thought that about my dad, during the divorce."

"Understandable. You were just a kid." Elisa hesitated. "I can relate, myself. There was a little more to the culinary school ex-boyfriend than I told you."

"What happened?" He leaned back against the bench, his posture stiffer than a moment before. Did he not want to hear this?

Well, he asked. Elisa took a breath. "This guy not only sabotaged my job, he cheated on me."

A muscle flexed in Noah's jaw. "That's horrible. What a creep."

Elisa shrugged one shoulder. "It's been years now. But back then, when it was fresh, I wondered why I wasn't enough for him. Or honestly, it was probably more like I was too much." As was the case with other men in her life, namely, her dad.

Noah's voice came out low. "You don't deserve that."

"What's this?" Elisa bumped her shoulder into Noah's, hoping to lighten the mood. "A Hebert wishing good things on a Bergeron?"

"Stranger things have happened." His jaw relaxed, which helped her own shoulders release.

"Enough about my ex." Elisa rubbed her hands down her jean-clad legs. "Let's go back to the Bible you found. Was there anything else with it?"

Noah held her gaze a moment, as if double-checking she really wanted to change the subject. Then, thankfully, he obliged. "Not that I saw. But that note in the margins really brings up so many questions. Like, if Grandpa didn't leave her, then why did everyone talk about it the way they did? Why blame it on Grandpa? And to that point, why would Grandma Edith choose to leave him?"

Elisa didn't think Noah expected an answer, but she wished she had one to give. "I'm sure divorce can be complicated. My parents stayed together, but my mom died, and . . . well." She swallowed. "Nothing was quite the same after that, either. I guess in some ways divorce is like a death, you know? And people grieve differently."

Noah's eyes shifted from wide to slightly lazy as he tilted his chin, contemplating her. "That's really wise. Thank you."

"You're welcome." Movement behind Noah caught her gaze—a woman approaching the walking trail that wove past their bench, a heavy tote bag on one shoulder. "Oh look, here comes Sadie." Was it her imagination, or did Noah scoot farther away?

He casually tucked the clue card into his back pocket. "We keep running into her."

"Hazards of a small town." Elisa waved as the woman drew closer. "Hi, Sadie. Did you hear today's weather report?"

"Cade warned me earlier." Sadie laughed as she slowed in front of their spot. "But I'm desperate. I'm in Chug a Mug every morning at six before opening up my shop, and most afternoons at three for my caffeine fix."

Noah chuckled. "A woman of routine. I can respect that."

Elisa cast him a glance. He'd definitely moved farther away. "Maybe the weather has changed since this morning. Just don't try the mocha." She wrinkled her nose. "Good luck!"

"You too." Sadie shot them a knowing glance before adjusting her bag strap on her shoulder and picking up her pace.

Noah's brow furrowed as he watched her leave. "Did that seem . . . weird?"

"A little awkward. But probably because you were about to fall off the bench over there."

He flushed. "This hunt is a need-to-know basis, remember?"

"I know, but I warned you about the small-town hazard. Some things are inevitable." She tried not to look at Noah's lips as the word lingered on her own. But he was sure looking at hers.

Then he abruptly tugged the card from his pocket. "Let's figure this thing out so we can move forward."

Elisa wasn't sure if he meant literally or figuratively, and this wasn't the moment to clarify. He read the clue out loud, competing with the Golden Doodle's eager barks across the field, while Elisa mouthed the words silently over his shoulder.

The origin of that fateful command
Lives among us even today
Search the books if you want to find
The truth to end a fray. (UJC)

And like gears sliding into place, it hit her. "The origin of that fateful command." She clapped her hands together. Why hadn't she gotten it sooner?

Noah jerked back against the bench. "Huh?"

It made so much sense now. She gripped his arm. "Who gave Paul Revere the order to ride?"

"Grandpa was the history buff, not me." Noah thumped the card with two fingers. "I know Hamilton lyrics, at best."

"Then Google it." Elisa flapped her hand toward him. "Quick."

Noah's fingers flew over his phone keys. "Um . . . Joseph Warren?"

"Warren . . ." She snapped her fingers. "Why does that sound familiar?"

"He wasn't in Hamilton, I know that much." Noah shrugged.

"Not like that." Elisa fought to keep from laughing. "I mean familiar around town. Isn't there a famous Warren in Magnolia Bay?"

Noah stared at the playground again, eyes narrowed in concentration. "It does sound familiar, like maybe I've seen it on a plaque somewhere. But I've been gone so long, there's no telling."

"A plaque . . ." Her mind raced. Plaques were on park benches. Memorials. Gravestones. Office doors.

And statues.

Elisa clapped her hands together again. "The statue!"

Noah jerked again. "You've got to start warning me before you do that."

"There's a statue of Thomas Warren at the library." Elisa could barely get the words out fast enough now. "He was the man who donated money and a bunch of first edition novels decades ago, when the library was in danger of closing."

"You mean that life-size statue of a man smoking a pipe and holding a stack of books in the courtyard?" Noah asked.

"Yes! And the next line of the clue. Look." She jabbed at the card.

"Search the books." Noah met her gaze. "That fits with the library."

"And your grandfather was a big reader, too, right?"

"The biggest." A grin started across Noah's face, and he jumped to his feet. "Nice work, Sherlock." He extended his hand toward her. "To the library?"

She eyed his hand. His instincts cautioned *no*. But some things were inevitable, right?

"To the library, Watson." And she slid her hand into his.

Fifteen

I DON'T GET IT." FRUSTRATION MARRED Elisa's face as she stared up at the bronze statue. The setting sun sent streaks of crimson and coral across the sky behind her. "We were so sure."

Noah planted his hands on his hips as he followed her gaze to the statue's carved expression, which stared blankly across the quiet library lawn. More like *Elisa* had been sure. He hadn't been sure of much of anything from day one of this hunt, but he trusted her instincts. The way she put stuff together was brilliant.

He'd be intimidated if it didn't bring him so much joy to watch her light up that way.

Right now, though, Elisa's scowl was dark as she circled the statue for the tenth time, her hands running so thoroughly over the concrete Mr. Warren that she'd probably have blushed if she'd thought about it long enough. "Are we missing something?"

"Like what, a trap door?" Noah knocked against the stack of books Mr. Warren clutched to his side. "There's nothing here."

"What if it *was* here, but isn't anymore?" Elisa's eyes widened with horror. "What if the clue was found by someone else first? These cards had to be stashed months and months ago, right?"

"That, or maybe Grandpa arranged for August to plant them after he...you know. After." Noah busied himself with a crack in one of the concrete book spines until the pressure in his throat eased. Man, that needed to stop happening.

Elisa stepped back, hooking her fingertips into her back pockets as she surveyed the library grounds, free of people now as closing time drew near. But the massive oak spreading shade across the yard, the bubbling fountain filled with wishing pennies, and the newly striped parking lot didn't seem to offer any hints as to their next move.

She began ambling toward the fountain. "Maybe we got the wrong Warren. Maybe it's specific to Joseph, after all—the guy who actually gave Paul Revere the command to ride."

Noah followed, mimicking her movement and shoving his own hands in his pockets. "If there's anything local around here about that particular Warren, you would know before I would." A handful of change jingled under his fingertips, and he pulled free a penny. He smirked as he handed it to Elisa. "How desperate are you?"

"I don't really believe in wishes." She held the penny up, squinting at it in the setting sun. "But it's fun, I guess."

He watched her watching the fountain. "What do you believe in, then?"

"Prayer." She rolled in her lower lip. "Though I admit, sometimes it feels almost as futile as wishing on a penny."

"I've never heard a believer confess that before." He thought it was just him. The urgency to find the next clue faded, replaced by an urgency to know more of Elisa's thoughts on the matter.

She stepped closer to the flowing water, looking down at the coins cluttering the fountain's concrete bottom. "I prayed hard for my mom when she got sick." She rolled the penny between her fingers, her voice trailing to a near whisper. "It didn't work."

He knew what that was like. "I didn't even know about my

grandfather's cancer returning until it was too late to pray." Noah sat on the rim of the fountain, stretching his legs in front of him. "But when my parents divorced, I sure tried everything."

Those weren't nights he ever wanted back. Begging God to change his dad's mind. To fix his parents' marriage.

He stared at his crossed ankles. "But instead of witnessing a miracle, I only witnessed yelling matches, ones that sent me cowering to my closet. Witnessed my dad driving away. Mom's mascara leaving permanent tracks on her cheeks."

"I'm so sorry." Elisa joined him on the edge of the fountain, still holding the penny. The warmth of her body radiated into his side despite the fact they weren't touching. Comforting, like a summer memory.

She cast him a sidelong glance. "You never talked about your parents when we were . . . you know, when we . . ."

"*Dated*?" He quirked an eyebrow at her. "It's not a dirty word."

"Depends on who you ask. Sure feels like it these days." A blush crept up Elisa's cheeks, turning them irresistibly pink. She sobered. "Semantics aside—why didn't you talk about it?"

That was easy. He let out a sigh. "I was eighteen and with you."

She turned questioning eyes on him, her face close enough to bring back all sorts of teen angst.

He should put the brakes on this conversation, but the truth rolled off his lips. "That summer was perfect, Elisa." He held her gaze. "The last thing I wanted to do was bring up my childhood drama."

She licked her lips. "But it found us anyway."

He nodded slowly. "I guess it did."

They sat in silence for a moment. Then, with her gaze fixed on the piece of copper in her hands, she angled slightly toward him. "Do you think my mom getting sick, and your parents divorcing anyway, means God didn't hear us?"

"No." The word left his mouth before he could fully process it,

WHERE I FOUND YOU

and he paused. Did he mean that? "I guess I haven't thought about it one way or the other."

"But you don't go to church anymore." Her voice lilted, inviting more detail that he somehow didn't mind giving.

Maybe it was the way the sunset created a stunning backdrop to the west, or the way the wind whispering through the oak leaves overhead protected their hushed tones, but for the first time in a long time, he didn't feel like hustling to the next item on his to-do list.

He felt like maybe he was supposed to be sitting right there, right then.

"I'm not mad at God, if that's what you mean." He lifted one shoulder. "I guess it's more a keep-my-distance type thing. I catch myself assuming God is like my dad, which I don't think is true. But then I'm not sure what to think, so I just . . . don't."

"I get that." Then her eyes widened. "I mean, my dad is great and all. He just . . . didn't handle losing Mom well, you know? He changed after that." She sniffed. "Understandably."

So she still made excuses for him. Not that Noah could blame her—he hadn't seen his own father in person in years. Easy for him to say what he would or wouldn't do if he ever did again. He wasn't dealing with the guy day in and day out.

Maybe there was some grace to his absence, after all.

Elisa held up the penny and let it drop from one palm to the other. "I think God hears our prayers and cares. It's just that things are often beyond our ability to understand this side of heaven."

Ha. He twisted his neck to look at her. "That's a church answer."

"Some answers are cliché, but they can also be true."

"I've heard plenty of those, trust me," Noah scoffed as he stretched his legs out in front of him. "Then I realized the church wasn't incredibly kind to divorced adults."

She kept slowly tossing the penny from one hand to the other. "Your mom?"

"And my grandfather." He pressed his lips tight, watching as a library worker exited the building and headed for the nearly vacant parking lot. "Let's just say the D-word is frowned upon in religious circles—even when one party wasn't at fault and wanted nothing to do with it."

Like his mother. She'd filed for divorce from his father, understandably so after word of the affair became public. But Dad hadn't tried to stop her, and their congregation at the time hadn't rallied around any of them.

But now they were getting dangerously close to the details of that event, the same event that had indirectly ended his and Elisa's perfect summer together. Were they really going to go there after all this time? He couldn't decide if the idea was necessary or foolish.

Elisa's hands stilled around the coin. "So you're not mad at God. You're mad at the church."

That wasn't where he thought she was taking the conversation.

He automatically started to deny the claim, then paused as her words rolled around his heart. "Maybe I am." Finding Grandpa's Bible had clearly stirred up old resentment he'd long left undisturbed.

Elisa's expression sobered. "What went on at the church?"

He let out a slow breath. "The congregation didn't exactly help my family out when Grandma and Grandpa split." A fog of memory swept through his mind. "There were a lot of whispers and not-so-discreet pointing."

Long dress hems and shuffling feet. Grandpa, head held high in his best suit. But he hadn't lasted long, had he?

Noah felt the bittersweet smile coming before it grazed his lips. "After that, most of my childhood Sunday mornings consisted of store-bought donuts, pirate-watching from the roof, and cardboard surfing down the lobby stairs." No more clip-on ties or

Grandpa attempting to swipe Noah's cowlick down with a wet finger. As a kid, he hadn't minded in the least.

Now . . . he wondered what he'd missed. If he'd have had faith like Elisa's if he'd kept going.

Elisa smiled back. "Your grandpa seemed fun."

"He is." Noah coughed against the knot that was back. "Was."

"I guess things weren't any better when your parents followed suit with their divorce." She shifted on the edge of the fountain, tilting her head toward him.

"Yeah, and as you and everyone knows, that was for much more scandalous reasons. By then, people didn't even bother to whisper."

"That's awful."

"That's why my mom moved us to north Louisiana so quickly." Noah stood abruptly, shoving his hands in his pockets. "Isn't church the place where people are supposed to be the *most* loving? The *least* judgmental?"

"I think so, but people disappoint." Elisa shrugged as she looked up at him. "That was a long time ago, right? Pastor Todd wouldn't have been there then."

"No, he wasn't. I've met him briefly through Owen, but I haven't heard him preach yet." Of course, he didn't plan to take the time now, either. Not until the inn was up and running, mold-free. Which meant either finishing this treasure hunt or getting his loan—whichever happened first.

Still sitting in front of him, Elisa silently met his gaze and reached for his hand.

He hesitantly allowed her touch, watching as she turned his palm up and pressed his fingers out flat. Then she set the penny in the middle of his hand. "Maybe you should try again."

He snorted, even as that familiar weight pressed behind his eyes and into his throat. He swallowed. "Prayer? Or church?"

She gently closed his fingers around the coin. "Why not both?"

Noah's Adam's apple bobbed in his throat, and Elisa had the sudden thought to press a kiss against it.

She quickly released his hand and stood, putting a little distance between them along the fountain edge as the tree frogs began to sing their evening chorus. Noah had made it clear the other night at the inn that their near-kiss was a mistake. And hadn't she all but agreed when talking with Delia at Chug a Mug? Two old friends connecting over shared trauma did not have to mean anything more.

Even if hearing Noah's childhood hurt made her want to wrap her arms around him and hug him until the pain went away.

"What about you?" Noah kept his fist closed around the penny, avoiding her gaze—or maybe she was avoiding his—as he edged toward the water. His navy cap was pulled low, preventing her from seeing much of his expression. "Do you go to church regularly?"

She opened her mouth, then slowly closed it. This was her turn to reciprocate. She owed him that much. But opening up about her mom . . . about culinary school and Trey . . . about her dad . . . it would all create an emotional firestorm that he didn't want to hear.

No one ever did. Except Delia.

"Of course I go to church." She rolled her shoulders down and back and found her practiced smile. "Every Sunday, sugar. Third pew from the front."

Noah eyed her, then the penny in his hand. Without any pomp or circumstance, he tossed it into the water. Then he closed the distance between them so fast, her breath hitched. "You're not getting out of it that easily."

"Out of what?" Bless it, but she sounded breathless. She tried to regulate her breathing instead of focusing on Noah's warmth, on his proximity pressing the side of her leg into the fountain wall. She could ask him to step back, to give her room, and he would.

But she didn't.

The scent of cedar and something else undeniably *Noah* wafted over her. His eyes searched hers, the beckoning twilight casting long shadows over his tanned arms. He reached up, and she thought he was going to touch her face again. Leaned into it, even, anticipating his touch.

But he didn't.

He held up another penny. "Your turn."

She snorted, half with relief and half with disappointment, as she plucked it from his fingers. He never did play by her rules. "Funny."

He didn't let go, though, only used their shared grip to tug her an inch closer. The somber expression on his face was anything but joking. "I get the feeling I haven't been the only one hurt by people not doing what they should have done."

She risked a glance into his eyes but didn't trust herself to speak.

Compassion and regret mingled in his dark brown gaze. "In fact, I think I might have been one of those people." He relinquished the penny, but didn't step away.

Elisa looked down, shook her head a little as her heart thudded loud. The coin burned hot in her hand. "We were kids, Noah. It's all in the past."

"Is it?" He raised her chin with one finger, his gaze dipping from her eyes to her lips and back again.

Her own gaze sought a safe place to land as her pulse hummed. She should step away, should definitely *not* open this door. Hadn't she opened it with Noah once before? And then again with Trey? This door should be dead-bolted and triple-locked by now.

Yet here she was, fingers on the door handle and ready to turn. She was going to kiss him, heaven help her. Wasn't there a Bible verse about fleeing temptation? Not that kissing was wrong.

But kissing Noah Hebert would be very, very wrong.

She shifted her weight, though moving too much would send her into the fountain. Maybe dousing them both with cold water was the answer.

Move. But her body wasn't listening to her brain, and she watched as if from a distance as the penny in her hand fell to the ground. Her fingers naturally curled into the sleeves of Noah's shirt and dug in tight.

He drew another inch closer, bumping his ball cap higher up his forehead with one hand as his other one found her waist. He leaned toward her, slowly, as if waiting for full permission, or perhaps in disbelief she was giving it.

Last chance. She swallowed. This was happening.

Unless . . .

Her gaze registered on his navy cap. On the gold stitched logo of legal scales and a pelican that created a triangle for three words to sit inside.

She took Noah's face in both hands, his permanent five-o'clock shadow rough under her palms. "Don't move."

"Um, okay . . ." His voice trailed off as she angled his head down for a better view of the tiny print above the bill. She squinted.

Union. Justice. Confidence.

"Your hat! That's it." Elisa stepped back, and Noah's hand slipped from her waist, leaving an immediate chill in its stead. But that was okay. She was safe again—and had their next move figured out.

Temptation avoided.

Noah's brow furrowed, and the heated look in his eye suggested he was still about three steps behind her. "What are you talking about?"

"Our next clue." She pointed to his hat.

He tugged his cap off and stared at the front. Then understanding registered in his expression. "UJC."

Elisa recited the end of the clue. "'Search the books if you want to find the truth to end a fray.'" She grinned, triumph crowding out any remaining disappointment over the missed moment. Well, almost. "We went to the wrong kind of books."

"We need legal books." Noah nodded. "The courthouse." Then he checked his watch with a frown. "They're already closed."

Drat. "And tomorrow's Saturday." Elisa groaned. "I hate to lose momentum when we're this close."

"I agree." Noah shot her a hooded look, and heat flushed Elisa's throat.

She coughed and he blessedly looked away as he dug in his pocket for his phone.

He wiggled his cell. "I have an idea."

Elisa bent down and picked up the penny she'd dropped as he made a call and put his phone on speaker. Soft ringtones mixed with the gurgling sounds of the fountain, and Elisa pretended to examine the raised head on the coin as she hid behind her short curtain of hair. That had been close—again. Too close.

Was she destined to be burned?

"Hey, man. Sup?" Cade's voice suddenly echoed from the speaker.

"I need a favor."

Cade laughed over the sound of the road noise coming from his end of the connection. "Doesn't everyone these days."

Noah shot Elisa a look. "Elisa's here with me."

Cade's laugh broke off mid-chuckle. "Wow. I mean, hey, Elisa."

"Hi." Flustered, Elisa waved toward the phone, then awkwardly lowered her hand at Noah's smirk. She stuck her tongue out at him.

He turned back to the phone. "Listen, we need to get into the courthouse."

A blinker clicked. "It's after hours."

"I know." Noah rolled in his lip.

"So?" Cade asked.

"*So* we were hoping you could help us out." Noah switched his grip on his cell, wiping his other hand down the leg of his jeans.

Elisa squinted at him. Was he nervous Cade wouldn't help? Or was he reacting to their second near-kiss?

Her own palms could use a good swipe, but she wasn't about to let him see that.

The road noise grew louder. Cade must be on the interstate. "You guys can't wait until Monday?"

Elisa shook her head as Noah confirmed the sentiment. "It's sort of an emergency. You know that treasure hunt I told you about? We've got to get the next clue—ASAP."

Cade exhaled. "Man, I don't know."

"We were thinking since your dad's the mayor and all . . ." Noah met Elisa's gaze and winced, as if holding his breath. Brilliant move. It was Cade's favorite line. But would it work?

They stared at the phone together. Silence ticked off several beats.

Then . . .

"Meet me there in twenty."

Noah fist pumped the air. "See you soon, brother." He slid his cell back into his pocket.

"Ready, Sherlock?"

"Ready, Watson." Then she hesitated as Noah turned to head to the parking lot. "Hey, about—you know. Earlier."

He turned back around to face her, walking backwards a few paces. "I know." His expression was gentle, but the openness on his face that had been present during their conversation had fled. She'd locked him up with her hat interruption—which he was surely interpreting as rejection—and understandably so.

But the truth remained. "I can't keep—we can't . . ." Her words weren't working, and her voice pitched. *Be a good girl and calm down.* She flexed her fingers and took a deep breath, bringing her tone under control. "I can't keep inching so close to a fire and then wondering why my shoe is melting, you know?"

Noah snorted, a bit of light returning to his eyes despite a hint of disappointment. He took a step toward her, hands lifted in surrender. "I promise to protect your Nikes." He glanced down at her feet and raised his eyebrows. "Pumas?"

She kicked out one foot. "Adidas, actually."

"They're safe with me."

Elisa followed Noah to the parking lot, eyes lingering on his shirt stretched taut against his broad shoulders. She believed him—about her shoes, anyway.

Not so much her heart.

Sixteen

NOAH WIGGLED THE MOUSE AT THE computer hub he'd sequestered, blinking against the bright light that suddenly flooded the dark room of the clerk of court's office. "I'm in."

Meanwhile, Cade paced the carpeted hall outside the cubicle, passing back and forth in front of Noah's work station. Even this late in the evening, Cade was still wearing his fancy loafers. "I'm going to get fired."

Elisa hovered halfway between them, as if torn over who to help first. She pointed at Cade as he wore a track in the carpet. "You most certainly are not. We won't let that happen, sugar."

Noah clenched the mouse tighter. The use of Elisa's common nickname shouldn't have bothered him—she talked to everyone that way. But that didn't stop the fleeting urge to drive his fist directly into Cade's face.

He shot his friend—he needed to remember Cade was his friend—a smirk on his next pass by the door. "And if you did get fired, it's not like you can't talk your way out of anything."

"That's right." Elisa's face suddenly lit in the dim room. She tugged at Cade's arm, halting his pacing progress. "Remember that time in Mrs. Green's class?"

Cade smiled down at her, his matching dimples breaking free. Noah frowned. Women always loved those on guys.

"I almost forgot. First grade, totally busted for breaking into Mrs. Green's candy cabinet . . ." Cade chuckled.

"And what did you say?" Elisa returned his laugh, still holding onto Cade's arm.

He winked. "That I was doing inventory."

Elisa turned her smiling eyes on Noah. "She was so impressed Cade understood the concept of inventory and used it correctly in a sentence, she didn't get him in trouble."

"Cute." The mouse beneath Noah's hand made a popping sound, and he quickly released his grip. "Our Cade, the scholar."

Cade shot him a quizzical glance, but Noah ignored him as he typed in his company access code. "I've got it." He quickly pulled up the search engine for Magnolia parish records, denying himself the indulgence of looking up as Elisa settled into a rolling chair next to him. At least she'd finally let go of Cade's arm. Knowing him, he'd probably been flexing, too.

The familiar hum of the computers sounded much louder in the still of the evening without the typical bustle of a courthouse to silence them. No murmurs at the water cooler, no rustling pages from parish workers or slamming doors and elevator dings. Only weighted silence . . . save for the whooshing of Cade's footsteps on the carpet and the steady *tap-tapping* of Elisa's fingers drumming an anxious rhythm by the keyboard.

He moved his hand to cover hers. Her erratic movement stopped, but her shoulders tensed. "Sorry."

"Did you sneak an energy drink on the way here?" Not that he felt entirely calm, himself. And he hated to admit it, but it had little to do with their delinquent escapade and much more to do with Elisa.

"I think I'm absorbing Cade's energy." Elisa gestured to where Cade had taken his pacing to the stretch of hall between their research station and the front lobby door. His gelled hair stuck up in the back as if he'd forgotten about his designer products and stabbed his hand through it.

Noah smirked. "He'll be okay. He secretly likes misusing his authority."

"I heard that," Cade called. "And for the record, accessing a candy cabinet without permission is a different penalty tier than breaking into a government building after hours."

Noah tilted his head toward Elisa to whisper, "He probably had to Google that."

Elisa snorted before clamping a hand over her mouth.

Man, he liked making her laugh. Which was trouble. All of this—the way the computer screen cast a soft glow over Elisa's features, the way her eyes sparkled as she leaned in close to hear his whisper—was so much trouble.

Elisa nodded to the computer, seemingly oblivious to his churning thoughts. "So these are the online records, right? Don't we need the actual property books for the next clue?"

"If Grandpa hid the clue in one of the physical books, like we're thinking, then yes. But we have to figure out which book to check first—unless you want to start turning random pages." Noah jerked his head toward the bookshelves on the other side of their cubicle, laden with dusty tomes and spreading the entire width and depth of the room.

Elisa shuddered. "No thanks. If we take that long, Cade might end up in the ER with a stroke."

"Heard that, too." Cade paused in the doorway, a dark silhouette in the shadows. "Can we wrap this up? That'd be great."

"You can't rush genius, sugar." Elisa flashed a grin and Cade smiled back before resuming his pacing.

Noah was going to owe the clerk of court a new mouse. "Where were we?"

He knew where he still was, personally. Back at the library courtyard, leaning in for a kiss a decade in the making before Elisa had to go and figure out the next clue so fast. Couldn't her brilliance have waited about five more seconds? Not that five seconds would have been enough. It hadn't been when he was eighteen, and he was fairly certain nothing had changed in the last twelve years.

But maybe sneaking in even five seconds of a kiss would have stopped her subsequent declaration of not needing one at all.

"We decided we weren't turning random pages." She tossed back her hair, and her honey vanilla scent provided relief from the competing odor of musty books, old carpet, and the faint remains of air freshener. "So, where *do* we start?"

"I'm thinking with instrument numbers, which is the number assigned to an individual record."

"What kind of record?" Elisa asked.

"Well, here, there will be records for civil suits, property deeds, mineral deeds, gas contracts, and so on. But everything is also cross-filed via book and page." Noah opened the search bar and pulled up a conveyance record, attempting to remember how his job worked and not the way Elisa's warmth penetrated his right side. "See how they're formatted? Newer instrument numbers are usually seven digits, but older documents will have much shorter instrument numbers."

She leaned closer to the monitor. "Goodness gracious."

"Yeah. It's a lot. And on top of that, book and pages could be any combination of length of numbers depending on what year it was filed. So an older document will have a smaller—or shorter—book number because they go in numerical order."

She gestured behind them. "So somewhere out there is a Book 1?"

"Somewhere. And as the books get more current, the book

numbers obviously get higher. This parish currently has books into the two hundreds. But the page number could be a single digit, double digit, or triple digit."

"This could take forever." Elisa's eyes opened wide.

"Please don't let it," Cade called from the hallway.

"Bro, you think there's a vending machine in the building?" Noah stood and pulled his wallet from his jeans. "Here."

Cade reappeared in the doorway, eyebrows perked in interest.

"Load up." He passed Cade a ten dollar bill—probably the last guy on the island who needed it, but Noah would pay a lot more for a few uninterrupted moments. They had to focus, and it was hard enough to do that as it was.

Cade folded the cash, his gaze landing on Elisa. "Want anything?"

"I'm all set. Thanks, though." She smiled sweetly.

Noah sat back in his chair, landing a little harder than necessary. "Get her some M&Ms."

Elisa grimaced. "I just can't eat the blue—"

"I know. They're not part of the original color pack." Noah let his eyes meet hers briefly. "I remember."

He felt her gaze hover on his profile, but he forced himself to stay focused on the computer as Cade's footsteps fell away and the lobby door eased open and shut. Finally, they could work.

"How do you remember that?" Elisa's hushed voice was barely audible despite sitting two feet away from him. "I think I ate M&Ms with you, what? Twice that summer?"

Three times. He swallowed. "I remember a lot of things." Could replay that entire month of July like a home movie in his mind if he flipped the right switch.

She nodded slowly. "So you're like an elephant."

"Something like that." More like a fool. He cleared his throat. He'd made her a promise about her proverbial shoes, and if he was going to keep that promise, they had to stay on task—even though

Elisa's eyes were asking him a dozen questions he wished he could answer. "First, we need to think of some numerical combinations that might have meaning and correspond with the clue and these instrument numbers, or book and pages."

Ideally, they needed to figure it out before Cade came back—and before the keyboard melted under Noah's suddenly heated palms.

"Hmm." Elisa drummed her fingers again as she focused on the monitor. "Longfellow wrote Paul Revere's Ride. So what was Longfellow's birthday?"

"November 1905."

Her head swiveled to face him, her mouth a perfect O. "You have that memorized?"

Noah tried to keep his expression steady, but failed and chuckled.

"You liar." She slapped lightly at his arm, and he couldn't help but flex under her touch. Okay, maybe he should let Cade off the hook.

"I'll Google it." He pulled up an internet window, but she was faster with her cell.

"February 27, 1807." She pursed her lips at him. "You weren't even close."

"So for the instrument number, that'd translate to 2271807." He pecked the number into the search field and hit enter. "That's a mineral deed for a Mr. Keats."

Elisa lifted one shoulder in a shrug, her expression crestfallen. "That name doesn't sound familiar."

"Agreed. But . . ." Noah held up his finger. "Grandfather could have tucked the next clue into that book. The actual document details might not matter. I think we're only looking for the holding place."

"That's true." She brightened again. "I'll go look."

"Let's think of a few more potential hits and then I'll show you how to find the right book. Every courthouse has its own filing system on the shelves."

"Sounds good." She leaned close again, her arm brushing his. "What else?"

"Paul Revere's birthday?" Noah pulled up the date and typed it in. "That'd be 12211734." He frowned. "No, that's too long to be an instrument. Or a book and page."

"Maybe we're going about this wrong with the birthdays." Elisa leaned back in her seat. "The clue read 'the truth to end a fray.' What day did the war end?"

There she went again with the brilliance. Noah quickly ran the search. "April 19, 1775."

Elisa hesitated briefly. "So, 4191775."

Bingo. "That's two good leads."

Hope pitched in her voice. "You think?"

"Absolutely." He turned to look at her. Mistake. She was much too close. The barely suppressed excitement in her eyes reminded him of standing in line at the Magnolia Bay Festival for a roller coaster ride. Of foot-long corndogs that left a streak of mustard across her dimpled cheek. Of counting to three and jumping off the dock hand-in-hand.

Noah abruptly pushed back his chair. "Let's give it a try." And give him a bit of space in the process.

He and Elisa might be in a room surrounded by old documents, but the only history he could think of was theirs.

Elisa shut the conveyance book, then sneezed into her elbow. Noah had explained to her how the courthouse kept the conveyance records organized on the shelves, but for the life of her, she couldn't remember anything except for the way his eyes sparkled when he got to teach her something. He'd been pretty business-like since the park, so seeing him in his element brought a hope that maybe her shooting down that near-kiss hadn't done any lasting damage.

And if she didn't know better, she'd have thought he was acting jealous of Cade—a concept that had both her mind and heart buzzing.

She shut off her phone flashlight that she'd been using to skim through the pages, since Cade had insisted they not turn on any overhead lights, and lifted the heavy book into her arms. Dust coated her fingers.

"Find anything?" Noah looked up as he slid another book onto the shelf a few rows over. His phone, balanced on the shelf beside him, cast a halo in the dim room.

"There's nothing for the date the war ended." She attempted to hoist the heavy tome back on the shelf above her head where it came from. "Any luck with yours?"

"Nope. I flipped through several pages before and after my number, too, just in case."

"Same." Elisa fumbled to reach the book's proper shelf slot. "I guess it's back to the drawing board."

The book slipped from her fingers. Elisa shrieked as she ducked and threw her other arm up to protect her head. But Noah was there, catching the bound volume and easily sliding it into place. "Careful."

"Th-thank you." She slowly straightened, her gaze lifting from his shirt stretched tight across his chest to the permanent stubble etching his chin. Her gaze rose another inch to his lips, the ones she'd almost kissed twice now in the last week.

She suddenly couldn't remember why she hadn't.

His right arm remained lifted to the shelf above their heads, and that, combined with the surrounding shelves, provided a barricade that somehow felt much more comforting than suffocating. In fact, the whole vibe made her think of soft hoodies and cut-off shorts by a bonfire. Snuggling on driftwood and roasting marshmallows. Her pulse thudded.

The summer of Noah.

His voice dipped low. "I guess the courthouse is dangerous this time of night."

"Very."

He was right. But the entire bookshelf could collapse on her right this second and it wouldn't be nearly as dangerous as what Noah was doing to her heart rate. She dared to look into his eyes, which were hooded with caution. Most unfortunate.

She reached out, trailing her finger down his forearm still lifted above them. Goosebumps immediately pebbled his skin.

"Elisa . . ." A warning echoed in his voice as his entire body stiffened.

"Yes?" She inched closer and tilted her face toward him, the near-kisses from the past cheering her on. It'd be a shame to waste such chemistry, right? Unforgivable, really.

All the reasons she'd turned Noah down a few hours ago hovered just out of reach, and she mentally batted them away like the pesky gnats they were. No longer important. She offered a soft smile. "I'm right here."

"I'm very aware of that." His tone, coated in gravel, sent a shiver of motivation up her spine.

She edged closer. "So what are you going to do about it?"

"Your shoes." His voice cracked.

"I can get new ones." Then she closed her eyes and launched into his arms.

Her lips found his by pure muscle memory. Time stopped. His right arm came down from the shelf to wrap around her, his other hand landing firm on her waist and gripping tight. His lips worked with hers in a choreographed dance they hadn't practiced in years, but had never forgotten. Joy and shock jolted through her like lightning bolts—no, like lightning bugs—beautiful and hard to explain.

Elisa's fingers clenched his biceps, which tightened under her grip. Then her hands, as if with a mind of their own, crawled up his shoulders and latched around his neck. She nudged his hat out of the way with her fingers, and he let go of her with one hand long enough to knock it off to the floor, out of the way.

She couldn't get close enough. Someone was groaning. Was it her? No, him.

Maybe both of them.

With a quick side step, Noah turned them, pressing her into the shelf of books, the hard volumes providing a convenient back support as her hands found their way into his hair. He growled deep in his throat, briefly coming up for air before reclaiming her lips.

But they'd always been his, hadn't they?

Her breath stuttered, mingling with his as Noah's lips teased their way across her jaw to her ear. Color exploded behind her eyes. The scent of cedar and something earthy, like the beach after a hard rain, worked their way through her senses and lit her stomach. If that Noah-scent could be bottled, she'd go broke on cologne purchases.

He returned to her lips before she had a chance to miss him, deepening the kiss and pulling her hard against his chest. Confidence radiated from every movement, but the slight tremble in his arms testified to the contrary. A fact that sent her reeling.

She'd never felt this way with Trey. Or with the few other men she'd kissed. Even kissing Noah back in the day couldn't compare with this version of him.

How had she lived the past twelve years without it?

Then a thought occurred, and she mentally flicked it away. But it came back, sticky and persistent. She pulled away, gasping for a full breath as Noah pressed another kiss against her cheek. "Noah?"

"Hmm?" His lips trailed to her ear and she shuddered.

Maybe a few more minutes . . . no. "Noah." She gripped his shoulders and pushed slightly, giving them enough space to breathe even though his arms remained around her. She hated the thought of him leaving. But . . . "Cade still hasn't come back with our snacks. He could walk in any minute." And see her mussed hair and swollen lips. Was that lip gloss on Noah's shirt?

Noah's eyes met her, glazed and unfocused, until her words sank in. Understanding registered. "Right. I better go check—"

The thought of his absence, even for a moment, was enough to undo her. "Maybe one more." She pulled Noah back in, and he immediately acquiesced.

A sudden beam of light cut through the room and landed directly on them. "There they are."

Noah stepped back, bumping into the shelf as he jerked one hand up in front of his eyes. Elisa blinked rapidly, shielding her eyes as the beam swept the room and then darted back to them.

"Found 'em." A brusque voice was interrupted by the squawk of a walkie-talkie. "Roger that. We're clear."

Another flashlight clicked on, illuminating Cade standing in the doorway of the room, surrounded by Sheriff Rubart and two policemen. Cade shrugged sheepishly, then held up a pack of M&Ms and a bag of Cheetos. "Hungry?"

Elisa glanced up as Noah's face blanched white. A rock settled in the pit of her stomach, and she pressed her fingers to her lips as she surveyed the officers and their hard stares. "Looks like that 'need-to-know list' just got a bit longer."

Seventeen

H E'D HEARD A COUNTRY SONG ONCE about falling in love in the back of a cop car, but Noah's real-life take on the matter sure was looking different.

"Dude." Cade gestured out the window of the police cruiser as the blue and red lights flashed, sending colored shadows across the deserted parking lot. The package of chips in his lap rustled with the sudden movement. "Don't worry. As soon as they get my dad on the phone, this will all go away."

Noah wrung his ball cap in his hands. "Or not. Pretty sure Sheriff Rubart hates me."

"Why? The whole feud thing?" Cade frowned. "He wouldn't put you in jail because of your ancestors."

"No, but he might if he figures out I was one of the middle-schoolers who filled his car with Jell-O that one spring." Noah winced.

"I almost forgot about that. He smelled like watermelon everywhere he went for weeks." Cade snorted. "Remind me, why haven't I ever used that against you?"

Noah shot him a look. "Because I was a kid watching my parents' marriage crumble. Maybe that was why?"

Cade sobered. "Right. Probably so."

"Why did these guys even show up, anyway? You were supposed to be finding a vending machine." Noah craned his neck to catch a glimpse of Elisa, who was perched in the back of the second car several yards away. Did her car smell vaguely of sweat and criminal activity like theirs did?

She wiggled her fingers in a wave, and he waved back. She seemed okay. Thankfully, Sheriff Rubart hadn't cuffed anyone. The older man now paced the lot between the two cars, cell phone glued to his ear as he periodically glared at Noah and Cade.

Hopefully Mayor Landry talked fast.

"I apparently set off some kind of silent alarm." Cade shrugged, crossing one ankle over the other. "But hey, after what we walked in on, I'm surprised they didn't turn a water hose on you two."

Heat surged up Noah's neck. "Whatever." Not an exaggeration, though. The second Elisa had touched him, he knew he was toast. Then when she practically leapt into his arms, well... He'd spent twelve years trying to forget how good she felt in his embrace, and clearly, he'd not forgotten a single thing. His body and heart had responded as if they were both eighteen again, and not a moment of time had passed since their last kiss. Maybe with the exception that this time, his heart thrummed a fearful warning to appreciate it a little more.

And boy, had he.

"You told me *near-kiss* the other day." The continual flashing of the red and blue strobes lit Cade's face, highlighting his arched brow. "New evidence indicates that was a lie."

"It wasn't at the time." They'd finally gotten it right. His lips still tingled, and he swore her vanilla honey scent lingered in his nose. His stomach churned... be it from lingering adrenaline or anxiety over what was next, Noah couldn't quite tell. It felt like another of Grandpa's favorite lines from *The Count of Monte Cristo*, one Noah had memorized during their frequent fishing adventures.

"Come now," he said. "Have you anything to fear? It seems to me, on the contrary, that everything is working out as you would wish."

"That is precisely what terrifies me," said Dantès.

Kissing Elisa after all these years had been exactly that—a terrifying wish granted.

"Would have been a lie tonight. That was something." Cade popped a chip in his mouth. "I wasn't flirting with her earlier, by the way. I could tell you thought I was."

Noah shot him a sidelong look. "Because you were."

"Okay, maybe a little. But we're old friends, it didn't mean anything. I didn't realize you two were . . . you know. *Hose-worthy*."

"We aren't." Noah frowned. "Weren't." He didn't know what they were now, since they were abruptly escorted to police cruisers before being able to figure it out. And now the whole town would be dissecting their relationship status—whatever that might be—before Miley could even fire up the espresso machine in the morning.

He leaned his head back and groaned. Elisa had been right. The need-to-know list for the hunt had just gotten significantly longer—with a second page attached that would be the juiciest gossip the town had devoured in years.

Maybe since his own father's scandal.

"Sorry about the flirting." Cade held up his bag. "Chip?"

Noah reluctantly accepted a Cheeto as Sheriff Rubart made his third or fourth pass by their car. "How do you think it's going out there?"

"I've been trying to read his lips." Cade squinted out the window. "He either said *rich pretty-boy* or *pretty rich boy*."

"Would it make a difference?"

"Valid point." Cade shoved a Cheeto in his mouth.

Noah narrowed his eyes at his friend. "Why are you so chill about this? Earlier you were worried about getting fired if we got busted."

"I always pre-panic about things. But when I'm actually *in* the horrible situation that I feared, I get all 'Ecclesiastes' about it. You know—all is vanity? Owen would know the exact verse." Cade lifted one shoulder before crunching another chip. "I do tend to stress eat, though. Where did those M&Ms end up?"

"I snuck them to Elisa before they hauled her away."

"Aww." Cade batted his eyes at Noah. "How sweet."

"Shut up, and keep reading lips." Noah shifted his position on the ripped upholstery, trying not to think about who or what had sat there before them.

"He might be calming down. It's hard to tell." Cade leaned closer until his nose practically grazed the window. "The man has one expression, and it's annoyed."

Movement from Elisa's car caught Noah's eye. He peered around Cade to see Elisa tapping on her own window and gesturing wildly. "I think Elisa is trying to tell us something."

She lit up when she realized she had their attention, and flapped her hand, dramatically pointing to her mouth.

"I think she wants us to read her lips." Noah would much rather be back to kissing them, but this wasn't the time—country song or not.

Cade nodded. "That, or she's out of M&Ms."

Noah shot Elisa a thumbs up sign. She mouthed several words, over enunciating to the point it made it harder to decipher. He shook his head and held up his arms in an exaggerated shrug.

Cade rotated his hand in a circle, urging her to try again.

Elisa shifted a little, leaning closer to the window, and mouthed again, a little slower.

"Origami." Cade held up his fisted Cheetos bag in victory. "She definitely just said origami."

Noah tried to watch her say it again, but Cade's head was in the way.

Cade's hand stilled mid-air. "Or wait. Maybe she said Aurora Pinot." He tilted his head. "Is that a wine?"

"Oh for heaven's sake." Noah shoved Cade backward with one arm, clotheslining him against the seat, and moved closer to the window. "One more time." He pointed at Elisa with his free hand.

Elisa mouthed the words and Noah watched carefully. *Origin.* And something else . . .

The origin of.

He leaned back against the seat, releasing Cade. "She figured out something about the clue." Of course she had.

"Too bad it wasn't about ten minutes ago." Cade glanced at his watch.

Thump. Thump-thump-thump. Noah peered around Cade again in time to see Elisa frantically banging on her window. "Uh-oh. What is she doing now?"

"She's getting the cop's attention." Cade's voice turned equal parts impressed and shocked. "Dude. You think she's going to ask to go back in to find it?"

Surely not. But then again . . . this was Elisa.

The dark-haired, lanky deputy, who barely looked old enough to be on the force, motioned at her to stop. But she only pounded harder.

Cade grimaced. "I say we draw straws now on who gets to tell Isaac Bergeron his daughter needs to be bailed out of jail."

"Not it." Noah watched as the officer wrenched open Elisa's car door, his young face a mask of irritation. A pile of blue M&Ms fell to the concrete at his feet as she leaned out of the car, talking ninety-to-nothing and gesturing toward the courthouse.

"This can't be good."

But Noah had seen her in action enough this week to know otherwise. "Wait for it."

The officer's face softened as she talked, and he didn't move away as Elisa touched his elbow. She then ended her spiel with wide eyes and a big smile, the same look she'd given Captain Sanders earlier in the week—and Cade earlier tonight, for that matter. The look that always made Noah want to buy her a pony and a private island and anything else she wanted.

Apparently it worked on the policeman, too, because he stepped back to let her out of the car.

"No way." Cade shook his head. "That's next level."

Elisa practically skipped back toward the courthouse. The uniformed man jogged to keep up, while Sheriff Rubart barked something after them that they both ignored.

Oh, man. Noah sagged against the seat as they disappeared inside the courthouse. "Definitely not it."

Cade's voice pitched. "What is she thinking?"

"I'm learning Puzzler Elisa is a different beast." Noah dragged a hand down his face. "Once that light bulb goes on . . ." He flicked his hand in the air to imitate a bomb exploding. "Nothing can stop her." Good thing Sheriff didn't have any K-9s out there.

Suddenly, the door on Noah's side jerked open. He startled and Cade jumped even higher, scattering Cheeto crumbs across the floorboard.

Sheriff Rubart gestured sharply with one hand. "Out."

Noah quickly obliged, drawing a deep breath free of the car's disconcerting odor. He tugged his hat back on his head.

"How's Dad?" Cade smiled sheepishly as he slid across the seat after Noah—a grin the sheriff didn't return.

"You're not in any position to give lip." The older man's gray brow furrowed into one thick line as he stepped back from the car. "I know your type, and I'm not impressed. Besides, I have a meat loaf at home you're keeping me from. Bottom line, your story checks out and your father vouched for you."

Noah could almost hear his silent *unfortunately.*

"I can't imagine why. And you." Sheriff focused his laser beam stare on Noah.

Noah straightened his shoulders. "Sir?"

"The courthouse is not, and never will be, Make Out Point."

"We have one of those?" Cade whispered.

"*Bro*," Noah hissed back.

The sheriff kept his eyes on Noah, ignoring Cade. "I suggest you find somewhere else to do your necking in the future. Preferably not in public."

Noah bristled. "I would never—"

"I know your type, too." Sheriff's brows drew even closer together. "Hebert men."

A rock lodged in Noah's stomach. He nodded stiffly. "Yes, sir."

Sheriff adjusted his belt around his girth. "You never know what mess you all are gonna leave behind, but you always guarantee one thing—you're gonna leave something."

Noah lowered his gaze to the sheriff's shoes, working his jaw in an effort to maintain control. But how could he argue? His last name was a brand he might as well tattoo on his bicep. His great-great-grandfather was the source of a never-ending land dispute his own grandfather had encouraged. Noah's own father had a scandalous affair and left town with zero remorse. Great Uncle William, Grandpa's brother, had been a known womanizer before finally moving away from Magnolia Bay decades ago. And Noah's however-many-times-removed cousin Jacob sat in a prison cell in east Texas for another ten years with a string of multi-state offenses on his record. All things the sheriff knew—things most of the town knew.

Noah was starting to forget why he was fighting so hard to keep the Blue Pirogue open.

"You're both free to go..." Sheriff Rubart squared his uniformed shoulders, turning his gun-holstered hip slightly forward as he leveled in on Cade. "...on the condition that you never break into a government building—or any property that's not your own—again."

"Not to be contrary, sir, but I'd like to point out I did have a key." Cade shoved his hand in his pocket and produced said key.

The sheriff glowered. "Fine. Make that unauthorized access."

"That's fair." Cade grinned again as he slid his key back into his pants pocket. "Then we'll be going. That must be one good meat loaf Mrs. Rubart makes." Then he stage-whispered to Noah as he clapped him on the back, "I get grouchy when I'm hungry, too."

"We can't leave until Elisa comes back." Noah elbowed him in the side. "She rode with us."

On cue, they all three turned toward the courthouse just as the front door opened and Elisa and the policeman emerged. She triumphantly waved a rectangular card in the air.

She'd done it.

"Well, look at that." Cade shook his head. The sheriff muttered something mostly unintelligible about pesky kids.

Relief and more than a smidge of uncertainty warred for top billing. Now, Noah wouldn't have to quit the hunt. There weren't many clues left to go, thanks to Elisa. They actually had a chance at finding the prize.

But did he still want it?

The sheriff's words echoed in his thoughts, the rock in his gut morphing into a boulder. What did he have to offer long-term besides heartache and failure? But he was too far in now to bail on it. He just needed to get back to his plan to get the inn fixed up and under quality management so he could move back to Shreveport as soon as possible.

The officer trailed behind Elisa, shrugging his arms wide in response to Sheriff Rubart's wide-legged, intimidating stance. "She promised five minutes, sir," he called out, as if afraid to come much closer.

"Didn't even take that long." Cade slowly crossed his arms over his chest. "Beauty *and* brains."

Noah shot him a glare.

"Just saying, man." Cade held up both hands in surrender. "Just saying."

Elisa pointed at Noah with the card, a hopeful smile lighting her face.

The moon served as a crescent-shaped observer, lighting the inky black sky over Bayou Beignets. Elisa looked up at the wooden Bayou Beignets sign swinging under the sage-colored awning as Zoey fiddled with the key on her ring. Beside her, Noah impatiently looked over his shoulder, as if the fear of getting busted still lingered. Cade's stomach growled, interrupting the cricket's song from the bushes next to the door.

"I wouldn't do this for anyone, you know." Zoey unlocked the front door of her shop, then stepped inside and flipped on the lights. The soft glow illuminated the chairs turned up on the tables, the floor so clean it squeaked under Elisa's shoe as they filed in behind her. "But I realize you guys need a place to brainstorm the next clue."

"With snacks," Cade pointed out.

He stopped short as Zoey turned and pointed at the three of them.

"If you get powdered sugar on something, you're cleaning it up yourself."

"Of course." Elisa bounced a little on her heels as Cade headed eagerly for the display case. "I'm still so keyed up from our—"

"Near arrest?" Noah filled in as he began pulling chairs off the table tops.

"Well, that, too. I was going to say victory." Elisa waved the clue card she hadn't yet read in front of her.

"I say that's cause for celebration." Cade grinned from the pastry case, his hands plastered against the glass. "Man, these look amazing."

Zoey snapped her fingers toward him. "Down, boy. Those are plastic. The real stuff is in the back after hours."

"Didn't you eat in the police car?" Noah cast Cade a sidelong glance as he settled the fourth chair on the ground. "Because we can say that now. We were *in a police car.*"

"Chips are savory." Cade frowned. "This is a totally different craving. Besides, Elisa didn't share her M&Ms."

"You could have had the blues."

Elisa and Noah spoke simultaneously, and she shot him a grin that he returned only half as brightly. Hmm. He'd been acting strange since she found the last clue. Maybe the near arrest had bothered him more than she realized.

"I respect a man with a good sweet tooth." Zoey waltzed behind the front counter. "I've got some leftovers from earlier today that I was going to discount tomorrow, but this seems like a worthy cause."

Within minutes, all four were settled at a table with a plate of raspberry lemon beignets and a pile of napkins. Elisa wasn't hungry in the slightest, but she pulled one of the sweet treats from the plate and nibbled on the edge. Delicious, as always.

"At least this time when we went somewhere after hours, we had a key *and* the owner." Cade snorted at his own joke and sent a cloud of powdered sugar straight into his face. He leaned back, blinking rapidly as white streaked his mouth, cheeks, and shirt.

Zoey sighed as she pointed to the bathroom. "Second on the left." She gave the seat Cade vacated a quick swipe with a napkin. "So, Elisa filled me in on the whole escapade on the way over here when she called and begged me to open the store."

"I didn't beg." Elisa gestured with her beignet. "I passionately requested." She glanced at Noah, expecting a smile. But he remained silent, his face stoic as he folded a napkin between his fingers.

Something was definitely up. She frowned. Was he upset she found the clue without him? They'd teased about that before, but he'd never seemed truly jealous of her puzzle solving ability. Or was he regretting the kiss?

Her stomach twisted into an ache.

Zoey pinched off a bite of beignet between her fingers. "As soon as I heard *Sheriff Rubart* and *held in a cop car*, I was all in. So have you read the next clue yet?"

"Not yet." Elisa laid it on the table between them. "I'm not sure we can have help, though. There were rules."

"August didn't specify," Noah finally spoke. "He only said you and I had to work together." His gaze darted briefly to hers, and a rush of warmth crept up Elisa's chest. As eager as she was to solve the next step, to get that much closer to finishing this hunt and helping Delia, she was just as eager to pull Noah aside and discuss what had happened.

Or better yet, talk it out thoroughly without words.

"Great." Zoey leaned in, scooting the plate of dessert out of the way. "Let's have a look-see."

Cade returned, sans powdered sugar, and settled back at the table. "What'd I miss?"

"Nothing." Zoey turned so he could read the clue. "We were about to see what's next on their little adventure here."

A grin stretched across Cade's face as his gaze darted between Elisa and Noah. "I think I might know what's next—OW." He leaned down and rubbed his shin under the table.

Elisa shot Noah a glance, but he kept a straight face as he looked down at the card. "Someone read it out loud," Noah said.

"Wait." Zoey clamped her hand over the clue. "How did you find this one? It was at the courthouse?"

Elisa quickly updated her on the filing system, casting periodic glances at Noah to make sure she had gotten it right. A smidgen of pride crinkled the corners of his eyes, and he never corrected her explanation, so she must have been pretty close. If he was proud of her, he couldn't be jealous, right?

Ugh. She hated this early part of relationships—or whatever this unlabeled thing between her and Noah had become. The guessing. The uncertainty. The eggshells. Though with Trey, that stage hadn't ever really ended.

Noah looked at her straight-on for the first time since her exit from the courthouse a half hour ago. "Where was it? Which book?"

"The origin of . . . it was Paul Revere's ride date." Elisa shrugged. "April 18ᵗʰ, 1775."

Noah nodded. "Instrument 4181775."

"Thankfully you'd left that computer logged in, so I could search which book and page."

"Nice going." Some of the tension left his forehead, his eyes warming. Yep, that was definitely pride in his gaze.

Elisa relaxed a smidge. Maybe she'd misread his earlier silence and he was just tired. She slapped Zoey's hand out of the way and slid the card across the table to Noah. "You read it."

He picked up the clue and cleared his throat. "Here goes nothing." His gaze darted low as he skimmed it. "We're back to the Longfellow poem."

"Read it." Cade picked up his beignet, and at Zoey's glare, he leaned forward over the table and took a careful bite.

"Then he climbed the tower of the Old North Church, by the wooden stairs, with stealthy tread, to the belfry-chamber overhead."

Silence hovered over the table. Cade swallowed. "That's it?"

Zoey frowned. "Only part of a famous poem?"

"They've all been like that." Elisa twisted her lips. "Except for this past clue, that was *about* the poem, but didn't contain any actual stanzas."

Cade tapped the card. "Could it be as simple as somewhere at the church?"

"They've never been quite that obvious. But even if—which local church?" Elisa asked.

Noah set the card on the table. "Yeah, we already determined Magnolia Grace doesn't have a bell tower."

"Celebration doesn't have one either. Nor the Methodist or Catholic churches." Zoey ticked off the options on her fingers.

"Well." Cade dusted his hands over the table. "This one's impossible."

Elisa snorted. "We've thought that about all of them at first. But something always clicks."

"For Elisa, anyway." Noah gestured toward her. "Usually right when she's in the middle of something else."

There was no mistaking his meaning that time. The warmth in her chest blazed into an inferno. If they didn't talk soon, she'd never be able to focus on the clue.

"It'll come to us." She stood and wiped the table with her napkin. "I'm getting pretty tired. Noah, would you take me to my car?"

He must have gotten her hint, because he stood so quickly, his chair overturned. "Yep." He bent to straighten it, his hip bumping into their table.

Zoey's eyes narrowed as they flicked between him and Elisa.

Cade snickered. "You have no idea, do you?"

Zoey zeroed her gaze on Elisa. "You better call me tonight. I have a feeling my update earlier wasn't a full update."

Elisa opened her mouth, then closed it. Her flush expanded. "I—"

Noah's phone vibrated on the table. He frowned. "It's August."

"Why would Mr. Bowman be calling this late?" Her throat tightened. "You don't think all that with the police got us disqualified, do you?"

Cade frowned. "How would he even know?"

"He said he'd be watching." Elisa nibbled on her lip as Noah answered.

"Why don't y'all head out, then, and we'll clean up?" Zoey tossed Cade the napkins.

He accepted them and wiped the table, while Zoey carried their empty beignet plate to the kitchen. Elisa began turning the chairs back over onto the table, heart hammering as she tried to subtly eavesdrop on Noah.

"*What?*" He paced by the door, one hand plugging his other ear shut as he listened. "You've got to be kidding."

Elisa's hand froze around the upturned chair legs. "What'd he say?"

Noah shook his head, still listening. "I understand." He nodded. "Okay, you too." He hung up and sighed.

"How bad is it?" She winced.

"Depends on how confident you're feeling about this latest clue."

"What do you mean?" Zoey returned from the kitchen, and Cade stepped up to join their huddle, paper towels still in hand.

"We've been given a deadline." Noah's Adam's apple bobbed in his throat. "We have one week to finish the hunt."

"One *week*?" Elisa sputtered. "But we still have another clue to find after this one—and zero leads."

"I know." Noah took off his hat and ran one hand through his hair. "He apologized for calling so late, but today was the date specified in the will to let us know, and he almost forgot."

Leave it to Mr. Bowman to be more worried about propriety than the bomb he was dropping. Elisa drew a tight breath. "Okay, we can do this." She nodded as she tried to wrap her mind around it. "We've already come this far in less than a week, so it's doable. Right?"

"I think so." Zoey linked her arm through Elisa's. "You're brilliant, Elisa. This will be no sweat for you." She gestured in Noah's direction. "No offense."

Cade tossed the napkins on a table. "I agree—not with the offensive part." He chuckled. "More like the 'you guys totally got this' part."

"I don't think y'all understand." Noah tugged his cap back into place and crossed his arms. His gaze found Elisa's, and her heart dropped in her chest at the graveness in it. "If we don't complete the hunt, we get nothing."

"Nothing?" Elisa's mouth went dry. Delia . . . the café . . .

"One week—or August will be legally obligated to donate the treasure to a charity Grandpa has picked out."

Eighteen

THE MAGNOLIA BLOSSOM ON A SATURDAY morning was, as Grandpa used to say, "busier than a church fan in July."

Noah hesitated in the doorway of the crowded diner, giving the yellow tables and shiny countertops a quick scan. It was hard to tell a fire or flood had ever happened. If anything, the place just seemed cleaner.

He wove around the clustered tables toward the serving counter, where he assumed Elisa would be helping pour coffee or any other task that wasn't in her job description. But she was nowhere in sight. Maybe the kitchen? He wanted pancakes, but more than that, he wanted the conversation that had yet to occur between them.

After August's phone call, Noah had driven Elisa back to her car at the park, and neither had discussed the elephant between them. Granted, it was hard to focus with the new ticking time bomb looming. That had taken precedent.

But the longer they stared at the clue in the pool of light provided by the lamppost, the more Elisa rubbed her red-rimmed eyes, and the more he'd raked his fingers through his hair until it stood on end like he'd been electrocuted. They finally agreed to sleep on it and Elisa drove away, leaving Noah kicking himself for not initiating the much-needed conversation.

Now, he rerouted toward the kitchen, lifting one hand in a reluctant wave to Peggy, August's secretary, who waved back so big she almost knocked over her water glass. Farmer Branson was back at his usual spot, frowning at a folded newspaper next to his plate of bacon. Owen's father, Pastor Todd, sat at a table in the corner, hunched over his Bible and a mug of coffee, while Peter devoured a cinnamon roll at the counter, pants still stained with slate blue paint splatters. The clank of silverware and the hum of conversation washed over Noah as he continued on his path . . . until suddenly it didn't.

He reached the kitchen door and paused, glancing over one shoulder. A dozen pair of eyes stared back, some accompanied by grins half-hidden behind coffee mugs and others accompanied by furrowed brows.

Oh, boy.

Before he could escape inside the kitchen, Trish sidled up, hair tied back with a ribbon. She cast him a searching look as she cocked one hip to the side. "Is it true?"

"Is what true?" But he already knew. And judging by the pointed gazes directed his way, so did the rest of the town.

"That kiss everyone is talking about." She arched a brow. "You guys stayed in the courthouse all night?"

Noah's eyes widened. "Definitely not." Was that what people thought? He released a tense breath. With him being a Hebert—no, more than that, with him being Russell Hebert's *son*—that wasn't going to look good.

Trish prattled on. "I know you and Elisa used to be together once upon a time, or something." She lifted one shoulder in a shrug, her eyes curious. "But she also said all that was in the past . . ."

A burning sensation filled Noah's throat. "Is that right?" It wasn't like Elisa to be gossiping with co-workers. But if the kiss last night hadn't meant anything, if it was all in the past . . .

Maybe that was the cause of the awkwardness last night in the parking lot—Elisa regretted kissing him and didn't know how to say so. After all, *she'd* kissed *him*, after having been the one to go on and on about her "shoes." Of course it'd be hard to tell him she had messed up by launching herself into his arms.

And launched she had.

"There are a lot of rumors this morning." Trish shifted the coffee carafe to her other hand. "No one knows what to think."

Including him. He glanced between the kitchen and the front door, debating his options.

Trish flashed him a flirty grin. "Can I get an exclusive?"

He blinked at her. "A what?"

"An exclusive. You know, be the first to know the scoop. That is, if there's anything to tell . . ."

Noah shifted his weight against the unpleasant emotions tumbling through him—namely, disappointment. It pressed hard against his shoulders, despite the small, inner voice attempting to console with reason. It was better for Elisa to dismiss last night, wasn't it? Less complicated.

Less painful for them both when he inevitably *left a mess behind*, as he was destined to do, according to Sheriff Rubart.

He cleared his throat. "Listen—I'm not a story." And it sounded like if Elisa had her way, there wouldn't be one between them at all. "I'd appreciate it if you could try to toss some water on those rumors and not gasoline, okay?"

Trish pressed her lips together. "Fair enough." Then she paused. "To be clear—does that mean there's nothing to the rumors, or that you don't want the truth spreading?"

Oh, brother. He didn't have time for this.

Apparently the look on his face told Trish what she needed to know, because she quickly took the coffee pot to a nearby table, leaving him with a dozen questions he didn't think either of them could answer.

But there was one person who could.

He pushed his way through the swinging doors into the kitchen. "Looks like word got out before the morning paper did."

Elisa turned from the open oven, wearing a cloth mitt on each hand. "Noah." Surprise lit her face as she deposited a cookie tray onto a waiting cooling rack. Then she nudged the oven door up with one foot. "What are you doing here?"

He was no expert in body language, but she seemed stressed. Over his sudden appearance? Regardless, it didn't look like there'd be any launching today. "We need to talk—because apparently everyone else is."

"What do you mean?" She finished shutting the oven door with her hip, then reached to stir something in a steel pot.

"The diner is buzzing with gossip. Everyone is staring. Trish asked me for an exclusive story like a rogue journalist. And—" He cut himself off as the scene before him registered. "You're cooking."

Elisa let out a strangled laugh, using the back of her oven mitt to swipe a tendril of hair from her face. "If you want to call it that."

The kitchen doors opened and a young waiter rushed inside. His eyes were frenzied. "Table four?"

"Warmer." Elisa pointed to the dishes waiting under a row of lights. "Can you take this one to twelve?" She handed off another plate, and the anxious kid left as quickly as he'd appeared.

Noah crossed his arms. "What's going on?"

"Lucius is gone." Elisa kept stirring the contents of the pot, even as she craned her neck to check the time on the wall clock.

"What do you mean?"

"He's . . . missing. Didn't show up to cook today." She waved one mitt in the air.

Noah frowned. "But he was so invested in the Blossom after the fire. That doesn't make sense."

"It makes a lot more sense when you consider there's also a substantial amount of petty cash and an expensive collection of cookware missing."

Oh, man. Noah closed his eyes and let out a slow breath. "So, you're cooking."

"I'm cooking." She swallowed, her voice tight. "We're short-handed on waitstaff again today, and I can't help because I'm back here. And Delia is out because the kitchen isn't wheelchair accessible, and if she knew about *any* of this, she'd roll in here anyway and hurt herself worse." Elisa's voice cracked and she cleared her throat, then squared her shoulders. "But I'm fine. It'll be fine."

Noah fought the urge to wrap her in his arms, elephant and all. But he didn't know what *she* wanted, and after Trish's update, he definitely didn't want to assume it was physical comfort from him.

But he did know what she needed.

He headed for the industrial sink and started washing his hands. "Where are the extra aprons?"

Elisa sniffed as she stared at him. "The what?"

Noah spied them hanging on a rack by the walk-in freezer, and grabbed one before she could protest. He quickly knotted it around his waist before heading for the warmers. "Where does this go?" He nodded to the waiting omelet.

"Table seven."

That part was going to be a problem.

As if reading his mind, Elisa pointed. "The table closest to the back hallway, on the left."

"Got it." He grabbed a carafe for good measure and started for the doors, plate in hand.

"Noah?"

He turned, pressing backward into the door, and raised an eyebrow.

Her eyes shone. "Thank you."

He nodded, avoiding her gaze so he wouldn't be tempted to go for that hug again, and spun to face the café.

There might still be an elephant between him and Elisa, but he was heading straight into a diner full of piranhas.

Elisa rested one hip against the kitchen island, untying her apron with stiff fingers. Her feet hurt. Her lower back ached. But the kitchen smelled delicious, the Blossom's customers were happy, and Delia, to the best of her knowledge, had no idea Lucius was a thief. She'd have to tell her so she could file a police report and an insurance claim.

But for a moment—just one—Elisa could take a deep breath and feel like maybe she'd accomplished something this morning. She'd cooked at the Blossom for the first time since her mom had passed.

And she hadn't hated it.

It was a lot to process.

She took a bite of the cinnamon bun she'd nibbled on throughout the breakfast rush. Of course, this recent theft might clinch Delia's decision to sell the café and that was an even harder thought to process, so for now, she simply chose not to.

The door swung open and Noah breezed through, brown tub full of dirty dishes braced against one hip. She set down her dessert and brushed off her hands. Speaking of a lot to process. Not only had Noah been filling in as a waiter for the past two hours, he'd started bussing tables when he saw the need.

A rush of appreciation swelled in her chest, and she checked her watch. The breakfast rush was over, and lunch wouldn't start for another hour. They had a brief lull, and she planned to take full advantage.

She smiled. "Didn't you say something earlier about us needing to talk?"

So much was left hanging from last night, and this morning's discovery of the missing cash and cookware had sent her on an anxiety detour she'd had a hard time hiding from her employees. But now that the emergency had passed . . .

"I did." Noah set the tub of dishes in the sink, then turned on the water, drowning out any chance of conversation.

"Nuh-uh." Elisa ambled over to him as fast as her cramping calves would allow, and tugged at his sleeve. "You've done enough. Someone else can load the washer. Let's talk."

He didn't face her, only remained standing at the sink with arms braced as he stared at the running water. "It can wait."

Elisa frowned at his hardened profile. "It seemed pretty important earlier."

Wasn't it? Wasn't *she*? She fought the urge to give into the fear of rejection. She shouldn't jump to conclusions.

But good gravy, he was making it hard.

"It's not a big deal." A muscle in his jaw flexed. "You've got a lot going on today. Speaking of, you should call Delia and file a police report. Lucius needs to be stopped."

"I'll get to that." Was he stalling, or trying to be selfless? She inched closer to his braced arm and angled to face him.

He kept staring at the running water.

Definitely stalling. Her stomach clenched. "What did you want to tell me?" She'd gone from looking forward to this conversation to dreading it in a matter of seconds.

Noah finally shut off the faucet and turned to face her, one hip leaning against the sink. "It might be irrelevant now."

For a man who hated riddles, he sure was puzzling. "Why?"

He let out a sigh. "Call me crazy, but I thought that kiss last night was pretty good."

Elisa blinked. "Then I'm crazy too."

"But Trish said that *you* said that we ... that this ..." he gestured listlessly between them " ... was all in the past."

Trish? Why was he talking to her co-worker about them? Elisa struggled to keep up. "I don't understand."

"I don't either." Noah shrugged, his face drawn tight. "Because, not sure about you, but last night feels pretty recent to me."

Frustration and confusion waged a battle to take over. She struggled to keep her feelings off her face. "Noah ..."

Then it clicked. Her words to Trish and Delia in the diner's kitchen that day Noah met with her dad for the inspection report. What were the exact expressions she'd used about her and Noah? *Once upon a time ... past tense.*

Elisa groaned. "I said that to Trish when you first showed up here with my dad last week." She lifted her brow. "I was referring to our *actual* past."

His lips pressed together, his gaze narrowing then widening as understanding registered. "Oh."

"Big *oh*." Elisa tilted her head. "You're telling me that all morning, you thought I regretted what happened last night?"

He lifted one shoulder, eyes averted. "I suppose so."

"And you still helped me?" Her heart cracked a little. She reached for his arm, and this time, it relaxed under her touch.

"I suppose so." He met her gaze, eyes cautious.

She traced a design on his arm with her finger, her pulse racing. "You still hauled away soggy waffles and cold eggs?"

A grin tilted his lips. "I suppose so."

"I want to say something very not nice about Trish right now." Elisa trailed her fingers down his arm until their hands joined. His fingers threaded with hers and her stomach flipped. "But I won't." Trish must have been confused, at best, or speaking from jealousy, at worst.

"I think we've given her way too much consideration already." Noah moved their joined hands behind Elisa's back and pulled her closer. Her free hand rested on his chest, his heart beating a runaway rhythm that matched her own. "There *was* something I really wanted to tell you."

Elisa lifted her face toward his, their gazes tangling. "Yeah?"

His brown eyes deepened from morning blend to dark roast as they dropped to her lips and back up. "Yeah."

Him looking at her like that . . . oh, bless it. The stress of the morning melted away under his gaze until theft didn't exist anymore. Betrayal, worry over the hunt and the café and the future . . . it faded into black. There was just Noah, and the scent of his cinnamon gum and her cinnamon buns surrounding them, and the assuring weight of his hands on her waist as he studied her up close.

He felt like coming home. Which was sort of silly, considering how he'd left home once.

Left her . . .

No. She shook away the thought, searching his gaze, seeing no remnant of the young man who once hurt her. This time was different. *He* was different now.

Right?

Noah was going to kiss her again. Her back arched, ready. Her toes twitched, eager to propel her up and closer to his lips. Her fingers gripped his arms, steadying her as his gaze threatened to sweep her away.

But this kiss would be different, wouldn't it? Every fiber in her tingling body knew it, and despite the urge to launch forward, logic kept her grounded. The kiss at the courthouse had been an impulsive chemical reaction, an inevitable simmering over of mutual desire and shared history.

This one would be intentional. No one could blame this time on hormones or familiarity or the past. If he kissed her this time, it would be full of promise . . . a whisper of a promise they hadn't dared yet voice.

Memories of their time together lapped like the bay against the dock. Her shoulders stiffened. He had voiced it once, hadn't he? Promised her forever.

And then quit.

She hesitated in his arms. "Noah, I don't . . . we can't make another mistake."

Noah had been wrong—about a lot of things, and especially about whatever mess Trish had tried to create. But holding Elisa felt like righting every wrong he'd ever made.

Yet her comment about a mistake rang true.

Noah loosened his grip, struggling to decide who had just rejected whom even as he kept his hands on her waist. He couldn't reel her in, but couldn't let her go.

And hadn't that been the case for twelve years?

Elisa allowed a few inches of space between them as her eyes searched his. What did his gaze reflect back? Did his face match the worry sketched across hers?

"I guess we still haven't technically talked." He eased back another inch and Elisa didn't protest, gently sliding free of his arms until she rested both hands against the sink.

The moment had officially passed.

"Guess not." She grinned half-heartedly, and his eyes followed the movement, a piece of him already missing the imagined contact with her lips.

But he had no business going there again with Elisa. The sheriff had a point about Hebert men. Wasn't Noah living up to his lineage already? Now there were inappropriate rumors circulating around town, and while in this case they weren't true, people wouldn't notice that. They'd only remember how they were true about his father.

"I'll start." He drew a breath. "The kiss at the courthouse . . ." He shook his head. "Maybe I don't have the words."

"I'll agree with that." A shy, cautious smile edged across her lips.

"But the facts are . . ." He swallowed. "You're probably right. Anything else would be a mistake. I've got my hands full with the inn, and I live in Shreveport now."

Her smile sobered.

"I don't want history to repeat itself." If it did, he couldn't blame anything on being a naïve teenager.

He could only blame his legacy.

"You mean, the part where you left? Where summer ended as you walked away from me with a sunburned neck?"

"Yeah, that part." Noah released a sigh. "We were kids."

"We were in—" Elisa rolled in her lip.

"There's more to that ending scene than my sunburn." Noah crossed his arms over his chest.

"Maybe so. But it doesn't matter, if you're still moving back to Shreveport, does it?" Her eyes glistened. "When you finish fixing the inn, you're leaving. Right?"

"That's the plan." He hesitated. "I don't know that I could do anything differently."

"I understand." She offered a stiff nod. "I guess neither of us are in a good place for anything more than what it was. Just a kiss for old times' sake."

That landed like a gut punch. It was way more than that to him, but how could he express that to her without getting her hopes up for more?

He didn't deserve her, and Magnolia Bay reminded him of that at every turn.

Noah's phone buzzed in his pocket, but he didn't dare wrench his eyes from Elisa's to check it. He reached to touch her hand, then thought better of it. "Do you need to say anything else?"

"No. I didn't want to fight, anyway." She pressed her fingers against her temples and massaged, and his arms ached to wrap her back up. To fight the reality they both knew was true. "But I will say thanks again for helping out. You're quite the hero lately."

"I don't know about that." Her words, obviously meant to encourage, to put them on calmer waters, only shone a light on the dark corners of himself he wanted to keep secret. "And for the record, I don't want to fight either."

His phone buzzed again, then twice more. He reached for his pocket. "I'm sorry, I really need to check this."

"Of course." Elisa waved him off, relief pouring off her delicate features. "I'll head to the floor, see if anyone needs anything." She pushed through the swinging doors and was gone before Noah could protest.

That hadn't exactly gone as he'd hoped. But had anything between them?

With a sigh, he pulled his phone free and checked the display of missed messages. All from Owen. His hopes lifted. Finally, news about his loan request. Maybe this day could be salvaged after all. He eagerly clicked the message box.

Owen
_____

Sorry, bad news.

Or not.

Owen
_____

The bank is spread too thin. Your request was rejected.

He wasn't surprised. But this, along with the deadline August had sprung on them, put a lot more pressure on finding the last few clues.

Noah closed his eyes. What was he going to do if they couldn't pull it off in time? At this point, he couldn't cover the cost of the mold mitigation crew coming to work on the Blue Pirogue Monday. The deposit was already on his personal credit card.

Dad couldn't have been right when he warned him about the inn and Grandpa's will. Noah refused to believe Russell Hebert was right about *anything*, but especially this. He opened his eyes and read the next message.

Owen
_____

Approvals are like catching Unicorns right now.
🦄

Noah shook his head. They should wrangle Owen in with the emoji usage.

Owen
_____

I used every connection I had and could only get
you approved for a grand. 💲

He winced. A thousand bucks was something, but not enough to make a dent. Not enough to make it worth the additional hit to Noah's credit.

But none of that was Owen's fault.

Noah typed back his response.

_____
Noah

I appreciate it, Bro. Don't worry about it. I'll figure
something out.

He pocketed his phone and headed for the mostly deserted café floor. There was nothing to tell Elisa—she didn't know about the loan request, about his previous temptation to ditch the hunt, or how much pressure all of this added. Elisa had too much on her own plate to worry about.

But now they *really* needed to find clue four—even if that meant combing all of the local churches from top to bottom. Hopefully, they could still work together after the awkward conversation just now. Maybe tomorrow afternoon they could meet up and get started. Maybe once they started looking, something would magically click for Elisa like it had before.

Funny how fast she'd become his only hope.

Noah spotted her standing by a table in the corner. He headed that way, hoping to further clear the air between them, then realized about two footsteps too late it was Pastor Dubois's table. Had the pastor heard the courthouse rumors about him and Elisa, too?

A rush of shame worked its way up Noah's chest. But that was ridiculous. He hadn't done anything wrong. Maybe they wouldn't see—

"Noah!" Pastor Dubois rose from his chair, tucking his Bible under his arm. "I thought I saw you swoop past me earlier with a tray. Are you working here?"

Noah approached, intentionally keeping his head lifted. Maybe if he thought of the man as Owen's father and not as the pastor whose church he'd been avoiding . . . "No, sir. Just helping out while Delia is laid up."

Elisa's smile was genuine as she beamed up at the reverend. "Pastor here is one of the Blossom's best booth warmers. He'll stay from one rush to another every Saturday and give me a reason to keep the coffee on."

"Well, *He-brews* is my favorite book in the Bible." Pastor Dubois winked, and extended his hand to Noah. A smattering of gray sprinkled his otherwise dark goatee. He was fit, with close-cut salt and pepper hair, and laugh lines that hinted his age was a bit higher than he looked. "It's good to see you. You're friends with Owen, right?"

Noah nodded as he returned the firm shake. "Yes, sir."

"I'll grab that to-go cup for you, Pastor." Elisa darted off before Noah could figure out a facial expression that would ask her not to leave him alone.

Mr. Dubois rocked back on his heels, arms crossed over his

dry-fit polo as he surveyed Noah. "I hear things aren't going very well over at the Blue Pirogue."

"That's one way to put it." Was that too negative? Noah was rusty. How was one supposed to talk to a pastor? He quickly added, "But I'm sure it'll all work out. God's plan and all."

The pastor's assessing gaze never left Noah's face. "I've been praying for just that."

"You have?" Noah stilled. He wasn't sure why that surprised him, but it did. Had Owen asked his dad to pray when Noah requested the loan? "Thank you."

"Of course. That's what I'm here for—and to talk about anything bothering any of my parishioners." He clapped one hand on Noah's shoulder and looked him in the eye. "Anything at all."

His eyes, wise and discerning, implied something specific, but what, Noah wasn't sure. His rotten family tree? The recent rumors with Elisa? The inn's financial woes?

Noah dipped his chin. "I appreciate that." Not that he'd take him up on it. But the gesture was friendly—not at all judging.

It was a nice change.

Elisa returned, to-go cup in hand. "Here you go, Pastor."

"Great, thanks." The older man smiled as he took the coffee. "So, I'll see you two in church tomorrow?"

Noah stiffened. The pastor hadn't seemed like he was church-hunting during their conversation, though. He'd seemed authentic. Noah felt certain he could say no and the man wouldn't think less of him.

Elisa's gaze darted to Noah's, as if seeking permission before answering. He appreciated that, too. But it also added to the pressure.

Then her words spoken from the library courtyard echoed in his head. *Maybe you should try again . . .*

He decided to listen to that voice and not to the one taunting him, reminding him that he would never be worthy of Elisa. She'd all but rejected him again in the kitchen. But this wasn't about them.

This was about something bigger.

Something about *him*.

Noah swallowed. And to add to the growing list of shocking things happening that Saturday morning, he nodded slowly. "I'll be there."

Elisa and Mr. Dubois turned matching surprised expressions in his direction, ones that mirrored how Noah felt. He offered a little shrug.

"Glad to hear it!" The older man recovered quickly, saluting Noah with his coffee cup. "I think you'll be glad you did."

Noah averted his eyes from Elisa's curious assessment as they told the reverend goodbye. They had to look for the next clue anyway, right? Maybe they'd find it at Pastor Dubois's church.

And he had the sudden sense that maybe, just maybe, he'd find a little something else.

Nineteen

O F COURSE TODAY THE CHURCH WAS packed.

Elisa clutched her tumbler of coffee a little tighter as Noah leaned in close, ducking his head to whisper as they hesitated at the top of the center aisle of Magnolia Grace. His breath tickled her ear and sent a rush of shivers down her back. "I realize I haven't been to church in a while, but I'm assuming we can't crawl around under the pews to search for our next clue."

She forced a smile at the rows of eyes peering at them from behind raised bulletins, trying not to get lost in the nostalgia of Noah's cologne wafting over her. Bad enough he'd worn a light green collared shirt that did dangerous things to his eyes. "I think that would make everyone stare more than they already are." She normally sat third pew from the front, but with Noah at her side, that suddenly felt like fixing a giant target to her back. She also typically sat with her father, and that, too, felt like a horrible idea.

For a moment, she recognized what Noah might be feeling—out of place.

The gray carpet stretching toward a stage containing a pulpit, acoustic guitar, and a few stools for the worship team offered zero leads on where they should start searching. She winced. "Then again, we might get desperate enough for a pew crawl before the day is over."

"We don't know if the clue is even at a church, much less this particular one." Noah frowned, adding to the stress lines already crinkling his forehead. He pulled the Bible he held tighter against his chest. "But I guess we have to start somewhere."

"Exactly. Time is ticking." She held up her wrist, then gave it a double take as her smartwatch alerted her to a high heart rate. Looked like Noah wasn't the only nervous one.

Or maybe he was making her nervous.

After their conversation with Pastor Dubois yesterday in the diner, Elisa had gone back to the kitchen to prep for the lunch rush while Noah had headed to the Blue Pirogue. They'd exchanged a few texts, brainstorming ideas for the next clue, but had come up with no real leads.

And had never finished the interrupted conversation in the kitchen. Though she'd pretty much been done, hadn't she? Not much else to say after they both declared any further relationship a mistake. The best thing to do was move forward with the hunt, and try to guard her heart as much as possible before he moved away.

Again.

She cleared her throat. "We should find a seat." Get away from the stares, and this train of thought that wasn't beneficial to a Sunday morning.

Elisa rose on tiptoe and searched the crowded pews for Zoey or Mama D, hoping they could squeeze in with either of them. She spied Farmer Branson, who had claimed his usual spot on the far side, wearing his best overalls. And there was Sadie in her brightly patterned sundress and denim jacket, sitting on the same row with Miley from Chug a Mug, who'd sprung for ripped jeans and a black choker necklace today. They looked like two mismatched book ends for the pew.

But there was no sign of Zoey or Mama D amidst the throng of floral-print dresses, diaper bags, and giggling children playing tag around their parents. Zoey might have had nursery duty today.

"Dude! You made it." Cade appeared at Noah's side, wearing a fitted navy sports coat and a hot pink tie that would have looked silly on anyone else. On Cade, though, it only made his "straight off the pages of a men's magazine" vibe even stronger.

Noah shook his hand. "Yeah, you might not want to get too close. Lightning strikes, and all that."

"I'm good at ducking." Cade grinned and clamped one hand on Noah's shoulder. "Seriously, though, I'm glad you're here. I'd offer to sit with you two, but I don't want to get in trouble with the cops again."

Noah snorted as his eyes darted around the church. "That's fair." His tone held steady, but his smile wobbled, betraying his nerves.

"I *can* tell you the nursery has the best snacks, though." Cade leaned in like he had a secret. "Animal crackers and apple juice."

Elisa grinned. "I've always wondered where you run off to halfway through the sermon."

"Hey, it pays to know the PK. I get the insider info." Cade glanced over his shoulder toward the front row. "Speaking of Owen, I need to catch him before the service starts."

Elisa glanced up at Noah. Was it her imagination, or had Noah stiffened at the mention of Owen?

Cade pointed at them as he walked backwards a few steps. "We've got a community softball game tomorrow night. I locked down a donor for concessions, so all the snack sales go to the hurricane recovery fund. Pastor is supposed to announce it from the pulpit today . . . you guys in?"

Noah winced, shifting his Bible to his other hand. "I haven't played in years."

"Perfect." Cade switched his pointing finger to a thumbs-up. "I'll put you on the opposite team from me. Elisa?"

"If I'm in, she's in," Noah answered before Elisa could open her mouth.

"You any good?" Cade raised his eyebrows at her.

Elisa rolled in her lower lip. "Define good . . ."

"Sweet, so that's two for the *other* team. Got it." Cade winked. "See you guys after the service." He was gone before Elisa could remind him she'd fielded in high school.

"Well, you can tell he's a politician's son." Noah rubbed his hand down his face. "Sorry I roped you into that without asking."

"It'll be fun." She shot him a look. "I'm more surprised you agreed."

"It's hard to tell Cade no, especially for a good cause. Though he should have remembered that softball in particular is difficult because—never mind." Noah's gaze flicked across the room again as soft piano music began to play. "Did we decide where to sit?"

She wanted to ask what he was going to say, but those still milling around began moving to their seats. Elisa nudged Noah toward the back row on the left. "This will work."

"So what's the plan?" Noah asked as the music picked up in tempo. "After church, we nose around? See if anything jumps out at us?"

"Works for me." Elisa set her purse on the floor by her feet. "I'm sort of hoping God gives me a better idea during the service, but so far, that's all I've got." Then she spotted her father down on the third row, and she sank a little lower in the pew. Hopefully he wouldn't turn around.

Noah followed her gaze. "I could have sat by myself, you know."

"It's okay." Elisa shook her head. "I know it's not easy for you to be here in the first place."

His gaze softened. "It's not all bad."

She swallowed, looking away. Refusing to give in to the push-pull between them that never seemed to end. "Good."

The music minister motioned for everyone to stand as the first phrase of the chorus began. Elisa closed her eyes, letting the joyful voices of the congregation swell around her, calm her heart. She wasn't just here for a treasure hunt—she was here for worship.

As the closing strains of the chorus receded, the congregation resumed their seats. Elisa tried to make sure she landed far enough away from Noah to not risk brushing his arm, but also not be obvious she was creating distance.

She had to play it cool around him. He didn't need to know how she felt—that their courthouse kiss was a mistake, yes, but also the best thing that had happened in over a decade. Or that every time she saw Noah, she wanted to merge the past with the future and create a new timeline. One where they didn't screw it up.

But he was leaving. And she wouldn't be left standing alone again, watching him walk away and choose a different life without her in it.

No, best to, as usual, *be a good girl*.

On the stage, Pastor Dubois greeted the congregation with a hearty welcome and read a few announcements from the bulletin before opening his Bible.

"I prayed about what to say this morning for our Scripture reading time, and I'll be honest, I had something pretty eloquent prepared." He adjusted his tie with a sheepish grin. "But I felt the Holy Spirit nudging my pride away and giving me a new direction. Figure I better go with that."

The congregation chuckled.

"Turn with me to Romans 8, please."

Pages shuffled. Elisa opened her own worn Bible, noting Noah struggling to find the designated book next to her. She gestured toward the back, and he dipped his head in acknowledgment.

Pastor Dubois cleared his throat away from the mic, then began to read. "Romans 8:35 and following. 'For I am sure that neither death nor life, nor angels nor rulers, nor things present nor things to come, nor powers, nor height nor depth, nor anything else in all creation, will be able to separate us from the love of God in Christ Jesus our Lord.'"

For I am sure . . . Elisa ran her finger over the words on the page, smooth under her finger. The congregation fell silent, save for Noah's shifting on the pew next to her. Across the room, someone coughed.

The pastor looked up from his Bible, a peaceful smile on his face. "Can we let that soak in? God loves us." He paused. "We might not all have ideal father figures, in fact, I'm sure we don't. I know I fail my own adult children daily."

Noah shifted again, the pew squeaking under his weight. She shot him a sideways glance.

Pastor Dubois tapped his open Bible on the podium. "But God loves with a *perfect* love—one we can't lose because it's not dependent on us to earn it or keep it. And one that never quits."

A muffled *amen* sounded from the back of the room.

"Don't get me wrong, God hates our sin—but he dealt with that through Jesus." Pastor Dubois gestured toward the cross mounted in the baptistry behind him. "And if you're a believer, then your debt is paid, and you're accepted. Right now. Just like you are, flaws and all. The real you . . . not the image you present on Sunday."

Elisa's heart beat faster. Those were almost Delia's exact words from Chug a Mug. *You know the right man will love you for who you are . . . not the image you present . . .*

Maybe that's where she'd gone wrong so far—trying to please men and earn love. Her father. Noah. Trey.

Yet God beckoned with a love that came with zero conditions. Did that mean she wasn't too much? That God didn't find her dramatic and exhausting when she shared her feelings?

Somewhere along the way . . . after her mom's death . . . she'd stopped praying regularly. She'd assumed she'd become gun-shy, afraid to ask for anything else after her pleas for her mom's health hadn't been answered.

But maybe she'd stopped praying because she was afraid God wouldn't want to see her disappointment.

"I hope you're warmed by the embrace of God's love for you today." Pastor Dubois's voice quieted.

Elisa traced the bold number 8 on the page with her fingers, her heart racing. Maybe she could risk being real again. With God, anyway.

Just to start.

Noah gripped the back of the pew as the united voices of the congregation swelled around him in song. He'd made it through the reading from Philippians and the first praise chorus fine, distracted by the curious glances aimed his way and the scent of Elisa's shampoo to his right.

But now, as everyone settled in—leaving Noah no choice but to do the same—the words of the next hymn pierced the defenses he'd carried for years.

I was sinking deep in sin
Far from the peaceful shore

That was him. He knew it as surely as he knew the best bait to use for sea bass. He tightened his grip on the wood beneath his hands.

Very deeply stained within
Sinking to rise no more

Noah might be an avid swimmer, but these past few years, he'd been sinking. The weight of his family's legacy, the financial stress of the inn, his father's shame. His own bad decisions along the way.

All of it had tied tight around his ankles and dragged him down.

Sinking to rise no more.

Noah stared without seeing toward the screen, the lyrics of the hymn blurring together. He'd spent so much energy attempting to outrun his family name and attempting to correct his family's name that he hadn't accomplished either. So the toxic cycles of denial and resignation continued, churning like a whirlpool, spraying accusations from so many voices over so many years—his mom, Isaac Bergeron, Sheriff Rubart—that he couldn't even separate them anymore.

He was a Hebert.

He was sunk.

But the master of the sea

Heard my despairing cry

Noah raised his head, Elisa's clear soprano singing loud beside him.

From the waters lifted me

Now safe am I.

Emotion clogged his throat. His own words from his conversation with Elisa mixed with the rhythm of the hymn. *"I catch myself assuming God is like my dad, which I don't think is true. But then I'm not sure what to think, so I don't."*

Maybe that was his problem all along. What had they read in Philippians 2? He squinted as he fought to recall. *"Therefore God has highly exalted him and bestowed on him the name that is above every name . . ."*

That was it. He'd been trying to come to terms with his own name rather than focusing on the Name above all Names.

The hymn continued, and he mouthed the words, unable to put voice behind them. Unable to fully believe they could be true.

Love lifted me

Love lifted me

When nothing else could help

Love lifted me

Elisa glanced up at him as the chorus continued. Her delicate brows drew together into a furrow, concern filling her pretty blue eyes.

He offered a smile as she sang, his heart clutching at the words like a drowning man would cling to a life preserver.

Love lifted me
Love lifted me
When nothing else could help
Love lifted me

If God could give Noah a moment during an old hymn, of all things, He could surely give them the next note card they needed in the hunt.

The service ended faster than Noah anticipated, even as the words of the hymn looped through his mind on repeat. He felt lighter—more bobber than anchor—and actually hopeful about their search.

"You okay?" From beside him on the pew, Elisa touched Noah's arm as boisterous piano music signaled the end of the service. They stood at the same time.

"I am." He took a deep breath, cracking his neck to the side, and released a short breath. "More so than I have been in a while, I think."

"I'd love to hear about it later." She tilted her head as she hitched her purse strap on her shoulder, and a wave of nostalgia mixed with longing swept over him. He might have figured out a few things today, but he had yet to figure out the puzzle that was Elisa Bergeron.

And there wasn't a single clue for that search.

"Sure. Later." He stepped back as the congregation filed out of the church in pockets. Zoey waved at them from across the center aisle, her dark bangs clipped back on one side. Then before he knew it, she had scooped Elisa into a big hug complete with hushed whispers that he could only assume was girl talk.

He gave them space, lingering in the back row, and paused to run his fingers over the family Bible he'd taken from Grandpa's closet. For the first time in a long time, he wanted to go home and crack the cover. Learn more about the name that mattered.

Maybe learn how to let go of his own.

"Noah Hebert." The creak of a wheelchair punctuated Delia's firm voice.

He looked up. "Hey, Mama D." She'd fluffed her gray hair that morning higher than usual. Her red lips matched her nails. He sat back down at the end of the pew so he could be eye level with her. "How you feeling?"

"Are you truly sitting in front of me right now, or did I get my med dosage wrong?" A teasing smirk lit Delia's face and she reached out and clasped his hand with her own. Her grip was strong, but a hint of pain hovered in her eyes as she shifted in her wheelchair.

He squeezed back, carefully. "I'm here."

"Well, glory be!" She gestured with her free hand to the worn Bible in her lap. "Answered prayers abound."

"Am I that much of a heathen?" Noah chuckled. "Apparently Pastor Dubois has been praying for me, too."

"Not that much of a heathen." Delia squeezed back, tighter. Her gaze captured his and held. "That much loved."

Love lifted me. A knot formed in Noah's throat as the remnants of the hymn continued to play in his head. His earlier wondering of what he'd missed all those years being away from the church had been answered, right there in the frail grip of bony knuckles and the gentle resonance of a song.

"Thank you." He wanted to say more, but the words wouldn't come. They wouldn't be enough, anyway.

Mama D seemed to understand, offering a smile and a final pat of his hand before she let go.

Elisa came up behind Delia, pausing to rub the older woman's shoulders. "There you are. I didn't see you before the service."

"I figured you were avoiding me, seeing how you're keeping secrets again." Delia lifted her chin and sniffed. But the teasing sparkle in her eyes gave her away.

Elisa plopped on the pew in front of Noah, wincing. "Sheriff Rubart called you?"

"He did. Wanted to know if I wanted to file official charges."

Elisa winced. "Did you?"

"I did. Hated to, but there was no way around it. And I filed the insurance claim." Delia reached up to fiddle with her gold necklace. "Sad part is, I would have given that young man that cookware if he'd asked."

"He doesn't know you like we do." Elisa rubbed Delia's arm.

"Which is his loss." Noah cleared his throat. "Is there anything else we can help with?"

"I heard you were bussing tables yesterday." Delia pursed her lips at him, pink lipstick slightly smeared. "You've done plenty."

That was the least he could do after all Mama D had done for him, but he had a feeling if he got mushy, she might smack him.

He caught Elisa's eye and gestured toward the podium. "By the way, I had a thought during the service about the next clue."

Delia sat up straighter. "You two still doing the treasure hunt?"

"Oh, don't pretend you didn't hear about the cops coming to the courthouse Friday night." Elisa pointed at Delia. "I know the sheriff didn't leave that out when he called you."

"Well of course I knew about that. But wasn't sure if you were still working on the hunt . . . or working on something else." She eyed them both beneath her lashes.

Elisa's eyes widened. "Mama D!"

Noah snorted.

"I'm just saying." She held up both wrinkled hands in defense. "Now, be a dear and turn me toward the stage. I see someone I need to speak with."

Elisa huffed and obliged, wheeling Delia around in the right direction as Mama D muttered something about save the date cards and getting on with it already.

"I would apologize for her, but . . ." Elisa shook her head as she took a seat on the row in front of Noah.

He watched Delia wheel herself purposefully toward the front of the church. "No one is changing Mama D. And no one should."

Elisa's eyes flickered to meet his. "I guess we really gave the town something to talk about."

"We did, indeed." He took a deep breath. "Look, I'll be honest—I've been worried about my family name. This feud, the rumors. My dad . . ."

"I know it's a lot."

"What I'm trying to say is . . . it's me."

She quirked an eyebrow. "Are you really giving me the *it's not you, it's me* speech?"

"*No.* Well, sort of." He scooted back on the pew. "What I'm *saying* is that I'm grateful we reconnected. I always hated how things were left between us. But today, during the hymn . . ." His voice cracked and he cleared his throat. "I think maybe God is working on me, after all."

"That's great, Noah. Really." Elisa squeezed his hand.

The lump in his throat eased a bit. "And . . . I think I have an idea where to search for clue number four."

Her blue gaze held his. He could have easily drowned in their depths. Would she let him off the hook that easily? She deserved more explanation—assuming he could find the words to give it to her. He didn't have it all figured out himself yet, but he'd found something on the pew this morning that had nothing to do with the treasure hunt.

But he would try to give her more, if she asked.

But she only shook back her hair and offered a mildly flirtatious smile. "So where is this next clue, Watson?"

Noah pointed to the baptistry, trying to decide if he was relieved or disappointed. "The song today—love lifted me. Made me think of the wording my childhood pastor used to say when he'd do baptisms."

She tucked her hair behind her ears. "Raised to walk in newness of life?"

Noah nodded. "He'd say that, and add the scripture about lifting me from the slimy pit and onto a rock."

"Yep. I think that's in Psalm 40."

"The baptistry has stairs, and the clue mentions 'wooden stairs with stealthy tread.'" He shrugged. "It's a thought. Grandpa attended this congregation years ago when he did go, so the odds of it being this particular location *are* good—if the clue really is talking about a church."

Elisa stood, brushing the slight wrinkles from her dress. "To the baptistry, then. It's as good a place as any to start."

Noah grabbed his Bible from the bench and stood with her. "Just like that, huh?" He grinned. "You're not going to argue this time about why my theory is probably way off?"

"I didn't say it wasn't." Elisa winked. "But I'll humor you."

Friendship established. He relaxed into a smile before tapping her with his Bible. "Get moving, then, Sherlock. You're wasting daylight."

Laughing, they turned into the aisle.

Straight into Isaac Bergeron, wearing a pale blue tie and a scowl.

Twenty

AS ELISA LED THE WAY BACK THROUGH the side door and into the designated dressing area for baptisms, her father's words echoed in her head. *Would you like to go to lunch?*

Leave it to her dad to make a casual question hold about a million pounds of subtext. His not extending the invitation to Noah was pointed and rude, if not surprising.

"Sorry about my dad."

Noah followed her through the doorway, catching the door before it could slam. "He's like a pop-up book."

"No kidding." At least the unnamed project they were working on had given her a viable excuse as to why she declined—and why she was with Noah after church ended.

Elisa navigated around a small couch toward the back of the cluttered dressing room, used partly for storage. The baptistry had yielded nothing except a bit of leftover water from the depths of the drained tub. The stairs leading up either side were solid. No cracks or crevices, no accessible underside for a clue to be taped to like at the lighthouse.

They were back to square one.

Noah stopped beside a row of white baptismal robes, dangling from sturdy hangers atop a portable cart. "Your dad doesn't know about this treasure hunt yet, does he?"

"He doesn't need to." She hated how her father could throw off her emotions so easily . . . and how hard she had to work to hide that fact lately. To *be a good girl.* "Though I'm a little surprised he hasn't heard from someone else yet." Though to be fair, the entire town would draw straws before volunteering to tell Isaac Bergeron anything unpleasant about a Hebert. "Regardless, there's only two more clues to go, then all this will be done and—"

"And what?" Noah waited, one hand resting on an empty clothes hanger.

She crossed her arms over her dress. "And then you leave. You move back home."

Noah's eyes flickered. "Maybe I won't."

She scoffed. "You've changed your mind on that in the time it took to cross the sanctuary and check a staircase?"

"You have a very convincing walk." He edged closer to her, a hint of a smile on his lips.

She backed up, only to find a wall. There he was, flirting with her again. Catching her off guard before she could do it first. That wasn't supposed to happen. She was supposed to be the one in control.

She lifted her chin as her heart raced. "Noah Hebert, we can*not* make out in a church."

"Who said anything about making out?" He stopped a respectable distance away, then reached out and skimmed his knuckles down her cheek. His voice deepened. "I'm just here looking for clues."

Good gravy, but the room was warm.

How did this man manage to kiss her senseless when he was still standing an arm's length away? Elisa's hands trembled as the push-pull began, beckoning her toward Noah's patient gaze and somehow pressing her back into the wall away from him, all at the same time. *Mistake, mistake, mistake.* The word echoed like an alarm.

His face sobered. "I could do better this time, you know."

Her gaze slammed into his, and her breath hitched at the gravity in his eyes.

"I realize the future is uncertain. But we're not kids anymore, Elisa. I was young and dumb back then. Kind of a hot-head."

She raised her eyebrows at the *kind of*.

"I know it's hard to trust me." Noah took a few steps back, returning to the cart full of robes. He absently ran one hand down a thick white sleeve. "After I found out my dad had cheated on my mom with your Aunt Rhonda . . ."

Elisa flinched.

" . . . when it felt like everyone knew but me—I didn't handle it well."

To put it mildly. He'd left Elisa standing on her front porch, crying as he stalked away and never looked back. She stiffened. "You bailed."

Noah ran a hand through his hair. "I didn't know what to do. You were hysterical over the fight you and your dad had. And there had already been so many years of whispers and judging stares. I felt stupid for not knowing—for making things worse by being me." He swallowed. "By being a Hebert."

The heat that had flooded her moments ago waned, leaving a chill in its wake. Elisa hugged herself, rubbing her bare arms with her hands. "I had no idea you didn't know the connection, or I'd have tried to break it to you a little more gently."

"Sometimes I wondered how I hadn't known, too." He fiddled with an empty hanger on the cart, eyes averted. "I think my parents tried to keep the details of their issues from me at first. Then Mom moved us to Shreveport so suddenly, the rumor mill didn't have time to reach me. I was a middle-schooler, more focused on how all of this affected me—not nearly as concerned about who else was affected, you know?"

He didn't seem to be expecting an answer, but she nodded anyway.

"And when I came back every summer after that, I stayed close to the Blue Pirogue. Fishing, reading, doing chores around the inn. In hindsight, Grandpa kept me pretty busy—maybe on purpose." He met her gaze, a season of memories filling his eyes. "Until that one summer, anyway."

The warmth was back.

Noah crossed his arms over his chest, mirroring her posture. "I know the fight with your dad that day was about me."

"He was upset we were hanging out. I tried to tell him the full story, help him see you weren't who he thought you were." Elisa closed her eyes. Even now, twelve years later, she could see the fire in her dad's eyes. The betrayal radiating off his face. A glimpse of the inevitable choice she would have to make. It'd been one of the only times—the *last* time—she hadn't calmed down like a good girl.

But Noah hadn't left her with a choice, after all.

Elisa opened her eyes, hugging herself tighter. "I'd been emotional that day—really stuffing a lot down. When you came to pick me up, I . . . I don't know, I finally felt *safe* enough to let it all out with you. Be honest and vulnerable, for the first time since Mom died."

Noah's eyes softened. He reached for her, but she edged backward.

"Being real hadn't gone over so well with my dad. He didn't appreciate how I felt or what I said about you. And then it seemed like being vulnerable with you went even worse."

"I handled it poorly." Regret filled Noah's eyes. "But I knew your dad was jaded, after everything that happened with my dad and your aunt. I guess that's why I thought it better to walk away.

Take myself out of the equation." He dipped his chin. "And then there were the letters."

Elisa frowned. "What letters?"

"Someone sent threatening letters to the inn that summer, warning me away from you." Noah shook his head. "They were pretty intense."

Her mouth opened. She scrambled for words through her surprise. "Why didn't you tell me?"

"Your dad had made up his mind about me. I knew how much losing your mom affected you—I sure wasn't trying to get in the middle of you and the only parent you had left."

The information absorbed slowly, filling the cracks of her memory. So much was starting to make sense, like the last pieces of a puzzle finally coming together. "Noah . . ."

He took a ragged breath. "I had planned to talk to you when I came over that day. Tell you that we were obviously at a dead end . . . that your dad was too hung up on this old feud to ever give us a chance. Then he was sitting there cleaning his hunting rifle, and you dropped that bomb about your aunt . . ." He shook his head. "It was too much."

How well she remembered the explosion. Then her breath hitched. "You're saying my *dad* sent those letters?"

She didn't need to wait for Noah's confirming nod to realize that was exactly something her father would do. Controlling, passive-aggressive—getting the final word without causing a public scene.

Being the master puppeteer.

"Now I'm the one who feels stupid. I had no idea." She reached for Noah's hand, her thoughts churning. "I'm sorry. You didn't deserve that."

"Well, you didn't deserve for me to walk away." He turned his palm so their fingers threaded. "But as I was saying . . . I know I can do better."

Resolve, along with a surge of frustration Elisa struggled to hide, flooded her veins. She might have been eighteen and dependent on her father back then, but now—like Noah said, things could be different. She just had to trust him.

It was as simple—and as impossible—as that.

Elisa tugged at their joined fingers, pulling him a step closer. "Sign me up for that whole 'do better' thing, too."

"I've got a permanent marker right here." Noah smiled, lowering his head so his forehead rested against hers. Then he eased back. "But if your dad doesn't sign off on the inn after this mitigation, I'm going to *have* to sell the Blue Pirogue. Which means I'll most likely not be able to stay in Magnolia Bay."

Elisa reached up with her free hand and pressed her fingers into the crease forming between his eyes. It relaxed beneath her touch. "I won't let that happen."

His gaze expressed his doubt that she had that power with her dad, and honestly, she doubted it too.

But she couldn't stand to see him worried. "I guess it's only fair you know the whole truth, too."

He tilted his head. "About?"

"The treasure hunt." She tightened her grip. "I never told you—but I'm hoping to use my part of the inheritance to help Delia."

Understanding lit his eyes, followed by gentle admiration. "No wonder you've been so fired up to finish this hunt." Then he chuckled softly. "You know she'll never let you, though."

"I'm going to cross that bridge later." Elisa arched her neck. "She's not the only one who can be stubborn—even if I have to make an anonymous payment to the hospital."

She exhaled as her gaze roamed the room behind him, bouncing off the baptismal robes and the old wooden table holding a stack of towels and a slightly warped mirror. "That is, if we can finish in time."

"Right. We should probably start looking for a new lead, since my baptistry stairs idea flopped." Noah held up their entwined fingers between them, a magnetic grin splitting his face. "But what about this?"

She grinned back. "I can search one-handed if you can."

He pulled their joined hands to his lips and pressed a kiss against her knuckles. "I'll never be able to focus."

Whew, same. What treasure hunt, again?

Noah's teasing tone reminded her of sunlit waters and pastel skies. Of that summer she'd claimed his sole attention for months straight and neither had complained. She traced his stubbled jaw with one finger.

He turned his chin into her touch. "Remember, you're the one who said we can't make out in a church."

"Did I?" She squinted at him.

"I'll make you a deal." He slowly slid his fingers free, letting his hands come to rest on her waist. The imprint of his touch left a fiery hot brand, emphatically replacing her earlier chill. "A kiss now . . ." He tugged her an inch closer, his hand coming to cup her cheek. "And one after we find the clue."

She searched his gaze, seeing a dozen promises inside. This was her last chance to back out, to keep her heart safe. Swimming in Noah's eyes felt like that first time that she'd jumped off the dock into Magnolia Bay as a kid. She'd been absolutely terrified of the water sure to rush over her head.

But she also couldn't fathom not jumping.

Elisa drew a fortifying breath, then took the leap. "Deal."

And oh, what a jump.

Noah took his time kissing her, lips moving gently, intentionally, as if he had all day. As if the treasure hunt and black mold and angry fathers and time itself had stopped to give them another chance.

A chance to do better.

Last night, when he'd been tossing and turning in bed, Noah had imagined they might find the next clue in their hunt.

In his wildest dreams, he *never* imagined he'd find Elisa again.

Now, as Elisa's hands pressed into his chest, wrinkling the collar of his shirt he'd spent ten minutes ironing that morning. He didn't care. He also wasn't worried about messing up her silky hair as he cradled her head in one hand.

That kiss at the courthouse might have been hose-worthy, but this one was Noah's favorite. Slow. Savoring. Steady. Good grief, Elisa and her vanilla scent and coconut lipgloss had him thinking in alliteration.

There wasn't any urgency to this kiss, as if either of them were afraid the moment might end before it started. No, there was a security here that Noah hadn't felt in . . . well, maybe not ever. He'd been too immature to notice it during their one summer together. And no one had ever come close to bringing that assurance since Elisa.

It'd always been her.

Suddenly, the door near them opened. Noah stepped back, giving Elisa space as a gray-haired man wearing dark coveralls strolled inside, humming off-key. Elisa quickly wiped her lips with her hand.

The familiar-looking gentleman stopped his tune short when he saw them, the loaded key fob jangling from his utility belt. "Uh-oh." His eyes twinkled and he adjusted his hold on the folded towels he held. "Am I interrupting something?"

"Hey, Mr. Bolding." Elisa smoothed her hair before tucking it behind her ears, that familiar flush Noah loved being responsible for working its way up her throat. "No, sir. We were just looking for something."

Her eyes darted to Noah's and he fought his grin. They'd certainly found it. He cleared his throat as he adjusted his shirt collar.

"A lost Bible, I'm assuming? We got a whole stack of them over in the lost and found." Mr. Bolding pointed back toward the direction he'd come from. "That's in the closet in the foyer, though."

"We're actually looking for something else." Noah had a hunch as he studied the man's mildly stooped posture. He used to see Mr. Bolding tending the churchyard when Noah was a pre-teen, while he'd been out running Grandpa's errands on his bicycle. "You've worked here a long time, haven't you?"

"Only thirty years, give or take." He lifted his chin with pride as he set the towels alongside the others. "I do a little bit of it all. Cleaning, stocking, groundskeeping. Whatever and wherever I'm needed."

Elisa smiled. "No one could imagine this congregation without you."

"Well, that's mighty kind of you to say, Ms. Bergeron."

Noah relaxed. If Mr. Bolding had taken sides during the feud, he wasn't letting it show. Zero judgment clouded the older man's eyes.

"I can imagine you've seen a lot over the years." Noah shot Elisa a look. If anyone at the church would know what they needed to know . . .

Mr. Bolding's bushy eyebrows rose as he turned back to face them. "I've had to stay overnight in that cemetery out yonder, son." He let out a belly laugh. "You've got no idea what I've seen. What are you two looking for, specifically?"

At Elisa's encouraging nod, Noah continued. "This might sound weird, but is there a staircase around here?"

Mr. Bolding frowned. "There are the entry steps out front. And the stairs here, going into that big ol' tub."

Noah shook his head. "Not those. This staircase would be bigger."

"And maybe hidden." Elisa's voice trailed off and she shrugged at Noah's look.

"A secret staircase?" Mr. Bolding scratched his throat. "Sounds like something out of a crime novel."

Disappointment draped over Noah. Maybe they had the wrong church, after all. "I figured it was a long shot, but had to ask." He gestured for Elisa to head toward the door first. "We appreciate your time."

"Now hold on a minute, son. I didn't say there wasn't one. Only that it sounded like a book." Mr. Bolding chuckled. He pointed toward the cart full of robes. "This church used to have a bell tower, years ago."

Noah's heart thudded. *Then he climbed the tower of the Old North Church, By the wooden stairs, with stealthy tread, To the belfry-chamber overhead* . . . The words of the clue rushed back at him as he shot a glance at Elisa. Her eyes widened big as the dessert plates at the Magnolia Blossom.

Mr. Bolding gripped the handles and gave the cart a shove. The wheels, which probably rarely ever moved, creaked in protest as they reluctantly obeyed. The sudden lack of robes in the space revealed a door that had been painted over, though recently cracked as evidenced by the dark ribbon running along the frame.

Elisa joined Mr. Bolding at the door before Noah could even tell his feet to move. He'd been standing right there mere minutes ago, with absolutely no indication the stairs they were looking for were on the other side of the wall. His hope soared.

"It's locked." Elisa turned from the painted knob, casting Mr. Bolding's key ring a pointed glance.

"Of course it's locked." Mr. Bolding crossed his arms over his broad belly. "Some decades ago, there was an accident. A staff member got hurt tending to the bell, and then a few months later, some kids got curious about it, started playing around up there. The church didn't want the liability." He waved one hand in the air. "Don't rightly blame 'em. So, they had the bell removed, repaired the roof, and locked this all up." He tapped the door with one knuckle. "Only us old-timers know it even existed in the first place."

Noah stepped forward. "Can you let us in?"

"We won't tell," Elisa quickly added.

Noah caught her eye, shared a smile. Between the three of them in the room, they'd be keeping all kinds of secrets. The blush started back on her neck.

"I'd love to." Mr. Bolding patted the bulky ring on his belt, then shrugged. "But someone borrowed that particular key a few months back, and I don't believe they ever returned it."

Twenty-One

"I KNEW I'D SEEN THAT KEY BEFORE." NOAH slammed the truck door and slung his duffel bag brimming with baseball gear over his shoulder. The sun, low in the sky, cast a warm glow over the community ball field—and Noah's clenched jaw. "You found it?" Elisa tilted her face to the coming twilight, drawing a deep breath as she leaned one hip against her car door. The warmth of the evening did wonders to relax her tension. Before meeting Noah for the game, she'd spent the day at the Blossom, cooking for the lunch rush and giving the police her statement on Lucius. Now she wanted nothing more than to soak in a bit of Vitamin D and forget how the fate of the diner hung—

He shoved a piece of paper in her hands.

She glanced down. The words on the card swam together and she blinked as realization dawned. Her breath hitched. "The next clue? You already got it?"

"The key was in Grandpa's desk drawer. I knew I saw it that day you picked me up for the lighthouse." Noah set his bag on the gravel and pocketed his keys. "I ran back up to the church this morning and Mr. Bolding let me in the baptistry area again. Sure enough, the clue was taped on the staircase railing."

She jerked her head up.

He lifted one hand. "The only reason I didn't call you was because I knew you were at the Blossom."

Warmth spread through her chest. He thought she'd be mad at being left out. Before she could wonder if it was a good idea to do so in public, she stepped into a hug. "I'm not mad."

His arms came around her immediately, embracing her with muscle and masculine soap and all things Noah. She spoke into the space where her mouth pressed against his neck. "That was a good call. I couldn't have gotten away from the diner today, and I would have been stressing making us wait."

"Good. I'm glad you're not upset." He pulled back a little, smiling down into her face. Tired lines creased his forehead. She knew the feeling.

His voice drew husky. "I missed you today, by the way."

The admission warmed her more than the sun. "Same." Guess he wasn't worried about anyone seeing them—though they were partially hidden from the field by the cars.

Just in case, she stepped back a little and held up the paper. "I'm really proud of you, for the record. And you didn't even have to sledgehammer your way through the wall."

"I was considering that, if the key didn't show up." Then his flickering smile waned. "But did you read it yet? Because we have a new problem."

She was so excited he'd found the clue on his own, she hadn't even thought to. She looked back down at the scribbled cursive writing.

How quickly Time passes
On tiny wings of Silence
Oh how it Waits
And oh how it Hopes

Cloudy as a silver lining.

She looked up and pursed her lips. "This is even harder."

"Exactly." Noah shouldered his bag again. "This whole hunt has felt like nothing but two steps forward, one step back."

That last clue actually felt more like *three* steps back, but she didn't see any point in raining on Noah's already cloudy parade. She studied the words again. "It's obviously not from the Longfellow poem. And this one doesn't even seem to reference the poem like the others."

"I thought the same."

She read it through three more times, the words bouncing around her brain but refusing to land anywhere. "There's some odd capitalization going on—maybe that's something."

"Like an acrostic?"

"Yeah. TSWH." She tilted her head.

"Treasure Seekers Were Here?" He snorted.

"Maybe its directional? Like North, South, East West. So this could be . . . The South West . . . Hill? Haven?" She frowned. "I feel like we're getting colder."

"Maybe it stands for This Seriously Was Hard."

Elisa elbowed him. "That Seriously Was Horrible."

"Agreed." Noah snapped a picture of the clue on his cell. "Let's look at it again tonight when this is over." He nodded toward the ball field. "Ready?"

"Sure." Elisa shoved the card into her back pocket. The thrill of the hunt still lit something in her, but over the past twenty-four hours, it had felt more like a smolder than a spark. The clue deserved her full attention, yet one thing chafing the back of her mind was the fact that she'd had to cook again—which meant Delia wasn't trying to find another replacement chef. Was Mama D feeling gun-shy after Lucius's betrayal?

Or was she closer to selling than Elisa realized?

She tried to shove aside the wondering and fell into step beside

Noah as they headed across the parking lot toward the bleachers peppered with pre-game fans. A handful of kids rushed past them clutching snow cones, and the scent of hot dogs hung heavy near the already-buzzing concession stand.

"The missing key worked out, and we've come this far. We'll think of something." She forced brightness into her words that she wasn't feeling. One of them had to stay positive, though, and of the two of them, she was the most equipped at faking it.

"If anyone can figure it out, you can." Noah navigated them past the row of concrete bathrooms and the announcer's stand, where Mayor Landry was putting on a wireless mic. "I believe in you."

No pressure. She smiled even as her stomach flipped. His pronoun choice was clear. *You.* Not us. She appreciated the vote of confidence, but she felt off her game lately.

And too much was riding on this deadline for her to be less than sharp.

Elisa stepped through the field gate Noah held open for her, glancing up as he stopped and adjusted the brim of his hat. His motions were jerky as his gaze flicked over the growing crowd.

He was definitely stressing over more than the final clue.

Elisa shifted her bag to her other arm. "Maybe a fun break will help us reset. Get the mental juices flowing again." Across the field, Cade stood in the dugout with a clipboard while Linc took a few practice swings with a bat.

Noah didn't seem to be in a hurry to join them as he slid on a pair of dark sunglasses. "Maybe." A muscle in his jaw tensed as he looked over his shoulder to the dugout. Owen and his brother Sawyer had joined the players packed inside, along with Zoey, Pastor Dubois, and Trish. "Not too sure about the fun part. Like I tried telling Cade earlier—I haven't played since I was a kid."

"No one will judge you if you're rusty." Elisa nudged him with her elbow, hating the strain in his expression. "They'll be too amazed at my skills in the outfield to notice, trust me."

He didn't smile like she'd hoped.

"Hey." She frowned, catching his sleeve. "You okay?"

He lowered his glasses, looked at the filling bleachers, then positioned himself so his back was to the stands. "It's going to sound stupid."

"Not any more than me bragging about my fielding ability from fifteen years ago."

That got a tiny smile from him. "It's just . . . bad memories. I quit baseball right before—" He swallowed.

Elisa turned to face him, shading her eyes from the sun now shooting crimson and violet hues across the sky. "Before what?"

Several seconds passed. Then he slid the shades back on. "Before my dad quit on us."

Ahh.

Elisa nibbled on her lower lip. There was so much she wanted to say, but he probably didn't want a sermon—or a psychologist. Still, he needed truth. "You know . . ." She touched his arm. " . . . just because you stop doing something doesn't mean you're a quitter."

"That's not what I was told."

She couldn't read his eyes behind the glasses. "By who?"

"Teachers, my mom. Pretty much anyone who knew my dad." Noah crossed his arms over his chest, spreading his feet wide. "I refuse to be like my father."

"Your father?" Elisa reeled back. "You couldn't be more different than him."

"I'd like to think that."

"Whether you believe me or not, you don't have to play softball against your will." She raised her eyebrows at him. "Both of those things can be true, you know. You can have noble goals *and* not play a sport you don't like."

"I never said I didn't like it." Noah's phone chimed from his pocket, and he pulled it free. He glanced down at the screen, then over at the dugout. "We're being paged."

Elisa followed his gaze across the field to where Cade waved the clipboard and pointed dramatically to the dugout, then his watch. "Better keep him happy. His dad *is* the mayor, you know."

Finally, a full smile from Noah. Mission accomplished.

Elisa started to head toward the others when Noah touched her shoulder, halting her progress. "Hey."

She turned to face him, glad he'd taken the glasses off again.

"Thanks." His gaze, soft but serious, swept across her face, darting once to her lips before landing on her eyes. "I'm glad you're here."

He was going to be okay. She squeezed his hand. "Me too."

Noah slid his glasses back on. "And not only because you're allegedly a wonder in the outfield."

"Oh, sugar, just you wait." She winked at him as she pulled her glove from her bag and thickened her accent. "I've got moves you've never seen."

Noah shouldn't have worried about being rusty. But Elisa definitely should have.

So far she'd caught two of the fly balls that headed her way, dropped two others, and missed three entirely. But the crowd rallied, cheering every time she made another error. She'd finally stopped turning red and started bowing instead, causing even more uproar. They adored her.

He knew the feeling.

Noah bent over, bracing his hands on his knees as he led off from first base. They were only playing six innings, thanks to Cade's common sense prevailing. "Come on, Trish!"

Bottom of the sixth now, they were down by two, and Trish was at bat. She was the only woman there playing in a micro tennis skirt, but she sure could run.

Cade buffed the ball on the sleeve of his shirt. "You know you only get three strikes, right?"

Trish smirked back at him. "Won't need them."

Cade wound the pitch and Trish hit an easy grounder past first base.

"Yes!" Noah hauled himself to second as Linc scooped up the ball in the outfield and threw it to Sawyer—but not before Trish pounded past the bag.

She tossed her flaming hair over her shoulder as she sidled back to take position on the base, winking at Sawyer. "Maybe you'll get me next time."

Oy. The woman never stopped, but at least it seemed like she'd given up on flirting with Noah. He turned his attention back to the mound, where Cade pitched the next underhanded ball to Zoey. It hadn't gone unnoticed that Cade had stacked his own team with Linc, Pastor Dubois, and Sawyer, while Noah was given Zoey, Trish, and Miley—who surprisingly made a mean short-stop. Cade's lead would have been much higher if not for Miley's defense.

Zoey struck out, leaving him stuck on second and Trish on first with one out.

Noah clapped his hands. "It's all right, we'll get it back." Hopefully, or Cade would never let him live it down.

Anticipation pulsed in Noah's veins, and he shifted his weight, wondering how far he could lead off to third before Cade noticed. The earthy scent of the field was like a long-forgotten cologne, the adrenaline rush a legal stimulant. His heartbeat pounded in his ears, mixing with the murmurs of the crowd and the echo from cheap static-filled speakers.

He'd missed this.

Elisa stepped up next to bat, pausing to tuck her hair behind her ears. Mama D hollered something encouraging from the stands that got lost in the wind. Elisa shot him a look, and Noah nodded his confidence in her. Good grief, but she was cute in her ripped jeans and T-shirt. He kind of wanted her to hit a homerun so he'd have an excuse to publicly scoop her up on his shoulders. That parking lot hug hadn't been enough.

She wiggled one sneakered foot into the dirt for grip as the crowd began to drumroll-stomp their feet on the bleachers. Cade threw the pitch.

"Strike one!"

Noah led off another foot. Cade cast him a warning glance over his shoulder and Noah shuffled a few inches back toward second. Pastor Dubois, playing shortstop for Cade's team, shook his head and grinned.

Maybe Elisa had been right. Maybe stopping something didn't equate to quitting. Noah was here, wasn't he? He didn't have to look back on those days on the diamond with defeat. He could simply recognize how fun it was to play. Could choose to remember who *had* shown up for him all those games—Grandpa—rather than on who hadn't. In fact, if Noah closed his eyes, he could almost still hear Grandpa's husky voice rising above the others. "That's my boy!"

He'd always had a home, even during those years he'd been gone from Magnolia Bay.

Maybe it really was time to make this place home again.

Crack.

He opened his eyes in time to see Elisa's second pitch flying hard and fast toward right field. The crowd screamed. "Run!"

Noah let out a whoop and took off to third, sensing more than hearing Trish flying behind him. He slid into third, his knee scrubbing hard on the dirt as the ball whizzed past him—and kept going.

Owen, playing third baseman, had missed.

The crowd lost their minds. "Go, go, go!" Noah jumped to his feet. Even Farmer Branson stood, frantically waving a straw hat and hollering with the others.

Noah headed hard for home plate, glimpsing Elisa rushing to second from the corner of his eye. He slid again, already anticipating his need for some Tylenol, as the ball flew by and smacked soundly into the catcher's glove.

"Safe!" Mayor Landry roared, the mic buzzing with feedback.

Noah half-limped toward the dugout, grinning despite the mild throb in his leg as Zoey slapped him a high five. He grabbed a Gatorade and tipped his hat to Cade on the mound, who pointed at him in warning. As he chugged a long sip, his gaze roamed the stands. Sitting behind Farmer Branson's wide hat was Isaac Bergeron, eating popcorn near Sadie and Pastor Dubois's wife.

Mental note—no scooping Elisa on his shoulders after all.

He turned his attention back to home plate. Miley was up next. Two strikes later, she hit one over the back fence that brought both Trish and Elisa home with her.

They'd won.

Mayor Landry shouted the final score over the speakers, and Mama D let out a piercing whistle between two fingers as the crowd bellowed. Noah rushed from the dugout toward Elisa, his knee a distant distraction as he hauled her into his arms. Forget Isaac in the stands. This was more important.

"We did it!" Elisa came eagerly into his embrace, lifting her feet off the ground as Noah tightened his grip around her waist and spun.

He didn't want to put her down. "Nice moves out there."

"Told ya." She didn't seem to be in a hurry to leave, either, sneaking a quick kiss on his cheek. She must not be worried about her father seeing, either.

Though he probably shouldn't push his luck. Noah reluctantly returned her feet to the ground, the impression of her lips lingering on his flushed skin. "You were right about a couple of things today."

"Oh yeah? Can't wait to hear." Her eyes shone up at him, and his earlier feelings about home shifted up another notch in priority. Yeah. He was about to make some changes. He'd wasted enough time.

Heart light, Noah turned to receive the various high fives and fist bumps offered from the other players, laughing at Linc's genuine scowl and Cade's mock frown.

"Good job, Mr. I Haven't Played in Forever." Cade fist-bumped him. Somehow, the guy's white T-shirt and faded jeans had stayed pristine, while dirt caked the length of Noah's entire left leg.

"Not bad, huh?" Noah clapped Owen on the shoulder. "Like riding a bike."

"That explains it, then." Owen stumbled forward under Noah's hand, grinning. "I fell a lot as a kid."

The din subsided as those in the stands began shuffling off the bleachers. The players in the dugout gathered their gear and discussed which pizza joint to hit up next. Cade walked backwards next to Mayor Landry, who wore a patient expression. "Concession sales were hot tonight, Dad. We exceeded expectations by almost double."

Elisa waited by the dugout entry as Noah threw his glove into his bag. He wanted to go for pizza with the others, but he also really wanted to take her somewhere alone. Not that he was dressed for it—and not that he could currently afford it—but images of a steakhouse and candlelit tabletops filled his thoughts.

But that was okay. If his new goal went as planned, they'd have plenty of time for that later.

Suddenly, a slow, rhythmic clap rose over the surrounding conversations, until the chattering around Noah stopped. He zipped his duffel bag and turned toward the sound.

A lone figure leaned against the field gate, still applauding. The man straightened when Noah met his gaze and strode toward the dugout, hands now shoved confidently into the pockets of his athletic jacket.

A sudden freeze washed over Noah, shooting ice into his fingers and toes. He blinked, but the image didn't vanish.

The silver-haired man, roughly an inch shorter than Noah, stopped in front of him with a cocky grin. "Looks like I finally made it to one of your games."

Dad.

Twenty-Two

THE LIGHTS OF THE BALL FIELD BLURRED into a kaleidoscope against the inky black sky as Noah's heartbeat pulsed heavy in his ears. "What are you doing here?" His dry voice caught in his throat as he pushed past Elisa and met his father outside the dugout.

The remaining players quietly slipped past them, heads ducked as if anticipating what was coming. Across the field, those still oblivious to the sudden shift in the atmosphere chattered as they clomped down the bleachers, the scent of popcorn and hot dogs hanging thick in the air.

"Can't your old man come for a visit?" Dad—Russell—spread his hands wide, his performance smile fully locked and loaded. He'd gone gray early in life. Growing up, Noah had heard him referred to more than once as a "silver fox." He hadn't known back then what that meant, but always figured at least the cunning part was right. Today, a smattering of gold rings—none on his actual ring finger, of course—and Ralph Lauren jacket boasted of the success he'd always shot for and usually achieved.

Just never in the things that mattered.

Noah stared hard at his father and tried to reconcile the impossible with reality. "Actually . . . no. I mean, you never have before."

"Well, times can change." Russell lowered his arms, apparently accepting Noah wasn't coming in for a hug. "Good game, son."

A myriad of thoughts flung themselves at his brain so fast Noah couldn't catch any of them. He hadn't prepped for this.

Not that he could have if he'd known.

"You can't walk in here and say that." He clutched his duffel strap, frustration welling in his chest. "You didn't even come to Grandpa's funeral."

"Couldn't get away. Don't worry, I lit a candle." Russell shoved his hands into his pockets, rocking back on his heels. The smile Noah used to believe was genuine still hovered in place like it'd been painted on. "Been busy with the hotels. You know how it is."

Russell's rote answer reminded Noah of the response he'd given to old friends in Magnolia Bay over the past several months. *Been busy with the inn.*

Noah's chest tightened at the comparison and he backed up a step, swinging his bag across his body so its bulk filled the space between them. He glanced over his shoulder at Elisa, who had frozen in the doorway of the dugout, eyes wide as she watched them. Maybe he should introduce them—scratch that, his dad didn't deserve to meet her.

But no, she wasn't staring at his father. She was staring at *hers*, stalking across the field toward them with fists clenched at his side.

The inevitable registered two seconds too late. Isaac charged at Russell, his face and throat as red as the color he was surely seeing. "How dare you show your face here?" He muttered a name Noah couldn't quite make out but could easily guess.

Russell held up both hands, his ever-ready smile still firmly in place. The one that had gotten him out of or justified so many contentions over Noah's lifetime. "Hey, I'm just here to see my kid."

Noah's stomach tightened. *Lies.* Had to be. Why now? Why not

WHERE I FOUND YOU

six months ago for his own father's funeral? Where was he then? Probably locked in another failing relationship.

Isaac stepped a foot closer. He pointed an inch from Russell's nose, his own nostrils flared. "Then you'll have no problem getting on a plane and going back to whatever havoc you came from."

Russell smirked even as he eased back. "I appreciate the travel tip, but I've got unfinished business to attend to here."

"Oh, there's plenty of unfinished business, trust me." Isaac's chest heaved with each breath. He swung around to face Elisa, his voice brittle. "We're leaving. I'll walk you out."

"I—I'm not ready to leave yet. Noah and I still have some work to do." Elisa darted a glance at Noah, then hesitantly pulled the clue card from her back pocket.

Oh, no. Noah flinched. "Elisa, I don't know if this—"

"Let me guess." Isaac's lips thinned as he drew himself to his full height. "That blasted project?"

"It's not a project, exactly. It's more like a treasure hunt." Her words faltered, stammering.

Isaac snorted, his fists still clenched. "Don't be ridiculous."

"You don't understand." Clearly flustered, Elisa gestured with the card. A warm breeze stirred the air, raking her hair back from her flushed cheeks. "It's all part of Mr. Hebert's will. He included me in his inheritance—"

"Gilbert Hebert had no business including you in anything." Isaac's eyes turned to slits. "You know what? That's enough. It was one thing for you two to mess around when you were teenagers, but this—" He waved a finger between her and Noah. "This is too much. You know better, Elisa."

Pain flashed across her face. She kept her chin up, but her lips trembled, fighting back tears. The hand holding the card drooped to her side.

A rush of anger welled inside Noah. It wasn't remotely fair for Isaac to take his rage out on his daughter. This wasn't how he'd wanted Isaac to find out about the hunt—especially not with the inn's inspection still unresolved.

But he couldn't stand by while the man berated his daughter. He drew a tight breath. "Sir, with all due—"

"Wait a minute. She's *yours*?" Russell pointed to Elisa, then at Noah. "And you two . . ." He leaned his head and laughed. "Man, that's ironic. Apparently I've missed the good stuff."

"That's it." Isaac launched, issuing both a curse and a wild swing toward Russell's jaw.

Russell ducked, but took Isaac's second hit on his shoulder as he attempted to sidestep. "Hey!" He shoved him. "Watch it."

"Dad, no!" Elisa rushed forward.

Noah threw out his arm to stop her, but she slipped under it, grabbing at her father's shirt. The men wrestled upright, exchanging blows and ignoring Elisa's feeble attempts to break them up.

"Elisa!" Noah reached to yank her back just as she wedged between the two men, straight into the thick of it.

Straight into the danger.

"Stop!" Noah lunged into the fray and caught a fist on the chin—from whom, he wasn't sure. He reeled backward, straight into Elisa, who went sprawling to the ground. He stumbled over her leg and went down hard next to her.

But the sound of a solid fist connecting with flesh demanded his attention more than the throbbing on his face. He regained his balance and leapt to his feet in time to see blood pour from Russell's nose. All pretense and arrogance was long gone from his face. He swiped at his jaw, then turned and spit blood. "You're going to regret that, Bergeron."

"You killed my sister." Isaac's tone could have chiseled steel. "I'm not going to regret anything."

"What?" Noah's head jerked toward his father, who kept his eyes on Isaac. "What is he talking about?"

"Dad, let's just go. I'll go with you." Silent tears tracked Elisa's cheeks and her voice wobbled. "Come on."

"What did he mean?" Noah directed the question to Elisa now, but she could only shake her head. His own head spun, and not only from the blow to his chin. He knew her aunt had passed away, but had no idea when or how.

Apparently those details mattered.

"You never told your son what you did to Rhonda? Figures." Isaac's eyes were wild as he paced in front of Russell like a caged tiger. "Go ahead. Tell him. Tell him how you lured my sister into an affair, then dumped her before she even had time to get her head on straight."

"It takes two to tango, and you know it." Russell growled, wiping his nose again. "I've sure made some mistakes in my life, but I didn't kill anyone."

"She called me." Isaac was yelling now, either oblivious or not caring that they weren't alone on the field. "Rhonda called me. That night, on her way home from where you had invited her over just to use her and send her packing. She was beside herself with guilt."

Russell scoffed. "I'd finally come to my senses and called it off. Not my fault she couldn't see the wisdom in that."

"It *was* your fault you let her leave that way." Isaac's voice rang with years of pain. "You'd both been drinking and she'd been crying hysterically for half an hour, at least. How dare you let her drive?"

Noah stared at his dad. He was responsible for Rhonda's death?

"That was fifteen years ago!" Russell raised his voice to match Isaac's. "Are you really trying to have this out now?"

"We would have sooner if you hadn't run away. Like a coward." Isaac's eyes filled with disgust. "But yes, you're right. This ends now." He jumped at Russell with another wild swing.

"No!" Elisa's cry blended with a sudden shrill whistle that rent the air. Sheriff Rubart and the same dark-haired deputy that had been at the courthouse burst through the field gate toward them. "Both of you, hands where I can see them! Now!"

Sheriff Rubart wasn't playing. Noah had never heard that tone before, and he hoped he never would again.

Noah took several steps away from Isaac and Russell, reeling. Processing. Had Elisa known about Rhonda? Of his dad's involvement? Wouldn't she have told him? But how could she have not known how her aunt died . . . He searched her face. Her expression reflected tears. No confusion. No shock.

She'd known.

His stomach felt squeezed into a vise. The past was replaying itself in vivid color. Blindsided with news about their families at the worst possible moment. Elisa, crying. Isaac, in a rage.

He refused to let this end the same way again.

Noah reached for her. "Elisa, we need—"

"I said both of you." Sheriff Rubart pointed at him, one hand resting on the gun holstered at his side. His eyes shot fire. "Right now."

"Me?" Shock flashed through Noah's veins and he automatically lifted his hands. "I thought you meant them. I didn't do anything."

"I don't want to hear it. It's clear what's happening here." He gestured between Noah and Russell. "You're both under arrest."

"What?" Russell sputtered. "This man attacked me! I was just standing here."

"Oh, I'm sure." Sheriff grabbed his cuffs. "Hands behind your back, Hebert. I've got you both for disturbing the peace and assault."

Russell spit another round of blood as the Sheriff wrenched his hands behind him. "What about him?" He kicked one leg toward Isaac.

The cuffs clicked into place. "Leave the police work to the police."

The lanky deputy hesitantly approached Noah with another set of cuffs, his eyes pleading for Noah to take it easy on him. Noah bit back his protest as he reluctantly moved his arms behind his back. They weren't going to clear up this miscommunication here, not with the sheriff refusing to listen to reason.

"I know your type. Both of you." Sheriff grabbed Russell's bound arm and turned him around toward the gate. "Your son was in the back of my patrol car a few days ago. Nothing ever changes with you Hebert men."

The words pierced Noah's heart with all the finality of a death knell. Arms behind his back, he allowed the deputy to propel him across the field behind his dad. He cast Elisa a desperate look over his shoulder. Surely she'd say something. She'd witnessed the entire thing. She knew the truth over who had attacked who.

But she stood quietly with her lips pressed together, visibly shaking as Isaac draped one arm around her shoulders and pulled her in close.

And just like last time, she didn't say a single word as Noah walked away.

"You have to do something." Elisa followed her dad inside her childhood home, catching the door he swung shut behind him. The house smelled like nostalgia and leftover spaghetti.

Her dad dropped his keys on the entry table, his tone low. "You're upset. Go home, Elisa."

"This isn't fair." She fought to keep her voice in check. It wouldn't do any good to get emotional with him, but it felt impossible when every fiber of her being screamed from the inside out. She crossed her arms over her chest as she attempted to hold herself together. To stay calm. "You can fix it."

"How?" Dad turned in the hallway to face her, his face distorted with leftover anger. "By turning myself in? Taking Russell's place in the cell?" He shook his head hard. "No, this is the least that horrible man can do after everything else. He deserves it and more."

Elisa pressed her lips together, holding back the truth she was dying to release as she followed her father into the kitchen. The same space where she'd cooked with her mother over the years, tasting various sauces they'd created and adding cayenne pepper like confetti while dreaming of the restaurant they'd open together.

The same kitchen where she'd fixed her mom endless cups of hot tea with honey and experimented with different flavor combinations after the chemo made everything taste metallic.

How had their family come to this?

Tears, born of memory and regret, pressed against Elisa's throat until she couldn't breathe. The look on Noah's face as he was being shoved across the field burned in her brain, an image she might never forget. She'd started to open her mouth a dozen times on that field, but her father's firm grip on her shoulder kept her silenced.

But not any longer.

She steeled herself. "Maybe Russell deserves it, but Noah didn't do anything. What about him?"

"A night in a cell might teach him a few lessons, too." Her father opened a cabinet and pulled down a mug before walking stiffly to the single-serve coffee pot. "That boy is trouble."

Maybe she needed that advice when she was eighteen, but she wasn't anymore. "He's thirty, Dad. So am I. We've been over this."

"Watch your tone. I'm not in the mood." He shoved a pod into the machine and jerked the lid down harder than necessary.

"Well, I'm not in the mood either. I watched a good man get hauled to jail for no reason because you wouldn't say anything." She swallowed hard, guilt bubbling up her chest. "Because I wouldn't say anything."

Dad jabbed the start button. "Family comes first."

"Not when something is unjust." She shook her head. "You of all people should know that."

"What are you trying to say, Elisa?" He turned, his voice cold as he braced his hip against the counter. The coffee pot gurgled to life.

She couldn't do this again—wouldn't. And maybe she didn't have to. Maybe she could risk being real because she would be loved anyway. By her heavenly father, if not her earthly one.

"I didn't stand up for Noah twelve years ago when you found out about us, and tonight I failed him again. Yes, I was being loyal to you—but not because you were right. Because I was scared."

He scoffed. "That's ridiculous. I'm not a threat to you."

"Yes, you are. I've played by your rules for my entire life, even when I knew they were wrong." Her hands shook and she folded them tightly under her arms. "But what you're doing isn't right."

He stared at a space on the linoleum floor between them, jaw clenched.

His silence gave her courage. "Russell Hebert didn't kill Aunt Rhonda."

Her father's gaze jerked to meet hers, fire lighting his eyes. "Watch your mouth."

"It's true, Dad." Now her whole body was shaking. But it had to be said. All of this had gone on long enough.

"You don't know anything."

"I know that a man who wasn't there isn't responsible for someone else's car wreck." She infused a strength she didn't know she had into her voice. "He made bad decisions that night but so did Aunt Rhonda. Everything that happened was the result of *both* of their choices."

"So you're siding with the Heberts now? Abandoning what's left of our Bergeron family name?" He ran one hand over his head and released a short breath. "I can't believe you. First your mother, now this."

Elisa froze. "What about Mom?"

"She always thought this feud was ridiculous."

"It *is*. It's not even about the land so much anymore, is it? It's about Aunt Rhonda."

He turned and grabbed for his full coffee mug. "Life's not fair, Elisa. The Heberts took things that weren't meant for them. And they profited off it, making the rest of us sacrifice. Then that jerk's affair with my sister." He practically spit the words. "To me, this is poetic justice."

"So to get revenge, you're going to let a good man and his father sit in a jail unjustly?"

"It's not unjust. Russell did hit me."

Elisa narrowed her eyes. "You hit him first."

"Life's not fair, remember?" Her father raised his coffee mug to his lips, his expression tight.

She bit back a frustrated sigh. She wasn't getting anywhere, and meanwhile, Noah was sitting in prison. Because of her. Because of her family.

Regret thrummed through her veins, sending a wave of nausea coursing through her stomach. If she hadn't told her dad about the hunt when she did, he wouldn't have gotten so upset. Maybe none of the fight would have happened.

She'd never know for sure, but she could do everything in her power now to fix it. She could speak up for once.

She could be a good girl by *not* calming down.

"Fine." Elisa lifted her chin, matching her father's haughty tone and returning his glare. "If that's how it's going to be, there's nothing else I have to say to you right now."

"You need to calm down, Elisa." He frowned. "You're making too much of all of this. Let it play out."

"*Me?*" she shouted the word, and the release felt freeing. In fact, it felt amazing. She shouted louder. "I'm not the one who started a fistfight on a ball field!"

He glared at her. "Watch your tone, young—"

"That's just it, Dad. I'm not young. And I don't have to cater to you anymore. All of this is wrong, and you know it." She bit down on her lower lip, then released the next words begging to be spoken. "Mom would be very disappointed in you tonight."

Then she spun on her heel toward the entryway, her heart pounding and hands trembling. But the block that had been sitting on her chest for the past half hour was gone, and she could breathe. She'd done it.

Maybe she should have done it sooner, but at least she'd done it.

"Get back in here, Elisa Bergeron. Where do you think you're going?" Her dad followed from the kitchen, coffee splashing over the sides of his mug onto the worn rug.

She yanked open the front door and shouted her reply—simply because she finally could. "To do the right thing."

Twenty-Three

NOAH HAD VISITED THE LOCAL JAIL once during a fifth-grade field trip. The deputy had walked the class around the small facility, shown them the lackluster meals the inmates received, locked them briefly in a cell with their teacher, and basically tried to scare illegal activity out of them from an early age.

Ironically, he was now trapped in the exact same cell, but not with his wide-eyed, giggling classmates. He was with his father.

He'd much rather be in solitary confinement.

Noah paced in front of the barred door, leaving a trail of dried dirt that flaked off his pants from his slide on the softball field. Russell sat on the wooden bench running the length of the holding cell wall, his expression grim as he tapped one hand on his knee. The fact it was only a holding cell should have given Noah hope, but the smug expression on Sheriff Rubart's face as he'd clanged the door shut an hour ago brought very little.

"They can't hold us for long." Russell crossed one ankle over the other as he leaned back against the concrete wall. "This is all for intimidation."

Noah refused to sit next to him—or sit at all. This place hadn't been wiped down in who knew how long, and while he wasn't as germophobic as Cade, he could easily let his nose make the decision for him. "I take it you speak from experience."

"I've crossed the wrong person a time or two—much worse than Bergeron." Russell's face crinkled at the name. "It always worked out for me in the end."

Noah had wondered how much of his father's business success in the Golden State had been legitimate. He paused his pacing and faced his dad. "Let me guess—you paid them off?"

Russell cut his eyes to Noah, a flicker of amusement in his gaze. "You always were a sharp one."

"Not that you were around to notice." The words slipped free, bringing a sense of relief and regret at once. Not that his dad didn't deserve to hear them and more.

More like he didn't deserve the acknowledgment.

Russell frowned as he sat up straight. "You know, I really didn't expect this much animosity from you. I thought you'd be glad to see me."

"Glad?" Noah scoffed. "You got into a fistfight with my girl—with Elisa's dad. At a public ball field."

Russell cursed. "That wasn't my fault."

"It never is, is it?" Long-dormant fury stirred in Noah's chest. "I guess next you'll say it wasn't your fault that you had an affair. Wasn't your fault your *mistress* died."

Russell was on his feet and in front of Noah in seconds. His dark eyes flashed. "It wasn't. You don't know anything about that—you were a child."

"Exactly. And you were my dad." Noah held his ground, staring him in the eye. "Emphasis on *were*."

Russell flinched. "So I make one mistake and you cut me off forever?"

"Pretty sure you made that decision when you cut Mom out.

And moved to the west coast to start a new life, leaving her to deal with your mess all alone."

Russell stepped back and ran a hand over the back of his neck. "I asked her to take me back. She wouldn't. So I left."

"Am I supposed to feel sorry for you?" Noah had never been more torn between laughing and punching someone in the face. "You ruined her life and reputation with your selfishness. You ruined mine!"

"Hey!" Sheriff popped around the corner of the hall, hands on his hips as he glared. "Keep it down in there." He kept his level stare on them for several moments before disappearing once again.

Noah lowered his voice, hissing through clenched teeth. "I had to move. I didn't get to go to high school with my friends. Everything changed because of you."

"Well, it looks like you and Elisa figured it out just fine." Russell shook his head. "I can't believe you ended up with a Bergeron. After all that."

"We're not . . ." Noah didn't know what they were now. Or maybe her silence on the ball field told him all he needed to know. Maybe it was like she'd said at the Magnolia Blossom last week before dumping coffee on their table—some things never changed.

He should've known better. There was too much water under their shaky bridge of a relationship. What had he expected? Thanks to the man sitting across from him, Noah's name was all but trash in this town. Hadn't the sheriff confirmed that with the click of a lock? Elisa had chosen sides, and she'd clearly chosen her father.

He couldn't fully blame her for it, either.

Noah squared his shoulders. "Elisa and I are none of your business. You don't have the right to know anything about my life."

"Fine." Russell raised both hands as he sat back on the bench. "I didn't come here to fight with you." He ran his hand through his hair, much like Noah often did, and then released a heavy sigh. His father was still silver, cunning, and narcissistic.

But he also looked more and more like what he truly was—an aging man living out a lifetime of bad decisions.

Speaking of tired, Noah's legs hurt. He'd run all evening at the game, and his knee still ached from his dramatic slide into base. He took a seat on the edge of the bench next to Russell.

Forget it—he was probably going to have to relegate these pants to yard duty anyway. Noah slid back into a comfortable position, then looked at his father. "What are you really doing here?" He racked his brain for any details from their last phone call nearly a year ago, only remembering one. "Did Bambi break up with you?"

"Her name was Bailey. And yes." Russell snorted. "She found someone with as much money but fewer years on the calendar."

"Again with the sympathy." Noah rolled his eyes. His head was pounding, and there was no telling how much longer they'd have to sit here. The more time he spent in his father's presence, the more uncomfortable he grew just being related to him.

This wasn't the legacy he wanted. But he wasn't ready to sell the inn and move back to Shreveport, either.

He didn't want to run away and quit—or become anything more like the man at his side than he already was. And the only way to prove that was to finish the hunt, with or without Elisa, and save the Blue Pirogue.

Russell crossed his arms over his chest. "Before you say anything about karma, don't."

"I wouldn't. I don't believe in karma." The hymn from Sunday's sermon flooded Noah's mind.

Love lifted me
When nothing else could help
Love lifted me

He stared at a crack in the tiled floor as the song ran on repeat in his head. Loving his father . . . that was a leap. So was forgiving. Maybe he could baby step toward that goal one day. The first step wasn't going to happen in a jail cell.

But maybe Noah could offer him something.

"You know that's not love, right?" He refused to meet his father's eyes, even though Russell's gaze bore directly into his profile.

"What's not?"

"The Bambis of the world."

"*Bailey.*"

"Her, too." Noah finally looked at his dad. "I'm just saying there's more to life than the next woman and greener pastures and money."

"Says the guy without any of those things." Russell smirked. "Nice try, son. If you're about to whip out a religious tract from your pocket, save yourself the trouble."

He was incorrigible. Noah leaned back against the wall, turning his face away. He'd tried.

A stiff quiet filled the cell, save for the hum of the fluorescent lights above.

Russell finally broke the silence. "So what's this your girl was saying about a treasure hunt?"

Noah leaned forward, bracing his forearms on his knees and sending more dirt skittering to the floor. "Grandpa set up his will to include additional inheritance six months postmortem."

"And you have to hunt for it?"

"Yep. Follow the clues."

"Such a quirky man." Russell shook his head. "Leave it to my father to saddle you with that inn and its mortgage, then make you work to find the money to pay for it."

"We're pretty close to the end of the hunt." Forget that this last clue was impossible and his partner had all but sent him to jail. He swallowed. "It'll all work out."

"Maybe it won't have to."

Noah turned his head slowly to his father. "What do you mean?"

"You asked why I was here." He shrugged one shoulder. "I'm here to take over."

He snorted. "I don't need your help."

"Sounds like you do. Black mold?"

Noah narrowed his eyes. "How'd you hear about that?"

"I keep tabs."

So he could bother to keep up with what Noah was doing, but not bother to keep up with Noah himself? Seemed about right. He clenched his fists. "I'm not asking to borrow money."

"I wasn't offering to lend it. I'm here for the inn."

"You want to take over the Blue Pirogue even with a mold issue?" Noah frowned.

"I can handle that." Russell waved one hand in the air. "Who's doing the mitigation work? I'll assume the payments."

A wave of protectiveness swept through Noah's body, tightening his shoulders. "Thanks, but no thanks. The inn isn't up for grabs." To Isaac Bergeron or to his dad. The last thing he needed was for his father to sink his cursed claws into Grandpa's legacy, just to have it taken over later by a loan shark or a lawsuit from a scorned west coast husband.

Not. Happening.

Russell leaned forward, matching Noah's braced posture. "I don't think you understand." His voice dipped as he leveled his gaze at Noah. "I'm taking the inn."

His ears flooded with heat. "It's not yours to take." He was starting to understand why Isaac had punched Russell square in the nose. This man and his arrogance were infuriating. "There's a sentence in Grandpa's will you might be interested in. *All my assets revert to Noah.*"

"On the contrary." Russell lifted his chin. "You know what trumps a will?" He didn't wait for an answer. "A mortgage with my name on it."

His heart skipped. "What?"

"I was the co-signer some years back when Dad needed help."

A co-signer? Noah stared blankly. Then Owen's words from

their bank meeting last week flew through his head like a bat in a cave but twice as scary. *If you had a co-signer, like your grandfather did for that second mortgage years ago, it'd be no problem.*

"I was getting bored in Cali. My hotels can manage themselves for a bit. Thought I'd take a change of scenery—catch up with my son." All smiles again, Russell clapped his hand on Noah's shoulder.

Noah ducked out of the grasp. "That's bull and you know it." He studied his father's carefully arranged expression. "Let me guess. Bailey didn't find another man. You *were* the other man, and now he's after you."

Russell clasped his hands together. "Like I said, you're sharp. Don't worry. I'll get you a job at the Blue Pirogue if you want."

Over his dead body. Noah abruptly stood and turned, towering over his father on the bench. "I'm not going to let this happen."

Russell laughed. "As soon as I can get to the bank, you're not going to have much of a choice. If I pay off that thirty grand, the inn is mine." He spread his hands wide with a grin. "You're welcome to find a probate lawyer and fight me on it, but I hear that's expensive."

"Fine." Frustration knotted in Noah's throat as he turned away from his sorry excuse for a dad and stalked to the door. "Then we'll see who gets there first."

With money he didn't yet have.

Noah gripped the cell door with both hands and stared down the hall, chest heaving as reality crashed. Elisa had abandoned him. He had no leads on the next clue. Had just been handed an even tighter deadline than the one Grandpa had initiated...

And he was literally stuck behind bars.

Clouds bulging with the threat of rain covered the night sky.

Elisa banged on the front door of the Magnolia Bay Parish Jail, shivering in the unseasonably cool wind blowing in from the bay. Sheriff Rubart looked up from the front desk, long abandoned by the receptionist this time of night.

He frowned at her, but rose from the rolling desk chair and ambled to the door, opening it just enough to poke his head out. "Is this an emergency, Ms. Bergeron?" His pinched brow affirmed his strong opinion that it wasn't.

"Yes, actually." Elisa slipped through the opening before he could block it. "I need to make a statement about what I saw at the ball field tonight."

He rolled his eyes. "How convenient."

"Noah didn't hit anyone. In fact, he *got* hit trying to keep me out of it."

"So you're saying you belong in that cell back there?" He raised his brows.

"No, I was trying to break it up. Noah protected me." She took a deep breath, shifting her keys from one hand to the other. "I was trying to get my dad to stop attacking Mr. Hebert."

There. She'd done it. She'd turned in her own father.

Sheriff Rubart didn't look impressed. "Again—how convenient that you believe Noah and Russell are innocent."

She had a feeling that raising her voice at the sheriff wouldn't give her the same sense of liberty as it had with her father. She leveled her tone, trying to stay patient. "Sheriff, you've known me my whole life. I'm not a liar."

He crossed his burly arms over his chest "No, but you were recently caught canoodling in a government facility after hours with the man you're defending."

Her cheeks heated. "This has nothing to do with that. I'm speaking as a concerned citizen. Noah is innocent, and Mr. Hebert didn't strike first. I'm a witness."

He stared at her, as if trying to determine whether she was telling the truth.

"You have to believe me." Her voice pitched against her best efforts. "You've only got one of the right people in jail, at best!"

"Actually, I don't." He drew himself up to his full stature and gestured toward the hall behind them. "They've already been released. My deputy is getting their belongings now."

Released?

As if on cue, a uniformed officer, Noah, and his father turned the corner at the end of the long white-walled hallway. Elisa's hope soared. Noah wouldn't be stuck there all night. They could talk. She could explain how she finally stood up to her father, and beg Noah's forgiveness for not saying something sooner. They'd get busy working on the last clue, and everything would be—

Noah raised his head and met her gaze, his expression drawn as he clutched his bag of baseball gear. That expression didn't change as he continued his approach.

Elisa swallowed. He wasn't happy to see her, and she couldn't blame him. But she'd come. She'd done the right thing—she'd ratted on her dad.

That had to mean something.

In contrast to Noah's defeated gait, Russell's arrogance radiated from every pore. Elisa narrowed her eyes. Her Sunday school teachers growing up had always taught her not to hate, but good gravy, that man made it hard.

"As you can see, your statement is unnecessary." Sheriff held the door for her and nodded toward the parking lot. "Now if you all can kindly leave the premises, I'll be getting home to my impossibly late dinner."

"This isn't over." Russell tipped his hat toward the sheriff as he started through the door. "Wrongful imprisonment is a lawsuit waiting to happen."

Sheriff's steady expression didn't change. "You were held less than twenty-four hours. Get out of my sight."

Noah and Elisa filed out the door behind Russell. Her heart stammered in her chest, and she reached for Noah's arm. Then thought better of it and let her hand fall to her side. A misty rain had started, blanketing the dim parking light. She blinked against the cool drops. She hadn't anticipated this. She thought she'd be able to blast into the sheriff's office, speak for Noah, and prove she supported him. Make up for her earlier silence.

But they hadn't needed her. The confrontation with her dad—it had all been for nothing.

She was too late.

"My truck is at the ball field." Noah wouldn't look at her. Drops of rain beaded on his hair and forearms.

Russell pulled his phone from his pocket and started typing, covering the screen with one hand. "I'll get us an Uber."

"I'm good to walk." Noah stared straight ahead, one hand clutching his duffel strap. The hint of purple had already started on his chin.

Elisa's chest tightened until it felt hard to take a deep breath. "Let me drive you to your truck." She jingled her keys. "We can talk on the way."

"No thanks." Still not looking at her, Noah shook his head and headed toward the street, his bag of baseball gear bouncing against his hip.

He still thought she hadn't fought for him.

Rain misted around them, the air thick with humidity. Panic tightened her throat, clutched her stomach in a vise. It couldn't end like this. They had to finish the hunt. Delia . . . the café. Everything was at risk.

Not to mention her broken heart.

Helpless, she took several steps after Noah and called out, "At least let me take your bag!"

He turned, walking backward now, and finally met her gaze via the glow of a streetlight. Her breath hitched at the betrayal radiating off his expression.

Elisa froze.

Noah held the eye contact for several moments before darting a final glance between her and his dad. Then he gave a quick shake of his head. "I'm better off on my own."

"Noah, wait. That's not true." He couldn't believe that. He just needed to hear what happened, what she'd done to try to help. Tears slipped down her cheeks. "We need—"

"You made your position clear." Noah's harsh words cut off her protests. "I'm the one who thought things could be different this time, and I was clearly wrong."

"But that's just it." Elisa took several steps after him, even as he kept retreating. "You're not wrong."

"I'm never going to be what you need, Elisa." Noah turned back around, throwing his final words over his shoulder. "So just calm down and go home."

Then he disappeared into the shadows of the rain-sprinkled street.

Twenty-Four

SOMEONE HAD MOWED THE YARD RE-
cently.

The rich aroma of earth and grass stirred Noah's senses
as he stood before his grandfather's headstone under the cloudy
night sky. His shirt was plastered to his chest and his soaked pants
scrubbed his legs. But he didn't care. He shoved back his wet hair
and dropped his duffel to the muddy grass beside a nearby grave.

This corner of the cemetery was fairly dark, but the scattered
poles lining the paved road provided enough light for Noah to
read the markings carved into Grandpa's stone.

GILBERT RENE HEBERT
FATHER. GRANDFATHER. PUZZLE MASTER.

And then the quote from *The Count of Monte Cristo* that he
had requested in his will.

HE WHO HAS FELT THE DEEPEST GRIEF IS BEST
ABLE TO EXPERIENCE SUPREME HAPPINESS ... LIVE,
THEN, AND BE HAPPY.

"Well, I hope you're happy—because you've really got me in a bind now." Noah spoke to the cement block as steady rain continued to pour down his back. "The clock is ticking, and we're stuck on this final clue. And on top of that, I'm on my own."

Elisa's face at the police station, full of regret, tugged at Noah. Maybe he should have heard her out, but he wasn't mad at her. More like resigned. This is clearly how they—and their families— were meant to be.

"I guess I expected something else from her. Thought I had it, for a little while." A regretful smile tugged at his lips. "You probably just threw Elisa into the mix to give me a fighting chance at figuring out these clues, didn't you? But history tried to repeat itself." His smile faded. "In a few ways."

Images of his time with Elisa—from twelve years ago and from the past week—rushed together into a collage of sun-kissed, coconut-scented memories. For a moment, outside the police station, he'd considered her stricken expression and debated giving her another chance. He had no doubt she was sorry for her silence on the ball field. She'd obviously come to the police station to try to help, which said a lot.

But it didn't change that he couldn't trust her to be there. To put him before her family, when needed.

And the fact that he had needed her at all was more than a little unsettling. Both for the hunt . . . and for himself. It was best to cut it off now, before anyone got more attached or more hurt.

Heberts and Bergerons didn't mix. How many more lives had to be destroyed for them to accept that?

Noah took a deep breath. "I guess it doesn't matter anymore, anyway, does it? Dad—Russell—is going to ruin everything . . . as usual." There wasn't enough time to figure out the last clue before his dad paid off the inn and took over. He had no doubt Russell would be standing in front of the bank in the morning when they opened at nine.

His heart sank. "You know what the worst part is?" Noah slid to his knees in front of the grave marker. Cold pressed into his knees. "All of this was for nothing. I lost the hunt. I've lost the inn. And I lost Elisa—not that I ever really had her back." He swallowed, eying the headstone as a downpour of emotions stronger than the storm washed over him. He choked over unshed tears, his heart racing. "I lost you."

He sat silently for several moments, letting the tears fall and mix with the rain. Grandpa couldn't hear him—or maybe he could. That was a question for Pastor Dubois. Still, the ball in his chest had eased a notch.

Noah wiped his face with his arm as reality weighed heavy on his shoulders. "I'm going to fail. You, the inn. All those memories. Everything you stood for and built. Dad's going to run it into the ground, I can already tell." He sniffed, shaking his head. "For the record, I'd much rather have you back than have the Blue Pirogue. Or money."

Time passed—how much, he wasn't sure. He sat there as the rain slowly subsided, until it was only a sprinkle misting the limbs of a nearby oak. All around him were stone names of former lives. Organized, tidy rows of heritage—for better or for worse.

Were any of them sons desperate to be enough? Fathers bent on betraying everyone they were supposed to love? Grandfathers who filled in the gaps left behind?

His gaze drifted back over Grandpa's headstone. *HEBERT*. Noah might hate much of what that name represented, but it wasn't totally tarnished—no matter what his mom, Sheriff Rubart, or anyone else in Magnolia Bay thought.

He wanted the type of legacy his grandfather left behind—the kind left by a man who invested in his hurting grandson and took him on adventures. A man who put his heart and soul into a thriving business for the community, despite rumors and naysayers. A man who went through a divorce, yet still wrote that he loved his wife in his Bible.

A man who never quit.

In the silence, the words of the hymn played once more in his thoughts.

I was sinking deep in sin
Far from the peaceful shore
Very deeply stained within
Sinking to rise no more
But the master of the sea
Heard my despairing cry
From the waters lifted me
Now safe am I

Earlier Noah had imagined those words being for his dad, but maybe they weren't. Maybe they were for him.

He closed his eyes, the rain-scented breeze rustling his damp hair. Somewhere in the oak above, an owl hooted. And the song continued.

Love lifted me
When nothing else could help
Love lifted me

Love was stronger than blood. Stronger than family feuds. Stronger than revenge. Maybe that was why his grandfather put him and Elisa together—not because Noah wasn't capable on his own, but because he was trying to mend fences. End the feud he'd been a part of his entire life.

Noah opened his eyes, his gaze once more roaming the letters on the headstone. He was a Hebert, yes—but he was loved. By his grandfather. By his friends. Maybe, to some degree, once upon a time, by Elisa.

But definitely by God.

And if he lived under *that* name—under the label Loved—maybe he could finally quit sinking.

The tears had subsided. So had the rain. The deepening darkness of the night felt less suffocating now, more soothing. It was time to go.

Noah drew a ragged breath as he pushed himself to his feet. "I sure wish I could finish this. See what you left behind for me." He tilted his head. "But a wise woman once told me that just because you stop doing something doesn't mean you're a quitter. So I'm not going to think that way."

He grabbed his bag and started to turn, but the quote on the headstone caught his eye.

HE WHO HAS FELT THE DEEPEST GRIEF IS BEST ABLE TO EXPERIENCE SUPREME HAPPINESS... LIVE, THEN, AND BE HAPPY.

Man, Grandpa loved that book. What was the other quote that had taken Noah years to fully understand? He racked his memory. Something about luck. No, misfortune. He spoke the words out loud. "'*Misfortune is needed to plumb certain mysterious depths in the understanding of men; pressure is needed to explode the charge.*'"

He'd certainly had the pressure lately. Noah smiled at the tombstone. "We'll see if there's an explosion, I guess." He made a note to find Grandpa's missing collector's edition, so Noah could re-read it in his honor.

He started up the hill, bag slung over his shoulder. Quite the walk remained to get back to his truck at the ballpark, but he didn't care. At least the storm had stopped.

Both outside and in.

Noah crested the hill to the road as more quotes Grandpa had read him from that book filled his mind.

"For all evils there are two remedies—time and silence."

"Until the day when God will deign to reveal the future to man, all human wisdom is contained in these two words—wait and hope."

Why did that sound familiar?

Suddenly he stopped, his shoes squeaking on the wet grass. He dug in his bag for his cell, then pulled up the photo of the clue he'd taken before the ballgame, his eyes devouring the words written on the card.

How quickly Time passes
On tiny wings of Silence
Oh how it Waits
And oh how it Hopes
Cloudy as a silver lining.

His breath caught and his heart raced. Elisa had thought there was significance to the capital letters, and she was right. But not because of an acrostic.

They were from *The Count of Monte Cristo.*

Elisa's dad was sitting on her doorstep, a blue windbreaker zipped all the way up to his chin, an umbrella laying at his feet.

She turned off the ignition and groaned, briefly resting her head on the steering wheel as she mustered the energy to open her door. She couldn't do this—not again. Not after she'd lost everything.

I'll never be what you need.

Weren't they a pair? If Noah felt he wasn't enough, she was too much—even for him. After daring to believe he could be different.

She raised her head, squinting against the porch light shining on her rain-streaked windshield. Was her dad holding a plate of cookies?

Elisa climbed out of the car and took a hesitant step toward him, all her fight and fire left back at the police station. "Dad, I really

WHERE I FOUND YOU

can't handle any more conflict tonight." She just wanted to crawl into some dry clothes, get in bed, and not move until morning. Maybe the morning after that.

But she had to get up early for the breakfast rush. The Magnolia Blossom needed her—for however much longer. Her stomach twisted.

"I come in peace." Dad awkwardly clambered to his feet as she approached, extending the plate of cookies. "Here. For you and Zoey."

She silently took the plate as she fumbled for her house key, then did a double take at the pile of thin blond cookies nestled under plastic wrap. "Are these . . . ?"

His Adam's apple bobbed. "Your mom's tea cakes."

"You baked?"

"I'm trying to make a gesture."

Oh, boy. She pushed open the door. "Come on in." She hollered for Zoey, but then realized her car hadn't been out front. She was probably still enjoying post-game pizza with the others.

Had that only been a few hours ago?

Her father trailed after her as Elisa dropped her purse to the floor, set the cookies on the coffee table, and grabbed a blanket. "Have a seat." She wrapped up and settled on a chair opposite the sofa—the same spot she took when she and Zoey had that big conversation just last week.

So much had changed, it made her dizzy.

Dad perched on the edge of the sofa cushion and picked up one of the navy throw pillows. "I owe you an apology."

"I'm sorry I yelled at you." The words came automatically, but upon further inspection, she realized she meant them. She could learn how to express herself and create a new dynamic without being disrespectful.

"No, this is on me. It's a long time coming." He flipped the pillow end over end in his lap. "I finally see that I've put too much pressure on you ever since your mother . . . died." He swallowed and looked up. "For that, I'm sorry."

Tears pricked her eyes. How many times had she wished to hear those words? Here they were, yet she could hardly believe them.

Elisa clutched the blanket tighter around her shoulders. Her wet T-shirt pressed into her back. "I just wanted to make you happy."

"I know. And you did, I promise you." His voice shook and he cleared his throat. "You were the only thing that got me through that year."

"Odd way of showing it." Elisa huddled deeper into the blanket. "I never felt like I could be myself with you. Like I was always one emotion away from setting you off. I had to hold everything inside." So much so she could barely wait to move out when the time came, to get space to be herself. She tried to be herself with Noah, then with Trey. Both attempts backfired.

And here they were again. Except this time with Noah, it was her fault and she couldn't fix it.

"I see that now. And again—I'm truly sorry." Her father stared at the pillow. "I handled my grief poorly. You reminded me so much of your mom—your mannerisms, the way you wore your hair. Your emotions and reactions to things . . . I couldn't handle the reminders." He met her gaze, regret filling the depths of his eyes. "I failed."

She'd never seen him look that way before. Her dad might be a lot of things, but a liar wasn't one of them. He meant this apology with his whole heart.

Compassion surged. "You didn't fail, Dad." Elisa scooted forward on the chair. "You made mistakes, and so did I."

"Mine were detrimental. I distanced from you, lost my temper too many times. Held on to grudges." He shook his head. "Sometimes we get in the habit of doing something a certain way, then we keep doing it that way even when it no longer makes sense."

"Like with the feud?"

His posture stiffened, then relaxed. "Exactly. I carried a torch that wasn't even mine to carry for years, just because my family did. Then when it was time to let go, all that happened with Rhonda and—" He bit his lip. "Russell."

"He's a pretty awful guy. That part is legit." She drew a breath. "But Noah's different."

"I think I've known that, too. Just still living on habit, assumptions. Prejudice." He sighed. "It's easier to be angry than sad sometimes."

Her heart softened. "I know."

He shifted on the couch, crossing one ankle over the other. "But I'll give Noah a chance—a real chance, if he's important to you."

"He is." A fresh wave of tears beckoned. "But I don't think that's going to be necessary."

Dad tilted his head. "I take it your attempt at the police station didn't go well?"

"I was too late. They were already released, and Noah . . . well." She shook her head. "I don't want to relive it right now." Or ever. The image of his betrayed expression as he headed off into the rain would haunt her for weeks.

"Fair enough." Dad met and held her gaze. "I'm here if you do later—even if there are tears or emotions involved."

Elisa snort-laughed, one such tear slipping down her cheek. "Thanks." He really was trying. Then she hesitated. "I do have a question."

"Shoot." He reached for the cookies between them on the coffee table. "I owe you answers to whatever you want."

She took a breath. "Why did you send letters to Noah all those years ago?"

"Letters?" His brows furrowed as he settled back on the couch, cookie in hand.

"The ones that threatened him if we didn't break up. You

could've just talked to him." She snorted. "I mean, you're not exactly known for hiding what you want."

Dad stared blankly at her as he chewed. "What letters?"

Elisa pressed her fingers to her lips. "Wait a minute. You *would* have just talked to him, wouldn't you?" Her heart hammered in her throat as the truth registered. Her father hadn't sent them.

So who had?

Twenty-Five

ELISA STACKED THE HOMEMADE DONUTS
she'd pulled from the air fryer into the display tower at the serving
counter of the Blossom. She glanced at the clock on the wall
over the door, and fought back a yawn. 5:15 a.m. Between replaying
her interaction with Noah, and replaying her father's unexpected
heart-to-heart last night, she'd finally given up on sleep and gone to
the Blossom to get an early start for the morning rush.

Except her churning thoughts had followed her to work.

She gazed around the diner—at the chairs turned up on the
yellow tables, the way the overhead lights reflected in the windows
against the still-dark morning. The sun hadn't risen yet, but soon,
the floor would be streaked with sunbeams. The early risers would
hustle inside to claim their favorite booths. Farmer Branson would
order more bacon than he could eat so he'd have leftovers for his
hound dog. Pastor Dubois would get his standard black coffee
and settle in with his Bible.

Her throat knotted as she slid the final donut onto the stack.
Once Delia sold the diner, would the new owners keep things the

same? Would they keep her as manager? Who would cook? Would the menu change? What would the locals do if they couldn't order their favorites?

Too many questions, and not any answers.

The front door swooshed open, and Delia ambled inside on a walker. Her eyes weren't as cheery as usual, but her lipstick was as pink as the buttons on her oversized shirt. "Morning, sweetheart. You're here early."

"Delia!" Elisa rushed around the counter, wiping her icing-covered fingers on her apron. "What are you doing here at all? And where's your chair?"

Delia let go of the walker long enough to flit one hand through the air. "Surgery is scheduled for next week, so I thought it was time to part ways with the thing. Besides, I'm not doing a whole lot right now."

"You're still going to church and coming in here. That's plenty."

"I'm not crippled." Delia winced as she made her way to one of the tables. "Lower that chair for me, will you?"

Elisa obeyed, then took the seat opposite her once Delia was settled. "I tried so hard, Mama D. I really did. But I failed."

Delia pursed her hot pink lips. "What are you talking about, sweet girl?"

"I've been looking for ways to save the diner." She couldn't bring herself to admit to her plan to pay for the surgery. "But it's all falling through. You're going to have to sell. I fought with my dad. I've lost Noah." She rubbed her temples. "I might not even have a job soon."

Then Elisa sat up straight, her hands slapping down against the table. "I'm sorry. I'm not trying to make you feel worse. I know you didn't ask for any of this to happen." Great, now she sounded selfish. She dropped her head to her arms.

"Shush, now." Delia patted her hand. "Look at me, Elisa Bergeron."

Elisa raised her head just far enough to make eye contact.

"One thing at a time." Delia smiled, her teeth white against her lipstick. "Then you'll see it's not all that bad."

"Feels like it."

"Well, you're not a failure, no matter what plans you did or didn't have." She sniffed. "That's foolish talk. Secondly, I'm glad to hear you fought with your dad. That's progress, dear one."

Elisa sat up straight. "I guess it was." She updated her on the events of last night.

"See?" Delia shook her head. "Miracles abound." She gave Elisa's hand another pat. "What happened with Noah?"

She groaned. "We need donuts for this story."

"I always need donuts."

Elisa retrieved two of the fresh pastries from the display, and then took her seat. As Delia crunched her way through the sprinkled topping, Elisa filled her in on the treasure hunt status, the ball game, the fight, and the jail. "I blew it. He was starting to trust me again . . . I was starting to trust him . . . and I just stood there. I let my dad intimidate me, *again*."

"What your father said about old habits is true, love." Delia brushed crumbs off her fingers. "They're hard to break. And you've had decades of bad habits."

She winced. "That's not very encouraging."

"I wasn't done." Delia held up one finger. "If Noah is the man I think he is—and I really do think he is—he's going to see that we all make mistakes. And he's going to come around."

She was too scared to hope. After all, Noah hadn't come back the first time she failed to back him to her dad. "You think so?"

"I'm rarely wrong about these things." She lifted her chin. "Or much of anything, really."

Elisa snorted.

"Now, the diner . . ." Delia nodded slowly, her smile fading as she absently wiped a napkin across the table. "That's been a hard one for me too. But this is the lot the Lord has dropped in my lap, and trust me when I say I've prayed for alternatives. There just hasn't seemed to be any."

"I've prayed too." The whisper floated from Elisa's lips. "Almost as much as I did for Mom."

"I know your roots here run deep, honey." Delia tapped her finger on the table. "And I know that God is the God of the midnight hour. Maybe we'll get a stroke of midnight miracle."

"Maybe." Elisa rolled in her lower lip, fighting a wave of frustration. If Noah would just forgive her and work with her . . . if they could figure out the last clue before the clock ran out . . .

"But if not, I'm going to hold to something else I know is true." A smile lit Delia's wrinkled face. "That hands surrendered to the Lord are never empty for long."

She was right—as usual. "I agree." Elisa leaned back in her chair. "But it's sure scary in the meantime."

"Of course it is. For me, too. But look at all the good that's come already from this treasure hunt and from my fall." Delia brushed a rogue sprinkle onto the floor. "You're mending fences with your father. *And* with the Heberts in general. Big things are happening. Don't you see?"

It didn't make the inevitable much easier to swallow, but she could see it. And see there was hope for the future—whatever that looked like. A bit of the burden lifted. She wasn't alone, and never had been.

"Remember this." Delia raised a white eyebrow and pointed at Elisa. "Blank pages are only scary when we don't know the Author."

Elisa let that wash over her for a moment. She liked being in control. But she couldn't flirt her way out of this one, or conform her way back into Noah's favor. She could only be herself, and trust the Lord to work things out the way He saw best.

Even if that looked different than how she would've done it. She swallowed. "Sometimes it's hard to release the pen."

Delia reached over and tapped her walker. "Don't I know it, hon. But God is good, all the time. Even when there are hospitals and For Sale signs involved."

Her conversation with Noah at the library courtyard flitted through her mind. *"It's just that things are often beyond our ability to understand this side of heaven."* She had finally gotten to a place where she could mean that about her mother. She meant it for Noah.

Now she needed to mean it for losing the diner.

She closed her eyes, releasing the rest of the lingering stress. "Thanks for being here, Mama D."

"I wouldn't be anywhere else." Delia patted her arm again. "Now, what's an old lady have to do to get another donut around here?"

Elisa shoved her chair back with a laugh. "Hint taken." She stood just as her phone chimed from her apron pocket. She tugged it free, shot a look at the screen, and widened her eyes at Delia.

A text from Noah.

Noah
Meet me at Chug at Mug at 6 a.m.

Noah stood in the pre-dawn light just inside the front door of Chug a Mug, which opened every day at 5:30 a.m. Miley was already inside, yawning, furrowing her pierced brows and scowling as she worked the espresso machine.

Perfect. The coffee he'd already ordered would be good.

He glanced at his phone, bouncing a little on the balls of his feet as his stomach churned. Elisa hadn't texted him back. He could only hope, at this point.

Even if they were destined to be apart, he didn't want to do this without her.

Noah turned to check the sidewalk again just as she pushed through the doorway.

Elisa stopped abruptly in the entry. "Hi . . ." Her hair was swept back on one side with criss-crossed pins, and icing dusted the shoulder of her purple top. Matching streaks decorated her jeans.

He breathed in her vanilla scent like a starving man. There was so much to say. So much to explain. "You look like you fought a donut."

That wasn't what he meant to start with.

"Don't worry, I won." She grinned, but it faded as she crossed her arms over her chest and huddled into herself. "I got your text."

"Thanks for coming. I wouldn't have blamed you if you hadn't." His arms itched to pull her into a hug. But not yet. Not until they said everything they needed to say.

Not until he knew.

"I have to admit, I was surprised to get a text after last night." Her eyes searched his, even as she guarded her body with her arms. "After everything you said."

She deserved an explanation. The full story of all he'd realized at his grandfather's grave last night. All the "whys."

But they were on a time crunch.

There *was* time for an apology, though. He shifted his weight. "A lot has happened. But you need to know, I'm sorry for the way I responded last night. My father caught me off guard, and well—I fell into a pit. But that's no excuse. You were trying to do the right thing, and I stifled you."

"I was." She visibly swallowed. "And I'm sorry I was so late."

Speaking of—Noah pushed back the sleeve of his flannel shirt and checked his watch. 6:01 a.m. He grimaced.

Elisa still looked confused. "Did something else happen with Russell?"

"Yeah. Something big." He appreciated how she didn't refer to the man as his dad, but by his first name. Further regret over how he'd brushed her off washed over him. Elisa knew him—understood him.

And yet, even knowing that, he still couldn't bring himself to wrap her in his arms. He wanted to leave the same legacy of love by which his grandfather had clearly loved his grandmother. He wanted the happily ever after. The whole story.

But just because he wanted all those things and they had both apologized, didn't mean they were ready to trust each other on that level. And he couldn't let any more passionate embraces or fiery kisses cloud the issue until they were. He didn't want a repeat of their teenaged fling.

He wanted the real thing.

"I understand if you don't want to tell me." She picked at the dried icing on her jeans.

"That's not it." He shook his head as the coffee grinder behind them whirred into action. "I'll explain everything, I promise. But first—I think I figured out the final clue."

"Are you serious?" Her blue eyes flashed up at him with hope.

"It's just a hunch, but . . .." He glanced at his watch again, then at the door behind her. "We don't have much time."

"Okay." Elisa frowned. "Then why are we here?"

"Remember who said she *always* gets coffee at six o'clock and two o'clock?" Except today, apparently. It was 6:03 now. He bit back a groan.

Recognition dawned on Elisa's face. "You think the clue is at Second Story."

He nodded.

She tilted her head. "But Magnolia retail stores don't open until ten on weekdays."

"Exactly why we're here." He peered out the window behind

Elisa. No sign of Sadie. What if she didn't come? The bank opened at nine, and he had to beat his dad there.

His hopes were ticking away with each second hand movement on the clock.

"Hey! Lumberjack!"

Noah spun at Miley's bark from the counter. She gestured to the two cups of to-go coffee sitting at the pickup station before turning back to the milk frother.

"I'm assuming she means me." Maybe it was time for a wardrobe upgrade. He headed for the drinks just as he heard the front door open. He picked up their coffees, then turned back, his heart leaping at the sight of the curly-haired woman strolling inside.

Elisa, however, actually lunged. "Sadie!"

Surprised, Sadie stepped back, eyes wide, as Elisa grabbed for her. Noah rushed toward them both. The strap of Sadie's tote fell from her shoulder and the bag landed on the floor.

"Sorry." Elisa grinned sheepishly as she picked it up. "We've been waiting for you."

"How'd you know I was com—ahh. Every day at six, right?" Sadie darted her gaze between the two of them, then leaned forward. "Let me guess. Sunny weather report?"

"No, actually, cloudy." Noah held up his cup in a salute. "But we have a favor to ask . . . and the coffee is on me if you say yes."

Twenty-Six

ELISA SIPPED HER COFFEE AS SADIE unlocked the blue door of Second Story and stepped inside. Immediately, the scent of used books and incense hit Elisa's nose, followed by a waft of cinnamon. She drew a deep breath as Sadie flipped on the lights, revealing shelf after shelf of carefully organized tomes awaiting perusal.

She turned a circle, taking in the strands of twinkle lights draped over a cozy sitting area in the back corner, which boasted a set of end tables, deep armchairs, and a brightly patterned rug. A winding staircase led to the second floor loft. On a normal day, Elisa would have loved to stay and browse.

But this wasn't a normal day. In fact, it wasn't even seven o'clock in the morning and her day had already held multiple surprises. Some hard. Some good.

Some confusing.

She cast a glance at Noah, whose tense expression proved a stark contrast to the colorful children's area packed with boardgames and bean bag chairs. His apology had seemed genuine. But he hadn't moved toward her at all, hadn't touched her. Hadn't offered any hint that he was interested in more than a heartfelt apology and a desire to finish the hunt.

Maybe that was all he was after. And just like she had to surrender the diner, she needed to be okay with that too.

Even if the thought ripped at her heart more than losing the Blossom.

She shook off the melancholy. This wasn't about her right now—it was about Noah. About his grandfather. And hopefully, about a way to end this hunt and get both her and Noah what they needed.

Even if that wasn't all she wanted.

"This place is a reader's paradise." Elisa faked a bright smile at Sadie, who had been more than kind in opening early for them. "You've thought of everything."

Sadie surveyed her shop with a satisfied smile. "I certainly hope so."

Noah set his coffee on the front counter, then ambled toward one of the shelves, tilting his head back as he gazed up toward the loft. "I spent more than a few of my childhood summers pulling a wagon full of Grandpa's purchases back to the inn."

"I think Gilbert read everything in my American History section at least twice." Sadie turned a knowing glance to Noah. "You're here for that book, aren't you?"

His expression lit with hope. "You *know*?"

Elisa glanced back and forth between them. "I think you both know more than I do. What are we looking for?" Noah hadn't offered any answers on their brisk walk to the book shop, and she didn't feel she could press in front of Sadie.

"Your grandfather brought a book in a few weeks before he passed." Sadie motioned for them to follow as she led the way up the wooden staircase to the loft. "I was given strict instructions not to sell it. I thought it was a strange request at the time, but . . ." She shrugged, as if to finish her sentence with a silent "That's Gilbert."

The wooden boards creaked under their feet. Elisa shot a glance over her shoulder to check on Noah, but he didn't seem to mind this particular staircase. His gaze was fixed on the top, a man on a mission. They'd come so far since their lighthouse climb—in so many ways.

She swallowed. Not so much in others.

Sadie led them across the loft, also full of bookcases and lounge chairs, past the section marked Classics. A hanging tapestry with vibrant blue and gold threads decorated a quarter of the back wall, matching the rug tucked under the nearby reading nook. "Gilbert wanted me to keep this book safe. It was the least I could do for my favorite customer."

"Safe?" Elisa frowned. "Why not keep it in his study at the inn?"

Sadie didn't answer as she moved aside the tapestry to reveal a wall safe.

Good gravy. Elisa's eyes widened. "I guess he meant keep it *literally* safe."

Sadie shielded the keypad with her back as she punched in a code, then opened the small metal door. It groaned a little, as if it didn't get a lot of use. She shuffled through the contents, pulled a book free, and then handed it to Noah with a soft smile. "I believe this is yours."

Elisa stepped closer to Noah, her breath catching as he accepted the book. "Is that . . ."

"A collector's edition of *The Count of Monte Cristo*." Noah's fingers grazed over the brown cloth cover. "Grandpa must have known I'd eventually clean out his library. Didn't want me to miss what's inside."

He took a shuddering breath, then looked at Elisa with a little laugh. "What's potentially inside, anyway. I'm almost scared to look. If this isn't it . . . if I'm wrong." He swallowed, his eyes glassy. "So much is at stake."

Elisa started to slide her hand into the crook of his arm, then thought better of it. She kept her hands at her side, her vision misting. "You have good hunches. I believe in you."

He handed the book to her. "Do you want to do the honors?"

Elisa shook her head, pressing the brown volume back into his hands. "This is your moment. You figured this out." She smiled, hoping against hope he was right. "I'm sure the Puzzle Master would be proud."

This was it.

Noah gripped the book, hope and fear warring for top placement in his heart. His hands trembled. It had all come down to this. If he was right, what would be inside the book—a check? What if the amount wasn't substantial enough for him and Elisa to split? What if it wasn't even enough to keep his father from paying off the inn? Russell had mentioned thirty grand. If that number was even close to being the accurate balance on the mortgage, Noah might not stand a chance.

But he'd never know unless he opened it.

With a deep breath, he eased open the front cover, the faint scent of cigars wafting from the pages. How many times had he seen Grandpa nestled in his favorite armchair in the study with this exact book open on his lap?

Nothing was tucked inside the front cover. He flipped to the back. Nothing there either. He gently fanned a few pages. The last quarter of the novel felt different, and he flipped slower.

There. A thin envelope with his name scrawled on the front in familiar script.

Noah.

He swallowed. This would have been one of the last things his grandfather ever wrote. He closed his eyes, then pulled the envelope free and handed the book to Elisa.

She hugged it to her chest, eyes wide and lit with pride as she smiled. "Open it."

Sadie cleared her throat and took a step back, busying herself with closing up the safe. Giving them privacy. Noah tugged his finger under the envelope flap, opening it as he moved toward the reading nook.

Several handwritten pages, front and back, filled the envelope. He looked inside for a check. Cash. Some kind of bond, maybe.

But there was nothing else.

Noah frowned, then started to read.

My dear boy,

If you're reading this, that means I'm dead. Ha! I always wanted to start a letter that way. So mysterious, right?

Noah snort-laughed, then swallowed. Man, he missed him.

I might wish I was still there, but probably not. I'm not afraid of death. Not anymore. I grew away from the church, but these last several years, I've found my way back to the Lord. I hope you're doing the same. (If you're not, you should.)

You're probably a bit confused why I arranged the hunt the way I did. But you know I've never been predictable, and I couldn't bear to start postmortem. I intend to share with you my greatest treasure.

The first of which is my faith, already mentioned. It had to be first. Do me a big favor, and keep it first in your life, too. I wish I'd done that from the get-go, but better late than never, I suppose.

The second treasure is one I grasped much later in life than I should have. Which is where Elisa comes in.

Noah looked up and motioned for Elisa to join him. "This is for you, too."

She immediately came to read over his shoulder.

Elisa Bergeron, I owe you an apology. Yes, this old man can still say those words. Better late than never, hopefully. I let my pride and my stubbornness keep a feud alive between our families that should have ended decades prior. Your father should have never been my enemy. The Good Book talks about vengeance being the Lord's, and like Dantés, I had to learn that the hard way.

Both of our families mistreated the other for years, and it accomplished nothing good. Division, hatred, and envy never bring forth anything beautiful, and those are the rotten fruits I produced and sincerely regret. I invited you into the search because I wanted to right some of these wrongs.

Noah glanced at Elisa. Her lips moved slightly as she continued to read, her cheeks flushed.

Noah, I apologize to you as well. I did something years ago that created more division that I'm not proud of. The summer you were eighteen, I sent those letters to the inn, warning you away from Elisa.

He sucked in his breath. Elisa must have read the same line at the same time, as she jerked her head up. Guilt pricked. "I'm sorry, Elisa. I just assumed it was your father . . ."

Assumption. Prejudice. All the things his family had been guilty of for years.

The things his grandfather humbly tried to correct.

Elisa chewed on her bottom lip. "There's so much I need to tell you. My father and I talked last night—he's sorry for a lot of things, too." She pointed to the letter. "But first things first."

I let you think it was Isaac Bergeron, and that was wrong. I know you must be surprised, and it's all right if you're mad at me. (I probably won't know if you are, which helps.) I saw how close you and Elisa were getting, and I panicked. I didn't want to confront you directly, because I also knew how much you valued my opinion. Frankly, I was scared that would change if I shared it.

So instead, I went behind your back like a coward and betrayed your trust. And I regret it deeply. Maybe I'm still being a coward, only telling you this in a letter. But Noah, you were and are forever one of the best things I was ever granted in this life. I needed to go into the next one knowing that we were okay.

Tears pressed hard into his throat. Noah looked up at the ceiling, trying to swallow around the knot. He couldn't stay mad—not when he'd have probably done the same thing. When the emotion passed, he coughed and looked back on the page.

I hope all the time you and Elisa spent together solving the clues restored what I broke. (I realize I didn't go easy on you with this hunt, but rest assured, August was instructed to give you this letter, even if you failed.)

"Bless it." Elisa pressed her lips to her fingers. "We'd have gotten it anyway."

If you did find this letter the way I intended, make sure to tell August. This is probably not at all what you expected to find when I sent you on a treasure hunt, but here's what's important to remember, my boy.

The greatest treasures in life are as follows: Faith. Family. Forgiveness. (Also love, but that threw off my alliteration.) Hold these close, my boy. Never let them go.

Matthew 6:21, For where your treasure is, there your heart will be also.

With all my love,
Grandpa Gilbert

Noah slowly lowered the letter as a heady silence pulsed through the loft. At some point, Sadie had slipped downstairs, giving them further privacy.

"Wow." Elisa handed him back the book. "Just wow."

"Yeah." He didn't know what to think first. Apologies. Betrayal. Mysteries solved. He didn't expect to be this sad. But this was the last thing he'd ever receive from his grandfather. There would be no more surprises. As frustrating as the clues had been, they were over now.

It all felt so final.

He met Elisa's worried gaze, speaking what she clearly wasn't saying. "I know." Both of them had expected a monetary reward.

But one thing didn't make sense. "If there's no physical treasure, why would he throw that surprise timeline on us to finish in a week?" Noah asked.

"He said he liked to be unpredictable." Elisa offered a shrug. "Maybe it was just a tactic to keep us working together?"

Maybe. He might never know now, unless August could fill in those blanks. A sudden weight pressed on his chest. As much as he appreciated his grandfather's words, as much as he would treasure them—he couldn't help the rush of disappointment.

He was going to lose the inn.

Twenty-Seven

ELISA PRESSED THE DOORBELL ON AU-gust Bowman's ranch-style brick house and stepped back. The morning breeze tickled her hair, and she wished she'd brought the denim jacket still tucked under the counter at the Blossom. It'd only been a little over an hour since she left the diner to meet Noah at Chug a Mug, and she felt like she'd lived two lifetimes since then.

Noah shifted his weight on the step beside her. "Remind me again why we're bothering this man this early in the morning?"

"Because you said the banks open at nine. We need to make *sure* that we didn't miss something." Elisa leaned sideways to look inside the front window. "After what you told me on the way here about Russell's plans, I'm not letting the Blue Pirogue go down without a fight."

He dipped his head toward her. "Or the Magnolia Blossom."

Elisa's stomach twisted. "I think that ship has already sunk. Delia's pretty set on selling, and now there's no money for me to convince her otherwise." She drew a deep breath. "But August is a lawyer. Maybe he'll know something we can do to stop Russell from moving forward. There has to be another loophole."

The door opened, revealing a slightly disheveled August wearing a bathrobe and slippers. He peered at them before pulling his glasses from his robe pocket. "Noah? Elisa? What are you two doing here?" He checked his wrist, then must have realized he wasn't wearing a watch. "Did I miss an appointment?"

"No, sir." Noah stepped forward. "We came to tell you we finished the hunt—and to discuss a bit of an emergency."

"Oh, dear. Come in, come in." August ushered them inside the wood-paneled front room. "Have a seat, anywhere. I'll let my wife know you're here and put on the coffee."

Several minutes later, Noah and Elisa sat on the floral-printed sofa while August, now changed into his typical work attire of a dress shirt and suit jacket, perched on the armchair near the fireplace. A thick folder lay in his lap. "So . . . you read the letter."

Noah leaned forward. "Yes, sir. And we realize there's not a monetary treasure like we'd expected. Which would be fine, except I was counting on having money for the inn. The mold mitigation that's underway is potentially going to put me under before I can even open for tourist season. And now, I don't know if you've heard . . . my father came back to town."

August peered at them over the top of his glasses. "Oh, I heard." He sniffed in disapproval. "And I'm terribly sorry."

Elisa always knew she liked August. She started to touch Noah reassuringly on the back, then remembered their fragile status. She kept her hands in her lap, twisting the ring on her finger. "Tell him the rest."

"Russell is trying to take over the Blue Pirogue while laying low from some guy in California." A muscle in Noah's jaw flexed. "That's his problem. But I can't let him take the inn." He quickly explained the situation with the mortgage and how Russell was going to be at the bank to pay off the loan and claim the deed as soon as they opened. "We have less than an hour."

"Well, we'll just see about that." August flipped through the large folder. "Lucky for you, I keep duplicates of client paperwork in my home office. You finished the hunt, so, first of all—congratulations! I was instructed to give you a copy of the letter you've already read, just in case, but you didn't need the cheat. I applaud your efforts." His gaze drifted to Elisa. "Both of you. Well done."

"It was harder than I anticipated." Noah's jaw tensed again. "The hunt, *and* reaching the end. Knowing it's all over now."

"Losing a loved one is hard." August's voice gentled as he leaned forward, his arms braced against the open folder. "I know." He included Elisa once more in his steady gaze. "Your mother was quite the magnolia blossom, herself, if I do recall."

Fondness, tinged with grief, rose in Elisa's chest. She nodded, searching for words. "She was." Maybe Elisa was going to lose the diner, but that wasn't the only place her mother's memory lived on. Her warmth and light and influence lingered right here in Magnolia Bay—in the hearts of the people she'd loved.

Maybe she and her mother never got to open their own restaurant or take culinary classes abroad. But the memories they had shared were ones that would never be sold or demolished. And Elisa could carry them into whatever she did next.

It could be more exciting than sad, if she let it be.

"She would be proud of you, I'm quite sure." August sat up straight and shuffled through the pages before him. "Now, where were we? Ah, yes." He held up another sheet of paper. "You were saying it's all over now. But I'm afraid that's the one part you got wrong."

A wave of hope crested over Elisa. "What do you mean?" She looked at Noah, who had grown still.

August pushed his glasses up on his nose. "There's a check to be written."

Noah waxed pale. "A check?"

It wasn't over. Forgetting their unresolved status, Elisa grabbed Noah's hand and squeezed.

"Absolutely." August offered a brisk nod. "Quite a substantial one, at that. The check will be written to Noah, but you two are free to split it however you choose. Gilbert didn't specify who got what—I believe at this stage in the hunt, he trusted you both to do the right thing."

Tears shone in Noah's eyes. "I guess there was still a surprise left, after all." He shook his head. "Well played, Grandpa."

"He did write in the letter that he never wanted to be predictable." Elisa tried not to notice how Noah's fingers threaded through hers and held on. Tried not to let it matter. But oh, it did.

August patted his pocket and retrieved a pen. "Here we are." He meticulously filled in the check's various fields. "And here you are." He handed the check to Noah.

Whose face immediately fell.

The morning had held so many highs and lows, Noah was starting to feel seasick. He looked down at the slip of paper in his hands, the one that was supposed to fix everything, and fought back the sigh threatening escape.

The amount wasn't enough for both he and Elisa to have what they needed. In fact, it would barely cover the amount still due on the mortgage. It definitely wouldn't cover the mold mitigation on top of that.

Or leave anything for Delia.

Noah closed his eyes, his heart hammering in his chest. He had to give the money to Elisa. Delia's health, the diner . . . those were valuable to not only Elisa, but the entire town. This money would surely cover Delia's medical bills and let her keep her livelihood. Let Elisa keep her dream. Her connection to her mother.

It was the right thing to do.

He opened his eyes, folded the check in half, and held out Elisa's hand. "Here." He closed her fingers around it. "Do what you need to do."

"Noah!" She gasped, then immediately started shaking her head. "No. You can't."

"I can, and I will. You heard him." Noah gestured toward August, who watched them quietly with hands folded on the file. "Grandpa trusted us to do the right thing. That's what this is."

"I can't let you lose the Blue Pirogue." She shoved the check toward him. "This is your grandfather's money."

Noah dodged her attempt. "That he chose to do with as he pleased. And now so am I."

"Noah, you don't understand. I'll be fine." Her gaze turned pleading. She scooted closer to him on the couch and pressed the paper against his chest, holding it there against his heart. "I've come to terms with this. Delia is going to be okay—she's got several potential buyers interested in the Blossom. If this hunt has taught me anything, it's about what's most valuable in life."

August leaned forward in his chair, eyes attentive.

Elisa's hand slipped on Noah's chest, and the check drifted to his lap. "I can't let you lose your grandfather's legacy because of me." She swallowed, pressing her now-empty hands to her cheeks. "You're more important than my memories." She let loose a little half laugh, half cry. "You're some of my best ones."

Noah picked up the check, his chest burning from the lingering imprint of her touch. He stared at her in awe. *This* was the woman he'd been afraid to trust? The one insisting she kill her own dream so his could live? The one sacrificing herself and her desires for him—because she genuinely believed that was the right thing to do?

He'd assumed the worst again, like his family had always done. But he could break that curse, right here and now. By trusting Elisa.

He searched her eyes, all his feelings for her rising to a crescendo in his chest. How had he been so scared before? He'd do a dozen more hunts with her and for her. He'd climb a dozen more lighthouses. Heck, he'd go to the moon if she wanted, heights and all.

"I mean it." She whispered now, her eyes glassy with unshed tears. "This check is yours. I've gotten what I needed."

"Elisa . . ." He couldn't stand it anymore. He reached out and touched her cheek. The tears slipped over, dripping down her chin. If August hadn't been sitting mere feet away, he'd have kissed it away. "I don't deserve you."

"Finally something you and my father agree on." She grinned through the tears, reaching up and taking his hand in hers as they laughed. She threaded their fingers together, then tucked their joined hands against her cheek.

Emotion clogged the words he wanted so badly to say. He loved this woman. He'd loved her every day since he was eighteen. It was true then, and it was true now—only deeper. Wider. All-encompassing. He stared into her blue eyes, memorizing their depths.

They felt like home.

"Maybe I'll pour another cup of coffee." August lurched to his feet. "Take your time."

Noah only noticed his exit through his peripheral because he couldn't stop staring at Elisa. "Last chance on the money. Are you sure?"

"Positive." She briefly pressed her lips against his knuckles on their joined hands. "I have full faith it's the right thing to do."

"I'm pretty sure something else is the right thing, too. Something I was too afraid to say earlier this morning." Noah traced her cheekbone with one finger before letting his free hand settle into the ends of her hair. "Will you give me another chance? Officially?"

"I've heard about those Hebert men." Elisa leaned in closer. "You know, about how persistent they are. Never quit, that bunch. I don't think I have a choice." She batted her lashes at him.

Her words, while playful, settled like a balm over his heart. "Very persistent, I think. Especially when we see something we want." His gaze landed on her lips, which curved into an immediate smile.

Curse broken.

He leaned toward her just as his phone rang, startling them both. He reluctantly pulled away and checked the ID.

Sadie. He winced. "I should probably get this." Sadie had agreed to keep the book in her store's safe until he could come back for it later. He didn't need to tote it to the bank unprotected.

Which reminded him . . . he checked his watch.

Thirty minutes 'til nine. "Do me a favor? Hold that thought you were just having"—he grinned at her—"and go let August know we've got to leave."

"Hello?" He pocketed the check as he answered, unable to keep himself from watching Elisa as she headed for the kitchen.

"Noah." Sadie's voice sounded serious, snatching his full attention. "I'm so glad I caught you."

He stood. "Is everything okay?"

At the question, Elisa paused by the kitchen door, eyes raised as she waited.

"After you left, something kept niggling at me." Sadie's words raced faster. "You called the book a collector's edition."

"Right." Noah frowned. "Grandpa's favorite." He motioned for Elisa to continue on her quest. They had to get to the bank before Russell.

Sadie's anxious tone pierced his ear. "Noah, it's not a collector's edition."

He headed for the front door, patting his pocket for his keys. "What do you mean?"

"This copy is a first edition."

What? He jerked to a stop as the potential implications raced through his head. "Does that change the value?"

"Oh yeah." Sadie let out a laugh. "Adds a few zeroes."

His mouth went dry. "You've got to be kidding me."

"I never joke about literature."

He believed her.

"Listen, Noah. Your grandfather was like extended family. Let me keep the book in my safe and put out feelers at a few upcoming auctions for you. Free of charge."

It was a generous offer. But . . . Noah rolled in his lip.

Sadie persisted. "I could probably make something happen in a few weeks, max."

He hesitated. Could he really sell Grandpa's favorite book? The one that had soaked up more of his grandfather's time and memory than any other novel in that library? The one that had captured Grandpa's attention and helped mold him into the man he'd become—the man he'd tried to teach Noah to become?

Then he took one look at Elisa, rushing from the kitchen in her icing-smeared jeans, and he knew he could. Knew that was exactly what Grandpa would have wanted—an end to the feud. A big gesture. Heberts helping Bergerons.

After what Elisa had just done for him, how could he not?

Elisa stopped in front of him, her mouth forming a silent *is everything okay?*

Sadie cleared her throat. "Would that be okay?"

Noah cleared his throat, turning back toward the phone. "Absolutely not."

Silence filled the line. Then—"I'd really like to do this for you. For your grandfather."

"Oh, you can. But you're not doing it for free." Noah broke into a smile, which Elisa matched even though she had no idea what was going on yet. He couldn't wait to see her smile once she did. "You'll get a fair commission on whatever you bring in, and that's a non-negotiable."

Sadie's delighted cry still echoed in his ear as he ended the call and shot Owen a text.

Sadie
_____

Headed your way. 💰

Then he looped an arm around Elisa's waist and pulled her in close. Her breath caught, and he knew the feeling. He pressed a quick kiss against her lips, then rested his forehead on hers as joy flooded his soul. Deep as the bay. Endless as the ocean. "Call Mama D. Tell her not to sell the diner."

Twenty-Eight

ELISA RUSHED TO THE DINER AS NOAH rushed to the bank. Delia hadn't answered her phone, and now Elisa was worried she might have fallen with her walker. At least the waitstaff would be there by now. Still...

She hurried inside the packed café, nearly bumping into Trish, who crossed in front of the door with a tray full of pancakes. She barely saved the tray from tipping over. "Whoa, where's the fire?"

"Don't even joke about fire." Elisa glanced around the crowded café. "Where's Mama D?" There was so much to tell her, she thought she might burst.

"Table twelve. I just convinced her to sit down—she was in the kitchen, trying to 'put love into the pancake batter.'" Trish smirked, shifting the tray to her other hand. "Where have you been?"

"That's a long story." Elisa sniffed the bacon-scented air. "Wait a second. I got everything set up earlier for breakfast, but who's handling the hot orders?"

"Lucius, actually."

"*What*?" Elisa started for the kitchen, her chest tight. "He came back? Did you call the cops?"

WHERE I FOUND YOU

Trish followed with her tray. "He didn't steal. Had an airtight alibi—the police confirmed it when they brought him in for questioning."

Was *anything* as it seemed today? Elisa pushed through the swinging doors into the kitchen and there was Lucius, wearing an apron and happily flipping pancakes. What in the world . . .

"I've got to get these plates to table five." Trish backed out of the kitchen. "I'm sure Mama D can explain everything."

Good gravy, she'd almost forgotten why she'd rushed there in the first place. The wonder of the morning—and her new questions—drove Elisa's feet to table twelve. Mama D sat with her back to the wall, her walker propped beside the booth as she sipped a glass of orange juice.

Elisa plopped onto the seat opposite her. "You have some explaining to do."

"Lucius is a good boy." Delia adjusted her necklace. "The only thing he's guilty of is not locking up behind him when he rushed out of here last week. Someone else stole the pans while the diner was unlocked. I already talked to Sheriff Rubart, told him to reopen the case, but he said it's unlikely we'll get a lead at this point."

"I don't understand. If that's true, then where did Lucius vanish to?"

"Apparently his mother had called—they live in Florida. His father was in the hospital, heart attack, I think he said. In his panic, he just left. His phone died, but he thought the text he sent me went through. It never did." Delia shrugged. "He deserves another chance."

"I feel so bad I assumed." Elisa shook her head. "There seems to be a lot of that going around today."

"You've been gone several hours—is Noah okay?" Delia moved her juice cup aside and rested her arms on the table. "Are you two okay?"

"Better than okay. We finished the hunt." Her face flushed. "You should have seen the letter Gilbert wrote."

"I'd love to read it one day." Delia's voice gentled. "Does Noah have what he needs now?"

"He does. He's at the bank as we speak, trying to save the inn from his father. But there's more." Elisa sucked in a tight breath. Here went nothing. "I'm paying for your surgery."

Delia blinked at her.

"I know you're going to argue, but we don't have time for all that. Remember, I can always go to the admin office at Magnolia Memorial and handle it while you're sedated." Elisa pointed at her. "I'm doing this."

Delia raised her chin. "Gibberish. You young people don't make sense anymore."

"No, you're just pretending you don't understand because you don't want me to do it. But I don't care. I've come into some money and this is what I'm going to do."

"From the treasure hunt?"

She hesitated. "Not just from the hunt. It's a long story."

"Elisa Bergeron, if you robbed the bank, so help me I'll—"

"Of course not." She held up one hand. "I should be able to cut you a check in a few weeks, max. The hospital will take that long to send you the first bill, anyway."

"*Hmph.* I don't know about this." Delia leaned back in the booth, her eyes assessing.

"Full disclosure—this was my plan all along. It's why the hunt was so important to me." Elisa lowered her voice as one of the busboys walked past with a tray. "I was going to use whatever inheritance Mr. Hebert left to help you. I just didn't tell you because I knew you wouldn't take it."

Delia leveled her with a stare. "You knew right."

"But you're the one who has always encouraged me to stand

up for myself. To be honest about what I want, to communicate. So . . ." Elisa wiggled her hands in the air like a magician. "Ta-da."

Delia didn't move, just watched, her lips twitching. Her silence was more unnerving than her protests.

Elisa let her hands fall to the table. "Don't you get it? I can pay for your surgery. You don't have to sell the diner now."

"I'm afraid I still do." Delia ran one finger around the rim of her juice glass, avoiding Elisa's gaze.

"Why?" Her chest tightened. After all that...why had she gotten her hopes up? She'd finally come to terms with losing the Blossom, just for Noah to present it back to her on a silver platter. Now this.

Elisa swallowed the string of protests she knew would be futile. "To who?"

Delia lifted her gaze and met Elisa's eyes. A tiny smirk crossed her lips. "I'm looking at her."

"Me?" Elisa jabbed her finger into her chest so hard it hurt. She rubbed the offended spot. "What are you talking about?"

Delia's wise old eyes sharpened. "What do you say we work out a trade? This money you say you've got, for the title to the Blossom?"

"But Mama D—"

"I'm old, honey. I didn't want to lose the Blossom any more than you did, but I'm kidding myself if I think I'm going to come back to cook full time after a hip replacement. Even if it wasn't for the money issue, I'd have been thinking about letting it go."

Her words washed over Elisa. She was right. Of course she was right. But the Blossom without Delia . . .

"I'd like the downtime. Maybe I could start a new hobby, or finally have some time to read. Been wanting to check out this Charles Martin fellow I keep hearing about." She squeezed Elisa's hand. "If you own the diner, I'm not losing a single thing. It's a win-win."

"But I can't afford the Blossom. I'm sure you would have gotten a lot more from a real buyer than the money I'm proposing."

"Honey, I've never wanted to be rich a day in my life. I've got plenty of retirement set back. If you cover this surgery, I'll be golden." Delia gripped her hand harder. "The least I can do in return is give you the deed to the place you helped create. You and your sweet mama."

Tears throbbed behind Elisa's eyes. She pressed her fingers to her lips, holding back the wave of emotion. Earlier that morning, she had slowly come to terms with not only losing the diner, but potentially losing her job. Now . . . the Blossom could be hers?

Talk about a midnight miracle.

"I accept." She drew in a shaky breath. "On one condition."

Amusement sparked in Delia's eyes. "Look at you, being a shrewd business owner already."

"I accept *if* you're on payroll."

Delia waved one hand in the air. "Again, with the gibberish."

"You might not be cooking full time or even up here every day, but the Blossom will still need you." Elisa reached over and took Delia's weathered hands. "I still need you."

Delia squeezed her fingers. "The feeling is mutual, my dear."

She casually let go and brushed her hair back. "Besides, you'll have to teach me and Lucius more about how to put love into your recipes."

"You and Lucius?" Delia tilted her head. "But you haven't wanted to cook in years!"

"Now Delia, I thought we said we weren't going to keep assuming." Elisa shot her a wink, then sobered. "I think it's time I put some of me and mom's recipes to good use."

"She'd be so proud. Almost as much as me." Delia started sliding out of the bench seat. "Get over here so I can hug you properly. Are you going to make a crippled old lady walk to you?"

Elisa grinned as Delia lumbered to her feet. She met her beside the table, and Delia wrapped Elisa in an embrace that smelled like syrup and baby powder and all things home. She'd lost her mother young, but God had provided love where she needed it most. Just like Noah—he'd not had a father growing up, but Grandpa Gilbert had been there to fill in the gaps.

Love abounding. Miracles abounding. What had the letter said? Faith. Family. Forgiveness. They went all together. And it was truly the greatest treasure of all.

More tears—how did she have any left at this point?—slipped down Elisa's cheeks. "Love you, Mama D," she whispered.

"And you, dear one." Delia pulled back and patted her cheek, then sniffed. "Now. Hand me that blasted walker, and let's get to the bank. We need to see how your boy is doing."

Noah leaned against the exterior wall of the bank, slurping his second coffee of the day. Apparently Miley had cheered up during the morning, because this batch was almost undrinkable. But the bitter taste did little to ruin his mood. The spring sun was shining, the birds were chirping, and the deed to the Blue Pirogue burned a hole in his back pocket.

Humming, Noah propped one leg up behind him and checked his watch. 9:05 a.m. Any minute now . . . He took another sip, then debated pouring the coffee into the grass. Nah. He needed the caffeine.

A sleek sports car pulled up and parked on the curb. His father got out, wearing a fitted sports jacket and whistling. Then he gave Noah a double-take as he stepped toward the bank. "What are you doing here?"

Noah took another slow sip. "I live here." Those words tasted much better than the coffee. He said them again, trying them out. He lived in Magnolia Bay.

Yep, absolutely delicious.

Russell rolled his eyes. "If you're here hoping to change my mind, you might as well start the tantrum now. I've got business to handle."

Not anymore. Noah smiled. "For the record, you were wrong."

"Doubtful." Russell reached past Noah for the door handle. "If you'll excuse me . . ."

Noah kept talking. "The balance owed on the mortgage wasn't thirty grand. It was twenty-eight five." He offered a casual shrug. "I was given change."

Russell's hand dropped from the door and he stared at Noah. "What are you talking about?"

"Told you I was going to beat you here." Noah stepped forward, pulling the paperwork from his pocket. He tapped Russell on the shoulder with it. "You lose."

Russell scoffed. "That's ridiculous. You can't just assume ownership of a property by paying—"

"When there's a will stating otherwise, I can. Worst case, it'll come down to a judge. The Hebert name might not be golden in this town, but that's because of *you*." He tapped him again. "Not me. So I think I know which way the judge would lean."

Russell shoved the paperwork away and squared his shoulders. "There's no way I'm going to let—"

"Also, Grandpa's lawyer knows a probate attorney in the next parish over who owes him a favor. The guy already said he'd be happy to take the case if you want to start a suit to stop me." Noah grinned. "But I've heard that's expensive."

Russell's eyes narrowed to slits. "This isn't over."

"You're right." Noah tucked the document back into his pocket and crossed his arms. "It's not over—but it can be different." He gentled his tone. "Better."

"What are you talking about?" Russell glanced over his shoulder at a sudden din of voices drifting toward them down the sidewalk.

"I'm talking about giving you another chance. You can stay in town if you want, help me out at the inn for awhile." The idea had hit him about ten minutes ago while signing the papers with Owen, and it still surprised him. But it was the right thing to do. *Faith. Family. Forgiveness.* The last part didn't come naturally, but if Grandpa could do it, so could Noah.

"You're delusional if you think I'm going to work for you. Don't you know what I do for a living?" Russell spat on the sidewalk, then looked behind him again as the rush of voices grew louder. "What the heck?"

Noah followed Russell's stare to the crowd heading their way down the sidewalk. Was that—he blinked. Yep, it was Elisa, beaming, as she walked beside Mama D, who moved her walker with surprising speed. Half the waitstaff from the diner paraded around them, still wearing aprons.

They drew closer. Sheriff Rubart was with them, too, *not* scowling for once. And Linc, who was. Cade, wearing an electric blue tie that could be seen a mile away. Then there was Zoey, who toted a pastry box from her shop, walking beside Pastor Dubois and Isaac Bergeron. Even Farmer Branson ambled along, a bacon strip poking out of his front pocket.

They all came to a stop, surrounding Noah. He took in all their faces, an overwhelming sense of belonging welling in his chest. "What are you guys doing?"

Elisa slipped her arm through his. "I wasn't sure how this meeting was going to go, so Mama D and I brought backup."

"We're here for you." Delia scooted her walker closer to Noah. "You're one of us, you know. Always have been."

His throat knotted. Noah wrapped his arm around Elisa and pulled her in close. "You got everyone here—for me?"

"Of course." She smiled up at him before twisting her head toward Russell, who had been forced back toward the curb. "Lucky for you, we didn't have time to grab pitchforks." She glared.

Zoey popped her head out from behind Farmer Branson. "For

the record, I saw what was going on between you and Elisa before Elisa did." She grinned and held out her pastry box. "Beignet?"

Farmer Branson immediately turned to take one.

"So you're staying, right?" Cade pushed his way through the group. "You got the deed? Ohhh, beignets." He helped himself.

Russell glared. "This town is crazy." He cursed under his breath. "I'll take my chances in California. But I said what I said—this isn't over."

"I'm pretty sure it is." Sheriff rose to his full height as he started toward Russell. "You can join up and shape up, or you can get lost. Choice is yours."

"Fine." Russell lifted both hands as he eased toward his car. "I don't want that money pit of an inn, anyway. Keep it." Then he got in and peeled off, tires squealing. The group around him cheered.

Noah watched his father leave, until the only evidence he'd ever been there was the tread marks on the road. He looked down at Elisa and clutched her a little tighter. "I guess some things never change."

Isaac appeared beside Noah and clamped his hand on his shoulder. "And some things do." He held his gaze. "Man to man, I'm sorry. My brilliant daughter here helped me see some things I'd been blinded to, and—well, I'd like to buy you some coffee. Talk about it further."

Apparently things did change. But not the important things. *Faith. Family. Forgiveness.*

Noah's gaze darted over the group. At Farmer Branson, who'd sprinkled his beignet with crumbled pieces of bacon. At Linc, who swatted away Zoey's attempts to brush powdered sugar off his shirt. At Cade, who had snatched Mama D's walker and now hobbled circles around her.

At the beautiful woman beaming up at him, love pouring from her eyes.

He locked gazes with Elisa and smiled. Maybe this wasn't the family he'd been hoping to make amends with, but it was a family. *His* family.

He tore his eyes from Elisa to answer her dad. "You've got a deal. Coffee it is." Noah shook Isaac's outstretched hand, then grinned. "As long as it's not today. It's much too sunny over at Chug a Mug."

Isaac laughed as he backed away. "Fair." He pointed at Elisa. "I'll see you later, honey."

She nodded. "Dinner tonight?"

"Yep. Bring Noah. We'll celebrate the Blue Pirogue . . . and its rightful ownership." Isaac's smile lingered on Noah. "See you then."

Grandpa had done it. The feud was over.

The crowd slowly began to disperse. Noah thanked everyone for their support as Elisa snagged one last beignet from Zoey's box.

They were finally alone on the sidewalk. Elisa bit into the dessert, leaving a touch of sugar on her lip. She licked it off.

"You're a messy eater. First with the pizza, now this." Noah wrapped his arms around her, tugging her to his side. Thankfully Sheriff Rubart was gone, because Noah fully intended to kiss this woman in public again.

"I'm not worried. You're a pro treasure hunter now." She dipped her finger on top of the remaining beignet, then with a sassy grin, drew on her cheek with the powder. "X marks the spot, right, *sugar*?"

He pressed a kiss onto the powdered target. "You missed." Then he lowered his head until his lips grazed hers. She kissed him back, her sugary fingers coming up to wind around his neck. He didn't mind at all.

He was finally home.

Read on for more from the

Magnolia Bay

series

No Place Like Home

BETSY ST. AMANT

The girl he always loved ran away to join...the circus. But will a homecoming give him a second chance at giving her a reason to stay in this unrequited love romance?

Magnolia Bay's development director, Cade Landry, would do anything for his town—and his family. So when the mayor—who also happens to be his father—decides to retire, he talks Cade into running for his seat. But Cade is already up to his dimpled cheeks in the town's post-hurricane revitalization fundraiser—Magnolia Days, featuring a flashy Cajun Circus. If Cade can't put the bay back on the map as a tourist town, he'll let the whole community down...and worse yet, his father.

Rosalyn Dupree is a famous aerialist with a secret—actually, quite a few of them. Much to Cade's relief, she agrees to return to Magnolia Bay for the first time in years as a headliner for the Cajun Circus. But neither her charming former school rival Cade nor her parents know she's broke, in debt, and nursing a back injury...among other things. She'd love to move back to the bay for good, but the beloved sport that used to let her fly has become her cage.

Despite her best efforts at resisting, sparks fly between Cade and Rosalyn as they work together on the circus fundraiser. But when everyone's secrets are revealed and worlds collide, will Rosalyn find forgiveness and restoration in a town being rebuilt? Or will there never be anywhere to truly call home?

One

I F A GUY HAD TO EAT A FEW FROG LEGS to save the family legacy, Cade Landry better find a bib.

Still..."Frog leg food truck, you say?" Cade leaned back in his desk chair in the mayor's office building in downtown Magnolia Bay and propped his brown Sperrys on the desk. The phone cord snagged against the overflowing bin of papers awaiting his attention, knocking half the stack onto a red folder that teetered before dropping. More papers fluttered to their freedom.

He closed his eyes—would that make the mess go away?—as the Cajun drawl continued in his ear.

"That's right. I heard about that Magnolia Days festival you got going on end of the month, thought we could snag a spot." The man who'd introduced himself as Bruno, and who Cade imagined *had* to be tanned and burly, cleared his throat. "Best in Louisiana, we are."

"Uh-huh." Was that a flex though? How many frog leg restaurants could there even be on the mainland?

Then again...Cade squinted at the open spreadsheet of vendors thus far committed to Magnolia Days—and at the multiple empty rows that had been full just two years ago. Before the hurricane. Before the annual festival had taken a nosedive, and with it, the much needed funding for his beloved city still undergoing storm restoration.

Could he afford to be picky? His secret weapon for the festival had ghosted his emails. Two months and still no answer. Cade reached over and clicked refresh on his computer, hoping for a miracle.

Nope.

And now he was going to be late to meet with the balloon arch lady. "Listen, Mr...."

"Guidry. Bruno Guidry, at your service." *Clang.*

That sounded like a stockpot lid. Was he cooking the legs as they spoke? Cade grimaced, fighting the irrational urge to pinch his nose shut. "Look, I'm sure they're great—as far as frog legs go—but I'm looking for crawfish meat pies. Shrimp tacos. Cajun biscuits. Beignets."

"Tell you what," Bruno said. *Clang-clang.* "Why don't you come up to New Orleans for a tastin'?"

Cade swallowed, smoothed the front of his fitted button-down. "Um..."

His office door, cracked as usual so it didn't jam when summer heat swelled the wood, swung all the way open to reveal his father's secretary, Pearl. She fanned herself with an envelope as she clutched the neck of her floral blouse with her free hand. "Miley is here."

Without waiting for an invitation, Miley Mitchell, the twenty-something barista from Chug a Mug, pressed past Cade's overheated receptionist and plopped into the chair adjacent his desk. She wore fishnet leggings under denim shorts, an oversized men's button-down with the sleeves rolled up, and a sullen expression. He jotted the word *latte* on a notepad—the coffee would be good today.

But probably not the pending conversation.

He raised his eyebrows at her as he leaned back in his chair. "What now?"

Clang. "No, you don't have to come now. Anytime next week works."

"Oh, sorry. Not you, Bruno." Cade held up a finger at Miley as Pearl slipped back into the hallway. "I'm actually not sure I can get to New Orleans at all—"

"He can't. He's busy." Miley cupped her hands and talked loudly toward the receiver. "Fixing potholes."

"No, we don't sell tadpoles." Bruno sounded confused. "Frog legs don't work that way."

Oh, for Pete's sake. Cade's feet hit the floor as he lurched forward. "Just a second, Bruno. I'm putting you on a brief *hold.*" Not pole. Or hole. He jabbed the red button on the phone base and gave Miley his full attention. "You were saying?"

A second line rang. His cell buzzed. Cade ignored both.

Miley gestured, black nail polish contrasting her white skin. "I sent in a request to meet with you."

He looked at his chaotic desk. "When?"

She hiked a dark eyebrow. "This mess is organized by date?"

Fair point. He rummaged a little, carefully. Miley leaned over and rescued the red folder from the floor. "Man. You need an assistant."

He snorted as he continued to fruitlessly dig. "I *am* the assistant." The framed diploma on the wall behind Miley taunted him—Yale Law. Ha. And look at him now. Working for Dad, being the face of Magnolia Bay. He'd probably shaken more hands and kissed more babies than his mayor father.

"I can't find it." Giving up, Cade reached in the top desk drawer and rustled around for the bag of M&Ms he'd stashed. At least he knew where those were. "I don't know why my father thought making me town director was a good idea."

Miley thumbed through the folder's contents. "It *was* a good idea—three years ago. Maybe you've outgrown the job." She narrowed her eyes. "Sort of like your workload has outgrown your desk."

"I like my job." Besides, the only place to go in small-town politics was *up*. And he certainly wouldn't be taking on the role of mayor anytime soon. He ripped the bag of candy and palmed a cluster into his mouth. "The festival is just...a lot. More pressure this year."

"Found it." Miley tossed the folder toward him. It landed on his desk calendar, which still showed last month. "There's a chocolate stain on the corner."

That was probably from the Twix he'd inhaled last week while crunching numbers—more red than black. He picked up the meeting request. "What's the big deal? We've always had potholes." The phone blinked, indicating Frog Legs still waited for an answer. And he'd never gotten a quote for the extra festival chairs. Had he confirmed the porta-potties?

Miley snapped her fingers in front of her own face. "Hey, right here. Focus."

He zeroed in, though the blinking red light of the phone still teased his peripheral vision. So many things to do. The festival was in less than a month. He fisted another bite of candy, chewed fast.

"Have you seriously not noticed the potholes have gotten worse?" Miley crossed her arms over her chest. "Take a walk and check them out sometime. That storm last month apparently finished what the hurricane started. And let's just say my dad's not happy about the crater in front of Chug a Mug. He says it's deterring customers."

Miley's mood swings were more likely the cause of that. Still, Mr. Mitchell, the wayfaring owner of the coffee shop who occasionally swooped into the Bay to see Miley, was not someone you wanted to disappoint. Cade sighed. "You know what's ironic?"

Miley lifted one shoulder. "A duck that can't swim?"

"Well, sure." He pointed at her with the bag of candy. "But more so, the fact that everyone seems to need something that costs money, but asking for it is taking me away from planning the event that is going to bring in that money." He squinted at her. "Are you too young to know Alanis Morissette?"

She squinted back. "I feel like this is a trick question."

"Forget it. She has song about irony." Cade reached up and loosened his tie. "I am that song right now."

Miley rolled her eyes. "Regardless, Dad wants it handled. He keeps saying 'Tell whoever's in charge down there to make it top priority.'" She walked two fingers up the air on an invisible ladder.

Cade shrugged. "I'll see what I can do, but as you pointed out, there are a lot of potholes in Magnolia Bay."

"That could comfortably house a family of four?"

"I'm just saying I can't guarantee yours will be fixed first—or any of them right now. We're trying to *earn* money, not spend more of it."

"You really think people are going to come to Magnolia Days this year?" Miley's nose ring glistened, mocking him as much as her tone. But the girl had never been cruel, just brutally honest.

He eyed the phone, the frantic flashing starting to match his heart rate. "I have a plan."

"Hope it's not buried on your desk."

It might be the only thing that wasn't. Cade threw the empty candy bag into the trashcan full of gum wrappers and crinkled chip bags. "We're having a special event this year to go along with all the food trucks and face-painting and vendors. A big draw to get people's attention, put Magnolia Bay back on the map."

The intercom on the phone released a burst of static, then Pearl's voice squawked. "Cade, some exotic animal sanctuary is on line two."

Miley slid her hand down her face. "Is that your plan? Monkeys and bearded dragons?"

"*No.*" Cade mashed the intercom button. "Pearl, I told that guy he couldn't come—too much liability. Get rid of him."

"Get rid of who?" An offended Australian accent sounded from the speaker. "*Me?*"

Oh brother. "One moment." Cade jabbed the mute button. "Look, Miley. I'll fix it, I promise." He'd fix the hole. He'd fix the town budget. He'd fix *everything*.

"How exactly are you going to fix...this?" She waved one hand toward his desk that now strongly resembled what he'd imagine an office supply store would look like if a bomb went off.

"Easy. We're going to host a Cajun Circus." He smiled, waiting for Miley's grin of approval.

He only got a blank stare. "A what?"

Okay, not what had he hoped. It would work...right? Cade stood. "Cajun Circus. You know—clowns. Juggling. Aerial acts. Hoops of fire." He spread his arms wide like a game-show host. "All with a Southern flair."

She frowned. "What's aerial?"

"Like Cirque de Soleil. Where they perform those flips and elaborate moves on strips of colored fabric hanging from the ceiling?"

"Sounds dangerous."

"I'm sure it is. But it's also impressive. You probably don't remember Rosalyn Dupree—you're younger than us. She and I went to school together. We kind of had a back-and-forth rivalry thing." Cade waved one hand in the air, as if it was no big deal. As if Rosalyn wasn't a combination of his best and worst memories. As if she wasn't the one ghosting his emails. "She's made a pretty big name for herself in the industry—even internationally."

Miley crossed her arms again. "That's your plan to save Magnolia Bay? Your old high-school rival and clowns?"

"To save *Magnolia Days*," he corrected. "And hopefully Magnolia Days will help save the town."

"There won't be a town to save if the potholes get much bigger." Miley tossed the comment like a grenade, then left with a stomp of ankle boots.

Oh well. At least she'd left annoyed, which meant Cade was still on for his latte later.

He took his seat, picked up the desk phone, and noticed the exotic animal sanctuary had hung up. Oops. Though now he wouldn't have to try to tell him no. He clicked the line for Frog Legs instead. "Sorry about that hold, Bruno."

Even the man's laugh held a Cajun accent. "No problem. Already fried up another batch."

Cade winced. "Perfect."

"So you're coming, then?"

"I...well." Why was it so hard to say no? Cade didn't want frog legs. He didn't want to even *try* frog legs. And he doubted the rest of the Bay felt any differently. But they needed vendors. "I'll think about it."

Clang. "Trust me, boy, you can't just think about my unique Cajun seasoning blend. You must *taste* it."

This guy wasn't giving up. Cade ran a hand over his face, his five-o'clock shadow coming in early. Did stress grow hair faster? "Okay, yes. I'll be there sometime next week."

As Cade hung up, his cell buzzed with an incoming text—another food truck vendor canceling. Ugh. He winced, then scrolled up to the texts he'd ignored during Miley's visit. A form response to his dancing poodle inquiry, another from his father asking if he'd finished his third-quarter projections yet. Also one containing Mama D's Wordle score.

Buzz. Great. Now Miley, sending several emojis in a row of a family of four, a house...and a knife.

How had he ended up here, again? Cade's gaze landed once

more on the diploma on the wall, highlighted by the afternoon sun streaming through the window, and his chest tightened. Oh yeah. That was how. Was he going to be able to pull this off? The festival, the circus. Without Rosalyn or a special act—*something impressive*—he'd just end up with his fishing buddy Owen walking on stilts. Hardly marketing-worthy.

His heartbeat accelerated. He couldn't fail.

Pearl sounded on the intercom. "Cade, there's a visitor for you."

"Not *now*!" Oh, he hadn't meant to snap. But breathing was still difficult, and who had decided to squeeze his head between their hands? His vision blurred.

A blonde head poked into his office. "Bad time?"

He looked up with a start. Rosalyn Dupree.

Rosalyn?

Cade blinked rapidly, but the golden-haired woman, dressed in a white linen top and paper bag shorts leaning one slim shoulder against his doorframe, didn't dissipate. She'd showed up. Here. Back in Magnolia Bay.

He opened his mouth, then shut it.

"Guess so." Rosalyn winced, green eyes crinkling as she tucked wavy tresses behind her ears. "Sorry."

"Wait!" Cade leapt to his feet, finally finding his tongue. His manners.

But the door had already shut behind her.

###

She shouldn't have come. Her mother was wrong.

Rosalyn rushed past the secretary—Pearl, she'd said?—and kept her head ducked, hair curtaining the side of her face as she hurried to the elevator. *Don't talk to me, don't talk to me...*

"Where are you going, honey?"

Shoot. She couldn't be rude.

She forced a smile, turned to see the kind older woman posed with a stapler in hand, brow wrinkled. A desk fan hummed atop a tower of file folders next to a Chug a Mug coffee cup.

Where *was* Rosalyn going? Wasn't that the million-dollar question. "Just...away." She punched the elevator button with a shaky hand. Away...backward...in circles. Pick one.

Down the hall, the door to Cade's office rattled. Despite her mother's assurance, he had *not* been happy to see her—and why would he be, after she'd ignored his email asking her to perform at Magnolia Days? She hadn't *meant* to ignore it, of course. It'd simply fallen off her radar after a skim-read a few months ago. Before...well, before a lot of things.

Her gaze darted to the bandage wrapped around her knee. She'd have hidden it under yoga pants, but after so many years touring abroad, she'd forgotten how hot it got here in the Bay. Plus, she'd come home to heal. Physically and mentally.

Emotionally might be asking for too much.

The AC hummed and she tapped her sandaled foot, willing the elevator door to open. She'd been back in town several days now, and her mom had kept not-so-subtly leaving a flyer advertising "Magnolia Days' First Ever Cajun Circus—Details to Come" strategically around the house until she'd taken the bait.

"What's this?" Rosalyn had asked earlier that morning, watching her mother blend a smoothie.

Elegant as always, Mom wore a high-necked sleeveless blouse, patterned with a swirl of emerald that brought out her eyes. "The town's latest fundraiser effort could use a little help." Mom scooped in a handful of berries, poured a measuring cup of milk. "And how convenient to have such a talented performer back on home turf—right on time."

"But I don't even know how long I'm staying." The excuse sounded as weak as it felt. But what was she supposed to say—that she couldn't risk media attention right now? She'd just sound like a diva. She crossed her arms over her workout top, going for the stronger excuse. "I have to take it easy on my knee."

Mom's all-knowing gaze dropped to Rosalyn's bandage, then back to the bowl of blueberries. "I thought you'd been given the all-clear."

"That doctor didn't know what he was talking about."

"Ah, I see. Well, it's a good thing second opinions exist in Magnolia Bay." The whir of the blender cut off Rosalyn's protest, and the urge to see Cade again—to participate in something bigger than her that wasn't *about* her—had nudged until she couldn't resist. The next thing she knew, she'd changed clothes and driven to the mayor's office to find Cade exactly where her mother claimed he'd be.

Just not apparently where Rosalyn needed to be.

Down the hall, Cade's office door rattled again. *Where* was the elevator? Rosalyn jabbed the lit button one more time, despite logic proving it made no difference. She hadn't seen him since that Harvard–Yale football game five years ago, when they'd had a... whatever you call it. Near-moment? Maybe that's why he'd been so annoyed to see her. Or maybe he'd somehow heard about—

"Rosalyn!" Cade hurried down the hall, all sandy-brown hair and pressed clothing and...smiles?

Oh. She frowned, hesitant. So, not annoyed, then? "Hey..."

He passed Pearl's desk, clearly not noticing the way the woman's eyebrow hiked up her forehead. Then again, Rosalyn sure hadn't noticed the cut of Cade's designer button-down, or the way it hugged his biceps, when she'd glimpsed him from his doorway a moment ago.

Someone had started working out since college.

"Sorry about that. The door sticks." Slightly winded from his battle, Cade's smile shifted from brilliant to sheepish. Five-o'clock shadow graced his cut jaw line, his brown eyes sparking with the charm that had always kept him popular in high school. "It's a little low on the priority list of fixes around here."

"I'm sorry I interrupted. I should've made an appointment." Rosalyn shoved her hands into her shorts pockets, hating she wasn't sure where else to put them. Normally, poise and grace came easy for her—she was a performer. No one wanted to watch clunky and awkward ten feet in the air. But since coming home, she seemed to have slid back into the role of nerdy, unsure teenager.

The girl Cade used to have no problem ignoring until it was time to compete.

"Oh, that had nothing to do with you—just work." He waved one hand in the air, the movement as confident as he'd always been. "I'm really glad you're here."

A bit of tension eased out of her shoulders. Not that she ever cared *too* much what he thought. Not since that one time in sixth grade when he'd added too much vinegar—make that too much *arrogance*—to their volcano experiment and ruined going to regionals in the science fair competition for them both.

She shifted her weight off her knee. Tested a smile. "It's been a long time."

"Too long."

"I'm sorry I didn't email you back." She winced. "I was traveling, and I'll be honest—it fell through the cracks." For good reason, but that wasn't a story for an old rival and a delayed elevator. Where *was* that thing?

Though maybe she wasn't in quite as big a hurry as before.

Cade nodded. "I saw you were on a European tour earlier this year."

And Saudi Arabia. She fought the shudder that crept up her back, fought the urge to look over her shoulder despite the fact the only person behind her was a sixty-something-year-old woman playing solitaire.

Definitely not a mob boss.

"But hey, you're here now." Cade slid his own hands into his pockets, mirroring her. "You have no idea how relieved I am."

He might not be as relieved if he realized she hadn't committed to the circus. She was just here to get info. Get her mother off her back. Get...something. "About that. I'm not in town for too long."

"Long enough for the circus, hopefully. Name your terms." He held up both hands, that same charismatic smile tugging his lips. "If they're not within our budget, I'll make it happen."

"It's not about the money." Well, that was a partial lie. The fact she desperately needed money in the first place was still foreign. Rosalyn hesitated. So much she could tell him, and so much she shouldn't. She took the easy way out again and extended her leg. "I'm still on light duty."

His gaze dropped to her knee, to the flesh tone bandage that he clearly hadn't noticed before that moment. "*Oh*. Are you okay?"

She nodded. "It's healing. I just haven't performed since I fell."

"You *fell*?" His eyes bugged from his head, his mouth open. "From your...fabric thingies?"

"Silks." She pressed her fingers to her lips to hide her laugh, but was too late.

"Sorry. I'm a Muggle." He matched her grin, and more of the tension she'd worn for the last several months lifted off her weary shoulders. "You'll have to teach me the terminology."

There was that charm that had landed him two prom dates. Though she hadn't been either of them. "I might." The words left her lips and hovered between them, seemingly surprising him as much as her.

"I mean, at this point, you have to stay for a while, right?" Cade rocked back on his heels. "Teach me about this aerial thing. It's not often you know something I don't, Ace."

His old nickname for her lit a spark in her chest she hadn't felt in ages. "Ace. Now *that's* been a while. When did you first call me that?"

He looked up at the tiled ceiling, lips twisted. "Probably fifth grade, when I read more books than you for that class Reading Railroad Train."

"You most certainly did not." She crossed her arms over her chest, feeling lighter than she had in weeks. Months. Her knee didn't even throb. "I read thirty-one."

He nodded seriously. "I read thirty-two."

"Liar!" It was hard to pretend to be mad when she was smiling.

He harrumphed, eyes sparkling. "Prove it."

"Find me a yearbook."

Pearl's stapler smacked against a stack of paper. "He's got one in his office." She pointed down the hall.

"Now Pearl, that is not helpful." Cade took Rosalyn's elbow, steered her away from the receptionist and closer to a potted fern. "What do you say, Ace? Want to go talk terms?" He tilted his head. "*Not* in my office, near the yearbook that absolutely doesn't prove anything?"

Rosalyn hesitated, his touch warm on her bare arm. *Ding.* The elevator doors finally slid open, beckoning her back to her car. To her childhood home.

To the distressing memories of the past few months and the new urge to watch her back, even tucked away in Magnolia Bay. Could she risk the circus? Though honestly, how much media attention could it really get nationwide? It should be safe in that regard.

Not in others. Was she ready to try again?

"We could start with a post-hurricane tour of town. Show you why we're doing the circus in the first place." Cade let go, took a short step back—clearly giving her space to make the decision.

Huh. That was new. High-school Cade barreled ahead, expecting whatever he wanted to be handed to him if he couldn't nab it for himself.

She sort of wanted to know a little more about this Cade.

"I'll throw in a latte." He gestured toward her with one finger.

"Or a vegan matcha almond foam tea, or whatever it is you probably drink now."

Her laugh escaped, and there was no shoving it back in. "Fine. A tour it is." It couldn't hurt. Maybe the company would be nice.

Behind them, Pearl hummed in approval. Cade seemed to ignore her. "Let me grab my keys. Wait here?" The concern in his eyes that maybe she wouldn't was sweet.

She nodded. "I'm not going anywhere."

For now.

Acknowledgments

Some books don't take a village to complete, they take a whole galaxy. On that note, special thanks to my agent, Tamela Hancock Murray, who has partnered with me these past 15-plus years. You're my North Star! And huge thanks to Susie May Warren, for pushing me to soar at new heights with her editing prowess. You're the best!

Megan – Thanks for existing, first of all, but more specifically, for being there to crit this story for me and cheer me on along the way. Hugs!

Daddy – Thanks for helping me not only create the treasure hunt for this novel, but for fueling me with coffee and lots of laughter along the way. That was so much fun! I love you!

Mom & Mammaw – Knowing you both are eager to read my next published book helps me persevere through the days of writer's block and brain fog. Also, thanks for going in together approximately a million years ago and paying for that professional critique from Dee Henderson. I'm here today because of your support!

Micahla – Thanks for being so delightful at 5:15 a.m. and helping me stick with CrossFit, without which, my sanity would have never completed the edits on this novel. Also, I just wanted you to see your name in a book, you Buff Bunny, you.

Hubby – You're cute. The end.

Holy Spirit – Without You, I've got nothing...especially not 80-90 thousand words. #SoliDeoGloria

About the Author

Betsy St. Amant Haddox is the author of over twenty romance novels and novellas. She resides in north Louisiana with her hubby, two daughters, an impressive stash of coffee mugs, and one furry Schnauzer-toddler. Betsy has a B.A. in Communications and a deep-rooted passion for seeing women restored to truth. When she's not composing her next book or trying to prove unicorns are real, Betsy can be found somewhere in the vicinity of an iced coffee. She writes frequently for www.ibelieve.com, a devotional site for women.

Learn more about Betsy at www.betsystamant.com.

It's time to come *Home to Heritage*

"I love this small town of Heritage, MI . . . where gossip blooms like wildflowers but also where love, acceptance, and mercy flow like a wild river."

—MJSH, GOODREADS

sunrisepublishing.com

Connect With Sunrise

Thank you again for reading *Where I Found You*. We hope you enjoyed the story. If you did, would you be willing to do us a favor and leave a review? It doesn't have to be long—just a few words to help other readers know what they're getting. (But no spoilers! We don't want to wreck the fun!) Thank you again for reading!

We'd love to hear from you—not only about this story, but about any characters or stories you'd like to read in the future. Contact us at www.sunrisepublishing.com/contact.

We also have a monthly update that contains sneak peeks, reviews, upcoming releases, and fun stuff for our reader friends. Sign up at www.sunrisepublishing.com or scan our QR code.

Made in the USA
Coppell, TX
20 February 2025

46176189R00215